CHASING GRAVES

BEN GALLEY

CHASING GRAVES

THE CHASING GRAVES TRILOGY | 1

"This book is a work of fiction, but some works of fiction contain perhaps more truth than first intended, and therein lies the magic."

– Anonymous

CHASING GRAVES

CGHB1 First Edition 2022

ISBN: 978-1-8381625-7-3

Published by BenGalley.com

Edited by Andrew Lowe & Laura M. Hughes

Map Design by Ben Galley

Cover Illustration by Chris Cold

Cover Design & Interior Layout by STK•Kreations

For Rachel.

MORE FANTASY FROM BEN GALLEY

THE EMANESKA SERIES

The Written

Pale Kings

Dead Stars - Part One

Dead Stars - Part Two

The Written Graphic Novel

SCALUSSEN CHRONICLES

The Forever King

Heavy Lies The Crown

To Kill A God

TALES OF EMANESKA

The Iron Keys

No Fairytale

THE SCARLET STAR TRILOGY

Bloodrush

Bloodmoon

Bloodfeud

STANDALONES

The Heart of Stone

Shards

ANTHOLOGIES FEATURED IN

Lost Lore

Heroes Wanted

Lone Wolf

Inferno! 5

The Art of War Anthology

CHASING GRAVES

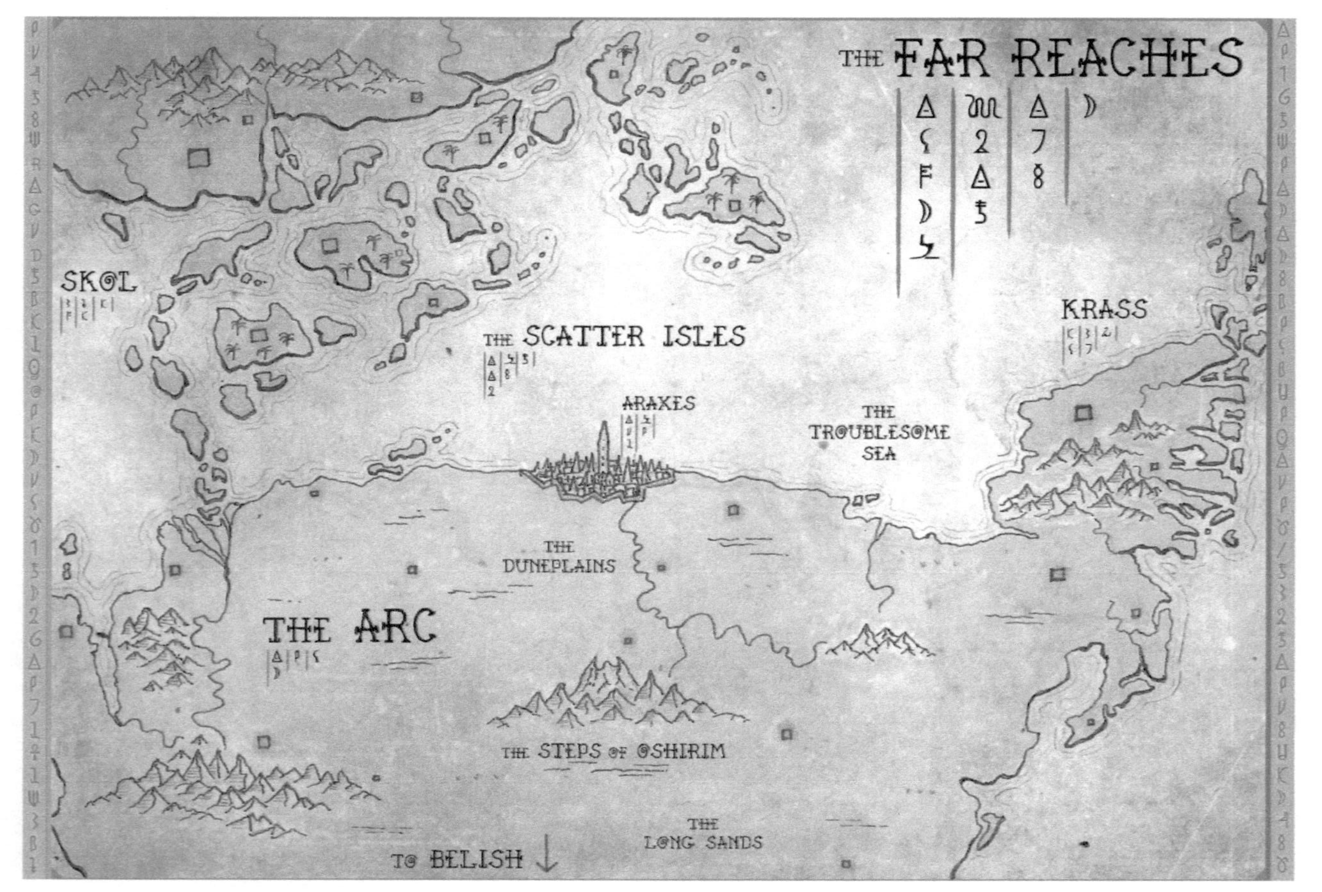
THE FAR REACHES
SKOL
THE SCATTER ISLES
KRASS
ARAXES
THE TROUBLESOME SEA
THE DUNEPLAINS
THE ARC
THE STEPS OF OSHIRIM
THE LONG SANDS
TO BELISH

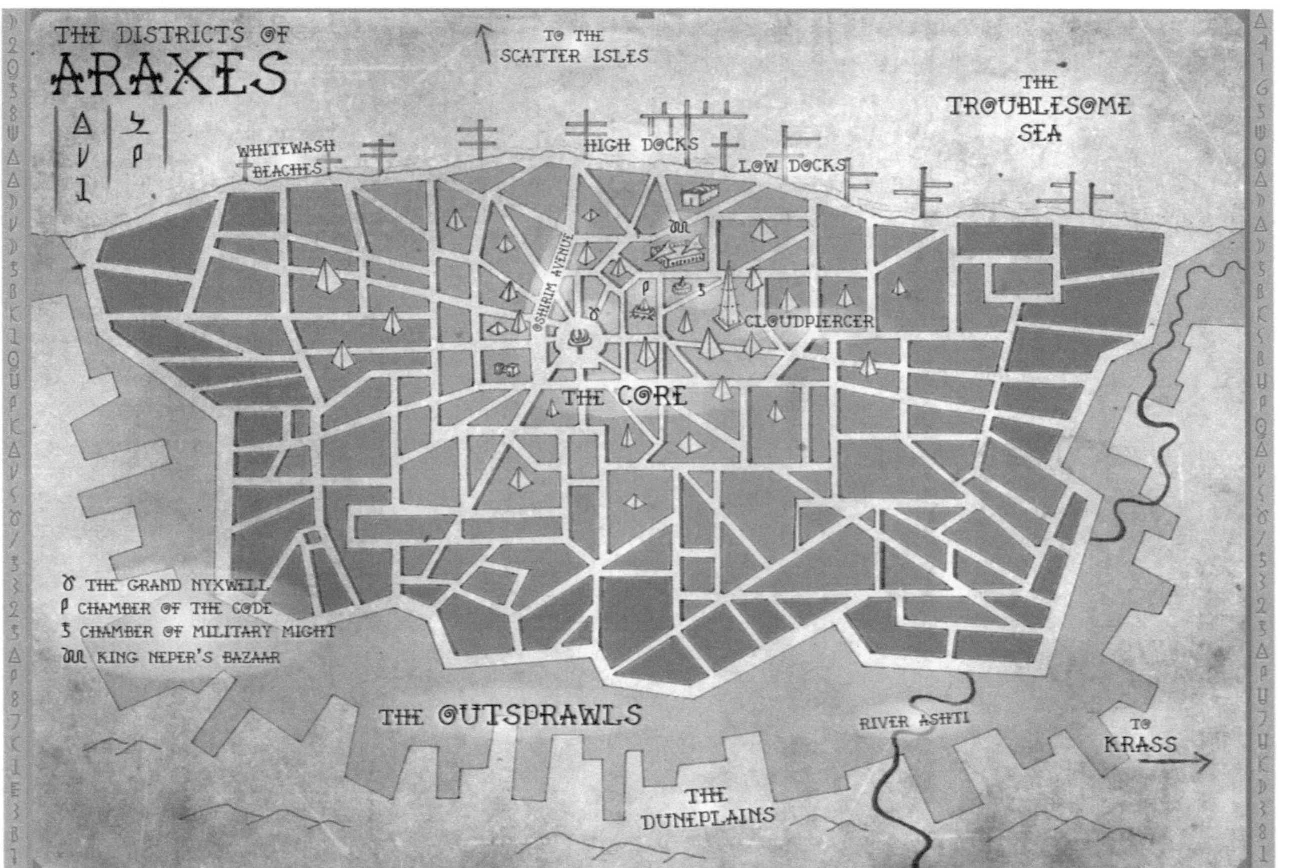
THE DISTRICTS OF
ARAXES
TO THE
SCATTER ISLES
THE
TROUBLESOME
SEA
WHITEWASH
BEACHES
HIGH DOCKS
LOW DOCKS
OSHIRIM AVENUE
CLOUDPIERCER
THE CORE
THE GRAND NYXWELL
CHAMBER OF THE CODE
CHAMBER OF MILITARY MIGHT
KING NEPER'S BAZAAR
THE OUTSPRAWLS
RIVER ASHTI
TO
KRASS
THE
DUNEPLAINS

TENETS OF THE BOUND DEAD

They must die in turmoil.
They must be bound with copper half-coin and water of the Nyx.
They must be bound within forty days.
They shall be bound to whomever holds their coin.
They are slaved to their master's bidding.
They must bring their masters no harm.
They shall not express opinions nor own property.
They shall never know freedom unless it is gifted to them.

PRELUDE

THE LAST DROPLETS OF WATER trembled on the lip of the flask, beads of dirty glass refusing to let go. She shook them, and one met her parched tongue. The other fell between her boots, striking the blistered sand with a hiss. She clenched a fist, buckling the tin flask.

The day was an oven, determined to roast her.

With an exasperated growl, she stared down at the dead things. One was considerably larger than the other: a horse with one leg bent at an unnatural angle. Splinters of bone poked through its piebald hair. Its chestnut eyes were bulged and clouded in the desert heat.

The other corpse was smaller, man-sized, and wrapped in leather sacking. It had been trussed in thick rope, the tail of which was tied in several knots about her waist.

Both had begun to stink.

The woman scanned the horizon once again, blurred as it was by heat. It was no different than the last time she looked. The golden dunes rolled out an endless and featureless carpet beneath a sky of overpowering blue: an upside-down ocean, beckoning to be dived into yet unreachable, and in that way cruel and taunting.

The sun was high overhead, beating down on her cotton shirt and the white leather hood which prevented the rays from baking her brain. Ash-rubbed leather trews, black gloves and boots saw to the rest of her.

When she could wait beside the corpses no more, she forced herself upright. Somehow it felt hotter further away from the sand. Not a breath of wind stirred. The rope came taut as she thrust herself onwards on foot. There were many miles yet to conquer. Far too many.

'Your funeral.'

The words came malformed, untested. He had broken his silence at last. She didn't deign to look at him, but she could tell by the cold waft of air that he was close. She wouldn't have admitted it aloud, but she longed for him to come closer, to escape the scorch for just a moment.

'I said it's your—'

'I heard what you said, you old goat. Go back to your brooding.'

Walking in the desert was not a joyful roaming, as one might enjoy on the high-roads of great Araxes. In the Long Sands, it became more a test of endurance. Every step was a parry in a duel between the ferocious desert and her determination. She had plenty of that. She leashed her mind to her task. As she trudged, the woman held onto a lump hiding beneath her coarse shirt: a coin dangling on a metal chain.

Hollow threats were spouted behind her. 'They'll find your body right next to mine. Bloated in the sun. All trace of that legendary beauty burned away.'

Trudge. Trudge. Trudge.

He chuckled; a wet, gnarled sound. His voice was still forming. She jerked the body, rope sharp against her cracked hands.

'They'll drag your corpse away like a piece of week-old beetle meat. Just as you have the temerity to treat mine.'

The woman whirled. 'SILENCE!' On instinct, she reached to grab his throat. Her fingers found only cold mist between their grip.

He stepped back, his blue throat untouched save for the jagged and broken scar where her knife had ended his life. It glowed a brighter blue than the rest of his swirling vapours, almost white at its edges.

'Forgetting something?' He smiled; a hateful little smile that in life had found its way to his face far too frequently. She'd hoped it had died with his body, but alas, no luck.

'Are you?' She patted the copper dagger hanging at her hip.

He shook a finger, baring teeth. 'You might have slain me once, but you wouldn't dare kill me twice.'

She tugged at the dagger's hilt. The copper blade flashed in the sunlight. 'Why don't you keep talking, and we'll see exactly what I dare, hmm?'

There came no smart reply, no spiteful, hate-filled remarks. The ghost slunk back to trailing his body, scowling as it slid without ceremony across the wind-rippled dunes.

The woman yanked her hood up to shade her face. 'See? You were always more enjoyable when you kept your mouth shut.'

CHAPTER 1

ARRIVALS & DEPARTURES

Whomsoever holds the greatest number of shades shall rule this kingdom.

Decree of Emperor Phaera of The Arc, 916 years ago

WHEN A WELCOME TO A city comes in the form of being chased through its streets by a bloodthirsty mob, you might assume you've done something wrong. Perhaps you're a murderer. A heretic. Maybe you're plagued, or owe silver to men who don't know the meaning of scruples.

I was no murderer. I was a thief, of course, but not a taker of lives. Religion had died in my country long ago just as it had in this one. I carried no disease, and my accounts were in scant but decent order. There could be only one reason I was somebody's quarry that night, I decided, between frantic looks over my shoulder, breath slobbering out over my lapels like a hound's. I had simply set foot on the wrong dock at the wrong time of night in a city where laws are laughed at and crime is king.

Innocence doesn't lend any more speed to legs than guilt.

Two hours earlier

'COME ON, COME ON, COME on…'

Burglaries are tense activities, made up of many heart-racing, sweat-inducing and lip-pursing stages. From the picking of the front gate to the dashing back through it, arms bulging with swag, it takes years of practice to not crumble under the pressure. It's what separates the dabblers from the daring, the lost causes from the true locksmiths.

I happened to belong to the latter camp.

'Hnnnnng!'

And yet, even the most seasoned locksmith can have a bad day. Sometimes the stress gets to a man, tightening him in areas where he doesn't want to be tightened. Then he thinks of the sand running through the hourglass, and he tenses all the more.

'Fucking come on!' I strained again.

Me. The best locksmith and thief in all the Reaches, clamming up like a freshpick. My only solace was that it wasn't my prized fingers that were failing me, just my unwilling arsehole. Tension is never useful when you need to take a shit in some imbecile's lockbox.

'Damn it!' I readjusted myself to see if a higher angle would help, and strained again.

I was rewarded with a precursory fart. I hunkered down and felt my bowels give way. I heard the splatter against the papyrus below, shook myself free, and used the nearby velvet cloth to wipe myself before shimmying up my trews.

Sparing a moment to assess my leavings before I slammed the lockbox shut, I couldn't help but wince. The documents were official business of some kind, judging from their wilted gold trims and grand swirls. They had all been thoroughly and gruesomely defaced. Possibly a bit extreme, I thought, but in my defence, the ship's cook had been producing a lot of salt-meat stews in recent days. Besides, the old hag who owned the chest had treated me like some Skol peasant for the entire voyage. It was her own fault for not having anything of worth to steal.

I shrugged as I fastened my belt. It would be a good surprise when she arrived at her destination; hopefully some sort of public family proceedings.

With two of my slender picks and a series of sharp movements, I relocked the box. I broke the rest of my tools into their respective pieces and slid them into the hidden pockets in the hem of my coat. I spared one to jimmy the door to lock when closed. That way I wouldn't have to bumble about in the corridor like a novice.

The door produced a pleasant click behind me and I adopted a nonchalant amble. I could have split my face with a grin when I saw my victim's fur-trimmed boots and velvet coat descending the stairs. I paused at their foot, my joy condensed into a polite smile. She snorted at me as always, and tilted her head away as if I reeked of farm work. Her lanky, leather-bound guard followed a step behind, giving me his usual blank but discouraging stare.

'Madam.' I met her grey-blue Skol eyes. Her lip wrinkled.

'You again. Lurking as always, I see.' She made her distaste clear with a swish of her coat, striking me in the chest. The guard pushed me back, and I found myself immensely pleased I'd finally found some lockpicking to do whilst aboard, even if it had taken three long weeks. I flicked the collars of my coat upright with a crack, and ascended to the top deck with a spring in my step.

The air had grown dastardly hot since passing through the Scatter Isles, and I went to the bulwark to replace the sweat on my forehead with cooler sea-spray. Whilst I lounged over the rail of the ship, listening to the seagulls mewing overhead and the waves slapping against the bow, I stared at the city that occupied half the horizon: my long-awaited destination. The City of Countless Souls.

Over the great stretch of seawater, Araxes had the look of a vast colony of sea urchins left to dry in the desert heat. To say the city was humongous was a dire understatement. Smoke-bound dockyards and piers stretched along the coastline for miles upon miles. Behind the sprawling warehouses, spires and pyramids reached up high, myriad and needle-pointed, all save for one bulging tower, poised like a column holding up the sky. Streaks of orange cloud stretched across its summit. Even from the sea I had to crane my neck to take it in.

The Cloudpiercer must have been half a mile thick at the base, and more than twice that high. The long tale of its construction was told by the bands of colour in its stone. Decade upon decade reached into the sky, tapering to a sharp point that shone like a diamond. At its very tip lived the emperor of the Arc, hidden away in an armoured Sanctuary – a smart decision when you rule an empire where everybody wants to kill you.

Word had it that if the Cloudpiercer ever fell, the heavens would fall with it. I'd scoffed at that when I first heard it, over a pint in some tavern, and I scoffed at it now. The tower was gigantic, true, but the Arctians were famed for having egos as bloated as their coin-purses, and I had no intention of feeding either on my first visit to Araxes.

The sun balanced on the ship's railing, and that meant we were running late. As I had strongly suspected since the moment I'd stepped aboard this cursed vessel, the captain had turned out to be a liar. I'd paid him an extra pair of silvers to set us in port during the daylight, as had many other passengers, no doubt. And yet, despite his repeated assurances, it appeared we would be landing past dusk. I should have paid him two pairs, or taken another ship west. One with a better name than *The Pickled Kipper*.

I cast a glance at the captain. He hadn't moved many degrees from horizontal for most of the day. He sprawled beside his wheel, yawning and flicking the rope tied about his big toe that held the spokes in place. I was not a violent man, and infinitely patient – in my line of work, patience pays – but at that moment I found myself aching to throw the fat fuck overboard. There was a reason Araxes had another name: the City of Countless Doors. In a city where you can kill a man, claim his ghost and everything he owns, or sell him for a profit, murder tends to flourish. Araxes' streets were dangerous after dark, patrolled not by lawmen or soldiers, but gangs and what the Arctians affectionately called soulstealers. It wasn't that they had no laws; just that with a city so huge, it was impossible to enforce them. I felt the sweat drip from my finger tip. For years, I had avoided working in the Arc, given their thirst for murder and their cutthroat politics. As the saying goes in the underworld of the Reaches: an Arctian would rather pay with steel than silver.

As the sun dipped into the Troublesome Sea, the sky to my left bruised to purple. The mouth of the port began to sparkle with ships' lights, and then the city followed suit with myriad oil-lamps. By the time the ship nosed into the busy waters, the adobe and sandstone of the buildings glowed almost as brightly as it had in the daylight. I wondered, somewhat aghast, at the number of whales that must have been speared each year to feed the city's thirst for oil. We had crossed wakes with a pair of whalers not three days out from Krass, and I scowled now as I had at them.

I paced impatiently between the masts as a boatful of armoured port guards came aboard from a skiff to conduct their checks of the passengers. Their questions were standard. My answers, as always, were lies. In my line of work it pays never to tell the same lie twice, even to a stranger. I'd always had a wonderful knack with fiction. In another life, perhaps I would have told my lies on papyrus, and sold scrolls by the thousand. But that was some other Caltro Basalt, and I was currently concerned with keeping this Caltro incognito.

The only truth I told them was my last name, and that my business lay within the Cloudpiercer. They snorted in disbelief until I showed them the papyrus summons that had appeared on my doorstep almost two months ago. I had almost tripped over the damn thing in my hungover exit from my pitiful excuse for lodgings. The document held only a smattering of words, written in green ink:

Mr Basalt,

Your presence is requested at the Cloudpiercer concerning matters of employment. Present this seal for admittance.

Etane.

I had recognised neither the black wax seal of daggers and desert roses, nor the name 'Etane', but it was official and intriguing enough to lure me to the mighty Araxes despite the city's blatant risks. I have done business with and robbed from some powerful names in my time, but none quite so prestigious as to call the Cloudpiercer home. Like a vulture drawn to a fresh carcass, I had sold my room and everything in it, bought a new coat, and boarded the cheapest ship to Araxes. It had absolutely nothing to do with the fact I hadn't been offered a job in months, and my coffers held more dust than they did silver. It was nothing to do with my desperate state of affairs whatsoever, and I had repeated that to myself for most of the journey.

The papyrus seemed official enough for the port guards, too, and they moved on to the next passenger. After half an hour of procedural horseshit, which I spent tapping my feet and eyeing the sinking sun, the ship was finally given permission to enter the port. Once the guards had disembarked, the rotund captain roused himself to steer the ship to an empty berth, somewhere amongst the press of vessels from every corner of the map. Several passengers cheered. The rest remained quietly uneasy, too busy clenching jaws, fists, buttocks, or if they were like me, all three.

Every moment the ship spent inching towards its quay, my eyes roved the dockside and the honeycomb alleys leading into the city. A few scores of ghosts glowed faintly here and there, working away. No signs of any living besides some bored overseers. Despite the clap of waves and the hum of distant industry, there were no screams. No baying gangs. No fact to the ghastly rumours I'd been told of Araxes. In truth, the only thing that concerned me was the overwhelming stink of fish and tar. My nervous heart calmed a fraction.

The other passengers gathered behind me. Some had loud complaints of their own for our captain, but he shrugged them off and occupied himself with his steering. Many didn't seem bothered, since they had bodyguards and soldiers arranged around them. The rest were too foreign, too naive, or too stupid to be paying much attention. The traders of the group were busy swapping stiff sheets of papyrus, and the Krassmen – my own countrymen – were too drunk for anything beyond standing still and trying not to vomit as the ship waddled up to the quay. Swarthy, stocky with muscle, they sweated in their furs and cackled in my harsh tongue. I wasn't sure whether they didn't know or didn't care about the fabled dangers of Araxes after dark. Perhaps it was the latter. Unlike me, they were big men, broad in the shoulder and thick in the arm. If I were to be honest, the only place I'm thick is the waist. I wondered if I could stick with them for safety, but a scowl from one of them told me I was not as much a countryman as I had assumed.

I caught the eye of the old Skol hag one last time. Her scowl was no deeper than usual, her eyes no more disdainful, and so I wagered she had yet to open her lockbox. If I wasn't deceived by the crowd, her guard appeared to be clutching it to his chest. For the first time, that bland, ivory face of his was wrinkled. I would have laughed had it not been for the ship knocking against the quay, and the dark, silent mouths of the streets beyond it.

I took another look at the purple sky and the faint remnants of sunset, and spat at my feet. 'Fuck this.'

As the sailors herded the stragglers towards the bulwark, I found a gap towards the mast and hopped up the greasy stairs to the aftcastle. The captain was still sloped in his chair. At the sight of me, he issued a half-arsed, half-mumbled order to show he was busy.

'Tie off! Ingrates! What is it, passenger? I'm very busy.'

'You promised a daylight arrival, sir. It is clearly nighttime. I wish to stay aboard for the night and disembark in the morning. You know as well as I do how dangerous this city can be after dusk. Otherwise I wouldn't have paid the extra silvers.'

That got him vertical. He waved his flabby arms in an effort to shoo me down the stairs. 'Impossible, just like I told the others. *The Kipper*'s being cleaned and loaded for a dawn sailing. Tide waits for no—' His bluster was interrupted by a yawn. 'You get the idea.'

An unsettling holler came from somewhere deep in the dockyards, and I set my feet against the man. We stood belly to belly for a moment, mine happily outmatched. I heard a few encouraging murmurs from the spread of passengers below us.

'Another silver for your smallest cabin. I'll be off before sunrise.'

He had the gall to push me. If not for the handrail, Araxes would have claimed me before I'd even touched its boardwalk. 'You heard me. No! Farn, get this passenger off my ship.'

A gruff sailor took up the job. 'Aye.'

Hands of calloused leather saw me back to the waiting crowd. 'Two silvers!' I yelled, but to no avail.

At the scrape of the gangplank, I was away, barging others aside so that I could be second off the blasted ship. In dangerous situations, it's always wise to let somebody else go first. That way you can scarper while they're busy screaming and dying.

It was working well until the line of passengers dispersed like smoke in a gale. I was left standing with three clueless traders, facing an empty canyon of a street that led vaguely south.

'After you.' I said, smiling and gesturing.

'To lodgehouse?' one said, in broken Commontongue. His accent was thick, of the Scatter Isles.

'Of course.' The odds were high that a lodgehouse lay somewhere in that direction. All things lie in all directions, if you're committed to walking far enough.

'Thanken,' chorused the three. Clutching their scroll-bags and coat-tails to their round stomachs, they led the way. I followed a few steps behind, using them like canaries in a mine to test the way, pointing and smiling whenever they turned around.

Sandstone warehouses, factories and granaries hemmed us in on either side, reaching high into the dark purple sky. The heat had not faded with the sun, as it did in Krass, and between the buildings it was muggy. Smoke was thick in the air, still creeping from the tall factory chimneys above. Foreign smells wafted in waves as we passed doorway after doorway, and with them came the various noises of toil. It seemed the working day was not over, at least not for the dead. Between slits in the stone walls, I glimpsed crowds of ghosts beavering away at mills or forges or various clockwork machines.

When I wasn't peering warily into the shadows, I kept my eyes on the glimmer of the Cloudpiercer, using it as a sailor uses the Undying Stars to navigate. I was eager to know the measure of my new employer Etane.

Despite a few ghosts that came ambling past with handcarts or lugging sacks, no others crossed our path. I was about to exhale for the first time since leaving the ship when a yell came ricocheting down the street and turned my blood to ice.

'Get ready!' it ordered me, though for what I had no idea. I assumed it would be something painful.

The traders stalled, swapping quizzical looks. I was already backing away, searching for nooks, crannies or any other apertures that would hide me. My heart was trying to punch its way through my ribcage. The rumours were true after all.

The sound of boots on sand was all I needed to hurtle back the way we'd come. I decided I would blabber something about forgotten luggage and hide on the *Pickled Kipper* until dawn. I'd give that oafish captain however many silvers he wanted. Being penniless was better than being murdered.

I made it around one corner before a door flew open and a pale-skinned man brandishing a curved blade jumped out to block my path.

Now, I am not a fighter. My hands are trained for more delicate work. But when death comes knocking, like most I'll do anything to frustrate its call, even if it involves tackling a gap-toothed bandit to the ground and kicking him in the face before his eyes can stop rolling around.

I was halfway back to the quay when his comrades took up the chase. I looked over my shoulder and saw a monster of a woman leading a bedraggled band clad in mismatched black armour. Half a dozen, I counted, and four more heading me off at the next crossroads. As I was forced to change direction, I threw a longing glance at the sliver of ship I could see between the buildings. Despite my shouts, nobody came to my aid. I would have bet a tooth the captain was horizontal once more, yawning as he counted his fee for putting in late, the fucking blaggard. He must have been in on it. Him and the port guards, no doubt.

Curses streamed from my mouth as I fled down a side street, men baying like hounds at my coattails.

SOULSTEALERS. THAT WAS THE ONLY explanation. I longed to

have stayed at home in Taymar, where most people stuck to chasing you for your coin-purse, not your soul. I cursed myself for not using Etane's invitation as tinder.

'Fuck it!' The infernal sand tricked my feet, sent me stumbling. Something swished behind me, far too close. I thanked the dead gods I had a penchant for tight and tidy laces. I've known far too many locksmiths who have been caught by the guards because of something so petty as a shoelace.

Only ghosts witnessed my harassment. They hugged the walls, daubing the sandstone a faint blue. Even fainter were their looks of pity. Even if they'd had the inclination, there was no help they could have offered. I found myself cursing the weak creatures in desperation. I looked up at the hazy swathe of black above me, bereft of all but the brightest stars. No gods to help me either. I was alone, and that is a deep and ancient fear to all.

I am not an athletic man. In fact, my build is that of a man whose only exercise comes from raising a pint glass to his lips. However, through terror alone, I managed to outpace most of my attackers. Only one stuck with me.

I swerved between a stack of crates, forcing the chaser to go around where I dashed ahead. An alley yawned and I threw myself into it. I fumbled into the dark before my eyes adjusted to the shadows. My breath came in panicked gulps. All I could hear was the panting of the man behind me and my heart vying with my heels to see which could pound faster.

Using the confusing nature of the streets, I weaved between the alleyways and the boardwalk, knitting an overlapping path for my would-be murderer. And yet every turn I thundered down, every zig I zagged, he clung on. His animal snorting stayed just a spear's reach behind me. With each violent swerve, the more my chest began to burn.

Every breath felt shallower than the one before it.

A courtyard sprawled between crooked old buildings, tarred black and dead of light. I ran for a street sprouting from its far side. At the last moment, I veered left for another, smaller street. I heard the crash and curse of a body against brick.

I skidded down another alley, thinking myself clever until I found it blocked by a wall of crab pots. I let loose a whimper as I collided headlong with them and fell to the sand. It was barely moments before I heard feet behind me once more.

'N—!'

The knife punctured me before I found my feet, cutting short my desperate cry. The steel came in through my back, to the left of my spine, and out through my belly. My shirt pulled around its point like a circus tent. I stared down at it, swaying on one knee and a hand, wondering why in dead gods' names I hadn't gotten a different ship.

The knife was dragged from me, and the pain came, blossoming like smoke over a Scatter Isle volcano. It crippled me, and I would have fallen had it not been for the iron arms that grasped me.

My head was yanked skyward. The steel raked across my throat, merciless. My chest and lap became wet and warm. Every time I tried to breathe, I drowned.

The arms released me, and I fell onto my back. A bloody-faced man stared back at me, standing against a backdrop of stars. He spat on me and bit his lip in a sneer.

I couldn't think of a more distasteful person to spend my last moments with, and yet here I was: the life eking out of me by the jugful, and my gurning murderer looming over me like a wood troll. There was blood at the corners of his mouth and nose. His dark hair hung in lank, greasy strands, making shadows of his lumpy face. I should have kicked him harder when I had the chance. I could have taken a different ship.

I should have stayed at home. That was all I had for comfort: should haves and could haves.

My fight was with the darkness now, and with his patience, which it turned out was thin. He was soon on his knees, knife at work once again. He cut me four more holes before my blood ran out and my body gave in. The shadows came swooping, and all I could do was scream silently at the injustice, the outrage and the hopelessness.

Fuck it.

CHAPTER 2
RITUALS

As per the Tenets of the Bound Dead, the soul of a body that dies in turmoil – whether through accident or unnatural causes – will naturally rise several days later. The shade has the chance to surrender its body to the Nyx should no other claim it first. In cases of the latter, only once said shade is bound can the master own all the soul's belongings and estates.

ARTICLE 1, S8 OF THE CODE OF INDENTUREMENT

WHAT IS THIS SLOPPY SHIT, Kech?'

The man gesticulated wildly at his split face, oozing with blood. His words whistled through the gaps in his teeth. There were a few new ones since he had started the night. "ave you seen my fuckin' face, Ani?'

Ani Jexebel had no patience for backchat. These newcomers needed to learn that. The back of her fist connected with the man's jaw and he performed a twirl before he hit the sand. He wiped a bloody smear onto the back of his hand and snivelled.

'Scars cost silvers! Boss Temsa wants clean kills only. You know how fickle buyers are these days?'

'Sorry.'

She tapped her ear irritably, like a fearsome school-madam picking on an errant child. 'What?'

'Sorry, Ani!'

'Better.'

Ani looked down at the corpse, throat splayed open to the white bone. Three – no, *four* – holes in his belly and chest. His sun-soaked skin was turning ashen as the blood bubbled from him. She made a furrow of her brow. He'd fetch twenty if they were lucky. Maybe with some shade-dust to cover the holes. She sheathed her axe in its leather loop with a grunt.

Ole Jenk liked to be quick with the rickety corpse-wagon. Time in the prisons made a man twitchy, but twitchy men made good lookouts. Despite his furtive looks and spasmodic movements, he kept the white horses still as desert bones as the men loaded the new corpses onto the older ones. Blood escaped in rivulets from the tail of the wagon. It had been a poor night for prey.

'Right, you fetid bastards. Back to the Slab before the guards get off their arses.'

Ole Jenk mumbled something between the matted wires of his silver beard.

'What?' said Ani.

'I said right away!'

'Better! You know how I hate mumbling.' And how she did. More so in recent months. Either her ears were not as clear as they used to be, or people in the city were talking quieter. In any case, it was great cause for irritation.

Ani stood on the back of the cart, watching the bodies shake as the wheels bounced through the myriad potholes. The others jogged alongside, the newcomers huffing and puffing louder than the rest. Too fat on beer and too fond of their bedrolls. She'd have the flabby fuckers mopping the cart until dawn. She ran a tight ship.

They curved away from the docklands and into the honeycomb sprawl of a housing district. Squares roofed with bright red awnings broke the monotony of the endless streets. Alleys flashed by, strung with clotheslines and bunting, and littered with the cornucopia of refuse usually found in a city's gutters. Now and again a scream would ring out into the dark night, or the concussive thwack of a triggerbow would echo across the stone: other soulstealer crews plying their labour.

Their road came to an open junction of five streets. A pyramidal building dominated one corner, and its great square door blazed with yellow lamplight. Pipe-smoke and noise poured out into the evening. Cackles of laughter and broken song flooded the junction. A steady stream of bodies came and went, the latter decidedly more unsteady on their feet. A band of stone sat above the lintel of the door, three words chiselled and painted into its weathered face: The Rusty Slab.

With great care, Ani's crew hugged the opposite street, heading for a squat iron entrance tucked into the building's backside. Ani knocked nine times, and with the crunch of a lock the door swung inwards. Jenk tapped the horse forward, down a slope and into a bare and lamplit room with a low ceiling. Two alcoves had been carved into the walls, occupied by wooden platforms held by curtains of thick chains.

Boss Boran Temsa was waiting for them as always. He stood alone on a stone platform, elbow on his cane, thumbing his oiled beard, eyes narrow and hungry. No matter how busy he found himself, he would invariably welcome his new arrivals. Attention to detail was one of his greater talents, vital in the business of soultrading. That virtue had been the reason Ani sold him her services. That, and he paid better than most.

'How many?' he yelled as Ani trudged up the steps of his platform, her weapons and leather-plate armour clanking.

'Six, Boss. From one of our captains at the Low Docks. *The Pickled Kipper.*'

Temsa banged his cane on the stone. 'Only six? Tut tut, gentlemen! I had expected better! Especially of you, Ani.'

Ani shrugged. 'We've only got so many ships, and they're away for weeks at a time.'

'Excuses are the hallmarks of failure, m'dear. We've been through this.'

They had. Many times. Ani wasn't in the mood for another of his lessons. She bowed stiffly. 'I'll play smarter.'

Temsa moved past her and she shuffled out of his way. It was more to avoid his copper claws than to be respectful. His left leg was missing below the knee, thanks to some old gambling debt gone awry. Temsa had rejected the customary wooden or ivory replacement in favour of a copper and gold version, carved in the shape of an eagle's foot. A hallmark that was known all through Bes District and beyond. It was so notorious that none had ever dared to suggest a nickname. The last man to do so had called him 'Goldylegs', and he had quickly found a dagger in his eye. Temsa preferred to be known simply as Boss Temsa, and that was final.

He clanked and tapped his way to the wagon, an odd rhythm of claws, cane and boot. His long coat of gold thread and purple silk swished about him. Ole Jenk stayed by his horses, but the other men parted like woodcutters before a falling tree as Temsa roamed the night's catch. They had been dumped in a rough line, lying on crude brushstrokes of blood.

Temsa's olive eyes moved quickly, hawk-like. 'Hmm. At least they're travellers, fresher than what we usu—What the fuck is this mess?' His cane stabbed at the stone floor again. 'Look at his fucking neck, Ani!'

Ani leaned on the railing, picking at her dirty nails. She knew exactly which mess he was referring to without having to look.

'Our new Kech got a little personal with that one, Boss. Wanted revenge for bootin' him in the face, apparently.'

Bloody-faced Kech had frozen. No complaints of a broken nose now.

Ani watched as Temsa pondered, his eyes distant. Boran Temsa was a man of quick decisions. She could tell he'd already decided to kill the man. He only nodded like that when mulling over *how* to kill something.

He spoke as he walked, taking a meandering route between men and corpses. Kech was undoubtedly at the end of his path.

'Forty silvers. That's the average value of a cleanly killed shade in today's market. Lowest it's been in six months despite this Nyxwater shortage. Top price – and I'm talking poisoned or smothered – is fifty to fifty-five. Old or young, thirty-five. But with a slashed throat like this poor soul? That's maybe twenty on the nose. Twenty-five with a bit of dust. Follow?'

The men nodded emphatically. Armour squeaked as heads bobbed.

'Ten of you to get the bodies. Coin a piece per body, that's sixty.

Then I've got to pay the binders at six coins a body. That's twenty-four. And another fifteen to the Nyxites for their Nyxwater. Can anybody tell me what that adds up to?' Temsa came to a halt beside Kech. 'Anybody?'

'Ninety-nine,' said Ani, after far too long a pause.

'Well done, Miss Jexebel. So, saying I get even one hundred and fifty for this lot, that leaves me just over one body in profit. Fifty silvers. A razor-thin margin, so the traders say. Do you think I got into soultrading to make razor-thin profits, Mr Kech?'

'No, Boss.'

The man was right to be shaking. Ani had seen men almost as big as her shake in Temsa's proximity. He might have been small in stature, but he cast the shadow of a daemon. His olive eyes, though small and pinched in wrinkles, held nothing in the way of predictability. Just the hunger and rage of a starving wolf.

The cane struck Kech hard across the backs of his legs. Its hook dragged him onto his arse, and his skull smacked on the stone. Temsa raised his foot above the man's torso, his four sharp talons hovering inches from his poorly-leathered tabard.

'I'm sorry, Boss! I swear I'll do better!'

'I've no doubt. You'll fetch a good price at the soulmarket, and what's more, I no longer have to pay you. You're doing better already.'

Temsa pressed down, driving the claws into the man's gut. Kech curled around them like a speared woodlouse, his mouth open in a silent, gap-toothed scream.

The copper came away bloody, and left streaks in the dust as Temsa left Kech behind to writhe and die. 'Load them up, gentlemen!'

Ani was waiting in the smaller of the alcoves. While the men went to work carting the bodies onto the other, wider platform, theirs fell in jerky increments and the *ratatat* of chainlink against pulleys. They descended into another domed room, this one twice as big. They stepped around two gangs of shades heaving on wheels and levers to crank the lift back up.

Ani had been pondering. 'You don't pay the binders six. You pay them four.'

'I think you're getting deafer and louder at the same time, m'dear.' Temsa waggled a finger in his ear. 'A little exaggeration is sometimes necessary.'

'Sure your mind isn't slipping? Forgetting your numbers?'

'Not a chance.' Temsa gave her a sly look.

The bodies floated down next, and the binders scurried forwards to unload them. Ani and Temsa followed the short train of corpses to an area lit by whale-oil lamps. There, the binders began their ritual, hands flitting about, sharp and quick. First, the hooded men picked the pockets and bags, digging for valuables before removing clothing. They piled belongings neatly at the heads of the bodies for later fencing.

Temsa always liked to poke, to see what extra treasures he could glean. Every so often, he found something he liked and saved it from the fence's piles. Ani pointed at the body whose throat Kech had slashed; the one whose belly sported four gaping holes.

'Why's this one got no stuff?' she asked. 'Who comes off a ship with no luggage?'

Judging by his dark skin and bright emerald eyes, the corpse was from the east. His hair was a few shades from black. Short, but shaggy and unkempt. Dried blood matted it over one pierced ear. He had the beginnings of a beard on his chubby cheeks. The man had no jewellery on his person, and nothing with him besides a smart grey coat, a folded document and a plain metal flask still sloshing with liquid. Palmshine, by the smell of it. She snatched up the papyrus, reading slowly.

'Mr Basalt. Krassman, I wager. Summons to the Piercer for a job, no less! Must be important. The name's all bloodied, but there's a wax seal on it.'

'Give it here.' The name was obscured by a dark smear. Something like *Etan* or *Eran*. Temsa thumbed the seal, a design of desert roses with thorns like daggers. He did not seem to recognise it. There were so many nobles in this city it was impossible to keep track.

Temsa snapped the seal from the papyrus and slid it into a pocket. There were so many nobles in this city it was impossible to keep track. He said something, but Ani's deaf ears didn't catch it over the shuffling of the binders.

'What?'

'I said a smith, by his trews and shirt.'

'You sure? What smith doesn't carry tools with him?'

Temsa felt around the lining of the coat, teasing a dozen small pieces of metal and springs out of the fabric. They looked like the shattered parts of some simple device.

'How peculiar.' He pieced a few of them together, making a small cross. One piece looked like a file. 'I'll have to see what Tor Busk makes of these.'

'That old fucktart? Prick gave me some bad advice on an axe.'

'No, he gave you good advice. You just didn't take it.'

The binders began to strip the undergarments with shears. They didn't bother to tend the darkening wounds. Instead, they wedged open the corpses' jaws with blocks of wood, then fetched a basket of copper coins bearing the royal seal of a spiked crown. Each coin was chiselled down the centre, and the binders snapped each one in two, placing one half in the open mouth of the dead while holding the other firmly betwixt finger and thumb.

With the blocks removed, the naked, bloody bodies were dragged towards a covered well at the edge of the room. The boards were moved aside and a pool of grey water revealed. Its ripples moved languidly, more like oil rather than water, but it had no sheen to it. No depth, either. The waters were too inky to see the bottom of the stone pool. Ani knew it was barely three feet deep. That was all the Nyx needed.

A body at a time, they were surrendered to the wet with a hiss, like virgin blades being quenched. It was not a matter of hot and cold; it was the sizzling of the magic in the coins as the bind set.

The Krassman's corpse was last, and once he'd slid into the waters, still with that gawping look on his face, the binders took their places around the stone rim. In silence they donned their copper-thread gloves and hovered, ready.

It took a moment for the shades to appear. First in, first out. Always the way. The shades always retched, too, as if they thought themselves revived, not yet realising their new state of being. Copper hands hauled their naked, vaporous forms from the ashen water and dumped them on the stone, where it shone with their blue colour. The shades wheezed and winced like newborns until realisation made them thrash. Their vapours, although bound to the shape and moment of their death, flowed and billowed as they struggled. The binders' gloves taught them stillness. Wherever they touched seemed to scald the blue vapour. The shades slumped to the stone, quivering.

Six had come out, including Kech, but the seventh was proving stubborn and taking his time. The Krassman. Some liked to hold on once they had glimpsed the gates of the afterlife. Ani snorted. The binding always dragged them back to the world of the living. Magic always outweighed will.

And yet, the moment stretched out. The binders' hands danced impatiently over the sloshing waters. Concerned glances darted under cowls. Ani looked to Temsa. His eyes were growing narrower, his good foot tapping with impatience.

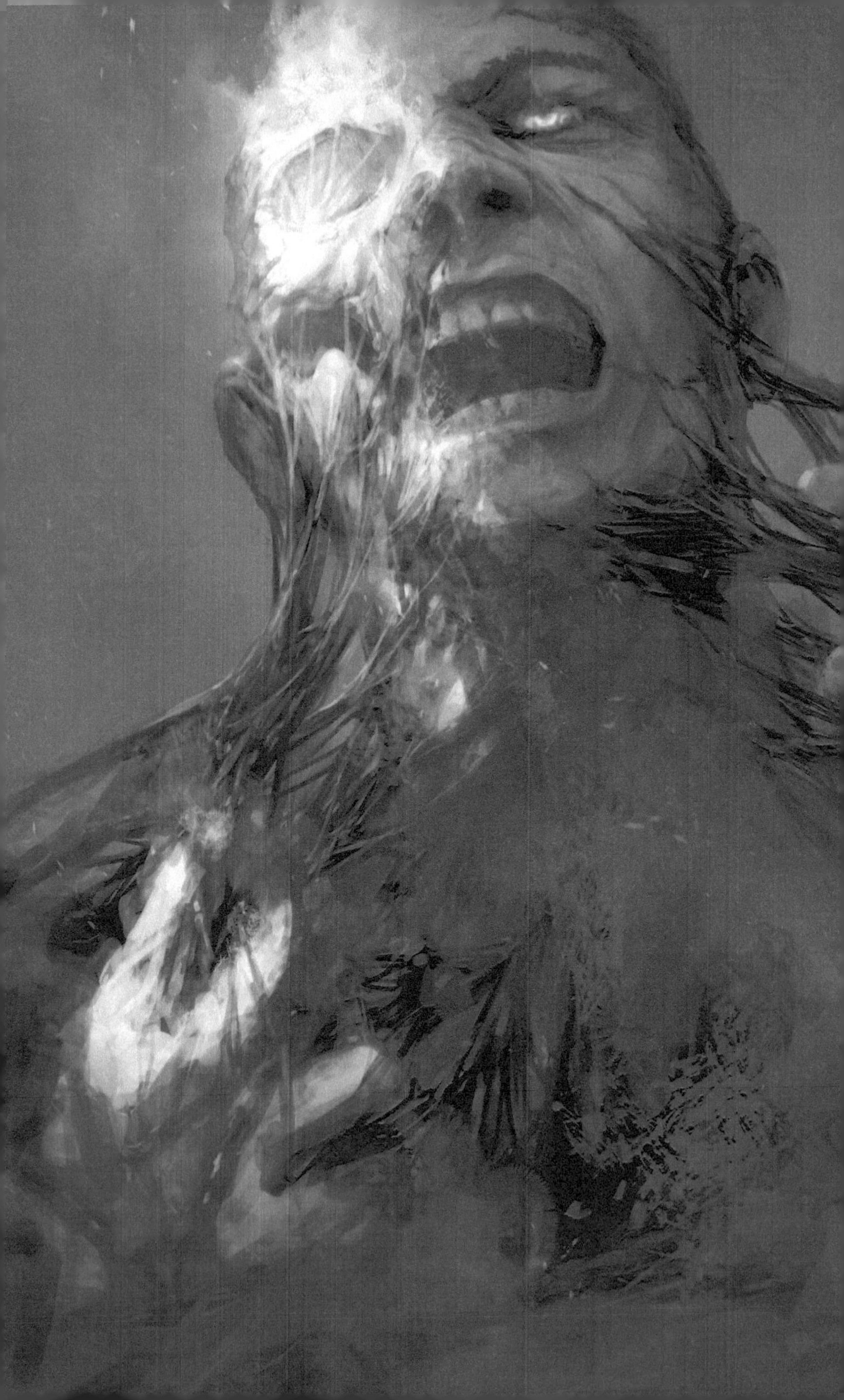

CHAPTER 3

CROWD MENTALITY

The Tenets of the Bound Dead were a parting gift from the dead gods. A last act of the god of chaos Sesh, almost a thousand years ago. He gave humanity the methods of binding before our old deities slipped from existence, and left us the afterlife, or duat in old Arctian. I mention the Arc only because it was they who pounced upon the opportunities binding presented. It was they who bolstered the Tenets with their Code of Indenturement. It was they who turned this world into a vale of the dead.

FROM 'A REACH HISTORY'
BY GAERVIN JUBB

DEATH WAS A CROWDED PLACE.

It had been cold and quiet at first. Nothing but an empty darkness. Although the stories of glowing cornfields and mountains haloed with cloud had been immediately proven to be yak shit, it was peaceful for a time.

Then the voices came. Just one at first, whimpering the same word over and over. Then another, angry, far too foreign to understand. As each voice broke out, a shadow of its owner appeared, outlines glowing softly against the blackness. I looked down, and all I saw were the faint edges of my own body. No wounds, just edges drawn in shadow and light, as if I was made of the purest glass.

The voices grew in volume and number until their clamour sketched a vast and crowded landscape. There were no trees, no constructions of man. There was nothing but intermittent angles of black rock, glasslike and shiny from a constant trickling of water. Sharp shale lay underfoot. Standing upon it in their thousands, nay, in their millions upon millions, were the dead. Endless ghosts, etched in shadow and lost memory.

The boundless crowd stretched down into a black valley so wide its fringes were lost in mist, so long its beginning was a smear of grey on a foreign horizon. The sky above was of the darkest night. I would have assumed I stood beneath a limitless abyss had it not been for the stalactites. They hung like upside-down mountains, breaking the blackness here and there, jagged and ominous. In the distance, a ring of five stars glinted, with a brighter star at their centre. I knew then I could have walked for a hundred years and never reached them.

I still trembled from my death, the memory of it so vivid behind my eyes. But it wasn't that particular injustice, nor the harsh reality of this so-called afterlife that disturbed me. It was the volume of the voices and the press of ghostly bodies. While I'd stood there all agape, countless newcomers had crowded in behind, their faint feet splashing in the puddles of inky water. As they pushed forwards against me, they too began to wail into my ear. Shouts for loved ones. Animal cries of pain. The constant, racking sobbing. The mumblings of hysteria or old age. It was unbearable.

I tried to push back, but it was like paddling through water. When I didn't move, the press carried me forward, inches at a time. I protested, but my feet slid anyway through the wet shale, unbidden. I was trapped in a nightmare that wasn't my own, and I will admit, in that moment, it drove me to madness. Clamping my hands to my ears, I gave in to screaming.

'SHUT UP! SHUT UP! SHUT THE FUCK UP!'

I felt the jolt of the ghosts around me. They stopped dead, pardon the pun. My shout faded on my lips. No echo returned to me. The silence was even more interminable than the voices. Without opening my eyes I could feel the weight of their gazes upon me. When I did, I saw a hundred ghostly faces staring at me. Somehow I knew countless more in the vast crowd did the same. Perhaps the whole damn ocean of deceased was staring at me. There was no emotion nor blame in those eyes. They were as impassive as glass marbles.

As any good Krassman would, I started to work on an apology. Before I could stammer anything of use, or inform them I was new to the area, they began to speak again. Not all, just one at a time. The first was distant, mumbling something about hunger. The second was closer, but unintelligible. The third was close behind, breath cold on my ghostly nape. This one, I heard.

'We call upon the locksmith. The harbinger of change.'

'The what?' I tried to turn around, but the press didn't permit me. I felt something akin to a cat weaving between my legs. *Do animals have an afterlife, too?* 'The who?'

A ghost in front of me spoke over his shoulder. His broken jaw hung loose, and yet his voice was somehow clear.

'Chaos shall not have his time.'

Another spoke next to him. 'The flood must not claim the world.'

'I'm afraid I have no idea what you're talk—'

'You will go back,' boomed a voice, deep in the crowd. 'With our gift.'

I tried to jump but I was held fast. 'Back! Yes, I want to go back. I was murdered, you see, and—'

A ghost beside me glowed green as it spoke. 'You will seek out the servants of chaos. Stop them.'

The last ghost to speak had wolf eyes, burning bright gold. 'Stop them. Save us. Save yourself.'

'I don't understand. Speak plainly! I—'

Words were stolen from me. The ground beneath me shook once before giving way. I tumbled into the hole that opened for me. Shale scraped at me. Water cascaded with me. The endless crowd vanished, giving way to black walls of rock rushing past, and then pitch-like darkness. I fell through that void until falling felt like flying, and just as I was imagining an eternity spent soaring, icy water filled my mouth, clogged my eyes and ears.

I exploded from the surface of the black water like a dolphin dancing in a ship's wake. Feeling half-drowned, I retched and coughed, dribbling the foul liquid from my cold lips. Weakness racked me. I felt numb from top to toe, and cold. Dreadfully cold. Rough hands hauled me up. I felt a pain in my arms, and for a blissful moment I thought it had all been a horrid dream. The ship must have sunk on its way to port, or I'd been pushed overboard by that old hag for shitting in her lockbox.

This is my rescue.

A stone floor suggested otherwise. I had expected wooden decking, perhaps sand. There was no pain, no thwack of meat on a butcher's counter. Just the deadened knowledge of something beneath me. I tried to open my eyes, but the light was piercing, setting my skull alight.

'Finally!' cried a voice in a burbling Arctian accent, though speaking the Commontongue. 'He reveals himself. Get him up. I want to see the damage.'

The hands came at me again, burning hot this time. I tried to cry out but only managed a wordless curse. The scalding hands held me upright and marched me forwards. I opened my eyes a crack to see who was holding me and where I was being marched to. Pain flooded me once more, and all I saw was a blur of blue.

I was shaken roughly until I could stand to bear the light. Somebody thrust my chin up. Before me, I saw a group of figures with dark robes and thick gloves, and a short gargoyle of a man with a golden leg shaped like an eagle's claw. He had a sharp beard on his chin and an ornamental cane in his hand. His sun-dark face was punctured with small olive eyes and shrewd lips. Gold-capped teeth glinted between them. His clothes were formal, fancy even: tight northern-style trews with a red silk shirt and a gold coat that brushed the stone.

He hummed at me, gaze roving over my body. 'Well, m'dear, he's not the trimmest, is he?'

I was about to complain when the hot hands released me, leaving me to kneel, body trembling, before the short man.

'And dust won't help that ghastly neck wound much, but we can try.'

I flinched at the mention of the neck wound. The dream shattered in an instant, and I remembered the cold steel jerking through the gristle of my throat. My hands flew up to check, but all I felt was cold and numbness. I looked down to find myself naked, my features and curves drawn in nothing but swirling blue smoke.

I was dead after all. Well and truly dead.

It was natural to try and scream, and so I did. I screamed at the top of my lungs, and yet all that came was a pitiful croak. I lashed out instead, but strong arms shoved me to the wet floor. I settled for pitiful mumbling, willing it all to be a nightmare, repeating a poor facsimile of the word, 'No!' over and over. It was almost as if the flesh I had worn throughout the years had dampened the soul's emotions, like cloth clamped over ears. Now I was bare, raw, deafened by terror and despair.

'He's a quick one, Boss,' hollered the woman standing behind the man: the hulking shape from the alley. Now I could see her better, I wondered if I had been lucky having my oaf of a killer instead of her. No doubt I would be lacking a limb or two by now if she'd been the one to bring me down.

Two axes hung from her belt, and another was slung over her shoulders, which were draped in a patchwork of leather armour. Her hair was tightly braided in three tails, pulling some of the wrinkles out of her weathered, scarred face. Angular swirls were tattooed across her neck, cheek and shoulder. Despite how much she looked like a barbarian of my own lands, her skin's lighter hue spoke of northern descent. Scatter Isles by her accent. That's a hard one to shrug off.

Her boss came forward, his metal foot clinking on the stone beside my head. 'You're too fresh to speak, shade. Takes a few days or so. Why do you think it is we bind you so quickly, hmm? So we get some peace and quiet while you accept your new fate. But where are my manners? A warm welcome to Araxes, the City of Countless Souls. Diamond of the Arc, city of cities, mountain of man's making!'

I wondered whether the dead could spit. If I couldn't kick or shout,

I might as well show my distaste in other ways. Unfortunately, saliva didn't seem to be a ghost's forte, despite all the mist and vapour.

'Bastard!' I cursed him, though it came out more as, '*Marra*!'

The painful gloves returned, hauling me into line with half a dozen other ghosts, each as naked as I. We glowed a faint blue, almost grey. I looked to my left to find none other than my oafish murderer. He wore a foul look, though not for me. For his displeased boss, most likely. I spotted the four holes in his bare sternum. Matching sheaths for the man's metal claws.

The traders had fared better than I, though they were even more boggle-eyed and forlorn-looking than they had been in life. They looked as if they were going to pop at any moment and descend into hysteria. I didn't blame them. One wore an ugly slash across his chest, nipple to waist. The other two had dark holes in their bellies, much like my own.

A couple I didn't recognise stood with us, and that was our small brigade of ghosts: cowed and shivering, still trying to understand our forcible transition. There was too faint a margin separating life and death, and our minds had not yet caught up. We were still entrapped in the horror of our murders. Even then, after mist and knitted vapours had replaced our mortal fibres, we covered our nakedness with our hands.

The gargoyle came to take a closer look at me. Even I, with a stature not worth boasting about, bested him by a head.

'To the cages,' he ordered, and those in hoods pushed us down an adjoining corridor. The traders began to wail in their foreign tongue, but they were beaten swiftly and sharply with metal rods. I flinched away from their hands; the gloves burned me every time they touched my vapours. With each flinch, I was thwacked for resisting.

We were shown to a squat, deep cage sandwiched between the hewn rock of the tunnel and its dust floor. More cages stretched into the smoky darkness. I could see spots of blue glowing here and there.

I was the last to be shoved inwards before the doors were slammed and locked up tight. I instantly went to the thick bars, but my hands jolted from the metal as if I'd been bitten by a flame. They were clad in copper, the only material that could harm a ghost. The parts that weren't covered in beaten copper felt soft and gelatinous to me, yet still immovable. I tried to shout again, but to no avail.

The big woman cackled at me. 'Try all you like, shade.'

Four more ghosts hovered in the cage's dark reaches, curled up in solitary balls. They glowed brighter than us. That must have meant they were older. A grim birthday, indeed, to be measured by how much time you've spent dead.

The man limped to the bars. 'Listen up! My name is Boss Boran Temsa, and I shall be your master during this brief period before you begin your new life of servitude. This here is Miss Ani Jexebel, my most trusted aide and one of the finest sellswords in the Far Reaches. It is our pleasure to inform you that your bodies are dead. Deceased. Deprived of life. Your souls, however, have been liberated. Through the glory of the Tenets of the Bound Dead, copper coin and Nyxwater, you are now an esteemed member of the indentured. A shade. A ghost. A half-life.'

Though it had been obvious the moment the knife-blade had met my flesh, hearing it aloud drove the meaning home like a fresh stab to the gut. I strangled the bars for as long as I could, battling the pain. Temsa pressed on with his speech.

'You should be excited. A new existence awaits you! Whatever ill-picked names your mothers gave you are no more. You no longer have to worry about possessions, or sustenance, or sleep. You have risen above such frivolous things as drinking and gambling and fucking. Leave them to the living, just like politics and religion and all the half-baked opinions you ever had on them. In fact, you can rest easy knowing that your existence is now out of your hands. That you need not bother yourself with the ideologies of freedom unless you are bequeathed it by some generous master. Because, ladies and gentlemen, you are now, for all intents and purposes, *property*.'

To make his point, Temsa held up a stack of seven halves of copper coins pinched between finger and thumb. I knew enough about the Arc to know they were our half-coins. What bound us to the living instead of death. A thousand-year-old perversion of the ancient tradition of paying the boatman for passage into the afterlife. Cheat the boatman. Cheat death. The Arctians had built their empire on the backs of those half-moons of copper.

I ached to yell. I tried, dead gods as my witness. I croaked and I hissed and I gasped. When that failed I threw every foul gesture I knew at the little man. Some I even made up on the spot.

The other ghosts joined me in our futile rebellion, but all the onlookers did was smile and chuckle. Temsa and his hillock of a bodyguard seemed to have seen it all before. He waved his hand dismissively. I could have burst into flame and he would have still paid me no attention.

'Detail them,' came the order.

Two men appeared, both in robes. One had a beard that had been braided down his chest, and he stayed mostly to the shadows. The other had a bald pate, and was brandishing a scroll and an inked reed. His skin was dark, of the deep deserts to the south. He cleared his throat before starting with the traders.

'Right. You. Name.'

The ghost with the cut across his breast flapped his mouth wordlessly. He needn't have bothered; the question was rhetorical.

'We'll call you "Amin",' the scribe suggested, reed already shuffling across the papyrus. Behind him, the bearded man began to scratch a name into the half-coin. Amin, the ghost, flinched with inner pain until the marks were made.

The scribe paused to look the man up and down. 'Thirty years of age. Coincounter for ten.'

Miss Jexebel grunted. 'Looks more like a cook to me.'

The scribe made a hurried correction. 'Cook it is.'

And so it went, one sorry soul after the next. A name was plucked from thin air and marked on the half-coin, and thrown together with an age and a profession. When it was my turn, I mimed something threatening involving a foot and an orifice. I'm normally not so confrontational, but something about my circumstances demanded it.

The scribe barely frowned. He had no doubt seen it all.

'Jerub,' he dubbed me. 'House-shade of five years.'

I doubled up as my half-coin was etched with the false name. It felt like an icicle retracing the stab marks in my chest, but it was brief. I was thankful they didn't bother with surnames or job titles. I was on the brink of collapsing. I had felt no pain like it in my life, and I have felt more than my fair share.

Temsa sighed. 'Get creative, man, I need to dress him up a bit. Look at that fucking neck. You know the buyers get squeamish over wounds like that. That's why we keep it clean; aim for the chest, the stomach, or the bloody arse for all I care! Anything, so long as a smock can cover it up.'

'*Fifteen* years, then. Thirty years of age.'

'Twenty-eight. Give him some stable experience, too. Beetles and horses.'

'Done, Boss.'

Temsa tapped his cane on the dusty stone. 'In that case, my new shades, we bid you a good night. We'll meet again on market day.'

With that, the group filed away into the corridor, murmuring about a fine evening's work. I watched until the last thread of robe had disappeared from view, then I found a stone wall at the back of the cage, far away from the copper, and thumped my head against it. It was more a soft tap, and did nothing to vent my frustration. I tried over and over, but the wall held no pain for me, only muted resistance. I was no ghost of ancient fables; one that could pass through doors and walls. I was as bound by reality as flesh was.

Buoyed perhaps by my invulnerability, I decided to whirl on my murderer instead. I found him staring at me, shoulders hunched and fists clenched. He had been watching my display, and was no doubt as frustrated at his plight as I was at mine. His glowing eyes told me he blamed me for it, as if stabbing me had somehow been my fault. If he could have killed me a second time, I surely would have been a puff of cobalt mist already. As it was, his rage was useless.

I shook my head at him and found a space to be alone. There, I adopted the position of the others: knees tucked into my chest and arms wrapped around shins. With my chin resting in the cold jelly that was now my kneecaps, I stared at my new skin. The vapours clung to the shape I had worn in life. Every bump and feature and edge were all there, just softened and made of blue mist. My ample gut still presided, and, somewhat pleasingly, even my cock and balls had survived the grave. However, I suspected they would be as useless in death as they had been in life.

My vapours had a slight flow to them, mimicking the old flow of blood. As I moved my hand, my form would drag and waver like a candle in a draught. My chest wounds glowed a whiter shade, just as I imagined my neck did. I probed them to find no pain, and half my finger disappearing inside my ribcage.

When I couldn't take any more examination, I tried to sleep, but it turned out sleep was a luxury reserved for the living. So, as any man is wont to do when he finds himself in the shit-heap of dire circumstances, I fantasised about what I should have done differently.

I re-ran the chase, cursing myself for not taking that left, or that right. I thought of all the clever ways I didn't know of turning a knife around in an attacker's grasp. I dreamt up witty lines that I could have parted with. I even wondered at how I would have recounted the near-death tale to my mysterious employer in the Cloudpiercer. The possibilities were unreachable, but they were distracting enough to be comforting. At first.

A person who longs to change the past will only see themselves as a product of what could have been. The longing changes nothing of the present. Every time I looked up, I was still sat in a grimy cell with immovable bars; my only company eight other ghosts, my only pastime pawing at my slit throat. The present was a miserable existence, if that word even still applied. That was how I spent several hours turning the beauty of hindsight into a tool of torture.

Save us. The nonsense of my death-dream bubbled up again. I'd assigned it to either some madness intrinsic to the binding process, or profound blood loss before death.

The point was, there were no gods to be saved by. That was the truth of it. If there were, I'd be the one asking for saving, right there and then, prostrate and howling at the heavens. The gods died the same day the dead began to roam the world, and some Arctian geniuses learned to bind them. Why bother offering yourself to the mercy of deities and slinging coin at church coffers when the afterlife is graspable and stands glowing before you? No religion, no guilt. No intangible authorities holding keys to immortality. You can just grab it yourself. All you have to do is die in turmoil, and stop anybody claiming your body before you do. *Indenturement*. What else would happen when humans are left in charge of death?

I remained hugging my shoulders, dashed by the weight of my situation. Once again, I thought of that thin margin between life and death. When alive, it's a precipice that's easy to slip over. When you're dead, it's a sheer cliff face without a handhold in sight.

Fighting a whimper, I did what I was good at and handled my problems piece by piece. I knew that I wanted the only things left to me as a dead man: my freedom, and justice for Temsa's sins.

The greatest city in the world might have been feral, but it was not lawless. The Arctian Empire was a society ranked by how many shades a person owned. Their precious Code dictated every area of binding and selling ghosts. If only a veneer, it was still a strict system; they simply lacked the ability or inclination to enforce it. But every system can be worked. If there was anywhere justice could be served on these soulstealers, it was here. It would take strength and patience, but I would have my deliverance, and I could return to being… *something*. A new me, at the very least.

A dead me.

I cushioned the sob against my glowing arm.

CHAPTER 4
OASES

A shade who wishes to make a claim of past illegal or wrongful indenturement may only do so if they are free or if allowed by their current master. They may submit a claim to the Chamber of the Code for review, and if such a claim is deemed trustworthy, evidence may be required and a hearing held. Should the shade's claim be proven true, and the original procurer of the shade found guilty of illegal indenturement, they shall be stoned until death.

AMENDMENT: Current time for review is set at three years.

ARTICLE 7, S2 OF THE CODE OF INDENTUREMENT

IT WAS A BRUTISH TRICK of deserts to be as cold at night as they were hot in the day. Her knees were half frozen, her feet as numb as stumps. Though breath escaped her mouth in plumes, the tough work of dragging the corpse kept no warmth in her body. It barely distracted her from the punishing cold in her chest.

The skull-faced moon was being lazy, hiding behind the horizon. Only the starlight bathed her tonight. Instead of the undulating horizon, she kept her eyes on the constellations, mouthing their old Krass names. In all her years spent living in the Arc, she had never forgotten them.

Mamil the Wanderer.

The Hook of Utros.

The Broken Pyramid.

Sothis.

And the five Undying Stars, circling the Stillstar, guiding her north to Araxes.

That fucking city.

Once again, her mind slipped to worry. Ever since the sun had set, whispers had plagued her. Every time a breeze moaned across a dune, every time something screeched in the darkness, she heard doubt. The woman turned to check the ghost was still trailing her. Her gaze was met with a foul stare, white eyes burning in blue sockets.

Time and the Tenets were against her. By the rules of binding she had thirty-four days left to make the journey to Araxes and bind his body in the Grand Nyxwell. Only the grandest would do, of course. Driving a horse to death could get it done in thirty. Four days: that was the daemon of a leeway she danced with. Arrive late, and the ghost would be lost to the void. He would vanish to nothing, and with it the chance to bind him. She had vowed over his bleeding and gasping body that would not be the case, and by the dead gods, she would keep that promise.

The pale sand at her heels turned blue. He was growing brighter now, more so every mile. It had instilled in him a boldness. Over the past hour, she had felt him warming up to another barrage of insults, working his limbs and muttering to himself. She had always been able to read him like a scroll.

'What cutting words do you have for me now?' she asked, and was rewarded with a tut.

His tone sounded jovial at first, soon slipping to hoarse rage. 'Well, Nilith, as it happens I find myself curious. You're still tramping north but it's been almost a day since your last drink of water. As the sun is due to rise soon enough, I was wondering when you were planning on dropping down dead!'

'How considerate of you.' Nilith let him wait for her answer. 'If you must know, I'm following an old riverbed, swallowed up by the sands.'

'And what good is that to us? You, I mean. What good is it to *you*? I could not give less of a fuck.'

She turned to look him in the eye, and at the gash her knife had drawn before his end. She recalled the blood bubbling over his lips as he gawped up at her like a hooked fish. He had muttered repugnant curses instead of the poignantly philosophical last words he had no doubt dreamed of. Farazar had been a fool in life and now he was a fool in death.

'It means an oasis further ahead, idiot. Oases rise from old riverbeds, because old riverbeds mean old springs.'

'And if there are people?'

'Then you will have to be extremely quiet, won't you? Otherwise you'll find out how much copper hurts a ghost.' Nilith tapped the hilt of her dagger, its cuprous blade catching the starlight.

'And you?'

'I will be even quieter.'

'I knew I should have married somebody from the Arc, not a barbarous easterner! The sun has cooked your brain, you foul wench.'

Nilith laughed at that, giving his body a sharp tug. 'If it's cooked mine in the twenty-two years I've spent shackled to you, then I hate to think what it's done to you and your ancestors over the centuries. Maybe that explains the Arc's lust for blood. Now quiet your tongue, before I cut it out. You may be dead, but I can still hurt you.'

She pressed on, letting Farazar hover behind her and test the limits of his boundaries. For anybody who was slain in turmoil – whether by blade or accident or disease – and not bound straight away, their ghost would naturally rise from their corpse several days after their death. The strange spell of death always tied them to their bodies. Twenty feet away from his corpse in any direction, and Farazar would hit a glass wall. If she moved onwards he would be hauled after his body. It infuriated him. He would poke at scrub grass and try to kick at stones, but he had not yet gained the form or control to have much luck besides nudging them.

Nilith decided to survey their surroundings, and after clambering out of the riverbed and to the top of a particularly tall and arduous dune, she was rewarded with the glimmer of torchlight. It twinkled, star-like, in the centre of a plain between the dunes, where a small village huddled around a burst of palms and ferns. Nilith could smell water on the breeze, sweet and full of minerals. Her parched tongue rasped in her mouth, like a sponge left out in the sun.

'People, like I said. I hope they catch you. Cut off your hands.'

Nilith drew the dagger and waggled it under the ghost's chin. She had half a mind to leave Farazar there, but if her sneaking turned sour, she didn't want to be running back on herself to fetch him. As a compromise, she approached the village by a curving path and left his body parallel to it, behind a wilted bush of some kind. The desert plants were all twig and thorn to her.

'You're going to abandon your prize? My body, here? In the dark? How dare you!'

'I dare how I please. You can't go anywhere, so why bother worrying?'

'What about wolves? Jackals? Foxes. They'll tear it… *me* to shreds, you inconsiderate trollop!'

'Oh, they would if they could get close enough. They can probably smell your corpse right now. Luckily, most beasts are scared of ghosts.' Nilith drew her knife. 'Unless it's you that's scared of the dark?'

'I…' Farazar trailed off, distracted by the shadows.

Nilith stalked away, crouched low and tense like a harp string. Her bones may have grown old, but they still remembered the wild steppes outside Saraka, hunting six-legged elk with nothing but a short blade. Krass she was, born and bred, and proud of it.

The village's torches were few, reserved mostly for the tiny streets between the mudbrick and plaster domes of houses. There were no guards or watchmen. With the desert awash with soulstealers and bandits, it seemed foolish. Hardly any of their windows were still aglow, but Nilith crept as though it were broad and burning daylight. She chose a darkened path, and was soon walking among the palms and wading through lush grass. She saw the oasis, black in the shade of the tall trees. Its waters bubbled gently.

Nilith darted to its edge and dipped her flask while she drank with her free hand. It was desperately cold, but it washed away the dust like an ocean wave. She took one last sip before dashing back to the sands.

Passing a larger dome, she spied a pen holding three horses. It was enough to make her pause, and after watching from behind a vine-wrapped trellis, she sprinted back to the oasis. Yellow berries hung like jewels between the thorns of a bush, and any fruit that was so jealously guarded must be safe to eat. She plucked two dozen, her fingers coming away spotted with blood. Clutching the fruit to her chest, she ran back to the horse-pen.

Its gate was a simple rope knot which her knife solved in a blink. She tied its ends into a makeshift halter and edged into the pen. The horses were skittish at a stranger, but Nilith knew beasts, and with low and open hands she calmed one enough to slip the halter over his neck. He was a short but sturdy creature, skewbald brown and cream like her last steed, with a black brush of a mane and bred for the desert. She stashed most of the berries in her pocket and held out a few in her palm. Rough, slobbery lips scooped them up in no time and soon she was being nuzzled for more.

Not wishing to risk the sound of galloping hooves, Nilith led the beast towards the desert at a walking pace. She left the pen closed, and after a moment of rummaging, left a cloth bag of gems on a post. Hopefully it would be a purchase and not a theft. As soon as she left the boundaries of the town, she broke into a run. The horse seemed content to trot at her side, probably keen for more berries.

Nilith found Farazar standing over his body with a length of scraggly desert bush in hand.

'I saw a wolf. Maybe a dog,' he said, noting her smirk. 'You're stealing livestock as well as souls now, I see?'

Nilith began to manhandle the body onto the horse's back, tying it in place with the rope. The animal almost fled at the smell alone, never mind the nature of the cargo. Farazar's ghost was already making him itchy. Horses were better than most beasts in the presence of the dead, but Nilith still had to spend a moment calming him. One hand pressed firmly on his coarse mane while the other stroked his neck.

His stubble-hair resisted her fingers. She could feel the shivers of his taut muscles, the rattle of his breath as he snuffled. The heat of his skin was welcome against her frigid hands. Calm whispers of nothingness spilled from her mouth, the babble of a gentle stream.

'I left a payment. Besides, it's for the greater good,' she replied once the horse had calmed. His unsaddled spine wasn't the comfiest seat in the world, but she was willing to swap it for four strong legs that weren't hers.

'And what the fuck is that supposed to mean?' asked the ghost.

'Nothing.' Nilith patted the horse's flank.

'Your greater good, perhaps.'

'I said shut it! Now, do you plan to float alongside the entire way?'

Apparently, he did. He'd already started walking. 'You know I detest riding with others.'

'Suit yourself.'

With a flick of her heels, the beast broke into a trot. She pointed him north, waiting until they were over a dune before kicking him into a gallop.

Farazar was clever. Once he grew tired of trying to keep up, he crossed his arms, adopted a regal pose, and let the spell of the bond pull him along. He would not be able to abandon his body until it was either pitched into the Nyx or Nilith's time ran out. For now it meant he followed behind the horse like a buoy trailing a ship. At least he was quiet. Nilith had only the rushing air for company, and the steady, if backside-bruising, gallop of the horse.

Anoish, she dubbed him. Her favourite of the old Arctian gods. Nilith had considered a Krass name, but he was a desert horse, not a steppe-hoof, and so he deserved a desert name. The god of the dead would no doubt have applauded her mission. Nilith had always harboured a private suspicion that the gods were not dead, just watching, but such notions were branded as madness in the Arc.

Anoish galloped until several hours past dawn until finally the heat got to him. His pace began to peter out, and he took to heavy puffing. Not wishing to be thrown by a horse twice in a week, Nilith rested him, walking while the sun ascended to its peak. Her buttocks thanked her, but every step brought back a new ache, or a forgotten sore between her toes.

Farazar kept his distance, pale blue in the harsh sunlight. He kept looking over his shoulder, seeming pensive.

IT WAS PAST MIDDAY WHEN they found the shallow ravine. It ran through the Long Sands in a north-easterly direction, and Nilith put it to good use, letting the horse rest in the shade while she took some water and dried meat. Anoish found some plants to nibble on, his rubbery lips smacking over their wiry branches. Farazar maintained his silence, no doubt cooking up more insults for later. She smirked at him as he paced. She had heard pretty much all of them over the years. It was always entertaining to watch him try to muster up something new.

Returning to Anoish's back, Nilith followed the ravine at a gentle trot. Every now and again, when a wayward dune blocked the way, they would pop up into the scorching heat and blink in the unfiltered sunlight. Around a fallen boulder, they spooked a pair of gazelles. Their hides were striped black and brown and their horns had the form of tree branches. The stick-legged creatures scattered in a puff of sand, vaulting clear out of the ravine in one hop.

When at last the path pointed too far east, they struck across the desert sands once more. Nilith called a halt at the summit of a dune to check her bearings. The Steps of Oshirim loomed on the horizon, sitting between her and Araxes. The mountains were naught but a black smudge, but they still filled her with dread. She would deal with them when the time came, and not a minute before. Between them lay the Long Sands: an utterly thrilling country of shallow dunes and rippled stretches of grassless plains. Bands of red, yellow and white salt flats ran through the landscape. Whirlwinds danced where the winds jostled shoulders.

Farazar's voice caused her to jump. 'Oh dear, Nilith.'

'What?'

When he didn't answer, she turned, finding him pointing back across the ochre plain they had just trudged across. Her gaze followed the trail of their footprints to three black dots shivering in the heat haze.

Nilith bared her teeth. 'Company.'

'Looks like you should have stuck to just stealing water.'

'Shut it. They're still an hour or two away.'

Farazar rubbed his hands gleefully.

With the ropes around the body tightened and Anoish calmed once more, Nilith drew her copper dagger. 'Mount the horse.'

'No.' There was a hint of a laugh in his voice.

'Get on the horse, or I'll cut off something precious.' Her eyes flicked down his naked frame to his painfully average manhood.

'Go ahead. It's not like I have any use for it now!'

'You never knew how to use it anyway, dear husband. Now get on the horse.'

'No.'

Nilith nicked the inside of his thigh with the flat of the blade, daringly close to more precious areas. He yelped, surprised at the pain.

'Fine!'

Farazar, with some difficulty, managed to climb onto Anoish's back, and sat hunched as Nilith followed suit. His vapour was thicker now, and she could almost feel the shape of a body against her chest. He was cold, and once again she hated herself for enjoying the relief it brought from the heat.

'Yah!' she cried, making the ghost wince.

They galloped until nightfall. Whenever Anoish slowed, Nilith pushed him harder. As the sun sank and bathed the world with gold, she saw the glow of metal on the distant figures. They had stayed level all afternoon, neither gaining nor falling back, simply following. It worried Nilith. It felt like time was being bided, and that was normally a luxury for those with the upper hand and the patience to wield it.

Night turned the blessing of Farazar's cold vapours into a curse. She leaned as far away from him as the galloping would allow, but still she shivered uncontrollably. Nilith made a mental note to switch places as soon as possible.

Anoish betrayed her as dawn's fingers came reaching over the black horizon. Despite Nilith's kicks, the horse's gallop ground to a canter, then to a trot, and finally a standstill.

Nilith slipped from his side, canteen in hand. With one hand cupped, the other pouring, she let him slurp the very last of the water.

Farazar was watching her. 'You won't outrun them. You'll be without hands by midday. Better yet, dead.'

'Keep hoping,' said Nilith. 'I'll keep disappointing you.' It pained her to admit it but Farazar was right, and it darkened her mood. Anoish might trot, but he would not lend her any real speed. She cast around in the faint light, looking for outcrops of rock. The dunes had flattened back into another plain, as if the landscape prostrated itself before the distant mountains. It offered not a scrap of shadow to her.

After another mile, in a shallow depression with pink salt encrusting its basin, she turned east to throw them off the trail. Nilith jogged alongside the horse, enduring Farazar's constant noise-making. His ghostly lips hadn't mastered whistling without lungs, so he hummed instead.

She was reaching for her dagger when Anoish whinnied and came scuffing to a halt. The halter jerked Nilith back, away from the edge of the pit she hadn't spotted. It was a shallow thing, dug by some weakness of the valley floor, but in the dawn light and growing haze it was practically invisible from more than forty feet away.

Nilith ran backwards to check once more and then rubbed her coarse hands together with a rasp. 'Down you go,' she ordered the ghost. He did as he was told, but with a snooty look.

'Never expected you to be the hiding type. It is cowardly.'

'That's rich, coming from you.'

Nilith made sure Anoish didn't break anything on his way down into the pit. His head poked above the lip, so she had to coax him to lie flat, easing his load a little to let him rest. 'Good horse.'

'Probably why they want him back.'

'Shut your mouth.' The threat came with a flash of copper. The dagger was already drawn and clutched in her hands. Farazar held his tongue, turning instead to watch the rippling tips of the distant dunes.

It took almost an hour for the black dots to catch up. Precious time wasted, and Nilith spent it baking like a hog on a spit in the rising sun. The turn in her path had not fooled them; she'd had no time to cover her tracks, never mind a palm frond to do the covering.

Nilith hissed, whacking the ghost on his arm, feeling cold, woolly air instead of flesh. 'Down! You glow too much.'

'And who's to blame for that, you murderous shrew? You're the one who turned me into this… this… *half-life*!'

She could see it hurt him deeply to use such a slur while talking about himself. It was strangely satisfying. She waggled the blade. 'Not now.'

Nilith hunkered down, stroking the hot flanks of the horse to keep him steady. His eyes were half closed in the heat, sand dusting his long, dark eyelashes.

The minutes inched past like lazy caterpillars. The black dots turned into quivering shapes sat tall atop horses. Their mounts were taller than Anoish, with reins encrusted with common gems. Those who lived beyond the Outsprawls of Araxes were too poor for silver coin. Nilith risked a peek and saw the glitter of blades, sweeping curves of steel and copper balanced on the riders' laps. Their sun-baked skin was wrapped in strips of yellow cotton, as though they were bodies ready to be surrendered to the Nyx. Pale spines, like the needles of a Krass quillhog, poked out here and there between the cloth around their heads. Desert-folk and nomads came from older bloodlines that had spent too long in the sands, or so the old fairytales said, and been changed by them. Most sported horns or goat-eyes, some had insectile features, but Nilith had never seen spines before. Though she dared not look any longer, she could hear them rattling softly as they rode.

She placed a finger over her lips as the men trotted closer, riding level with the pit in a wide line. The nearest of them came within easy bowshot. Nilith listened to the sound of hooves crunching on the tough salt, eyeing Farazar all the while. The copper blade hovered under his chin. Closer and closer they came, her heart rising with every hoofbeat, until they mercifully began to recede.

When they were beyond earshot, she finally let out a breath.

'Lucky,' sighed Nilith.

Farazar's face was sourer than a month-old lemon. 'Too lucky. It'll run out soon enough.'

She prodded at him again. 'You'd better get it into your thick head that whatever happens to me affects you. Feel free to enjoy indenturement in some desert hovel, or trailing a caravan for the next hundred years. Maybe they'll have you work in a desert colony.'

Farazar tried to spit but ended up spluttering viciously instead. 'Better than giving you the satisfaction of binding me!'

Nilith tapped the corpse beside her, smiling. 'We'll see. For now, you'd better hold that blue tongue of yours.'

Anoish was reluctant to get back on his hooves, but with some coercing and the help of a last handful of dried berries, he complied with a grumpy whinny.

With Farazar once again trailing behind at the leisure of the magic, Nilith rode with the body for an hour or two before dismounting to walk. The corpse had achieved a higher level of pungency. Before long, she was walking the horse at the full stretch of his ropes and breathing through her mouth.

And so the afternoon went: slow and weary for the both of them, spent largely looking over the shoulder and lip-biting. Nilith saw no more sign of the riders, and as the dune-shadows began to lengthen, she finally managed to relax.

THE EVENING'S CAMPSITE CAME IN the form of a small hollow on a rocky hillside. Even though she shuddered under her blanket and coat, Nilith risked no campfire. Starlight was their only illumination once more, and she had begun to find it a cold light. Even Anoish's warmth, pressing up against her back, did little to help. Maybe it was Farazar, sitting opposite, glowing sapphire like a starved oil lamp. Like the stars, he offered only cold air and beady eyes.

He was playing at his staring game again. His shoulder-length hair wafted about him at half-speed, like the tendrils of a jellyfish. Behind him, the hollow of rock shone a slate-grey with his light. Farazar was still as naked as the day he had risen from his corpse, peeling from his chest like a beetle outgrowing his carapace. He bore his neck wound proudly.

Farazar had now settled into his ghostly form, and that presented a new problem. He would soon be capable of holding things, touching things, even stealing sharp things from belts and plunging them into their owners' chests. Ghosts – or *shades* as the Arctians insisted on calling them, as if it somehow disguised their nature – were far from harmless, no matter what was preached. Although they were weak and no more solid than a feather pillow, they could still hold and use objects, such as rocks for bludgeoning, or sharp things for stabbing. Combined with a ghost's inability to sleep, it gave Farazar the capacity for revenge. He already had a heart black enough for it. The coldness of his gaze only affirmed that.

'Got more complaints for me?' she challenged him.

He narrowed his eyes at her. That little smile of his appeared. His words came calm and slow, but she heard the tightness of rage beneath them.

'At first I imagined my murder to be one of those wonderful lessons of yours; a final attempt to teach me the error of my Arctian ways. Decades you have spent giving me laborious, sanctimonious lectures. And yet here I am, being dragged along on some huge quest, a captive audience in every sense of the word, but I haven't heard one word of gloating of your great victory over me. That is most unlike you. It makes me curious.'

Nilith sighed. She was too tired for his manipulative games. 'This is no grand lesson, Farazar. There never were any lessons, only my points of view. They just happened to clash with your archaic Arctian traditions. Stop looking for excuses as you always do. We both know what this is: I killed you; I'm dragging you to Araxes; when we reach the Grand Nyxwell in Araxes, I will have you bound and claim what's yours.' She lifted up the copper coin that dangled around her neck and thrust it at him. 'It's as simple as that, Farazar, and the sooner you realise it, the more peaceful and quiet this journey will be. For me at least.'

'I was enjoying my own peace and quiet before you decided to track me down and murder me in cold blood.'

Nilith clicked her tongue. In Krass it was a sign of disrespect, and one she had never forgotten after her years living in the Arc. 'Whoring and drinking and smoking yourself into a shit-smeared heap is peace and quiet, is it? You could have stayed in Araxes to do that, instead of sneaking several thousand miles south to get away from me. Were the city's orgies boring you, husband?'

'Hmph. I had assumed that going all the way to Ede would keep my throat from being cut by scoundrels after my fortune, but look where that got me!' he replied. 'And to be accurate, they were not "whores". They were Duke Goljar's daughters. You would have found that out had you not knocked them senseless before proceeding to knife me.' He pawed his neck.

Nilith chuckled. 'I couldn't give a fuck. You could have surrounded yourself with an army and marched them past the edges of the maps, I would have still hunted you down. I've spent too long in your shadow, spent too long in that rancorous city. I long for change, Farazar, and your corpse is how I get it.'

Farazar's face fell into a bitter glower. His restraint was cracking. 'The things you learn even after two decades of marriage, hmm? I thought taking a wife from outside the Arc was a safe bet. I never thought you had the stones for murder. Now I see your greed knows no bounds. Perhaps there is some Arctian in you after all,' he hissed.

That needled her. Nilith got to her feet, forgetting herself and her surroundings. 'You prideful prick! You think it was for mere greed that I slew you? You're a bigger fool than I thought!'

As he too flew to standing, his face a snarl, she realised she had given him the reaction he had been digging for.

'And you're a filthy Krass peasant whose father couldn't marry you off quick enough! And now you dare to claim me as your own? Good fucking luck! I'll make every step of this journey a battle. I'll wave at ever nomad and trader. Shout at the top of my lungs through every street. You'll be lucky if you make it to the edges of the city alive! Whatever it demands of me, I will have my retribution for your crimes!'

'Ha! You have so much faith in the people of the Arc and yet you forget what a murderous, cut-throat empire it is. Go ahead. Shout away! You think they'll care for you? You're not special. You're a fresh ghost. They'll have you bound in a blink! I've known you for twenty-two years. Every flaw and sin. You're a man full of hate and spite and greed, but above all, you reek of pride. You could never be a ghost to some beetle farmer, and for that reason you'll stay quiet as your corpse!' Nilith patted her dagger in warning.

His blue glow had taken on a darker hue, almost violet. 'Then I'll tear my body to pieces if I have to, or throw it in the nearest Nyxwell, coin or not. You will never bind me, Nilith, I promise you that. None shall! I'll either be free, laughing from the afterlife, or in the void before I let you stand on my corpse and claim what is mine!'

Nilith's answer never made it from her lips. An arrow sliced against the back of her calf before burrowing into the sand. She half-fell, half-threw herself to the grit as another shaft buzzed through the air, clipping a rock. She stared down at the black fletching and the blood staining it.

Farazar immediately forgot his rage and curled up in a tight ball, flinching with every clatter of arrows. He was safe; they weren't copper-tipped. It appeared their attackers had no desire to harm their prize.

Anoish, tied to a rock further up the hill, had started to buck and whinny. Nilith stole a glance down the slope. In the starlight she saw three familiar shapes flowing over the scree and boulders. Two loosed their bows while the other climbed, who then took his turn to shoot as the others overtook him. It was clever work; she had no pause in which to flee.

Nilith grasped for her dagger and shuffled her feet, ready to spring. She didn't have to wait long.

The first figure bounded into the hollow, yellow tails of cloth streaming like banners. It was a man, judging by his stature, holding a curved sword high above his swaddled head. The ash-grey quills protruding from the cloth rattled as his gaze switched between the ghost and herself, crouching on the floor.

He paused too long. Nilith pounced, throwing her weight into his chest despite the searing pain in her calf. She rode him to the ground, hearing the crunch of his spiny head against the rock. Her dagger passed across his throat, drawing an arc of blood in the air. She snatched his bow from his shoulders, nocked an arrow, and as the second man burst into view, she let it fly. His neck snapped back, arrow planted firmly in his forehead and raised like a flagpole. He teetered for a moment before disappearing into the darkness.

Once the echoes of his tumble across the scree had died, silence fell across the hillside. Nilith's last foe was hiding somewhere below, waiting her out. The next arrow quivered in her shaking hands.

'Get up,' she hissed to Farazar, still curled up nearby.

'Excuse me?'

'Stand up and start walking! They're not copper-tipped, you idiot!' She glared at him, but he refused to move. She heard the crackle of pebbles below her.

'Do you want to spend the rest of your existence shackled to some goatherd? Move, Farazar!'

The ghost wrenched himself up and marched across the hollow.

An arrow hissed through him, making him yelp. It clattered on the stone beside him.

Nilith wrenched herself up and sent her arrow into the night. It was a messy shot, catching the man in the thigh. He began to hobble away, but she was already marching awkwardly down the scree, dripping dagger in hand. It was a wretched sort of race: both limping and lame, where the only prize was not dying.

The man took a stance on flatter ground, wrappings heaving around his mouth with each laboured breath. His crescent sword was out and shining. She beckoned with her copper dagger, and he cursed in a tongue she had never heard before.

With great windmilling swings, he advanced. Nilith weaved with them as she hobbled backwards. Her timing needed to be perfect. There was no fancy blade work to be done here, no flourishes or parries. Her copper blade would be cloven in two if she tried to block the thick steel.

He let loose his war cry, but it withered almost immediately as Nilith kicked at the arrow still protruding from his thigh. There was a snap and a screech, and it gave her time enough to drive her dagger under his blade and up into his belly. She stared into his dark brown eyes as she held the weapon in place. They rolled up to the whites as the life drained from him, his quills wilting with his strength. The words lingered on her lips, unsaid until it was too late.

'I'm sorry.'

As she let the body drop to the gravel, the pain caught up with her. One leg was aflame, and the accompanying boot felt hot and wet with blood. With much cursing of her own, she made her way back up the hillside, a new scimitar balanced on her shoulder.

Farazar was waiting with slack arms. His eyes were wider than when the arrows had been flying over his head. It was to be expected; in all their years of marriage, he had never seen her brandish a sword.

'Some more to say, husband?' she asked, seeking something to sit on after she gathered up the stray arrows. 'Feel like waving at nomads now? Shouting to the night?'

'No,' he replied, watching her pour the blood out of her boot.

Nilith caught his expression, and despite the throbbing pain and the gaping laceration across her calf muscle, she had to chuckle.

'You must be losing your memory now that you're dead, husband. You call me Krass as an insult and yet you forget what that means to me. Our mothers don't push when we're ready to meet the world. We have to claw our way out, and so we're born fighting. You call me peasant, but you forget my life before Araxes was spent in Saraka's training yards and hunting in pine forests. You have forgotten who I am, and in doing so, you have underestimated me, and that was a dire mistake. You wanted a lesson, husband, and there it is. So please, threaten me some more. We'll see how little of you makes it to the city.'

The ping of her nail against the scimitar's steel edge punctuated her threat. As Farazar held her stare, she saw the realisation dawn behind those white eyes. Not only how deadly she was, but just how determined she was, too.

Lip curled, Farazar looked away, seeking something in the stars. 'And you wonder why I didn't want to marry a Krasswoman,' he muttered.

CHAPTER 5

THE SOULMARKET

At current count, not including the Outsprawls, Araxes is comprised of three thousand and forty-six districts. Altogether they contain an estimated four million constant inhabitants, both alive and dead.

ARAXES CITY CHARTER,
ARCTIAN YEAR OF 1003

THEY CAME TO FETCH US at the crack of dawn. Men with robes and gloves of copper thread.

They called us out one by one, shouting our ghost names. I ignored mine until they were forced to come and grab me. A heavy rope was looped about our necks and something in its fibres itched me. When it was tightened, it pressed hard against my vapours, as if they were as firm as flesh again. It must have had a copper core.

Boss Temsa and his soulstealers had been busy. There were twenty of us now, the product of two nights of hunting. Some hadn't been dead more than two hours, still wild of eye and faint of vapour. They flashed me desperate looks, but I ignored them. My brief time in the cage had hardened me to any plight but my own.

Temsa was waiting in a domed hall beside two covered wagons. A wide, half-open door revealed a street and sunlight. He was leaning on his cane, his leer framed by his dark beard, freshly oiled and combed. His entire outfit was a deep sea blue, trimmed with gold and silver chains. Copper rings claimed every other finger. His cane was an elongated shard of obsidian. Coloured dust had been dabbed around his eyes and their wrinkles. Jexebel stood at his side with a broad-headed axe in her hand, and behind her loitered a gaggle of black-clad sellswords.

'Load them up,' Temsa ordered, thumping a wagon's wheel before addressing us. 'You'd better be on your best behaviour at market, you hear? Buyers pay good silver for obedience and mild manners in a half-life. Perfect temperament for a house-shade. Play the fool, and you might find yourself heading north to work in the docks or factories!'

The collective groan from my fellow ghosts was audible.

'Jexebel!' Temsa hollered. 'Get the butchered ones up front and get them some shade-dust. The sun's doing us no favours today.'

I was one of six picked out of the line. One had a sword-cut so deep into his collarbone that his head looked fit to topple. Another's guts peeked from a slash across his belly, all frozen in the moment of death. Kech was there too, with his glowing talon marks. He gave me the usual hateful and accusing glare, and I mouthed a polite suggestion to go fornicate with himself. It was his fault I was here. The second day in the cage, he'd tried to throttle me. All I'd felt was a cold waft of air at my torn throat and much amusement.

The robed men came at me with clay dishes of crushed blue powder. They flicked pinches of it over my neck and stomach, trying their hardest not to touch me. The dust stuck to my wounds, even swirling with the slow movement of my vapours. The white scars dimmed somewhat, but did not disappear.

I looked down at Temsa as he wandered close to inspect me. 'You won't get away with this.'

It was clear he'd heard these sorts of complaints countless times before. 'And so you have yelled for almost two days now. Tell me again how you have business in the Cloudpiercer! Of the injustice! The horror! Fear not, shade. It will sink in soon enough. That, or your new master will beat it into you.'

I muttered something foul.

Temsa wasn't satisfied with me. He waggled the sharp metal tip of his cane in my face. 'You curse like that at the soulmarket, shade, and I'll have you put through a copper mangle. You think pain's only for the living? Just you wait and see what death can hold.'

That put a good measure of fear in me, so I held my tongue and let Temsa's workers haul me away. We filled the interior of the wagons with our glow: ten ghosts and a guard apiece. With a whip-crack, we juddered out into the dawning daylight.

All I'd seen of Araxes at this point was a few alleys, the sharp end of a knife and a dingy cage. I craned my neck to see the grand spires above me. It was almost as if I needed to prove, once and for all, that this wasn't a nightmare, nor some devilish dream.

But there they were: the mighty towers of Araxes. Sandstone, marble and imported granite occupied half the sky. Some coiling and needle-pointed, others wider and pyramidal. There seemed to be an unspoken challenge between the buildings of the City of Countless Souls; every one of them competed to touch the sun. They stretched into the brightening sky, gleaming yellow on one side while their western flanks took on a colourless shadow. The beauty was far from lost on me.

Like a mountain range thrust up by some churning of nature, Araxes was not only mighty in its peaks, but in its foothills, too. Even at street level, buildings clambered atop one another. Houses and minor towers rose above in twisted shapes or clung like molluscs to older structures. Whitewash and adobe glowed pink and orange in the morning light. Ropes and cranes poked from every other rooftop. Billowing flocks of pigeons and starlings raced each other between pennants and spires.

Above that, the rich held sway. The towers cast their long shadows over the streets. Spiderwebs of lofty roads and bridges spread between them, leading to the core of the city. There the buildings formed a crown about the mighty Cloudpiercer, staggering even at that distance. No other tower reached more than half its height. It dominated all.

When I grew bored of the heavens, my gaze turned back to the gutters. I saw then how Araxes had earned its name. I watched the multitudes of ghosts flowing through the streets, swelling at every junction like tributaries of a gargantuan river. The living were flotsam amongst their numbers. Traders, citizens, beggars and travellers far luckier than

I, all beginning their days by jostling with the dead. It was a gruesome sight, and a far cry from the streets of Krass cities, like noble Taymar or the capital Saraka, where the dead merely peppered the cobbles instead of infesting them. Then again, in Krass, we did not measure wealth by the number of souls one owned, but in good old-fashioned silver.

I found myself wanting to see more of the living, and I searched for them among the glowing crowds. Copper and steel-clad knights took their places in guard-boxes, or on corners where headless statues of dead gods gathered sand. Bakers and smiths stoked their street-side fires. Shops and teahouses flung open their doors to set out cushions in the dust. Pipe and card-dens were already summoning a haze about their doorways. Some old bugger with a white beard wrapped around his head like a turban sat in a doorway, wailing away on some curly kind of flute. A yellow rat danced before him.

Here and there a wagon or cart would force its way through the crowds, led by stout horses or enormous insects. We saw few of the latter in my country. I stared at the beetles and their tree-like horns of deep emerald and black, the hairy spiders creaking as they took their ponderous paces, and the centipedes in their long traces. Every now and again one reared up, spiny legs flailing as they hissed at something in their way. Whips would crack, and they came back to the earth with a bang. The armoured plates along their backs rippled as they moved along, their legs undulating like waves approaching a shore.

I'd heard tales of the Arctian fondness for the large desert insects. We Krass trusted in smarter beasts: horses, ponies, goats, even wolves. There was more intelligence behind their eyes, instead of the black, deadpan gaze of a beetle. To me, it seemed the insects were constantly deciding whether to eat you or not. It was certainly true of their wilder cousins; the ones that roamed the deserts and gobbled up unwary travellers. Dunewyrms, they called them, giant creatures that had a frightful habit of hiding in dunes and luring in prey with a glowing tentacle.

A puff of coloured smoke distracted me, and my attention was drawn to a seemingly endless row of street kitchens. Simple coals and grates smoked in doorways or under dangerously low-slung tarpaulins. On those black and dripping grills I saw chunks of meat on skewers, quarters of chicken and waterfowl marinated in lurid red and yellow pastes. Haunches of what I suspected to be beetle meat roasted in beds of hot coals. Glass jars of rainbow-coloured juices lay on slanted tables, surrounded by their associated fruits and vegetables. I didn't recognise half of them.

Besides the intoxication of cracking locks and pinching other people's things, I am a man of simple tastes: fresh air, another body in my bed, and as my ample belly would suggest, beer and food. On the accursed *Kipper*, I had salivated over the idea of filling myself with western food. I had thought long and hard about the waves of heady spices and sugars Arctian cuisine was famed for. I sniffed, but found nothing but icy air in my nostrils. I snorted long and hard until the guard glowered, but the world stayed bland. My sense of smell was non-existent. *Another insult for the pile.* Strange, how one longs for something only after it is taken away. At that moment, I would have buried my face in a sun-baked gutter, just so I could smell again.

The wagons came to a halt in a wide square lined by old brick towers and overshadowed by awnings of bright crimson. Temsa clacked his cane on the bench-backs, ordering us ghosts up and out. I could already see sweat on his forehead. I imagined the air was growing hotter by the minute, but all I felt was cold.

We ghosts were poked into a smart line of height order, and I took the chance to look around the soulmarket, where thin groups of finely-dressed buyers hovered around clusters of stalls; merchants, eager to provide some distraction while the wares arrived. I could see sizzling pans for those who hadn't yet broken their fast, and all manner of ghost-related paraphernalia for the buyers. Whips and switches, shackles and gags, all of them gleaming copper.

Behind us was a squat wooden platform, standing about three feet high. A ring of gold rope had been stretched around poles on every corner. Packs of men and women wearing white silk cloaks stood about it with scrolls in hand and bags under their wrinkled eyes. They seemed official enough, and the fact that this wasn't some cellar-room soul sale but a legitimate and sanctioned soulmarket was actually more disturbing. The Arctians seemed to approach death and slavery with fewer questions than a drunk being offered another glug of palmshine. Had I not already felt deathly cold, I would have shivered, and only the fear of being thrown into a factory kept me from cursing them all at the top of my voice.

Other wagons were beginning to arrive. I stared at the ghosts filing out onto the sand. I wondered if the living who herded them were also soulstealers, and as cruel as Temsa and his crew. It shocked me to think the hundred or so dead that stood around the edges of the square could have all been murdered. Surely there had to be honest soultraders here, profiting off genuine accidents and illness. The Tenets' definition of "turmoil" was amazingly broad. I'd heard that in the Arc, it was considered fortunate to die at your allotted time at a ripe old age.

Boss Temsa stood nearby, deep in conversation with the white-cloak officials. He was bartering for something, though their hushed whispers were too rapid for my dulled ears. By the time they reached an agreement, the first threads of a crowd had begun to gather around the rope.

It soon became apparent what Temsa had been bargaining for: any position other than first in the schedule. The prospective buyers were sparse, and, like the day, barely warmed up. He looked confident as the first line of wares were marched onto the platform, closely watched by armed men. The ghosts were naked, just as I was. My eyes roved over their wounds, helplessly measuring myself against them. It was a sour blotch on my character, hoping somebody had suffered a worse death than me just to ease my vanity, but I was desperate for an upside to my situation.

One of the cloaked officials opened the soultrading proceedings in a shrill voice, greeting the market in Arctian first before permanently switching to Commontongue. Between every sentence his head bobbed up and down to check his scroll.

'Boss Ubecht's lot. Comprised of nine souls. Mostly fresh to medium-bound. Some skilled workers. Others good for hard labour. Do we have any interest?'

The bids came slowly and intermittently. Hands crept up cautiously. It took several minutes for a skinny pair of ghosts to fetch fifty-five, which made Temsa titter to his bulging bodyguard. Jexebel barely smiled.

Next came a sorrier-looking bunch than before. One ghost was particularly agitated, straining at his ropes and gurning at the crowd. If he hadn't been dead, I'd have guessed he was heavily constipated. Instead, he looked crippled by fear.

A woman in a fine leopard-fur coat came forward and waved the announcer away. Her eyes were smoky with ash and orange paint, and her lips were painted gold. Countless bangles clung to her skinny, tattooed wrists. She toured the ropes, teasing out the curls in her dark hair as she proclaimed her wares.

'Ladies and gentlemen, tals and tors, citizens of this fine city! I present to you some of Araxes' finest souls. Here we have a cook, trained in the Scatter Isles. A seamstress. A nurse. Even a tailor! Why wait to bid on lesser souls, when you can have one of mine instead? Barani guarantees every worker as a genuine death in accordance with the emperor's Code and Tenets. Never have I engaged in soulstealing, unlike some others here, and never shall I!'

The agitated ghost burst out screeching, unable to control himself any more. 'Help me! Somebody please help me! She—'

A copper gauntlet smacked the ghost onto the floor and into silence. When he was dragged up by the guards, he was hunched, sullen, and cross-eyed.

'Genuine death, she says!' barked Temsa, stamping his foot with a clang that made me jump. A smattering of laughter spread through the crowd.

The woman, Barani, was not deterred. She raised her hands with a flourish. 'Do I have any bids for my first shade here? Starting at thirty! Can you give me thirty?'

Her volume and patter had attracted some more buyers. The soulmarket's crowd was beginning to grow in number and in willingness. A low rumble of conversation sprang up.

'Forty from Widow Horix! Thank you. And forty-five from you, Tal Rashin. Fifty to Master Wafah.'

Temsa was busy grousing behind me. 'Fifty silver for that desiccated corpse? We should get into poisoning, m'dear. Apparently that's what these rich pricks want.'

Miss Jexebel growled an affirmation, idly thumbing the axe blade at her waist.

I felt a tickle at my elbow and found Kech standing next to me. 'I hope they put you in the fucking sewers and make you clean shit for a hundred years.'

Before I could retort, Temsa poked us both with his cane.

'Shut it, morons,' he hissed, and Kech sidled away.

With every bid, with every ghost that was hauled from the platform and shown their new master, my trepidation grew. Which of these rich folk would be mine? Would they believe me when I told my story? Would they even listen? Questions sputtered in my mind like water from a choked hose.

A shove dragged me from my thoughts, and before I knew it, I was climbing the handful of steps to the platform. The crowd looked different from up there, even just a few feet from the dust. As a locksmith, I was not one for attracting attention, never mind being the centre of it. The multitude of eyes felt scratchy, like spiders' legs crawling over my nakedness. And I abhor spiders.

Instead, I turned my gaze to the Cloudpiercer, ever-present above the rooftops. I wondered about that alternate life where I had made my appointment in its reaches instead of being murdered. You don't get to be the best locksmith in the Far Reaches without a bit of discipline. In twenty years I had only failed one job, and that was still a gaping wound in my pride. Yet here I was again, letting down a second employer, thanks to Temsa.

I tried to grind my teeth but they felt like a sea-sponge. I wondered at my mystery employer, and what they would have wanted from me. *Etane*. No doubt they were already in contact with my rivals. That damned Evalon Everass wench.

Temsa was already deep into his introductions, swaggering across the stage, blue coattails swishing.

'…so as you see, ladies and gentlemen, I peddle no torn and bedraggled souls this morning. Only clean-killed shades. Simply honest, hard-working shades that will do your house, shop, or factory proud. Ask anybody about Boss Boran Temsa, and they will tell you I deal in nothing but honesty and quality, as I have done for years. Let the bids begin!'

I felt the eyes searching every inch of my nakedness, examining me, measuring me. The pressure built inside my chest, and I understood then why the other ghost had been so distressed. The words spilled without thought behind them. Rather than for such noble ideals as revenge or justice, I blurted out of desperation, 'I was murdered! Bound against my will!'

'Ha!' Temsa chuckled, unbothered. 'We have a joker!' He motioned to Ani and something sharp poked me in the back. It felt like a hot poker, and it sealed my lips shut. The buyers shrugged and tittered to themselves. There must have been a hundred of them now, all richly dressed and sparkly-eyed with the idea of owning more souls.

Temsa continued. 'For Amin here, a skilled and trusted cook, do I have thirty?'

And so the bidding went, cascading down the line towards me at the end. It gave me some satisfaction to see Kech go for cheap, which I attributed to the fact his face looked like the arse end of a pumpkin. I held my chin high until Temsa called my new name. I even tried to smile, despite the emotions bubbling up somewhere in my vapours. If I was to be sold, I would be sold right. A noble master might be useful to my cause.

'And finally, we have Jerub, a Krassman who should not be dismissed despite his uncharacteristic outburst. He's a shy soul. A proficient manservant of fifteen years before death, and one year of his life already spent in servitude. One previous master since death, and in my expert soultrader's opinion he would make quite the excellent house-shade. Do we have thirty?'

I scanned the crowd. Not a body moved.

Temsa forced a grin. 'Twenty-five?'

One man called out from the back. 'Pretty cut up, Temsa!'

Irritatingly, Temsa played the man well. 'An unfortunate accident involving an angry butcher, I'm afraid. The easterners are barbarians compared to our civilised Arctian ways!'

'I'll give you twenty,' spoke an old woman, shrouded in frills of black.

'Do I have twenty-five?'

The calls rolled in, hesitant and muted.

'Twenty-two!'

'Twenty-three.'

'Twenty-four!' hollered a pale, noble-looking man wearing a conical hat and metallic silks. Cut copper medals adorned his breast. Despite the rest of him being rotund, his face was narrower than an axehead and he wore a pompous scratch of a moustache on his lip.

'Thank you, Tor Busk! Twenty-five?'

The woman in black raised a hand. I scrutinised her wrinkled, brown arms, trying to scour the face beneath her satin cowl.

'Twenty-five for you, Widow Horix. Do I have thirty?'

Busk's hat wobbled. 'Twenty-seven!'

Horix raised that winter's branch of an arm again. 'Twenty-eight.'

'Will any of you match twenty-eight?' Temsa cast about the circle, arms wide, cane searching for movement. Silence reigned. Stillness fell. He was wise enough to recognise a lost cause when one slapped him in the face.

'And sold! To Widow Horix!'

Strong hands muscled me offstage, under the rope, and towards a cloaked and bearded man holding a scroll. The other sold ghosts gathered around me. Kech was there, glowering as always. He'd been sold to the buyer named Tor Busk. The balloon of a man hovered nearby, eager to check over his new property. His moustache twitched as if he were on the cusp of sneezing.

Temsa came to ink his signature in three callous swirls and punched his basic seal into the papyrus with a stained ring. As a bidding of farewell, he offered each of us a smug look before clanking away to his wagons. I don't remember the particulars of what I silently vowed to him in that moment, but I know it involved plenty of torture and grief.

I was harassed into a line with the two other ghosts purchased by the woman Horix. I had only spied a limb of her during the proceedings, but she came to meet us now, and I gazed upon my new master.

The widow walked slowly yet purposefully, a rising tide of black cloth and frills. No flowing rainbow silks for this woman, no metal trimmings around her neck; just a cowl and a puffy gown. Her hands were clasped inside her sleeves like an ancient monk. They showed themselves only once to drop a fat leather bag of coins into a cloaked man's open hand. She didn't offer a single look of acknowledgement, even while scratching her signature and seal on his scroll, or snatching up our three half-coins from the man's palm. Her stare was reserved for us: her acquisitions. The two white orbs hovering in the shade of her hood switched between us and our wounds.

To the left of me stood a young, skinny lad, whose eyes were bulging out of their sockets. I wasn't sure if it was due to fear or the enormous section missing from the back of his skull. To my right was a woman with dark patches around her throat, and black veins climbing her cheeks like tendrils of ivy. *Throat-rot.*

'Stand up straight!' snapped Horix when she came close enough. We did our best, but she tutted all the same. Personally speaking, spending the morning being herded and sold like cattle didn't put one in the most acquiescent of moods.

'I see Temsa's given you no training.'

'No, ma'am,' said the croaky woman to my right.

'Ma'am? Such foreign tones. I am a tal. A noble of this city. What are you? Too pale to be Krass. Scatter Isles?'

'Skol, Tal.'

'Looks like you'll be needing some training, then. House-shade, was it? Or was that gold-footed swindler spouting falsehoods again?'

'Nanny, ma'am.'

'Close enough! Name?'

I saw her birth-name sputter on her lips and die. 'Lu... Bela, ma'am.'

Horix waved her aside and turned her attention to me. I looked down into her cowl, seeing a web of wrinkles across a brown face. I found the white orbs to have slate-coloured centres. She eyed my waistline, then the copper half-moons in her hand. She had my half-coin right there; the lock and chain that bound me to this world. I longed to snatch it and run.

'Jerub, if I'm correct?' she said, reading the glyph Temsa's binders had scratched into my coin. 'I forget what Temsa touted you as, but I can tell it wasn't a labourer.'

'Close. A bear tamer,' I replied in a flat tone.

She nodded, then slowly removed a long, spatula-like implement from her sleeve. It glittered in the morning sun, like her ruby-painted fingernails. Some of the nearby soulmarket officials hummed in a low tone, nudging each other.

Before I could dodge, the tool swished through the air and slapped me square across the face. The pain was intense, spreading across my skin like hot poison through veins.

Horix patted her palm with the implement, watching me wince. 'Let's try again, shall we?'

It took a while to get my jaw to work. 'Temsa said a manservant. Though in truth I worked with doors,' I added, hoping for a higher station.

The widow cocked her head. 'Guarding them or breaking them down?'

The spatula was good at eliciting pain, but not truth. This wasn't my first interrogation. 'Neither. I designed and built them. I was a vaultsmith.' A good lie dances close to the truth.

The widow cast a look back at Temsa, climbing aboard his wagon with Ani Jexebel in tow. 'That man,' she tutted.

I grasped for my opportunity. The words had been poised on my lips since I'd been shown the stage. Besides, I thought it best to be upfront. Why endure any more servitude than I had to? 'He's not just a liar, Tal Horix. He's a murderer. A soulstealer. He had men catch and kill me. I came here on honest business. I was on my way to meet my employer when I was accosted!'

Once more, the wicked tool was raised, but she didn't use it. Instead, the widow fixed me with a stare. There was no more kindness to be found in those wrinkles than on a windswept mountainside. I tried my best not to flinch as I urged her with my eyes.

The spark of hope was coldly squashed as she turned away, looking instead to the bug-eyed brat beside me. I hung my head.

'And you, boy. Mamun, was it?'

The boy worked his lips as if he was new to speaking. 'Mhm.'

'Fresher than the rest, are you? You look Arctian.'

'Mhmfl.'

'I see. Horse boy?'

'Grhmr.'

The widow took a step back to survey us once more and after a nod, we apparently passed her test. She motioned to somebody in the crowd and a bookcase of a man came wading toward us. His arms couldn't have touched his ribs even under duress. Dressed all in mail and black leather, he would have made an imposing character without the pirate's beard bursting from his cheeks, the raft of medals on his bulging chest, and the set of knives strapped to his thigh. He was the sort of man who made me want to suck in my belly, stand a little straighter and jut out my jaw, all in a vain effort to limit the damage to my masculinity. I knew it was a base reaction, instinctual, but until our animal nature is completely bred or educated out of us, it will always have first say.

'This man is Colonel Horat Kalid. Retired from the emperor's armies. He commands my guard, my house, and therefore you. Bow.'

I offered a shallow bow.

The colonel looked us over with a curl of the lip. He was almost as tall as Jexebel. 'The standard of stock is slipping,' he said in a voice that had the timbre of rocks colliding.

The widow tutted. 'They'll do, for what we need.'

'Suppose.'

She swatted at him with the spatula, but he didn't move. The touch of copper had no effect on living skin, never mind solid muscle and mail. 'Load them up, Colonel. Show them to Yamak and Vex. They'll get them settled.'

Rattling our half-coins in her hand, she walked away, unaccompanied and undeterred by the crowd. She spared only one glance and that was for me. It was cold and blank. I wanted to shout after her, make her turn again. Even if it resulted in another painful slap, at least I would know I had been heard and understood.

The colonel bound us with more stiff, itchy rope, and led us to a flat cart where we were told to sit in silence. I spent the jolting journey with my face skywards, watching the spires pass by and wondering how many ghosts it took to afford such lofty heights. I wondered if the widow would have such grand apartments, perhaps with a fine view. Anything to lighten the load of eternal indenturement.

I attempted to approach the problem the best way I knew how. A locksmith works on the principle of one set path. Although a lock has many tumblers, cogs, springs and traps, every lock has but one solution. The trick to being a good locksmith – nay, the *best* locksmith in all the Reaches – was honing in on that solution. If indenturement was my locked door, and justice and freedom lay behind it, then all I had to do was pick the lock. Currently, I felt like a freshpick, staring down a keyhole and sweating at the number and weight of the tumblers in front of me.

This city was even more fickle and uncaring than any rumours I had heard. Any hope that my new master would be concerned by a stolen soul had been crushed. Freedom and vengeance now seemed to be slipping further away. What had I expected of a nobility that revolved around tight lips and blind eyes? For all I knew, Horix could have had a share in Temsa's business. Why would she care about my murder, if that was the case?

'Fuck all, is what,' I said. I did not shout it, but I needed to hear it aloud to vent my frustration. The other ghosts stared at me, confused. They had a point, and it was illustrated by Kalid's fist slamming on the edge of the cart.

'Quiet back there!'

If this city was so dismissive of its living, extinguishing a recalcitrant ghost would be little more than a minor inconvenience. Twenty-eight silvers lost, and that would be the sum of me.

If I was to have my freedom, I needed to be quiet and clever, like any thief worth his salt. *And patient.* That gave me an ounce of solace. Say one thing for locksmiths: we're patient bastards.

I rested my cold head against the juddering wood, and waited.

CHAPTER 6

HER TIME

Strangebinding came on the heels of the phantom and deadbinding fashions, and required a slow immersion, with plenty of blind solitary confinement for a number of days until the subject was calm and had come to comfort in the host body. Domesticated animals were always preferred over wild, as the soul tended to blend somewhat with the body's natural tendencies. Hounds, felines, larger birds. No example of a fish strangebond ever survived. Compared to the deadbound, such as soulblades, madness was mightily decreased, and yet it was still spurned by the greater population.

FROM 'THE BINDING LIGHT',
BY THE NYXITE SHAMAS

HER FOOTSTEPS FELL WITH THE steady but fervent beat of a smith's hammer. They echoed along the voluminous corridor, making her sound like a dozen. Ahead stood a grand doorway of varnished foreign wood, copper and gold. On either side of it were stationed two Royal Guards. They stood at attention, with their wicked, hooked spears raised high and at arm's length. She watched them intently as she marched, daring them to move: a twitch, a shift of their features through their golden faceplates, a ripple in their turquoise capes. *Anything for an excuse to ruin their perfect poise.* To her annoyance, they remained like statues. On any other day, she would have walked leisurely down the sun-painted corridor and made them tremble with the effort. But on a day like today, Empress-in-Waiting, Sisine Talin Renala the Thirty-Seventh did not have time for such torture.

'Out of my way!' she yelled from a dozen paces away. The guards withdrew rapidly with bowed heads.

'The doors, curse you!'

'Yes, Highness!'

Shining gauntlets yanked at ropes, and the doors swung open just wide enough for her to enter.

After the opulence of the corridor, the antechamber beyond felt austere. A solitary bench, all sandalwood and silver swirls, sat in the centre of the circular room. Aureate lamplight spilled from plated sconces set into the plain marble. Another door stood in front of her, far mightier than the one behind her and far more decorative. It was not tall or square, but circular and formidable like the door of a half-coin vault. And rightly so, for this was the emperor's Sanctuary; her father's answer to the cutthroat tendencies of his family and countless subjects. A fine solution for the person inside it, but highly inconvenient for all those outside.

The Sanctuary was armoured with gold and copper, and across the flawless metal were engraved scenes of ancestral battles and hordes of subjects prostrate before pyramids. The royal seal of a spiked crown and half-coin hung above them, surrounded by a bloom of desert flowers made of steel. At the doorway's centre, five holes were arranged in a circle. No jewels were clasped there, and no jewels ever would be, for the gods were dead and these were keyholes for highly coveted keys. Only one jewel graced the door, and that sat between the keyholes: a diamond the width of Sisine's palm, glowing gold with the lamplight. A deadlock, they called it; a lock that would rip the soul from any that tried to tamper with the Sanctuary. Sisine's fingers traced its frozen, glasslike surface.

If one looked closely at the door, they might have seen fine gaps that betrayed hidden hatches. One such hatch was placed at the bottom of the door, and it was perfectly scroll-sized.

Sisine rattled through the ritual. First she knelt, then bowed to recite the salutation. 'May your reign be long and prosperous, my emperor, powerful of strength and mind, lord of all the sun touches. May both the living and the dead remember your name throughout all ages to come.'

Two knocks sounded and the small hatch popped. A stubby scroll was pushed through. No sooner had she grasped it did the hatch shut with a clang. She knocked twice on the door, and waited.

'Father?' she called softly. 'Can you hear me?'

No answer came. Just the whack of a hand against the other side of the door, several feet away.

'Suit yourself,' Sisine snarled. 'The Cloud Court awaits me.' With the scroll gripped in both hands, she swept from the room, her raven-coloured hair trailing behind her like a banner.

Several floors below the Sanctuary, a phalanx of Royal Guard waited to escort her into the court chamber. They added the clanging of armour to her staccato march, but it did nothing to drown out the court's bickering. Sisine heard it long before entering the cavernous hall. The soldiers peeled away from her, left and right, and with her skirts swishing against the marble, she took her place in the centre of four great pillars that held up the ceiling.

Sisine looked up at the gathered sereks of the Cloud Court. A hundred strong, they perched on high balconies and sat pretty in grand chairs. The multi-coloured swathe of silk and velvet and gold stretched almost halfway around the chamber. The sun pouring through the slanted windows made one half of the chamber glow and cast the other in shadow behind glare. Bold blue sat beyond the light, cloudless and empty. Not a single tower in the city was tall enough to peek into the Cloudpiercer's court.

She stood with her arms folded, scroll clasped to her breast, and waited for silence. It was a long time coming, and once the sereks' conversation and arguments had dried up, Sisine bowed to the throne at the southern side of the court as if her father were sat upon it. The grand sculpture of turquoise quartz was empty. Half a decade had passed since his backside had last graced it, but to bow was traditional. He had ruled since through that damnable hatch, his rulings delivered solely by his wife – and now daughter – to a court that was growing increasingly ambitious in his absence. In this city, ambitious had the same meaning as murderous.

'Sereks! I have our glorious emperor's latest decrees!' She lifted the scroll high. 'Perhaps they will put an end to your clamouring. I wonder if the court was this discourteous when it was the empress who delivered your emperor's words?'

As Sisine's tawny eyes wandered over their pouting faces, she noticed more empty seats than usual. For the most part, this was due to the fear of travelling even short distances across the city. Even the high-roads weren't completely safe. The richer an Arctian noble, the more skittish they became, and for good reason. A serek was a high prize indeed for a soulstealer.

Two minor nobles, Tal Askeu and Tor Yeera, had disappeared in the last month, along with their entire stocks of shades. Sisine was of the opinion it served them right. That's what they got for keeping their half-coins in their towers instead of in Araxes' great banks. It never paid to sit on one's fortune and trust too much to lock and key. She wished her father was aware of such wisdom. Her line had built a tower that could scratch the heavens, and still the emperor hid in a vault with his half-coins.

Disappearances weren't uncommon. The churn of Araxes' upper echelons revolved around unexpected disappearances, accidents and untimely deaths. What usually followed soon after would be a certain member of society receiving an equally unexpected windfall. A 'business deal' gone favourably, perhaps. Or a 'relative' dying. There were all sorts of ways to spin it, and that was the knack. As long as the half-coins were physically in possession to be Weighed, and the banks could be given good enough proof of a lawful exchange, somebody would climb the societal ranks. The truth would be told in whispers behind closed doors, but never spoken aloud. That was the great game of Araxes, only now it appeared that somebody wasn't playing by the rules.

Nobody had claimed the nobles' half-coins. That was highly unusual. Why play the game if not to rise in the ranks? Judging by the empty seats around the court, such events had made the sereks even more skittish than usual.

Sisine opened the scroll and scanned it before she read aloud. She held back her sigh. In the month since she had started standing before the Cloud Court in place of her mother the empress, her father's decrees had grown ever more bizarre. They seemed to focus almost entirely on his precious shade-claiming wars against the princes of the Scatter Isles.

'The emperor's decrees are as follows! Ten phalanxes of the Dead Rats to be reassigned to Harras to protect our ports there. Withdraw support from Prince Phylar and prepare for a siege on his fort on Corfin. We must also stockpile our steel reserves to increase their trading price.' She paused, gaze lingering on the last glyph. 'And that is all. His Imperial Majesty speaks.'

In the silence that followed, she watched the looks of dissatisfaction spread around the court, until at last one of them found the balls to shout out: a greying serek with a thin, braided beard bound with gold.

'And what of the Nyxwater shortage, Empress-in-Waiting? Surely—'

Sisine pointed the scroll at the serek, silencing him. 'I cannot decide whether you are accusing my father of ignorance, or of ineptitude? Which is it, Serek?'

'Neither, Highness.'

'I should hope not. My father is well aware of the rumours surrounding the Nyx. If he deems it to be an issue, he will surely take action.'

'Is there truly nothing else?' called another voice, one she recognised immediately. It was Serek Boon.

The shade was splayed across his chair, easy to see in the shadow of the western seats. A gleaming feather motif of white jewels sat on his chest, over where his heart should have been. The blue vapours beyond his puffy sleeves glowed darker than those of other shades, something to do with the fire that had claimed his body fifty years ago. Few free shades ever rose to the height of a serek unless they died in the position and managed not to be claimed. Boon belonged to this narrow minority.

Sisine stared at the shade, hoping he could see her simpering smile. The sereks were a prideful club. To be a serek was to be one of the richest citizens in the empire, bar the royal family. The title meant a serek was supposed to govern their own districts, but Sisine had come to realise they instead spent most of their time bringing her complaints. As the emperor still held the most shades, the sereks held no sway over the crown's decisions, but tradition stated they were the voices of the city. That made them dangerous to ignore or insult.

'Dissatisfied, are we, Boon?' she said, giving him the floor.

'Nothing about the real issues at hand? The rampant soulstealing? Or what about the empress' absence? Or, as the esteemed Serek Warast has already mentioned, the rumours of the Nyx drying up? Is there nothing being done about these matters?'

Others took up the cry. 'Hear, hear!'

Sisine fought not to scowl at the mention of the empress. There had been plenty of rumour and speculation over her mother's disappearance, but Sisine knew the truth: the woman had forsaken her duties and her family, leaving her belongings, her scant account of half-coins, and a slip of papyrus with the simple message of "gone east" inked onto it. Brief and cold, as usual. Sisine's mother had no Sanctuary of her own, but over the years she had become just as unreachable and detached as the emperor. Sisine was glad the bitch had finally given in. Instead of making her own gambit for the throne like a true Arctian royal, the empress' disappearance had left Sisine as the only royal voice in the Piercer.

In an effort to buy herself a moment of thought, she searched the scroll for words that were not there. Her father had been strangely brief today; barely half the scroll had been used. She pulled it further apart, revealing more virgin papyrus. Her eyes glazed. The temptation she'd harboured for weeks bloomed afresh. She chewed the inside of her lip. *What else was she to do*? Sisine strongly suspected her father was beginning to lose his mind. The emperor was obsessed with his Sanctuary, too afraid of daggers and deception to leave it. Perhaps justly so, seeing as his ascent to the throne had meant skewering his own father. And yet, for all his security, his reign was slipping from his grasp, slowly but surely, and like Sisine, the sereks could sense it. She would burn the Cloudpiercer to the ground before she let those wild dogs anywhere near her throne.

'Silence!' Sisine yelled, and when the sereks had given up their muttering, she prodded at the blank space at the bottom of the scroll. 'I see now that the emperor has included a footnote. His Imperial Majesty has decreed that the price of Nyxwater barrels is to be further increased to limit usage. It seems your fears are unfounded, Serek Boon! Are you content now?'

The shade nodded, speaking for the court. 'Somewhat.'

Sisine's eyes toured the half-circle. 'And the rest of you?'

A rustle of acquiescence came and went like a wind chasing leaves. It was not entirely convincing. Sisine raised her chin. According to the Code, fabricating an emperor's decree was treachery at its kindest. If the court smelled deception, it would be a fine excuse to decry her, and lay claim to her half-coins.

Growing up in a web of cutthroat politics – literally speaking – tended to teach a girl a thing or two about power. Power wasn't all about half-coins. Half-coins had a habit of bringing mobs to front doors. No, power was about controlling the mob. Sisine knew the best way to achieve that wasn't with steel gauntlets, or broad smiles, or charity. It was a matter of discovering what the mob wanted and then dangling it in front of them, like a beetle chasing vegetable scraps. For the sereks, in that moment, it was action.

Sisine held up her hands, forcing a smile. 'If it also pleases the sereks of the Cloud Court, I will also summon the commander of the Core Guard and order him to increase patrols around the central Nyxite storehouses and Nyxwells. I'm sure the emperor, in his everlasting wisdom, would see the sense of such action. As for Her Imperial Majesty,' added Sisine, with a forced smile, 'she is attending to family matters in the east and is no reason for concern. I'm sure she will return, and soon.'

'Let us hope so, Empress-in-Waiting,' Boon called out, rubbing his sharp chin.

Sisine swiftly made her exit, leaving the sereks to their chattering of Nyxwater and extra guards and stronger locks. Royal Guards tramping by her side, she ascended to her chambers.

When she came crashing through the armoured doorway, she found the chamber-shades were still busy polishing in her grand lounge. If shades were perfect for one job above all it was polishing things. The dead left no greasy fingerprints. And yet it didn't mean they did it with any alacrity.

'Out!' Sisine shrieked. 'All of you!'

As the shades gathered their rags and fled for the door, another emerged from a side room, hands clasped behind his back. This shade wasn't going anywhere. He had a scar in the shape of a V on the right side of his bald skull. There was a royal shape to his jaw, echoes of an older family line. He had chosen a charcoal suit today. It fitted him poorly; too baggy around the waist. Dark powder clung in patches to his face in an effort to give the effect of makeup. It fell away with every movement, no matter how small.

Sisine scowled darkly at him. 'Why do you insist on following the fashions of the free shades, Etane? You look frankly absurd.'

The shade frowned, more powder falling across the lapel of his suit. 'After ten decades dead it's nice to have something to occupy yourself with.'

'Do I give you no chores? Have you no sword training?'

'Call it individuality, then.'

Sisine scoffed. 'Wear a robe like every other chamber-shade of mine. I'll make it an order if I must. You are not the empress' property any more, remember? You are mine.'

'Robes feel too half-life for me. Too... *cultish*, Highness.' He sighed. 'I think I need a different tailor. If Serek Boon can manage it, I—'

'Bah! That fucking shade!'

Sisine moved to a window, eager to glower at the muddle of buildings and towers below. Her eyes darted over the sea of white and tan stone, interspersed with blooms of bazaar awnings, kaleidoscopic in colour. The streets were knit tightly, the buildings piled tall, the districts overlapping. No inch of land was wasted, and where the city collided with the turquoise sea, it bunched up along the coastline for a hundred miles both east and west. Even now, on this bright day, Araxes' distant reaches were lost in factory smoke and dust blowing in from the deserts. In all her life, she had never seen the city's edges: the Outsprawls.

'Have you any news for me, Etane?'

'Plenty as always in this city, Your Loftiness. What in particular?'

Sisine tutted. 'Of your Krassman locksmith!'

'Nothing, other than that he is still late. Unusual for a man of his reported reputation.'

'You made a mistake in choosing the Krassman,' she snapped, pushing open the windows to hear Araxes' roar. It was an ocean of noise: voices and footsteps, animals braying, birds keening, the banging and crashing of workers and toil. 'We should have chosen that Miss Everass instead.'

Etane came to stand by her side, eyes skyward. 'You said she was too well known, and unlikely to get involved.'

Sisine gave him a dark look. 'Must I remind you yet again of your station, shade?'

He shrugged. 'He's probably been caught in a squall. The summer heat tends to stir up the sea, make it as troublesome as its name. I wager he will likely dock within a few days. Then you can carry on with your…' He wiggled his fingers. 'Dealings.'

With any other half-life, Sisine would have fetched a copper poker and handed out a battering, but Etane Talin was not the average indentured. Irritating though he was, he was family: some distant great-great-great something, over a hundred years bound and as bitter as the day an arrow had found its way into his skull during a coup for the throne. He had served the Talin Renala line ever since. Until she had vanished without a word, Etane had belonged to Sisine's mother. His position as her personal shade and bodyguard fetched him slightly more respect in the Cloudpiercer than the usual chamber-shades were afforded. Not to mention he had practically raised Sisine in place of the empress, given she had been too absent to do so. For that, Sisine held no gratitude towards him, and only more spite for her mother.

Sisine swept from the window and wound an angry path around the chamber. 'Perhaps we shouldn't be putting our faith in a Krassman.'

'Old Emperor Milizan seemed to trust his sort.'

'Grandfather trusted a lot of people, especially the Cult of Sesh, and look where it got him. A sword up his arsehole, skewered on the latrine by his own son, my father. And banishment for Grandmother.'

'Don't remind me.' Etane grimaced. 'Not the most ladylike way to put it, but I see your point.'

Sisine pinched the gold and amethyst rings about her hands as she paced, teasing out ideas. 'Continue looking for the blasted locksmith. He might still be useful to us, but I will not wait much longer for him. Mother could still return at any time. The sereks grow too restless. I see them staring at the throne while I speak, especially that bastard Boon. If I cannot break my father out of his hiding place, then I will have to draw him out. Something unprecedented.'

'And what might that be, in a city such as Araxes?' asked Etane, quietly, as if he didn't want to hear the answer.

Sisine looked again to the city sprawled far below. Twenty years she had waited for the cold touch of its crown on her head. She could remember the idea blossoming when she was but two years of age, watching her father take the throne with blood still on his hands. That was when she learned her place in the world.

'I will create an uproar in the city; chaos. Something that finally drags him from his golden burrow. And I shall be there waiting for him with a smile and a triggerbow in my hand. Too long have I waited in the shadows, watching my father squander his rule and my mother become more like a shade each passing day. I refuse to be a messenger, a lackey, as she was. I was born into the Piercer to rule, and it is high time I did.'

The shade said nothing.

'A problem, Etane?'

'No problem, Your Resplendence. Just sounds like more blood is set to be spilled, is all.' He turned to face her, a blank look on his blue features. 'But what's more blood to a family line like the Talin Renala's?'

Sisine snapped her fingers. 'Precisely, and I will be trusting in you to be the one spilling it, when that time comes.'

'I died to serve, Magnificence,' he said as he bowed.

'In that case, have my spies look into these recent disappearances. They could be just what I need.' She sought an armchair and threw herself into it. 'And fetch me my luncheon. I'm hungry.'

'Of course.' Etane bowed again, already on his way to the door. 'I imagine all this scheming generates quite the appetite. Your mother and father would be rather proud if they could see you now.'

He shut the door before the pillow could reach him. It bounced to the floor, belled tassels jingling. Their musical notes hung in the air, interrupting the curse poised on her lips with an idea.

Mother.

In Sisine's private bedchamber, a steel chest sat at the foot of her bed, guarded by three thick padlocks. The keys from around her neck cracked them open, and inside, perched atop a raft of precious things, was a polished wooden box of mahogany and black iron. It held a slender silver bell, engraved with a design of fine copper feathers and storm clouds.

Sisine took it into an adjoining room, where gossamer curtains frolicked around an open door and balcony. With the wind dragging at her hair, she held the bell high and rang it nine times. A tiresome number, but it was what the spell demanded for the quickest summoning.

The air above the stone parapet crackled sharply, then came a burst of white feathers and dust. Sisine recoiled as grit flew in her face.

'You again,' said a harsh voice, like crab-shells being crushed.

When her vision cleared, she found a dishevelled falcon perched on the stone, feathers sticking out at all angles. His black and yellow eyes were narrowed, hooked beak parted in a pant.

'Me again,' she replied.

He fixed her with a stare, bright yet somehow cold as murder. 'I was halfway into a rat burrow. Scared the shit out of me. You can't just summon me after all this time with no warning. I thought you'd bloody sold me.'

'Actually, I believe I can.' Sisine held up the bell, letting it chime. The falcon screeched as if in pain. 'So you had best mind your impudent tongue, little bird.'

'It still works with six bells. Ring six bells, and I can come here at my own speed.'

'No. This is urgent.'

The bird clacked his beak. 'I'm a falcon, Princess. I'm pretty fucking fast.'

'You're here now. I have need of you.'

'That ain't how it works. I'm bound to the bell, not your uppity whims!'

Sisine dangled the bell over the stone parapet, craning her head to wonder at which street it would fall in. 'I know how it works, Bezel. The same as a half-coin, so you had better watch your tone with your master.'

The falcon strutted brusquely up and down the parapet. Sharp talons rasped against the sandstone. 'What you offering this time?'

'Food, naturally. Wine. Roost for as long as you want it. I shall even have all the messenger birds cleared out.'

'That all?'

'A female or two per week.'

'Better make it three.' Bezel puffed himself up. 'A day. Anything else?'

Sisine folded her arms. 'And I shall ring six bells.'

'And what is it that you want this time?'

'I need you to find my mother as quickly as possible.'

'She not dead, then? Rumour had it she was dead.'

'Hardly! You would have heard of such a... tragedy.'

'Princess, I was in Skol before you rudely summoned me. Believe it or not, the Reaches don't revolve around the Arctian Empire and your royal family.'

'Perhaps it should, but we digress. My mother is not dead, simply gone. A note she left mentioned going east and so I thought her homesick or finally tired of father and his Sanctuary. I need to know for certain. I need to know where she is and whether she is planning on returning. Whether she's up to something I haven't yet discerned.'

The falcon sighed. 'You Arctians have real problems with trust, don't you?'

'I am merely worried for this family's safety, of course.'

'Your own safety, more like,' Bezel squawked.

Sisine felt like backhanding the bird into thin air. He was half-mad as well as half-dead. Etane's cheek paled in comparison to Bezel's tongue. The uppity strangebound had been a gift from a past courtier, a Prince Phylar, seven years past. The Scatter Isle fool hadn't known what the bell could do, and she hadn't bothered to return it after refusing his hand. Father had skirmished with his princedom ever since, and Sisine had used the bird for all sorts of nefarious spying during her earlier years.

'Will you do as I order?'

Bezel put a pinion to his beak in thought. 'What does your father think of his wife leaving?' he asked. 'Still in his Sanctuary, I assume?'

'The emperor is still locked away. Nothing has changed except that I'm now the one who hands out his decrees.'

'He's a wise man, your father. They say you royals are born with daggers in your hands.'

Sisine tapped the silver bell with her fingernail. 'They say that for a good reason, bird. Now, do we have an accord?'

Bezel bowed his head, keeping his beady eyes locked on hers. 'We do. But you make it four females. A day.'

With that, he threw himself from the windowsill and plummeted from the tower. She lost sight of him in the sprawl, but heard his keening wail, scattering clouds of pigeons and parrots from their roosts.

Sisine stared out at the dusty horizon once more, finally able to relax a little now that Bezel's keen eyes had been bought. She sighed, and felt her stomach rumble.

Etane was right: all this scheming did work up an appetite.

CHAPTER 7
THE WIDOW'S TOWER

A master's will is absolute. A shade must do as he or she pleases. Should disobedience occur, it is the master's prerogative which punishment he or she sees fit to apply. A list of suggestions is available from the Chamber of Punishment.

ARTICLE 12, S1 OF THE CODE OF INDENTUREMENT

'LINE URRRP!' THE COLONEL'S BELLOW deafened me before we had been freed from the cart. I didn't have much time to complain as my ropes were yanked and I pitched onto the dirt face first.

I was dragged up and shoved into line as I wrestled to get my bearings. I'd been too lost in my hopeful daydreams to notice we had arrived at Horix's abode. I gazed up at the skinny pyramid stretching into the sky. Five faces, I counted. It was taller than most of the buildings around it, a sand-brown colour striped with marble and iron. The tower wore its windows like old pox scars, deep and sunken into the stone. Few balconies interrupted its slanted sides. I saw a few lingering halfway up and another near the spire's point. A gaggle of bright green parrots sat on the lower ones, cackling amongst themselves.

We had been brought to a courtyard made of simple pillars holding up colossal slabs. Ghosts hovered in every corner, dressed in grey servants' smocks embroidered with black feathers: the symbol of the indentured.

In front of us stood a bald and portly man, his skin shiny with grease and sweat. He had a clear fondness for silks. He was swaddled in them, head to toe. Dark patches had blossomed at his chest and armpits. Bracelets of bone and beetle carapace hung in their multitudes from his forearms.

At his side was a ghost with vacant eye-sockets. He too was bald, but comprised entirely of angles, like the facets of a cut gem. A grey smock hung on his sharp shoulders, also emblazoned with a black feather and presumably the widow's seal. Despite his blindness, I felt the pressure of his gaze on me as he surveyed us new arrivals. Perhaps he still had a sense for sight in death. His wizened grimace told me he didn't approve much of us.

'What arse-scrapings has the lady bought now, Colonel?'

'They'll do fine for what we need, Yamak. Don't worry your ugly head.' Kalid tossed the fat man a scroll. He caught it clumsily and passed it to the ghost.

'Read 'em, Vex.'

The ghost by his side cleared his throat. 'Jerub.'

I raised my hand after some hesitation. I didn't like playing my new character, but in all honesty, I wasn't keen on any more pain. Who knew being dead could be so unenjoyable?

'Bela?

The Skol woman raised her hand.

'So you must be Mamun.'

'Mfghm.'

Yamak threw up his arms. 'Oh, for fuck's sake, his voice ain't even settled in yet!'

'Calm, man,' said Kalid.

'Vex, get them clothed. Get that one a scarf. And the young'un a cloth cap.'

'Cleaning duty?'

'Aye. For now. Kitchen for the lad.'

'Right you are.'

Vex beckoned us forward, and after Kalid had released our ropes, we followed. Yamak stayed behind to whisper with the colonel.

The inside of the tower was grand and spacious. Great blocks of stone had been hewn into arched corridors and sweeping stairwells. We took the grandest of them, and as we climbed I found myself glad of my spectral muscles for the very first time. There was none of the usual burn in my underworked calves, no ache in my overfed sides, and besides the concentration of walking on vapour, which I was still growing used to, it felt easy.

Vex gave us our welcome as we climbed, pointing out places of interest on every floor. 'You will now refer to me as Vex. I'm the head of the house-shades, and report directly to Master Yamak, the master of this household. As such, you will obey me. Lower balconies are through there. Tal Horix, or Widow Horix as she is also known, expects a high level of excellency from her shades. You will call her tal or mistress. Storage rooms and laundry cupboards here. She does not tolerate tardiness, backchat, or excuses. Quarters for the living staff are here. You are to be silent until asked a question. When answering, speak loudly and clearly. Tal Horix does not like mumbling. Guards' chambers there. You're never to touch her, for she cannot abide the touch of a shade. Merely looking at you's enough of a challenge. Trust me, I should know. First and second libraries there. If you're confused, there is but one golden rule to abide by: you will do whatever is asked of you without hesitation or question. That is what the Tenets demand of you. The widow always abides by the Tenets and the Code of Indenturement. Ah, kitchens.'

Vex halted us in front of an archway, leading to a corridor beyond. Steam lingered on the ceiling, and I could hear the sounds of clanging and yelling.

'Mamun, report to Cook Hussa. He'll put you to work. Down there, boy. Go.'

Two floors up, Vex showed Bela and me to a series of honeycomb hallways, with alcoves no bigger than small cupboards and without doors.

'This is where you stay when not working.'

The question burst from me. 'And what work is that?'

Vex shot me a hollow look. 'As a house-shade? Cleaning, serving, dusting, washing, and more cleaning.'

I nodded, holding back all manner of sarcasm.

'You will find your new smocks in that chest there. I shall get you a scarf, Jerub. The widow doesn't want to see grotesque wounds about her tower.'

'Do I get a choice of scarf?'

Vex offered me a smile as he came closer. I stared into those dark pits, wondering who had plucked them clean. 'I can tell your sort. You think you're above this, that you've been wronged in some way. That this half-life of yours isn't fair. Well, sir, I can tell you that never goes away. The inevitability of your situation never goes away, either. Twenty years I've worked for the widow and no doubt more await me. This…' He paused to poke a finger into my chest. I felt gelatinous, and despite how freezing I was, somehow he felt colder still. 'This is your lot now. Save us all your witty jibes and smart remarks. You're dead. Hurry up and get used to it.'

I managed to nod, even as I silently reaffirmed my vow to do the exact opposite.

'Fine,' I said, following Bela to the chest. Now I had been offered clothes, I was eager to end my spate of nakedness. Bela was, too, it seemed. She saw to the lid, angling it up to reveal neat rows of folded cotton smocks with black feathers emblazoned on their breasts. They also bore the widow's seal: three skeletons hanging from nooses.

I grabbed at one, but my numb fingers slipped over the smock. I tried three times to no avail, marvelling at how my fingertips almost passed through the fabric. I looked to Bela, who was doing much better.

'Slowly,' she whispered. 'While you think about being solid. Alive again.'

'Trouble, Jerub?' asked Vex.

'No,' I lied, reaching out again. I thought hard about being alive. I had done nothing else since being tossed in the cell, so I was rather practised. To my surprise, it worked. My vapours seemed to flow down my arm, bolstering my touch. After several more tries, I managed to pinch the smock and pulled it over my head before I lost the thought.

'Creatures of will instead of flesh,' I muttered to myself, some old poem of childhood forgotten until now. The Krass have never been known for the cheeriness of their nursery rhymes. The eastern Reaches didn't dally in teaching the hardness of the world. I've always thought it had something to do with the climate. The steppes and mountains knew only scorching sun, mad storms, and slightly less scorching sun.

'Be glad we're not the sort of house that brands its shades, or leaves them naked! Now off to the dining hall with you! Chores await.'

Vex shooed us from the room and back up the stairs to a hall shaped like a wedge of cheese. One wall was almost entirely glass, sloping with the shape of the tower. Dominating the marble floor was a table that would have easily sat fifty people. Great loops and hammocks of silk adorned the sandstone walls, framing tapestries woven in metal threads.

Half a dozen ghosts stood around the table, already hard at work polishing a veritable sea of cutlery. They didn't stop working when we arrived, but their eyes followed every step we took.

'New shades. Put them to work,' said Vex, and with that, his work was done. He strolled from the hall without so much as a sniff, leaving us alone with the others.

Cloths and glazed bowls of greasy polish were handed to Bela and me without a word. The ghosts' gesticulations told us to get working. I caught a few of them glancing warily at the doorways leading from the hall. I decided to hold my tongue around these creatures.

Once I'd finally managed to manhandle the cloth, I jabbed at a nearby spoon. It came out in a shine at once. With some difficulty, I angled the cutlery to face me. I wanted to see the raking gash across my neck.

I almost dashed the thing from the table. I had no reflection. I thrust my nose into it, but all I saw was a melted whorl that resembled the wall behind me. The sight was a punch in the gut, and far more morbid than I'd been aiming for.

The others had begun to chuckle. I heard the word 'fresh' mentioned more than once in whisper. I turned my back on them and moved further down the table.

There is a pureness in tedious work. Time spent on nothing but a singular and repetitive task is holistic for the mind, much like sleeping while a wound heals. I occupied my mind with the simple battle of polish versus filth. Each object cleaned was a tiny victory in my own private war. It was the closest I could come to relaxation.

More so, it gave me time to practise my fingers. I knew ghosts could manipulate the world of the living – hold, lift, carry and all that – but I had never realised how tricky it was. The heavy cutlery slipped from my palms over and over, drawing narrowed looks from the other ghosts. For somebody whose hands had once been so dextrous, so clever, it was maddening.

After several hours, I got the measure of my grip, and by the time we'd cleared away the table, I could hold a tray of cutlery with only a slight wobble. Another small victory, but it buoyed me all the same.

Dusters appeared and we saw to the tapestries. After that, brooms for the leopard- and antelope-skin rugs. Then wax for the marble. It was almost evening by the time we were shooed from the hall by Master Yamak, and set immediately to cleaning the guards' quarters. Beds, drawers, cupboards, windows, I saw to them all like a creature of clockwork. By the time Vex came to take us back into our alcoves, everything we had touched gleamed. The war on dirt was over. Vex gave us a shrug, pointed out several areas of dust, and ordered it done again on the morrow.

As the ghost led us away, I began to understand the dour expressions I'd seen on the household dead. Until now, I'd thought it a simple by-product of being deceased; now I saw the burden wasn't death, but indenturement. Immortality sounds a wondrous thing with air in your lungs and freedom in your pocket. To one as dead as me, it was a hateful word. To a man enslaved, it is an endless war, the weapons of which are repetition, dullness and cruelty. Passing time becomes surviving time, and tomorrow becomes a curse-word.

'What now?' I said to Vex before he escaped again. I wondered what could be so important he was always running back to it.

'You wait until called for.'

'But we don't sleep.'

'No, we don't.'

'So I just stand here?'

'You can sit on the floor if you'd like.'

I crossed my arms.

Vex chuckled. 'What did you expect, Jerub? Ostrich feather beds and palm fans?'

'My name is Caltro,' I snapped, refusing to give up my name. It was the only tangible thing left of me.

Vex shoved me roughly into my alcove. A deeper cold and numbness spread across my chest, something akin to pain.

'No longer, shade,' he said before departing.

I stayed silent, listening to the soft brush of his feet on the stone stairs. Gradually, I met the eyes of my neighbours. They clearly saw no wrong in staring at me. Some were even leaning out of their alcoves to do so.

'What?' I asked. 'Can you speak, or only stare? Have they cut out your tongues?'

One of them nodded, but the rest just closed their eyes, letting their glow fade. Only Bela kept her focus on me.

'You're new to this, aren't you?' she asked.

'Aren't you?'

'No. That Temsa stole me from my owner. A year dead now, I am. Trust me, it's better to keep your mouth shut. Just get on with it, like Vex said.'

I shook my head, staring at the ceiling. 'I refuse to give up.'

'Give up what?' spoke another, a man, further down the line. 'You've already lost everything, friend.'

I scowled in his general direction. 'You're wrong. There's justice. Vengeance. My pride. My reputation. My sense of honour.' The latter was questionable, but it sounded good. 'I've been wronged and I refuse to lie down and accept it.'

Somebody down the hall sniggered. 'Reputation, he says!'

'Refuse quietly, then,' said another. 'Or you'll get us all copper lashes.'

Exasperated, I tried to grab at the cold roots of my hair. 'Surely there is a way of protesting? People of your Code that can help me?'

A voice rang out from the far end of the row. 'The Code? Ha! What indentured shade has the time or silver for such things? Even if you did, it takes years for a case to be reviewed!'

I threw up my hands. 'Some virtuous group of charitable fools, then!'

Their mocking laughter shut me up. That, and the pointlessness of arguing with such fearful souls. They had already given up and succumbed to their situation, their prison of death. Perhaps that was why there had never been a ghost uprising in the Arc.

Three hours, maybe four, I stewed like that. Outside the stone walls of the tower, the bustle of the city died to the creaking of night insects and the occasional muted scream. Inside, all was still, save for the coughing of a house-guard.

I have never been one for being told to sit and stay. My parents – may they rest whole and forever – tried that and it sent me running.

Though I have the patience to sit, it's the being told to do it part that niggles me.

The floor proved better than standing, and in that position I propped myself up like a beggar and half-closed my eyes in a forgery of sleep. Try as I might, rest did not swoop in and take me elsewhere. It didn't even taunt me, as sleep can often do, hovering at the edges of the mind.

Sometime in the early morning, I knew not when, I saw them. Ghosts, climbing the stairs in silence. In pairs, sometimes in small groups, they wandered past my sliver of hallway. For almost half an hour they did this, until finally a house-guard came to make sure none had wandered. He was thorough; he even came to check on our alcoves. Short spear in hand, he peered at each one of us, grunting as he tallied.

Curiosity never needs much in the way of an invitation. I've found even the most unremarkable things can bring it swooping in.

Once the guard had disappeared, I got to standing. Bela was sitting cross-legged on the stone opposite me, a questioning look on her face. I didn't offer a word of explanation. I simply stepped from my alcove and crept down the corridor.

'Hey, idiot!' hissed a ghost behind me. I could tell by the urgency in his voice that he was concerned for himself, not me. 'Stay put!'

I ignored him, following in the footsteps of the guard. My blue feet made no sound on the stone besides a faint whisper. I suspected I would have a brighter future as a thief if I ever managed to get my freedom.

'Oi!' another shout, louder now. I ignored that, too, coming to a halt at the spiralling stairs. No movement on them now. The tower had gone back to sleep. I bit my cold lip. I itched to descend and see what it was that had so many ghosts traipsing the stairs in the early hours.

Patience. I tore myself away and returned to my alcove, much to the glaring and grumbling of my new colleagues. I heard one whisper, 'Fuckin' idiot,' before silence fell. I did not reply. Their opinions weren't worth salt to me. Let them linger here, shackled to an eternity of cleaning silver spoons.

I had my own plans.

CHAPTER 8
VESTED INTERESTS

Shades in possession of their half-coins, and therefore their freedom, must display the white feather at all times. Any shade found wearing the white without their freedom shall be quartered with a copper blade.

ARTICLE 9, S13 OF THE CODE OF INDENTUREMENT

ANYBODY WOULD HAVE BEEN FORGIVEN for thinking Danib was the shade of a large bear instead of a man. He had the cold eyes of an animal, but he also had the height, the brawn. Fuck, he even made Ani look small. All he lacked was the pelt and fangs. He had his plate armour and his blades for that. No roar, mind. The killer was mute as a stone.

Temsa stared up at him like a climber assessing a rock face. 'What is it now?'

Danib mimed the door and a hood over his cracked-open head. The vicious white scar, spanning most of his skull and half of his face, was overkill when it came to looking menacing.

'Your old friends are finally here, are they? Good.' Temsa slammed the huge scroll shut and replaced the reed in its glass with a clink. 'About bloody time they gave us some more leads.'

The big lump of a bodyguard tutted.

'I don't care if they're the heads of the Cult. Or how old and wise they are.'

A grunt.

'I'll be hospitable, don't worry. Cheery, even.'

Giant hands clenched into boulders.

'I can be cheery.' Temsa pasted a smile onto his weathered face. Danib rolled his eyes, hunched some more and led his boss into the narrow corridor. Although his spectral feet made no sound, his armour clanked heavily.

A flight of stairs took them past the bustle of the tavern. Temsa paused to check the tables and eye his staff, ever the scrutinising proprietor. This tavern had been his first investment and a turning point in his career. Although the rest of his growing empire needed constant attention, he always managed to put the Slab first.

Somebody had broken out a skin drum. Another wielded a screeching arghul. The Rusty Slab was the largest tavern in Bes District, and could be relied upon to be rowdy at all hours. It was how Temsa liked it. Rowdy meant busy, and busy meant plenty of silver flowing into his pockets.

Danib grunted, reminding Temsa of their guests.

'Yes, yes.'

At the top of the stairs, where the noise faded to a dull vibration, Danib threw open the door to the meeting chamber. Temsa stomped inwards, claws ringing on the stone. The oil lamps had been lit and the brazier stoked. Ani loomed in the corner, eyes narrowed at the glowing guests that stood behind the table. She shared Temsa's sentiments.

Enlightened Sisters Yaridin and Liria waited with arms folded inside vacuous sleeves. Their blue faces were shrouded by their scarlet hoods. Temsa could barely tell between them unless they talked. Liria had a deeper voice. Their matching red robes were adorned with nothing but a silver rope belt and a stitched white feather. They were both gaunt creatures in death; the vapours hung in straight lines around their jaws and cheeks, and their mouths were narrow dashes.

Temsa's smile returned, this time needing some effort. He had little love for the dead gods. Less for the morons who still followed them a thousand years on. The Cult of Sesh were such morons. They were a strange organisation, almost as old as the Nyxites, the organisation that oversaw the usage of Nyxwater. Old Emperor Milizan had fallen in with the Cult and forged a close relationship with them. It was a relationship that had ended with Milizan being stabbed by his own son and the empress exiled to dead gods knew where. Since the current emperor had banished the Cult from the Core Districts, they had kept to themselves in the Outsprawls, content to deal in rumours and secrets. Recently, however, it seemed they had developed a taste for crime.

'Sisters, what a pleasure it is to see you again. Has it been a month already?'

'Boss Temsa, as we die and glow,' they chorused. They did not bow to him, but they did to the big ghost by his side. 'And Brother Danib.'

Danib returned the gesture, nodding curtly.

Temsa interrupted the moment with a tap of his cane. 'As I reminded you the last time you came here, he is your brother no more. He is mine. My property for five years now. Now, might I say how well both of you look? There's a healthy glow about you.'

He waited for the sisters to bow their heads before he continued. 'I must also thank you for the information you kindly provided. I was suspicious at first when Danib introduced us, but the tor and tal you suggested turned out to be somewhat… lucrative. My question is: have you come for your payment, or to provide me with more tidbits of information? I know which I prefer.'

The shades spoke in turn, Liria first. 'We have more information.'

'Though we have other matters to discuss first.'

Temsa had the feeling this conversation would be a lengthy one. He dug his pipe from his silk jacket; a long curve of brass and northern pinewood. He picked up a taper and stole a flame from the crackling brazier. 'And they are?' His voice was deep with the smoke that curled from his mouth.

'Our fee.'

He sought out a chair. 'I see. You want more silver.'

'No. We wish to take a portion of any shades that you acquire on the basis of the… *tidbits* that we provide to you.'

Temsa blew a great ring of smoke across the table. It framed the two sisters for a moment before it broke apart. 'Out of the question.'

'And why is that?' Liria rested her knuckles on the table. He could feel her cold wafting over him. His pipe dimmed.

Temsa leaned forwards. 'Firstly, because shades are worth a lot more to me than silver. And secondly, I don't like the idea of you buyin' them just to set them free. This city doesn't need any more free shades. It's bad for business.'

Yaridin sighed. 'We do not wish to free them, Boss Temsa.'

'We too have need of the indentured,' added Liria.

He let the fragrant smoke wreathe his face, hiding his curiosity and surprise. 'What needs would they be, I wonder? Rather backward for a cult that preaches for the betterment of shades, wouldn't you say so, Ani? Danib?' Ani apparently hadn't heard, but he could hear the scrape of metal behind him as Danib shrugged.

The sisters were unfazed. 'We prefer to be called a church, and if you dislike our practices, then perhaps we should hear what your competitors have to say.'

Temsa laughed at that. 'I have no competitors.'

Yaridin looked grave. 'Are you so sure? This is a vast city with many… *soultraders* such as yourself. Berrix the Pale, for instance? We wager he would happily pay for our information. Much needed in Quara District. Or Astarti, perhaps, of the Whitewash Beaches. We hear her days of stealing shades from hospitals might be coming to an end.'

Liria nodded. 'An astute young woman, she is.'

Tap. Tap. The pipe stem clacked against Temsa's teeth. 'How big a portion do you want?'

'Thirty percent.'

'Outrageous! I'm insulted. Eight.'

'Twenty-five.'

'Twelve. Nyxwater prices have risen by the emperor's decree. Supplies are tight, they say. I need to make my cut.'

'Twenty, then.'

'Seventeen, and that's final!'

The sisters spoke as one. 'We accept.'

'But I want bigger, better. No more dockyard snatchings and average-sized hauls.'

'Our thoughts exactly.'

'We see great ambition in you, Boss Temsa.'

'The ladder is there.'

'All you have to do is climb it,' whispered Yaridin.

Temsa jabbed his pipe at them like a sword. 'That depends on what you've got for me! If you want shades, then you tell me where to find them.'

'We shall.'

'How many?' asked Temsa.

'Eight more opportunities for profit.'

'What are we talking?'

'Mansions and towers outside of the city's Core Districts,' said Yaridin. 'Wealthy business owners. Important people. Tors. Tals. A Chamber of the Code magistrate. Even a serek.'

He narrowed his eyes through the haze. 'You must think me ambitious indeed. A Chamber magistrate? A serek? Talk will be rife. Panic, maybe. I don't know which will be tighter; the city's doors or its arseholes. More importantly, who are they to you?'

Liria answered far too quickly for his liking. 'Nobody. Strategically chosen for their wealth.'

'They do not entrust many of their half-coins to the banks. Instead they keep vaults in their homes,' added Yaridin. 'The easiest route to success.'

'And why should you care about my success?' asked Temsa.

Liria smiled. It didn't look like an expression that came naturally to her. 'Why, Boss Temsa, because of what we get in return. Our seventeen percent.'

Temsa waited to see if they had another lie to offer, but they held their blue tongues. He let them wait as he thought. The pipe-bowl was just ash when he broke the silence. 'Well.' He slapped his palm on the desk and got to his feet. 'I believe we have an accord. If it's shades you want, it's shades you'll get.'

They bowed their heads, and spoke in unison. 'We will give Danib the names and details, if we may have a moment alone with him. We did not manage to speak on our last visit.' They looked to Danib.

Temsa scowled. 'Speak about what?'

The sisters bowed again. 'Old times, Boss Temsa.'

'Simple things. Nothing more.'

After showing them the full depth of his displeasure, Temsa grudgingly left them to speak with Danib. It felt like letting a known molester have a quiet moment with one of his children. His ownership of the shade was absolute, but that didn't mean Temsa liked that his bodyguard had once been a member of the Cult. Or that he still showed them reverence despite choosing to leave their ranks and sell his coin as a mercenary.

'Come.' He beckoned to Ani, leading her into an adjoining study.

'I don't like it, Boss,' she said once the curtain was drawn across the arch, in a whisper as loud as a speaking voice. He held a finger across his lips.

'Nor I, m'dear. Nor I. But we have to think of the other eighty-three percent. The eight jobs we've been promised. If they're like the last two, or bigger, then they can't be ignored.' Temsa stamped his foot and a spark flew from the sandstone. 'I said I'd test the Cult's information, and I have. Tor Yeera and Tal Askeu were good hauls. Why not take the sisters up on more?'

'Because they're sneaky pricks, that's why, with their blue hands wedged up a lot of arseholes in the city. Push one of those sisters and you'd hear half the districts fart. Who knows who they're involved in, never mind the Chamber of the Code and the scrutinisers getting curious where all these riches are coming from. It's too big and too messy for my liking.'

'Messier than a goose with the shits, m'dear, but who is more used to playing in the muck than I? Isn't that what I have been doing for many years now? How I built this tavern? My reputation?' He sighed, knuckling his temples. It was an argument they'd had before. 'Far, far too many years, and what has it brought me? Middling profits. A few minor districts under my thumb, and yet all the while I walk under the shadow and gaze of nobles far less deserving than me. It should be me looking out over the rooftops, not them, and yet instead I lurk in cellars under the sand. No more! I will show this city who I am, show these tors and tals just how undeserving they are. If it takes the help of the Cult then so be it. They've seen fit to place this opportunity into my hands, and I would be a fool to ignore it. Do you know me to be a fool, Ani?'

It took her a moment to answer. 'No, Boss. You're no fool.'

'Good! Because I'll need you by my side on this endeavour,' he said. 'There'll be plenty of knife-work afoot. Plenty of noble blood that will require spilling.'

With a grunt, Ani was placated and the matter buried. She could always be swayed by the chance to cut a throat or two, especially a rich one.

'What do you suppose they want indentured for?' she asked after some time. 'The Cult, that is?'

'What does anyone want shades for?'

'What?' Ani cupped a hand behind her ear.

'To serve, to work or to build.'

'Right. Except—'

'Except most of the Cult don't eat and the other half wouldn't ever hold a shade as property. It can't be serving, and it can't be working, as the Cult don't own businesses. Not in the open. Emperor's decree, after all. Information and favours, that's all they trade in.'

Ani grumbled. 'So?'

'So they must be building something.'

'What?'

Temsa shrugged. 'They're calling themselves a church these days. Maybe that's what they're building. Good time for it, with the emperor stuck in his Sanctuary. Bah! Whatever the reason, the Cult is dependent on me. As we keep that balance tipped and keep smiling, we needn't worry. We'll follow their path for now, see what we can make of these tips of theirs.' He licked the corner of his mouth while he pondered. 'And in the meantime, we'll reap the benefits.'

Ani rubbed her hands, though her face remained as grim as ever.

'Get your men ready. No more fresh meat if we can help it. They need to be trustworthy.'

'Aye, Boss. When are we heading out?'

Before an answer could be given, the curtain was wrenched back and Danib's glow spilled into the room. He had to duck to negotiate the archway. Temsa eyed the thin scroll in the shade's humongous fist and tapped his cane with vigour.

'Tonight, m'dear. Tonight.'

As Ani vacated, Temsa snatched the scroll from Danib and held it to a nearby oil lamp. The ornate scratching of the Sisters was on the boundary of legible, and it took time to draw out the words.

'Tal Habish. Tor Merlec. Tal Urma. Tor Kanus. Magistrate Ghoor.

Serek Finel. Serek Boon… He's already dead but he's still richer than most. An audacious list, but then again, perhaps it is the time for audacity,' Temsa raised his eyebrows at another name. A certain Widow Horix, the old bag from the soulmarkets. 'My, my. Notes, too. "Hires cheap guards. Easily bribed. Break in watch at three chimes. Combination six, seven, eight…" Those sneaky Sesh-loving fuckers. I wonder how they gleaned all this. Hands up arseholes indeed.'

Danib shuffled, but Temsa put the point of his cane to the shade's breastplate.

'You hold them in far too high a regard for my liking. Especially for a group of people you turned your back on. They're gossip peddlers and tiptoers, you know that just as I do. That's what drove you out, no? The secrecy and ceremony? Their lack of will to swing a weapon? Or was it all that incessant prayer the old religions are so fond of? I forget.' He blew a sigh, shaking the scroll. 'Fuck them, I say. They've delivered all of this into my hands without so much as a handshake or a contract. The Cult might be useful, old friend, but they are weak. They have no teeth, just tongues, and that is not enough to get places in this city, as I intend to do. You made a good decision leaving them and selling your coin all those years ago. Don't doubt it.'

The big ghost bowed his head.

Temsa went back to the scroll, reading the names once more, matching them with their weaknesses. He thought out loud, laying bare his plan. 'Selling all these shades at market would be too difficult. Too suspicious. We already had enough trouble with Askeu and Yeera. No. No more dingy soulmarkets for us, Danib.' He rubbed his fingers together. 'I'll need a sigil to make these claims look legitimate. A good and dirty one, or at least one who can be threatened. Then I can have the half-coins Weighed, banked and put to good use. In time, maybe I'll need an entire bank. One that can handle this many coins and not raise questions. Suspicion is a bad guest to invite to a party.' He hummed. The noise turned into a low chuckle. A fizzing of anticipation built in his belly. His fingertips scratched at each other. 'Go get me Starsson.'

Danib left and returned with a pale-skinned man wearing a stained apron and long, greased hair tied in a tail. A tattoo of an octopus wrapped around his gullet and around his ears like a peculiar beard. The barkeep bared blackened teeth at Temsa.

'Alright, Boss?'

'Starsson. Tell me, is that whingeing coincounter fucker from Fenec Coinery still drinking here?'

'Proppin' up the bar as we speak. Still whinin' like a dying toad. Fenec this. Fenec that. Fuckin' borin' if'n you asked me. Should do 'im in, Boss. Just for some peace and quiet. Say the word and I'll go tickle his guts with my steel.'

Temsa cackled. 'See, Danib? You can always trust a Skolman to speak his mind. No steel. Just go fetch him for me.'

This excursion took some time, and resulted in raised voices and a crash of stools. Temsa had another pipe glowing by the time Danib reappeared with Starsson, and a wriggling man in the shade's grasp. The man was young and, like all financial types, he was dressed as sharp as a dagger. His eyes were underlined with dark paint and swirls. It had started running down his cheek now that he was sweating profusely.

'I haven't done anything!' he cried. 'I can pay for my drink!'

'Mr…?'

'Banush, sir.'

'You know who I am?'

'M… Master Temsa, sir. I mean, tor? Oh, fuck.'

'You can put him down, Danib.'

The shade obliged, dropping Banush so hard he fell to his knees. He blinked in the tendrils of smoke curling from Temsa's pipe.

'Boss Temsa. I'm no tor. Not yet.' That felt good to say out loud. *Finally.*

Banush had the look of a condemned man wondering why he was still gibbering excuses as they tightened the noose. 'We... They know that. They call you a tor because of the way you—'

'The way I what?'

'Er... conduct yourself, sir.'

Temsa mentally pocketed that for later. He watched the sweat pour out of the man. 'Here's the problem, Mr Banush. You come in to my tavern with a lot of words. Not only that, but you're rather fond of sharing them at a loud volume. Now, the Slab is a welcoming establishment. I might understand if you had something entertaining, or interesting, or even musical to say. However, all you bring to my tavern are complaints about your workplace and your apparently odious superior. Now that's the sort of patron that I don't much care for.' Starsson affirmed his words with an irritable grunt.

'I—'

'I'll let you know when it's time to speak.'

Banush bowed his head so fast Temsa heard cartilage pop.

'Something must be done about your incessant yapping.' Temsa arose from the desk while Danib yanked the man's head back by his hair. 'Either my associates here can cut your tongue out and solve the problem that way, or you can do me a favour, and I might let you keep it. So long as you learn the virtue of silence, that is.'

'Yes, Boss Temsa!'

'Which is it, man?'

'Erm, the second one. The favour. Anything!'

Temsa sucked his teeth, scolding the man. 'Be careful with that word, Mr Banush. It's a slippery one.'

Danib released him, and with much shaking, he got to his feet. 'How can I be of service?'

The pipe glowed, making Banush wait. 'You can tell me more about this superior of yours.'

There was a pause. 'Tor Fenec's son?'

Temsa raised an eyebrow. *Even better.* 'Is that the man you complain about so liberally?'

Starsson nodded. 'Trust me, Boss, it is. I 'eard all 'is bloody stories. Name's Russun. He's… how'd you put it again, Banush?'

The man's lips wobbled. 'The runt of the litter. Tor Fenec's third, no, *fourth* son.'

'Is he a coincounter like you?' Temsa came closer.

'No, he's a sigil.'

'Able to sign transfers, deposits, organise Weighings, that sort of thing?'

'Of course, Boss Temsa. He's set on following in his father's footsteps.'

'And where does Russun Fenec live?'

'He got a big house from daddy, over in Yeresh District. Dead gods know what he did to deserve it. He's forever talking about the sea views—*Erg*.'

Danib dug an elbow into Banush's ribs to cut him short.

'Has he a wife? Children?'

Banush gulped down whatever moralistic lump he'd just found in his throat. Temsa found people always squirmed at the mention of children, but unless it was their own children, almost always their own skin proved more important.

'A wife. And two young ones.'

A bare scroll and inked reed were shoved into Banush's hands.

'Write their street down before you get back to your drinking.'

The man hurriedly got to scribbling. Temsa could see the question hovering on his lips throughout, and it escaped only once he had laid the reed down.

'What will happen to Russun? To them?'

Temsa indulged him. 'If he is a good boy like you and does what he is told, then nothing. You should be happy, Mr Banush. Come tomorrow, he'll be too preoccupied to bother or berate you any further. Oh, but I'd keep silent if I were you.' He chuckled, tapping a finger to his nose. 'Or I'll have Danib rip your chords out and Starsson cook them up so you can physically eat your own words. He's quite the chef.'

Banush's weak smile withered immediately. Starsson met his horrified gaze with a blackened grin.

'I make a mean rat-meat hash,' remarked the barkeep, scratching at his octopus beard.

As Banush was hauled down the stairs, face ashen, Temsa waved his pipe. 'Enjoy the rest of your evening, Mr Banush! I know I will.'

THEY SAID FATHERHOOD TURNED EVEN the heaviest of men into the lightest of sleepers. While Russun Fenec was more scrawn than brawn, he'd learned that lesson all the same. Two small children could be brutal teachers. The slightest wail, moan, or cough never failed to drag him from his ever-shallow dreams.

So it was that the tinkle of glass awoke him in an instant. His hand reached out, feeling the outline of Haria, moaning in her half-sleep. His other hand went to the drawer, for the thin knife that lived there.

The stone was cold underfoot but quieter than floorboards. His fingers saw to each of the four locks on the bedchamber doors, then quietly peeled back the bolt.

The lanterns had either died or been snuffed. The orange glow of the city spilled through the shutters in crisscross patterns along the hallway. Russun slipped across the stone, knife at the ready. The children's room was around the corner, door just ajar as always.

He pressed his ear to the gap and it moved at his touch, opening with a creak. He saw the dark shape framed in the light of the window, and his heart froze in his chest. He thought of calling for his house-guards, but he wanted his wife to stay put and sleeping. *Out of harm's way*. Knife-tip wavering, he thrust open the door with teeth bared.

'All's well, Mr Fenec,' said the shape. A man with his back turned, surrounded by shifting curtains. His silhouette had a lopsided shape, short and hunched, and in the gloom below his waist, something shone dully. 'No need to worry.'

Russun saw both cribs empty. 'Where are my sons?'

The man turned with a thump of something heavy on the floor-boards, and showed Russun his face in the half-light, and what he held in the crooks of his arms.

'Guards!' Outrage trumping fear, Russun marched for the man, knife held high. His wrists were immediately seized by hands as cold and solid as iron, forcing them behind his back. A blue glow washed over him, along with a deep shiver up his spine. He arched his neck to find a giant shade towering above him.

'I'm afraid your guards are somewhat… indisposed.'

Russun struggled all the same. It was also said fatherhood breeds the fiercest of protective instincts.

'You leave them alone!' Despite his shouts, the small boys slept on soundly in the intruder's arms, curled up like the day they were born, thumbs in mouths.

The man rocked them, offering a smile and speaking softly. 'You should know I mean your boys no harm. But then again, we all do things we don't mean from time to time, eh, Mr Fenec?'

Russun's voice was tight and hoarse, but low. 'If you want silver or half-coins, I keep none in this house. It's all stored in my father's bank. I will give you all of it. Just don't harm my boys.'

The stranger smiled. 'Oh, I have plenty of my own, but thank you. No, Russun. I want *you*.'

'Me? Why?'

'More precisely, I want your right hand. You just happen to be attached.'

Russun felt the colour drain from his face. He struggled, looking behind him for a blade. His own still wiggled uselessly in his hand.

'Relax,' said the stranger. 'Although usually I would mean that literally, tonight I do not. As a sigil for one of the oldest banks in the Arc, you can help get me an account at your father's bank. I'll also be needing your signature on certain transfers and deposits, and a Weighing or two in the near future. One that does not require much scrutiny. I have my mind set on becoming a noble, you see.'

'It's against the Code. We won't have any part of criminal—'

The stranger stepped closer to the window so Russun could watch him run the back of his hand across his son's cheek. 'You can and you will. Or your pretty wife will come in one morning to find young…?'

Russun swallowed. 'Bilzar. And Helin.'

'To find young Bilzar's little face facing the wrong way. Maybe Danib here will snap Helin in half. Variety is a spice, so they say.'

'I…' Words failed Russun. He squirmed in the big shade's grip.

The stranger placed both snoring bundles in the nearest crib, but not before kissing each on the cheek with his wrinkled lips. 'There's a good man. Now, why don't you take a moment to say goodnight, get a hold of yourself, then we'll get started, shall we? We have a busy night ahead.'

'Started?' he said, before Danib tossed him to the floor. 'Tonight?'

'That's right.'

Russun's hands shook as he grabbed the crib bars. He was a stewing pot of emotion, clapped tightly shut, pressure trapped by impotence. All he could do was obey to keep his sons and wife alive. He left a kiss on his sons' foreheads before the huge shade muscled him towards the open window.

'I…' he tried again, but only air came from his mouth.

The stranger smiled as he showed Russun the grapples of a rope ladder. A group of dubious-looking characters and a covered wagon waited half a dozen storeys below. The young man threw a look back at the dark of the nursery, and received a sharp prod in the chest for his procrastination.

'No need to worry about that pretty wife. I can always leave one or two of my boys to guard her chamber, if you'd like?'

'No!' There was no pause in that reply. 'No need.'

'You'll be back before dawn, my good sir,' said the man, with another wicked smile. 'Unlike banking, in my business it pays to be speedy. Now move, before I change my mind.'

Russun grabbed the rope and put one gangly leg over the railing, silently berating himself for not asking his father for a bigger house.

CHAPTER 9
A GLIMMER

Churn, churn, stir it so,
Coin on tongue, stripped head to toe!

Dead god-wrought and god-forgotten,
Never still and never rotten.
Flowing ever, the gate of death,
Welcomes all who know no breath.

Churn, churn, stir it so,
Naked bodies, in they go!

Coin once for passage, now for key,
Binds them to immortality.
Lifeless in, come thrashing out,
'Til coin re-joined, a servant's shout.

Churn, churn, stir it so,
Out come shades, all a-glow!

Old Nyxite Poem
for prospective Nyxites

FUCK ME, JERUB.'

'I'd rather not, if it's all the s—'

The copper switch, Vex's favourite toy, struck again. It scored a mark across my cheek, stinging as sharp as a whiplash.

'You call these *polished*?' He poked at the candlesticks I'd been tending to for over three hours. 'The widow would be horrified to see these on her shelves. Start again!'

I looked to the ceiling, hunting for patience through a long breath. 'Yes, Master Vex.'

He strode away, making the others scatter. Once gone, they stared at me with the usual withering looks of *we told you so.* I went back to my polishing and kept my anger on the inside, far away from my face.

For the next few hours, I gave the candlesticks the thrashing of their lives, finishing up long after the other ghosts had been pulled away to other tasks. I was left alone in the great dining hall, for the first time untended and unwatched. It was in moments like those that my fingers and feet grew rather itchy.

The candlesticks were replaced in hurried motions and I swept the soiled cloths and empty vials of polish and other cleaning stuffs into a bag. Concentrating hard to hold it, I slung it over my shoulder and plotted a winding path around the hall, taking long looks at things I had not yet been allowed to touch.

The sun bathed the trinkets and metal-thread tapestries in a golden light. It would be hours before it sunk below the rooftops, but there was a tinge of orange in its glow. Decorative urns shone with it. Bejewelled mahogany boxes took on a molten quality. The craftsman in me – or to be truthful, the thief in me – wanted to salivate. I licked my cold lips instead.

I left the hall and went up the stairs instead of down. I had the excuse of finding the others or Vex if it came to it. That was all the license I needed to pry into the upper corridors at the pinnacle of the widow's tower.

My first impressions confirmed they were small and slanted, leading to rooms that glowed orange with whale-oil lamps. Spotted furs and sweeping silks hugged their walls. I wanted to tread the floors of each hall, but I couldn't linger. Instead, I found a large reception room with another wall of clear glass at its far end. The city beyond it was black and glittering gold. Only its myriad lamps and candles told me how vast it was.

Plants in varying stages of life and decay sat about the room, rooted in ornate pots ranging from tiny to back-breaking in size. Mahogany shelves lifted them high up the sandstone walls, and I wasn't surprised to find that the harder to reach vegetation was the deadest. Gold watering cans sat between the pots, a layer of dust dimming their metal. A few scrolls and tomes leaned here and there, lonely between the plants.

I thought the room empty until I heard the rustle of a reed on papyrus in the corner, and saw the shadows move across the shelves. A monstrous bowed head lifted, and claws flexed. I froze at first, then turned to bow.

'Lost, half-life?' croaked the widow.

Horix was hunched over a small writing desk, almost facing away from me. An oil lamp sat at her far elbow, burning brightly. Her attire was black and formal as usual, though this time she wore no hood. A cascade of silver hair fell in a waterfall down her chest and withered shoulders. I fancied she was a skeleton beneath all those layers of cloth and frill.

'I appear to be, Mistress. Please, excuse me,' I apologised, but my legs didn't move.

'Temsa's stock, correct?'

The old hag had a good memory. Her cruelty couldn't be blamed on senility. 'Yes, Mistress.'

'Settling in?'

I decided to play nice. 'As much as can be expected.'

'I see they found you a scarf. Good.'

My hand moved to my throat, and the scrap of black cotton wrapped around it. A 'scarf', indeed. One for a pauper, maybe. I had to keep telling myself I was in no better social standing. Maybe lower, in fact.

Play nice, the wiser part of me reminded. 'Yes, Mistress.'

She returned her reed to its glass inkwell and wiped her hands on a black cloth. 'And how is it, being dead? With my advanced years I grow curious, you see. I like to enquire of all my house and chamber-shades. Most have told me it's wonderful, not worrisome. But I can see they don't tell me everything.' She turned, fixing me with a glare. She seemed less craggy out of shadow, almost kind, were it not for the scowl and puckered lips. 'You seem to be one who speaks your mind. Tell me. Speak as honestly as you wish, with no reprieve.'

Explaining something to another is always harder than explaining it to yourself. You've all the vocabulary in the world in your head, but from your mouth it's clumsy. That's how I felt then, giving it voice for the first time.

'It's numb. Cold, both inside and out. I can't feel much apart from the sting of copper, which I seem to have felt frequently since dying. It's like I tread on frozen feet half the time. They're like stumps. Holding things is hard. Infuriating. I miss sleep awfully and I'd happily take a nightmare in an instant if it meant I could dream. Oh, but what hurts the most is the irreversibility and injustice of my situation.

To be nothing but a ghost. To own nothing but a scarf. To have the knowledge that I was murdered, robbed of my life and my freedom, yet know there's hardly anything I can do to change it. To know that I am a dead slave, and will be, most probably, for all of eternity. Unless somebody helps me.'

I realised I was panting, but it was just reflex and emotion; I had no breath to be short of.

'"Ghost", hmm? You Krass suit your name. We call them shades here,' said the widow with a tut. She jabbed the wood of her desk with a skeletal finger. 'And that's not *your* scarf. It is *my* scarf. Shades hold no property, as per the Tenets. Remember that.'

I pursed my lips so as not to curse her.

'My physicians tell me I have many more years left in me. Many more as a free shade, if I choose to slit my wrists and become a half-life of my own accord. The thought has sickened me until now, but you raise some interesting points. I prefer the cold. As for copper, I've always preferred gold. The stumps, well, I imagine they're no different from these bony callouses my physicians call feet. And of course, if I bind myself, I imagine my time as a shade will be very different from your situation.'

I preferred the word 'plight'. I drew myself up to my full height and tucked in my stomach. Perhaps it was too soon to push her, but with Vex breathing down my neck, I didn't know when the next opportunity would arise.

'Widow Horix. Tal. Mistress. Whatever. There must be a rule here in the Arc, as there is in Krass, against wrongful indenturement. We follow the same Tenets you do.'

She stared at me with those flint eyes. 'Indeed there is. Under the Code of Indenturement. Article seven if I remember rightly.' Sharp as a dagger, she was.

'Then I'd like to make such a case. I'd like to plead for wrongful indenturement. If I cannot have my body back then at least I can have my freedom, and justice for—'

A shout cut across my speech. 'There you bloody are, Jerub!'

It was Vex, bustling down the corridor towards me. His vacant eyes hadn't yet noticed the widow.

'I'll have you flayed for wandering. If you think I—' He cleared his throat at the sight of her and immediately bowed. 'Widow Horix, I beg your forgiveness. I shall remove this shade from your presence.'

'Calm yourself, Vex. He has been rather entertaining. Until now. You may see him out.'

'Entertaining?' I asked, as Vex pushed me to the hallway. I got nothing but another stony look from Horix as she picked up her reed again.

Once out of sight, Vex clapped me around the head with his copper switch. I yelped.

'To the rubbish heap with that bag of cloths, and then to the guards' quarters. There's a mountain of laundry with your name all over it.'

I was poked and prodded down every step. Vex even followed me all the way to the quarters to ensure I didn't wander off. He spent a whole hour watching me work, like a hungry owl poised over a rat's burrow. He tutted at every flaw in my methods, sighing every time I dropped so much as a thread. In the end, I made a game out of his noises, seeing which kind won by the time he escorted me back to the alcoves. It turned out to be a low grunt of disapproval, similar to that of a pig finding its trough unexpectedly empty.

'I have more work for you, first thing in the morning,' he hissed in my ear. He felt colder than I did.

'I look forward to it.'

There he left me, amongst a forest of disapproving faces and dry stares.

I turned my back on them, getting into the new leaning position I had adopted the last three nights. It faced me away from the dimwits and gave me a perfect view of the central stairwell. There I could sit and stew over the day, and try to reconcile the fresh disappointments until I could watch the ghosts traipsing up and down the stairs.

Over the past few nights, they had trickled down a few hours after midnight and trickled back an hour before dawn. Roughly two-score, and growing in number, if my eyes and brain weren't deceiving me.

There was plenty of stewing to be done that night, and before I knew it, I saw the waver of blue lights. Three-score ghosts came past that night, this time with two extra guards who looked pale and tired in the glow.

Choosing to stay put was easy. I had a feeling the nearby ghosts had gotten to the point where they would report anything to Vex just to keep me out of their group. They spent their days telling me what happened to recalcitrant indentured. It turned out they were beaten, for a start, then kept in a cellar or something called a sarcophagus. If they didn't mend their ways, they were sold at low prices and bought for manual labour in places such as building yards or distant quarries in the desert, like someplace they called Kal Duat, or the White Hell. I had been told that if I thought this housework was tough, I should wait until I was working under a sun so hot it could make even the dead sweat.

I did not fancy that one bit.

Patience, I told myself, as some distant bell struck five times. It would soon be time to see what Vex had planned for me.

AS IT TURNED OUT, VEX wanted me to do his shopping.

That was the summary of my 'punishment': a simple fetch and carry for the larders and the widow's whims. I couldn't understand it. Vex had made it sound like a terrible assignment. The ghosts in my alcoves had snorted and chuckled amongst themselves. Even when I lined up grinning with three indentured I hadn't seen before, I found them with sullen shoulders and bowed heads. If I hadn't known better, I would have assumed we were about to be whipped with copper lashes.

Vex swaggered up and down the marble before us. His hollow eyes were dark in the shade of the atrium. 'Listen up, smart arses. Get what's on your list and be back here sharpish. I expect you in the courtyard by noon. Noon, I say! And don't forget that we hold your coins. You impudent bastards can forget any ideas of making a run for it. Just see how far you get before *snap*!' He clicked his ghostly fingers, though no sound came forth. 'We break your half-coin. And therefore you. Off to the void for you. Understand?'

I understood perfectly. Vex was right: I had contemplated running for the nearest boat maybe a dozen times already. I supposed every ghost did when let loose for the first time. But I knew what a half-coin meant to a soul. It was its anchor, and when damaged, so was the ghost. If destroyed, so was the soul, despatched to nothingness. In Krass, they heat a half-coin in a pan, almost to the point of melting. It brings the ghost running, screaming bloody murder. No doubt the cruel Arctians had methods more devious and infinitely more painful.

A woven palm frond basket was thrown at my feet. It had a scrap of papyrus appended to its handle. A list, in Arctian glyphs and sloppy Common, along with a bundle of silver coins. My list was mostly fruits and vegetables, along with some wool, and a few strange objects Vex refused to clarify. They would be a challenge, he told me, but I welcomed a challenge if it meant a taste of freedom. However brief.

Four hours. I had four hours free in the city with nobody breathing a chill down my neck. I couldn't wait to stride out of the tower's armoured door. Vex had the guards crank the locks open, and a band of sunlight split the atrium in two. As the other ghosts moved forwards, Vex held me back. He pressed his palms together.

'Please, please make my week and try to run, Jerub. I'll make it swift, I promise.'

I stared into his sightless eye sockets, hoping he could see my sneer. I pushed away, basket swinging at my side as I stepped into the roasting sun.

The others split up a stone's throw from the widow's tower, leaving me at a crossroads that resembled a spider's web. I tried to remember the cart ride in and decided to head north-east for the Troublesome Sea, where the cold breeze was blowing from.

Four hours seemed a long time in a city, even to a stranger. But Araxes was a thousand years old, with every century building heedlessly on the last. If the city was a living, throbbing creature, it would have died long ago of vascular issues. Every road I took was clogged with people and carts and beasts. Goats, camels, horses, donkeys, and great armoured beetles on ropes; they all barred my path. Nobody made room for a shade. I was jostled and shoved aside, practically ignored by the living and the dead alike. I longed to take the steps to the high-roads standing tall on their sandstone stilts. Some journeyed alongside the main roads, only the height of a tall roof but high enough to be clear of the stinking press of the common people. Others stretched between spires, or crisscrossed over the buildings, using their square roofs for support. As always, the needs of the rich resulted in the poor being trampled in some way.

On the nearest high-road, I saw a clump of nobles on fine riding spiders, peering down over the stone blocks from their jet-black mounts. The arachnids' carapaces shone alongside golden reins and bejewelled saddles. I couldn't hear the nobles' tittering conversation, but I could see the contempt in their smiles. I pressed on.

After the dull monochrome of the widow's tower, my senses were assailed by the city. The morning sun beat down in angular patterns between the buildings. Every time I was forced from the shade I felt my vapours prickle. The streets were a riot of colours, from awnings, clothing lines, pennants, curtains and clothes, to the blue forms dotting the crowds. Silk-clad Arctians were second in number to the dead, but they were not alone. Between them I spied the redder skins and white cotton of Belish, and the paleness of Skolmen. Even the fur trappings and glass jewellery of my own countryfolk, all the way from the scorched east.

Araxes was a vast empire, built with war and trade, and to survive it had absorbed all it claimed into its own. The City of Countless Souls was a boiling stew of culture, a hodgepodge and yet unique at the same time. Ingredients from across the Far Reaches had been thrown together with Arctian grandeur stirred into something new. I saw the evidence all around me.

Hounds, hogs and miniature centipedes strutted by their owners' sides. Multicoloured cats lazed on traders' wares. Daggers, light mail armoured clothes littered one table. On the next, children waited to have palm frond dolls daubed with paints and glitter and animal faces. Carved skulls on strings and silver chains were sold as trinkets by beggars. The drone of hammers came and went as I passed shirtless men and ghosts chiselling at stone tablets. Beside them, tattooists prodded away at skin with sticks tipped with whale-bone splinters, inking angular patterns and glyphs into backs and arms. Here and there, steam and charcoal smoke arose from open-walled eateries, where meats sizzled and bread charred in stripes. The hungry and the hungover queued into the street to get a taste. I heard their arguments with the cart drivers over the horde of other voices, all with something to say. It was a din of half sentences and foreign tongues; of rattling jewellery and the clip-clop of feet. I battled on through the choked warren, one ear covered and a hand up to shield my eyes, basket bouncing against my ribs.

Every time I saw a guard, I thought about approaching, but their uniforms and armour had no continuity. They too were a spectrum of colour and style. From fur and leather scale to mail and steel plate. Some had seals, some had glyphs or symbols. None bore any insignia that looked like it belonged to the Arctian monarchy or the Code. *Sellswords and hire-bodies.* That's all they were. They wouldn't have given a fart for my plight, and so I wandered on.

The bazaars in the next district seemed to be all carpets and leathers, but no yarn, so I continued on until I caught a glimpse of flowers between the mighty buildings. Flowers and fruit often went together, I wagered, and in that instance I was right.

Past the strange and unfamiliar desert flowers, I found the fruit stalls. The merchants all babbled in Arctian until I showed them my list, and then they began to shout numbers at me in the Commontongue. They never once met my gaze. It was as if they bartered between themselves. I took the lowest price they reached and let a grizzled man fill up a cloth bag with fruits. I handed him one of the silver pieces Vex had gifted us and got nothing back. He avoided my eyes and shouted out for a new customer.

I took my basket, concentrating hard to keep it hooked on my shoulder, and found vegetables on the next row of stalls. There I received the same treatment, if not worse. Only two of the merchants bartered over me, and the loser cursed in Arctian as he handed over the bag and my finger grazed his own.

'Problem?' I asked.

'Touched me!' He spat at me, missing my bare foot by an inch.

'Fade away, half-life,' he said, in thick Common. To make his point, he twiddled a copper knife between finger and thumb.

I moved away, not wishing to feel another blade in me. I withdrew to a quiet corner, out of the flow of people and ghosts, and reviewed my list. I had wool, something called a *ki'thara*, two things I couldn't pronounce, and a weight of clay still to get. An hour must have already passed. I sighed, realising why the other ghosts hadn't jumped with glee at this job.

Weighed down by my basket, the going was slow but scenic. I wandered towards the lofty core of the city, hoping to find more textile and craft merchants among the taller towers. Secretly, my eyes were peeled for some great courthouse or other building of justice. I had seen a Chamber of Military Might between two spires, and so it was logical there would be a Chamber of the Code.

The buildings grew around me. The high-roads inched further from the streets. Compacted dust and sand turned to cobble. In the shadows of the spires, I found grand buildings with painted fronts. Guardsmen in full battle armour stood in the more opulent doorways, ones belonging to towers that soared high into the bright blue. Needle-pointed or ridged with crenellations, some looked as if they could have snagged clouds.

The busyness of the streets faded slightly, and I soon found my ghostly companions outnumbering the living. The flesh and bone that did walk the lowly flagstones travelled within circles of wary personal guards, while the rest clattered by in carriages plated with steel and ridged black leather.

I took a wide avenue south, where palms rose up and over the sand-washed streets. Jewellers and smiths worked the streets, wares glittering for all to see. Men and women stood silently between the tables. Some bulged with muscle beneath their chainmail, others were quick-eyed and lithe, but both kinds waited for somebody to be foolish. I didn't blame their employers for hiring guards. With murder so rife in this city, what was a little shoplifting?

I toured the shining tables, looking for a potter or something similar. I had to walk almost a mile to find one, and by then I had reached an immense opening between the crush of city buildings.

Thanking the man for the clay, and ignoring the meagre grunt I got in return, I turned to admire the vast greystone plaza. Spread around its edges, six knights carved from sandy marble bent a knee and bowed their heads. The statues would have stood twelve feet high if not kneeling, and though formidable, the spiralling plates of their Arctian armour were chipped and weathered. I imagined a battle-weary, glazed look behind their crownlike helms. One knight was receiving some much-needed attention. A scaffolding of palm wood had been built around him. Ghosts were spread across its levels, making a din with chisels and hammers.

The rest of the plaza was flat and featureless but for its very centre, which was hollowed out in steps like one of the Scatter Isles' amphitheatres. At its bottom, some forty feet below the street, was a short channel running north to south and occupied by a charcoal river. Spiked walls ran alongside its waters. Dark-feathered birds, maybe crows, balanced atop them and croaked out mocking songs. At the channel's centre was a raised dais crowded with soldiers and figures in grey robes. Above it, three enormous tusks of black stone soared high into the air. Each of them was etched with skeletal figures and glyphs taller than a man.

I knew this scene well. Almost every city and major town in the Reaches had one like it, though few could boast something as grand and formidable as this. It was a Nyxwell, a spring of the river Nyx. Or as we Krass called it, the world-river. The Arctians would call it the lifeblood of the entire soultrade.

The Nyx ran through every corner of the map, springing up in wells and marshes, always lingering just under the surface. Nobody knew where it began or if it even had an end. It was a vital constant across the Reaches and it was sacred as well as feared, for it was the gate to death and back again. Once upon a time, it had ferried the dead to the afterlife. We surrendered our dead to it or buried them in graves near its banks, always with a copper coin in their mouths for the boatman, and in doing so we had sent them to a better place with joy.

A thousand years ago, that abruptly changed. Something perverted the waters across the Reaches. Not long after, a bunch of sages supposedly received the secrets of binding from the dead gods, and decided to snap the coin in half. They say the greatest discoveries always come from the most capricious of circumstances, and lo and behold, binding was conceived. The Nyx became the key to trapping souls in the harsh light of day, and death and life became irreversibly intertwined. The Tenets were written by the Nyxites, then came the Arc's Code, which was adopted across the lands. Society was upheaved. Dynasties were built. The gods were declared dead. Murder became fashionable. Here we were, a millennium on.

Without Nyxwater, a ghost cannot be bound. Those that die before their time and aren't snapped up to be indentured rise from their dead body and are tethered to it for forty days. Their only chance for paradise is to drag their body to the nearest Nyxwell before they're claimed. If they fail to reach one, they fade away, lost to the void. No afterlife for them. It's the same if a half-coin is destroyed.

In that moment, I wondered if a void of nothing was better than spending a thousand years in that endless cave of shouting dead. That was the only afterlife I had seen, and if I thought of it for too long, I began to feel the trickle of water over my feet, the rising roar of voices. *Paradise.* I snorted. I would call that a paradise when I was the fucking emperor of the Arc. It was nothing but a great lie.

Feeling a cold shudder run through me, I watched the Nyxites – the robed fellows who were allowed to touch the waters – as they tested the river with cups on long poles. It was said that almost every Nyxwell found in civilisation or the wild was tended by at least one Nyxite at all times. I reckoned that was primarily so they could charge silver for it. Those humble caretakers had cleverly orchestrated a thousand-year-old monopoly that nobody had ever questioned. Being the only ones who harvested and distributed the Nyxwater, they were treated more like priests.

Rumour had it that the Nyx was drying up. It was one of those rumours that everybody laughed at, but then immediately shivered privately at the thought of. If the river ever dried up, so would the Realm's shade industry.

A long queue snaked back and forth on the far side of the Nyxwell. I wandered closer, inspecting the crowd of people. Almost all of them seemed to be accompanied by large bundles or boxes. Those who could afford it had guards to keep them safe. Those who didn't hugged their sacks and boxes to them, wary-eyed and cautious. It made sense. The best time to bind a soul is before it's been properly bound. At that point, whomever gets the body to Nyxwater first wins the claim.

I saw a few free ghosts amongst the crowd. As I watched, one was called forwards and up the steps to the Nyxwell's dais. He was clutching something to his chest, but I still saw the white feather on him. There was a moment of discussion between the Nyxites and an officious-looking man, and then the ghost stepped forward to the edge overlooking the black waters. I watched him throw his half-coin down into the Nyx. The coin met the waters with a hiss. In the same moment, the ghost deliquesced into a cloud of blue smoke. The wind wiped him away in moments. He had completed his payment and chosen the afterlife. I pitied his mistake. That endless cavern was not freedom to me. That was giving up.

'Next!' came the cry from a soldier on the steps, and it was then I noticed two black-suited figures leaning against the Nyxwell's base. I walked closer to see their insignia.

They both looked Arctian by their features, and they were busy muttering about something, punctuating their words by pointing. They seemed to be scrutinising the queue, looking on with what appeared to be mild amusement. A seal of a woman bearing scales and a star, stitched in gold thread, sat upon their chests. They had shaved heads, and black tattoos creeping from their collars onto their cheeks.

'Sirs?' I began. 'If I could have a moment of your time—'

'Whoa! Back up, shade!' one yelled, instantly shoving a gloved hand in my face. His voice caused some disturbance in the queue.

The other was also quick to shoo me away. 'Keep your distance! Back, I say! Better. What's your problem?'

'Well, sir—'

'That's *Proctor*, if you please, half-life!'

'I—' I had no idea what that was, but I assumed it was official. Perhaps related to the Code. My love for law enforcement was close to non-existent. For most of my life, these sorts of men had played the role of the enemy. Now, I was hoping they would be allies. 'What exactly do you, er… proct?'

The men chuckled between them. 'New here, I take it?'

'Can't tell, him being so blue and all.'

The first man sighed at my blank expression. 'We try to keep the peace, shade, what little of it is left to keep. Make sure nobody's causing trouble, like you currently are.'

'I'm not causing any trouble. I wanted to complain of a murder. My murder. And illegal indenturement.'

The proctors rolled their eyes. 'Yeah, you and every other shade.'

'But this is serious. A man named Boss Temsa sold me. He's a rampant soulstealer—'

A leather glove sewn with copper plates shot out and caught me in the sternum. I staggered, spilling half the basket onto the dust.

The proctors had gone back to their leaning. 'Go line up at the Chamber like all the rest. Or find a scrutiniser if you got tips on a particular boss. There's nothing we can do.'

Your jobs, for starters, I thought. That would have been refreshing. I suspected crime paid more than the law did in this city.

'Where is this Chamber, then?' I asked, already retreating.

A thumb jerked somewhere to the east, amidst the towers of stone and marble. Nothing remotely resembled a chamber to me. In my gazing I caught sight of the sun. It had risen quickly, and I realised I had little over an hour left to make it back to the widow's tower.

Not bothering to thank the lazy idiots, I headed west hurriedly. It occurred to me that a minute of lateness might be all the excuse Vex needed to be rid of me. I rushed through whichever markets and bazaars I found in my path, showing the list to whoever I could, noting the words I didn't understand. They snorted and spat and waved me away, and in the end I gave up in favour of haste. My task incomplete, and my victory over Vex unaccomplished, I ran back through the crowds as fast as I could, thankful I had memorised the shape of Horix's tower.

Vex was waiting calmly for me as I came staggering under the courtyard archway, feeling bullied and invisible after fighting the press of the crowd. Two of the other ghosts had already made it back. Dust clung to the vapours around their face and arms. One had a bright red stain splashed across his smock. Their baskets lay at their feet.

'Let's see how you did, Jerub!' Vex called, blue teeth bared in a wide smile.

I placed the basket and papyrus-wrapped clay in the dust and stood back to let him examine them.

'I didn't get the last few things,' I said.

He raised an eyebrow. 'Oh, no?' He showed me the list, fingers jabbing at the strange words. 'You have not come back with increased respect?' *Tap*. 'Humility?' *Tap*. 'Obedience?' *Tap*.

I wanted to roll my eyes at his little game. 'I suppose I have.'

'I'm glad to hear it.' He stuck out a hand, and I placed what few coins I had left in his palm. 'Hmph. Not very impressive.'

Vex made us wait for the fourth ghost, giving him almost an hour past noon before beckoning to a nearby soldier. The man came forward with a cloth bag, and out of it came the missing ghost's half-moon of copper. In the light, I could have made out the broken seal of a spiked crown and coin, and the etched glyph of the ghost's name. But all I could focus on was the bag, knowing full well my own half-coin was in there. I could have seized it and ran. Made it as a free ghost. *Worn the white feather*.

Vex produced a curious set of pincers with jagged teeth at the end of their jaws. He clamped the half-coin in them and began to squeeze. I could hear the metal squeaking as it was punctured.

For a long time, nothing happened. The other two ghosts and I winced together, but there was no screaming, no patter of hurried feet. Nothing.

Vex pressed harder, bending the coin crooked, digging a gash in it. The spell seemed to be protesting. That was when the scream came: not from beyond the courtyard, as we had expected, but from within the tower. A belch of dust came next, then ghosts in smocks dragging limp bodies out into the sunlight. They were painted red with blood and caked in sand.

'Fetch a physician!' shouted a ghost with a giant beard.

For a moment Vex froze, staring at the bent coin as if it had somehow caused the chaos. It hadn't, of course, and once he realised he yelled at the ghost next to me, 'Go! Fetch a physician!'

I stood by as four bodies were dragged into the courtyard, their faces and bones crushed by something heavy. They were house-guards, some of Kalid's men, and their chainmail hadn't saved them. I found them morbidly intriguing, to know that was all I lacked. *A body.* Just a complicated lump of meat.

The vacancy in the nearest corpse's eyes was mesmerising. They were frozen wide, bloated veins reaching through their whites to a dark centre. They said the eyes were the windows to a soul, and perhaps they were. I imagined the guard's ghost, trapped behind those small windows, throwing itself at them as a prisoner might at his cell bars.

'Out of the way, shade!'

Two more bodies were thrown onto the pile. These were still groaning, and I stared while a hushed conversation was carried out behind me between Vex and the bearded ghost.

'What happened?'

'I don't know, Vex.'

'Tell me! Has there been any damage—?'

'Not that I know of!' the man yelled as he strode back inside the building.

As Vex chased him inside, I was left alone, ignored. The two injured fellows were pulled into the shade and given water while I stayed with the corpses. I knelt beside one, head cocked. The dome of his skull had been caved in so that his forehead stopped just above his eyebrows. Beyond that was pink and grey mush littered with skull fragments. Dark blood still seeped from severed arteries.

I stayed like that for some time as I pondered where this man's soul was; whether it was stuck in that body, dormant until buried or bound, or whether it was already there, in that vast crowd waiting beyond the afterlife, staring at distant gates and stars.

The corpse's sand-caked lips twitched, and I recoiled with a noise I was not proud of.

'You're wasting time,' he rasped at me.

I looked around. The other shades and guards were still tending the injured. Nobody had heard the voice, nor my effeminate yelp.

The eyes were coming alive now, rolling about in their sockets until they found me. One was cloudy, the other a bloodshot blue.

He couldn't possibly be alive. No man could have survived his injury. I looked back and forth between the eyes and the red mess of his skull.

'You can't—'

'You're wasting time, Caltro. You should be fighting, not dallying in servitude.'

'Fighting? Fighting who? For what?'

'Damn it, boy!' The corpse's face compressed into a deep scowl. 'Fighting for us! Fighting to stop the flood!'

My mouth hung open. I was still busy trying to figure out whether I had become delusional. I didn't know ghosts could lose their minds, but here I was, chatting with a corpse.

'What are you?'

'Stop wasting time. Save us from chaos. Do what we ask of you!'

The corpse twitched again. This time its hand flicked out, limp and bending in places there shouldn't have been joints. I recoiled again.

'Take it!'

The urgency in the voice forced me to do it. I touched the still-warm skin and an image flashed across my eyes, all sideways, with a figure kneeling before me on a sunny day.

It was me. I was the corpse. In the time it took for a single grain of sand to fall through an hourglass, I was back in that vast space under the stars, feeling the press of the endless dead around me.

'You can't let us die…' the voice gurgled into nonsense. 'Can't let the river burst…'

With that, the corpse died, again. The mist returned to its good eye, and the lips twitched no more.

'Get out of the way!' another voice yelled at me. 'Bloody shades, always getting in the way!'

Dazed, bewildered, I stepped back as another body was hauled into the daylight. The man and the woman standing above it, both guards, took a moment to clear their lungs and stare at the pile.

'Fuckin' mess, this is!' said the woman.

I chose that moment to walk away. I wanted space. I wanted to shrug the feeling of being crushing out of my shoulders. I didn't care for their talk, nor to know the reason why those bodies had come out of the tower so crushed and broken. All I cared for was the tingle in my hand where I had touched the dead flesh, and the voice that had demanded I fight a flood.

I found shade and let the croaking words play over, again and again. *The flood is coming. Save us from it.* A peculiar turn of phrase, to my ears, and I wondered whether I'd misheard those bloody lips.

There I stayed until Vex came to fetch me. He seemed subdued but angry enough to send us packing up the stairs and into our alcoves. Not a soul came to check us or summon us for work. We were left to wonder in silence, as instructed, and trade no rumours. The other ghosts had no glares for me that night. I got the feeling whatever dues they felt I owed the household had been paid.

There came a wailing in the middle of the night, long and thin and far beneath us. It sounded like a falcon at first, but I could hear the wretchedness in it, and no feathered beast free to roam the open skies could be so miserable. It was cut short by a distant thud; perhaps a door, perhaps a boot. Whether it was the ghost that had tried to run, or some unfortunate stepping into the wrong alley, I did not know. But it kept me upright and rigid until sunrise.

CHAPTER 10
THE BELDAM

When a king, a man who was a despot, arrived at the great gates to gain his way into duat, the afterlife, all gods but Mashat agreed to let him enter.

'Surely,' she petitioned her brethren, 'this man is not deserving. Let him be cast back to the endless void, and taste the fruit of his evil ways.'

But the other gods scoffed. 'This is not the way of it, Mashat,' Sesh argued.

The goddess was not deterred. 'If no justice is served in life, then justice should be served in death.' Taking hold of the great and sacred chains of life, she bent them in a circle, end touching end. 'And so it shall be. What a man bestows, a man shall receive. Not in form, but in kind.'

The gods tore their robes in outrage. 'This man was a king in life. So shall it be in death!' said Oshirim, lord of the gods.

Mashat shook her head. 'King is merely a title when there are no kingly deeds to earn it.'

A FABLE OF THE DEAD GODS

NILITH DRAGGED HERSELF UPRIGHT ONCE more. Anoish's coarse hair, dusted with sand, was starting to scour away the skin of her cheeks.

The nausea came again, rising up like the swell of an ocean, dumping her on a shore of pain and dizziness. She tried to take a deep breath, caught a whiff of the nearby corpse, and retched.

Cracking open her eyes, she saw Farazar had wandered ahead. It was as if he too could smell it, and was trying to get upwind. Maybe he just didn't like seeing his body dragging in the dust, tied to an even dustier horse.

He certainly had changed since the attack. His silences were longer, his mood even more sullen. Nilith wasn't sure if he was busy plotting, or still brooding over her intentions for him and his corpse. In any case, she was finding it hard to care. She was in far too much pain for that.

A wound was quick to fester in the desert. The heat and grit made it hard to keep anything clean. The arrow injury had leaked poison into her blood and the fever had struck the day after. If she thought baking in the sun was tough before, with a burning fever it became unbearable. It made every hour twice as long, every jolt of Anoish a stab in the gut, every mouthful of water she slurped just something to sweat back out.

The day was almost over, and with the Steps of Oshirim now standing in their path, dark against the bruising sky, she had a choice to make. Her brain felt no good for choices, but she was out of time.

The shortest route through the mountains was over the Firespar. Though it was a monster of a mountain, it was the shape of a cone and thus easier to climb. It also happened to be the most dangerous route. As well as being treacherous underfoot, the Firespar had a healthy reputation for entertaining waylayers. Going around it or negotiating the craggier mountains would take several more days, and though they had travelled hard, they were days she would need. Araxes was still far beyond the horizon.

Nilith looked up at the distant mountains, jagged and misshapen like a pile of broken crowns. The Steps of Oshirim were mighty peaks: as red as a sunset and streaked with iron rust. The grand churning of the earth had built these gigantic protrusions, and the wind had carved them into whorls and pinnacles. The Firespar was their tallest: a dead volcano with a jagged, hollow peak. It dominated the range, sitting proudly at its centre like the Cloudpiercer lording over Araxes.

The people of the Long Sands spoke of an old god ascending into the sky by these mountains, using them as steps to climb into the heavens to re-join his brethren. The Krass had a similar fable about the Dolkfang, the peak that soared above the capital Saraka. The One-Eyed God was supposed to have climbed to the peak to spend nine nights and nine days watching the earth below, learning its secrets and spells.

Nilith was clearly becoming delirious, dreaming of wives' tales and dead gods. They were called dead gods for a reason: they were buried and forgotten to most. The enslavement of ghosts meant that man had built a new afterlife for himself, here in the Far Reaches. What use were gods when humanity had mastered death?

There she went again. Nilith hauled herself back to reality, eyeing the peaks once more. She would challenge them, but first she needed to rest. The deaths of the three men had brought no further followers, and they had seen few others on the road since. Their part of the Long Sands was largely untravelled. One had been a carpet trader on the back of a scarab beetle, taking the lesser roads to Hebus. Another was a camel-herder, eager to avoid the dubious-looking woman dragging a body through the desert.

The foothills of the Steps stretched for miles before the mountains thrust from the earth, almost vertically in some places. Gnarled rocks interrupted the rolling dunes, providing Nilith with a good number of nooks and crannies to camp and hide in for the next few days. She was not the only one who needed peace of mind; she could feel the weariness in Anoish, and how his muscles shook beneath her backside. His steps were shorter, his head lower.

'Almost there,' she whispered, patting his side.

By sunset, they had found a shallow cave to bed down in. At first it had seemed a simple cave, but they soon realised it was a kind of shrine. A hollow had been carved in the back wall. Within it, somebody had balanced two dozen stones in intricate, seemingly impossible piles. After sliding gradually from the horse's back, seeing to his reins and the reeking body, Nilith inspected the stones with weary eyes.

There were three piles, each made up of rocks about the size of her fist. They defied the world's laws, sitting upright on their sharp ends without falling. There was a fragile stillness to them that was mesmerising. They seemed frozen in the very last moment before tumbling, as if a mere breath could ruin their balance, and yet they endured. Nilith found herself holding hers.

'What is this peasant fuckery?' Farazar said from behind. 'Some sort of witchcraft?'

'It's a work of art.' She waved him away from getting too close. 'And you'll not disturb it.'

He muttered as he went back to the cave mouth. He crossed his arms and stared at the blazing sun that turned the western sky into liquid fire. 'Work of pagans is what it is. Some desert cult that worships rocks.'

Nilith followed him at her own pace, checking that Anoish had settled down for the evening. The horse watched her with his mahogany eyes. Was there wisdom or ignorance in his gaze? She had a sneaking suspicion it was the former. Sprawling beside the beast, Nilith let the rise and fall of his ribs relax her. She sighed as she watched the ghost.

Farazar was sullen, but he did not mope. He had taken on a serious expression instead of the slighted child's scowl he adopted so readily.

She let him stew, seeing to her leg and a fire instead. The wound had finally started to knit together but the pus remained. She spent some time wincing and squeezing the foulness out before redressing it with some cleaner cloth. She had no poultices, no plants to scrape together. Fresh water was the only thing for it. A scant dribble was all she could spare.

After collecting a bundle of brushwood from the surrounding crags, she built a small fire behind a stack of boulders and coaxed it to life. Once she had it crackling gently, Nilith leaned back and half-closed her eyes, feeling the rumble of the horse's heart and lungs in her back. She summoned up the map in her head. Weeks she had spent memorising the desert paths. The Long Sands and Duneplains shifted constantly, but the nomads, tribes and traders kept the mapmakers updated as best they could. Nilith's routes were based on landmarks that wouldn't change. The mountains, for example.

She spent an hour trying to decide which to take. In the end, she left the decision to the morning. All she wanted now was sleep.

Although Farazar hadn't tried any mischief in several days, it didn't mean he wasn't planning some. He spent the nights feigning sleep or wandering his boundaries while she drifted in and out of fitful, feverish slumber. Tonight, she felt the weariness dragging her down into a deep abyss. Inexorably, she fell, hard and fast into a dreamless sleep. It was short, but blissful. At least until she was rudely awakened by a fervent tapping on her shoulder.

'Someone's coming,' came the whisper in her ear. Cold air fanned her face. Her hand flew to the dagger and in a blink had it pressed to his side.

'Just try it,' she whispered, voice thick with phlegm.

'Someone's coming, you idiot,' he hissed again, moving away to be deeper in the cave.

'Who?'

He did not answer. Anoish whinnied as Nilith pushed herself up, dagger in hand. The fire was still burning, but its light had faded. She could barely make out the figure emerging from the boulders scattered around the cave mouth.

'Stay where you are!'

'I mean you no harm,' replied a woman's voice, curiously deep. At first, Nilith thought it was the glow of the fire, but as the woman came a step closer, she saw the orange colour of her cloth.

The woman held up a wrinkled forearm, showing a stump cut just above the wrist. Nilith imagined a flat hand. 'I only wish to share some warmth on this cold bitch of a night.'

'The fire's on its way out, I'm afraid.'

'No trouble.' The woman came forwards again, her hand delving into one of her pockets. Nilith flinched away, letting the woman see the dagger in her hand.

'No trouble.' Bending down, she gently threw a handful of blue dust into the fire. The flames danced higher, shining a bright green.

'Clever trick.' Nilith had a better view of her now. The woman's face was a topography of wrinkles and freckles, as withered and as cracked as the desert. Like her eyes, her skin was nut-brown, lighter than the usual desert-dweller's. Her skin hung in baggy jowls about her cheeks. Thin lips hid teeth like burnt fenceposts. She had little girth to her; her robe hung on a bony frame.

'Tricksters are ten a gem, young miss,' said the woman, her accent thick and southern. 'What you need is a fuckin' good healer, I think.' She gestured to the stained cloth wrapped around Nilith's leg. Already the stain of blood and pus had seeped through.

'Know any?'

The woman momentarily looked to Farazar, still hovering in the cave. He folded his arms and pretended not to be involved. 'Hmph,' she grunted, before gesturing to a spot across from the fire. 'Might I?'

Nilith gestured with the dagger and the old crone settled down into a strange crouch, hands outstretched to the heat.

'Do you always greet kind strangers so fuckin' rudely?' she asked.

'Apologies. It's a new policy.'

A slow nod. 'The Long Sands are full o' danger. Dunewyrms. Sandstorms. Soulstealers. Slavers. Bandits. I wager you've seen some o' the latter? That an arrow wound? Smells like shite.'

'Where are you from?' Nilith changed the subject.

The woman turned to face her. 'South of here.'

Nilith hummed. 'How far south?'

A shrug was her reply. 'You're pretty. Got all your teeth, at least. You're of the city, I'd wager.'

'Not originally, but yes. I am from Araxes. We both are.'

'The City of Countless Souls? You and your shade?'

'We call them ghosts in Krass.'

The woman laughed like a crow choking. 'I like it.' Another palmful of dust met the fire with a whoosh. 'More accurate. "Shade" softens the blow, like a bloody sword wrapped in a fancy scabbard. Still fuckin' steel beneath, right? Shade almost makes 'em sound human, instead of a monster.'

Nilith nodded, trying to decide whether this woman was wise or just plain weird. She had a mouth like a pirate, that was for certain.

'Saw the great city once. Just its edges.'

'The Outsprawls?'

'Saw the city stretchin' for miles. Beetle farms everywhere. Buildings like mountains in the distance. Bigger than the Steps. Far too big. Far too fuckin' big.'

Farazar piped up. 'A hundred miles of streets and buildings from there to the sea. More than a hundred from east to west. Greatest city ever built.'

The woman nodded to the ghost. 'You go to bind him there?'

Nilith tapped her teeth in thought, wary. The old crone pointed at the wrapped corpse stashed a stone's throw from the cave, downwind.

'Obvious, int it? His body hasn't touched the water yet. So what fuckin' else would you be doing with it? Don't worry 'bout me. Never owned a shade, never will.'

'I am going to bind him,' said Nilith, feeling the cold of Farazar's glare. 'In the Grand Nyxwell.'

The woman waved her stump at the cave. 'Have you seen the stones?'

'I have.'

'And you know what they are?'

'Works of art?'

She shuffled closer, and it took some effort on Nilith's part to keep the dagger steady on her lap. The crone's eyes had taken on a dark shine, gleaming like molten tar. Nilith tried her hardest to match her heavy gaze.

'A grave, young miss. Something this world has forgotten. We used to spend our lives only once, see. From the moment our bitch mothers squeezed us out into the wide open, we'd thirst for life, breath in yer lungs, grab it with both fuckin' hands.' She paused to roll her eyes at her stump. 'You'd never win, of course, but that was the point. The end of the chase made you work harder, try harder, live bloody harder. Cheat death until it came to catch you. People cared about life. Now we don't care. Now you just knife a man when you want what he's got. Now we care nothing to take what isn't ours, and keep what we kill. Nah. We ain't chasing life any more. Now we're just chasing graves. Fuckin' graves. The world's died another kind of death, don't you think?'

Nilith found herself sitting upright. 'As a matter of fact, I do.'

'Is that so?' Another rasping chuckle. Another sidelong look at Farazar. 'Three girls, I had. Fuckin' three. Taken by shite-brained soulstealers who marched them through the desert heat for four days. Raped them whenever they took a fancy. And when they were near the soulmarkets, they killed them cold in a gutter. Blundered it, though, so nobody would buy them. Save for me, o' course. I tracked those murdering cunts down. I bought my dead daughters at discount fuckin' prices, and then I set that slavers' camp on fire and watched them all burn.'

Nilith wondered if the knife would be enough. 'I can't understand the pain you must have felt.'

'Mm. Their coins are in the Nyx now. That's all that matters.'

'Well, I'm sorry,' Nilith replied, putting more meaning into it than she expected, thinking of other mothers who had recently lost children. She thought of how those children lay under a pile of rocks on a hillside, where their ghosts would eventually rise and be stuck there until they withered away or were bound by passing travellers. Nilith winced.

'No trouble, no trouble. Desert is a shite place. The sand carves you away, changes you in ways you don't fuckin' want. The more time you spend here the more you're worn away.' Those gleaming eyes searched Nilith's. 'Although there are a few ways to lighten that load. Stave it off.'

They sat there in silence for a time until Nilith bowed her head and began to rummage in a nearby sack. She withdrew a pouch tied with a strip of reed, and placed it between them. She could hear Farazar tutting. He had never been one for charity. Like most Arctians, he barely knew the meaning of the word.

What he didn't understand was that this was more like a payment. Nilith's blade had not taken the lives of her girls, but it had taken the lives of those three men. There was ill will that needed to be offset. A balance to be struck.

'May the dead gods reward you for your loss,' she said, speaking words she had only read in scrolls before now.

'You are kind.'

'And you are kinder.'

The ceremony abruptly over, the woman took the pouch and then gestured towards Nilith's wounded leg. 'As it happens, I do know a healer. A great fuckin' healer.' She raised a finger like a winter tree branch and prodded her own chest.

Nilith compressed her lips. 'Of course.' Another pouch hit the dust.

The crone shuffled closer, going to work. She sprinkled more dust onto the wound, a burnt orange powder this time, the colour of her clothes. The pain made Nilith gasp. She squeezed the hem of her sleeve between her teeth. Gnarled fingers poked at her, pressing it deeper and deeper into the wound. A tiny blade appeared, no more than a shard of black glass, and was used to cut away the rancorous flesh. Then the wound was set with a dark paste and sealed by twine and thread. When fresh bindings were wrapped around her leg, Nilith allowed herself to breathe. Anoish whinnied as she leaned against him once more.

The foul-mouthed crone had already gotten to her feet and was aiming for the night. Before the shadows and glare of the fire swallowed her, she raised a hand and made a closed circle with it. Nilith bowed her head once more in thanks, and then she was gone.

Farazar made sure they were alone before creeping forward, arms crossed and face a mask of disapproval. 'What do you care for three dead desert girls?'

'I don't.'

'Then wh—'

'Orange cloth in the desert. Doesn't that mean anything to you? No? She was a beldam.'

He thought for a moment before snorting. 'A sand-witch? You're even more foolish than I thought.'

'You should have spent less time fucking and drinking and read a scroll every once in a while, Farazar. You know nothing of your country.' Nilith closed her eyes for patience. The pain had begun to dim, at least. 'A witch, maybe, but haven't you ever heard of *ma'at*, as you Arctians call it?'

Farazar mouthed the words. 'Life is round?'

'Life is a *wheel* in the nomad dialects. The opposite of the idea of *ba'at*, a bound ghost. What goes around, comes around. A gift from the goddess Mashat when the Arc was just dust and dreams. You know her at least, right? She's ironically the symbol of your precious Chamber of the Code, after all. It's something they believe in Skol, but they call it *shuld*. It means balance, something Araxes seems to have almost entirely forgotten. I give the beldam gems for her children, and what I did to those men is paid for. Balanced out. She makes sure of it, and gives us good luck for the mountain passes.'

'That's what you get in the absence of civilisation. Pagan nonsense and superstitious shit-talk from people that don't know any better.'

'Suit yourself. But if you ask me, you got what was coming to you. Maybe *ma'at* does exist.'

'Says the murderer and the soulstealer. Let's see what it brings you, shall we?'

She didn't rise to him, and overcome by frustration, he threw up his hands and stormed back into the cave. Nilith waited for an irritable clash of stones, pre-emptively burning with anger at the idea, but nothing came. Just some faint scuffs of moody pacing. They lulled her into a drowsy half-sleep, where the dying fire and rock walls were muddled up with arcs of splashed blood and gurning faces of pain. Her fingers felt sticky. Arrows hissed past her ears.

It was an intermittent sleep that took her.

CHAPTER 11
DOORS

Nobody was more surprised than the banks when they realised the bond between master and coin still held true behind a vault door and a signature. Until then, for fear the Tenets were fickle and that ownership would pass to another who merely touched the coins, half-coin fortunes were kept in one's own possession. It took a brave master, one whom history has forgotten to record, to entrust a coin to a bank. No ownership was conferred. The bond seemed intuitive, keeping as rigidly to contracts and sigils' marks as it did to physical possession. A new age of indenturement was thusly born: the age of banking. Five hundred years later, the banks watch over the coins of millions of shades, handle thousands of transactions, and preside over every Weighing of every noble in the Arc. And yet there is no Chamber of Banking to govern them. The banks are trusted because they follow the Code to the letter. Or, at very least, they appear to.

FROM A TREATISE ON ARCTIAN ECONOMIC THEORY

'DO YOU KNOW THE SECRET to torture, Tor Merlec?'

The pathetic whimper of a reply told Temsa that no, Tor Merlec did not know the secret to torture. It was to be expected. The tors and tals of the city were usually more concerned with private balls and dainty cutlery.

Temsa's 'cutlery' was less dainty.

He reached into the case for another savage-looking hook, lying amongst the array of twisted knives and pincers. With his other hand, he used his handkerchief to dab away some of the blood and snot from the man's bare chest and the velvet couch they'd repurposed into a table.

'There was once a man in Araxes called the Butcher. Imaginative, I know, but what he lacked in names he more than made up for with his aptitude for prising information and apologies out of people. As it happens, he was the man who taught me everything I know about torture.' Temsa paused to scrape his talons across the floor, making Merlec wince. 'Though his price was high, he left me with one invaluable lesson. The secret, my dear fellow, is that the tortured, not the torturer, is in control.'

The tor's wild-eyed look was one of surprise, as if he had endured the last hour needlessly. He murmured words made almost entirely of vowels. Consonants are hard to make without a tongue.

'Or fuckih iyin!'

'No, I'm not fucking lying. Because you can stop this at any time. Sweet release shall be yours, Tor Merlec. Freedom from pain. All you have to do is relent. I lost a leg learning that. What will you lose before you give in, hmm?'

The man riled against his restraints. A scrawny man, with oddly pale hair and wide green eyes, he was breaking rather easily. 'I wom ehb ou! Fuck ou!'

Temsa looked to Ani, halfway across the room. 'It's nice the dead gods made us so that we can still say "fuck" after somebody's cut out our tongue, isn't, it m'dear?'

Ani shrugged, as she always did when she hadn't heard something.

Temsa tutted. 'Come now, Merlec. Not even to save this old skin of yours?' He twisted the thick hook into the tor's flesh, in and out so the metal held a band of skin over it. That made four now, spread across his chest and shoulders. Merlec's wiry white hair was stained with blood.

'I…'

'No? Well, then.' Temsa spoke as he worked, attaching thin chains to each of the hooks. 'You're an old man, Merlec. You've lived a good and prosperous life. Perhaps it's time to let somebody else have a chance, eh? Tell us how to get into the vault. It's your own fault for not trusting in our good banks like a clever man. That's what they're there for!'

'Fucking old-fashioned is what it is,' said Ani.

'I agree.'

'Maarua,' mumbled the tor, growing more nervous as Temsa clanged backwards, chains gripped in one fist.

'Was that a yes? Release his restraints, Danib, Ani!' Temsa tugged on the chains once the man was free. Merlec squealed as he scrambled to get up. He clung uselessly to his stretching skin.

Temsa threw the tor into the opulent hallway, where his thugs were busy liberating trinkets they fancied from mahogany cabinets and shelves. Temsa got the pick of their piles, of course, but it was cheaper payment than his own silver.

'Any luck, Tooth?'

At the end of the marble hallway was a wide room with one way in, one way out. A large circular door occupied one wall, the entrance to Merlec's vault. A woman standing up against its door spat as they entered. She was holding a papyrus cone to her ear, the other end flush with the decorative wood and silver of the vault.

'Ain't no uthe. Take a better lockthmith than me t' get in't 'ere, Both,' she said, with a thick Scatter accent and lisp. The woman had one tooth that poked from her upper gum across her lower lip. It made her whistle when she spoke. She turned from the door and froze when she saw the state of the tor, and the chains running from his naked, bloody back to Temsa's fist.

'Fine.' Temsa yanked the hooks again. One tore lose, making a hole of bloody flesh above Merlec's nipple. 'The combination, Tor, if you please.' He spoke calmly over the man's screams.

'Ou wom fuckih geh ewa wi is! Crimiha! CRIMIHA!'

Temsa stamped his foot, making everybody present jump. 'The combination, Merlec! I'm waiting! Don't test me further, man!'

With a sob, Merlec hung his head. Another tug on the chains brought it straight back up, grimacing with pain.

'I'm waiting! Or would you rather see how many hooks it takes to dangle you from the top of your tower?' shouted Temsa.

The tor got to his knees, reached for the handles of the vault door, and began to turn them left and right in an intricate sequence. Something deep within the wood and silver panels clicked and whirred, hidden cogs and springs winding. There came a great clang, and one half of the door edged open.

'Ahhh, that'th it,' whistled Tooth.

Merlec slumped on the floor, broken. Temsa released his chains and stepped over him into the vault.

Like the rest of the grand mansion, the vault bled luxury. There were silk drapes at the door, fine wood on its ceiling, and gold swirls on the floor. Small lamps of glow-worms filled the room with a greenish light.

Temsa tugged the curtains aside to reveal stacks upon stacks of shining half-coins spread around the walls, all bound with reed twine and gauze.

He heard a shuffling behind him, and a polite cough. 'That you, Russun?'

'Mhm,' came the mumbled reply. This was the second time they had plucked him from his home, and it had become apparent he was the quiet type. Temsa didn't mind. He liked silence in his men.

'Once we have his signature, you may start counting. After that, you're free to leave. Is that our tor's last will?'

Russun nodded and lifted up the scroll for him to look over. 'And transfer documents for everything else he entrusted to the banks. What little there was.'

'It looks good. Very good indeed. What excuse are you going with this time?'

'It's all aligned with the Code… Boss. Under section ninety-six, Tor Merlec bequeaths you his estate due to ill health. At the time of his death and after binding, you own his estates and half-coins.'

'And why me?'

'Several receipts for legal trade of shades, visits to your tavern, and family connections. They've all been put into the scrolls. It's good enough for the Chamber, should they ever investigate.'

Temsa banged his cane. 'Very good! You're a natural, Russun. Both your father and your family would be extremely proud if they could see you now. Ani, assist our young sigil here with Merlec's signature and seal.'

The woman led Russun away, leaving Temsa and Danib to admire the coin-clad walls. Even the shade's fingers reached out to touch the stacks. The more Temsa counted, the more he chuckled, until he was braying with laughter. Danib stood there scratching his head.

'I thought you'd be pleased, old friend. Twice now your old comrades have led us true.'

The big shade shrugged, waving his hands over the coins as if they were a meagre handful.

'You're wrong. This *is* what I've been working for. Of course it's bold, but bold is what I need to be if I want to claim my rightful place in this city.'

Danib met his eyes. Temsa stamped his foot in rage. 'I don't care what it looks like! I will deal with these uppity nobles how I see fit. If that means teaching them a lesson before they taste a blade, so be—'

A loud screech interrupted him. Temsa threw up his hands and limped to the vault door.

Ani had the chains in hand, almost hauling Merlec off the floor. The skin around each hook looked like the peaks of desert tents.

'He refused,' she said.

'Tut tut, Tor. You should know better than to refuse Miss Jexebel here.' Temsa took Ani's hand and lowered it. 'How is he supposed to sign if he's passed out from pain?'

'But you said—'

'I need him to sign. Then you can do with him what you want.' There came another sob from behind him, and Temsa looked in its direction. 'Now, Tor Merlec, are you holding us up again? Sign the document and this ugly business shall be concluded.'

Merlec offered a stream of malformed curses. A handful of them made sense: something about criminal, murderer, and thief. Temsa smiled.

'What else do you expect from a man who breaks into your tower in the early hours of the night with a handful of thugs?' The thugs in question chortled amongst themselves. 'You know I'll just take it all if I have to, with or without your signature. I'll do it the old-fashioned way and sell your trinkets and shades at market one by one. I'll have you bound, too, cut your tongue out and sell you to some desert quarry. But I have grander plans than that, my good man, and I wager you would rather spend the rest of your days either alive or unbound in some far-flung part of the Reaches. So why don't we make it look official, hmm?' Temsa thrust the document in his face once more. 'Fucking sign it!'

It was then that Merlec gave up his last vestige of rebellion. Perhaps it was the pain, or the pointlessness of it all, but in any case he took the reed with a shaking hand and managed to scrawl something legible enough to make Russun nod. A silver box, its insides black with ink-stained moss, was held in front of the tor. Temsa manoeuvred Merlec's hand like a puppet master, dabbing and pressing his signet ring to the papyrus.

'Good enough, sigil?'

'It'll get by,' whispered Russun, withdrawing. It seemed the man was not one for blood.

Temsa sighed, patting the tor on the head. 'Ani, Danib, take him away. I think he's earned something reasonably quick. Keep it away from the face, though. I want him sellable after we bind him.'

Merlec did not protest until the last words. He thrashed and bellowed like a drowning oryx. It was one thing to take his possessions, his house, even his life. But to bind him for eternity like one of his own shades? That was true damnation. The nobles were so sure of their ability to carry on being rich beyond the grave, it was almost a pleasure to cheat them of it.

As Merlec was escorted into the hallway and back to his bedchamber, the screams faded in increments until they stopped altogether.

Temsa concluded his work with a slap of his hands. 'You four,' he barked, pointing to a group of his men. 'You stay. Dress up in Merlec's livery. Keep anyone who comes calling at bay. Say he's gone south unexpectedly. You lot, help Russun get these half-coins counted, loaded up and back to the Slab. Take anything we can sell, too. Store it all with the rest, ready for when we pay Fenec's Coinery a visit. As for Merlec's shades, gather them up and keep them in the cellars. I'll own their half-coins as soon as we have Merlec bound. Then we can start putting them to good use. Got to keep up the appearance of legitimacy, haven't we, m'dear?'

'Aye, Boss.'

He oversaw their scurrying for a while until he realised Tooth was lingering beside him, like a lost column. She was a wiry thing, getting wirier all the time with age. She also watched the activity, biting her bottom lip repeatedly with her snaggle-tooth as she teased at her fire-coloured hair. No wonder she had such dry lips.

'What?'

'Pologieth for the door, Both. Combinathons are tricky beathtth. Thethe rich artholes get the betht vaultthmith. Thith wath probably Mathter Thulith's work. Recognithe the patternths. Deviouth fuckin' thmith 'e ith.'

Temsa stared at her flatly. 'I see.'

She appeared to be out of excuses, so she shrugged, bowed, and began to pack up her tools. Temsa watched her, examining each tool she chucked into a cloth bag. Some were not so different from his tools of torture. An auger there, a hammer here, and pieces of thin metal, like knife blades. His eyes narrowed as he pondered.

Ani had returned, as had Danib, now with a fresh corpse in tow.

'Something on your mind, Boss?' she asked.

'Always, m'dear. At the moment, it's a locksmith.'

Ani followed his eyes, seeing Tooth slip out with his men.

'Not the first time that scrawny cunt has failed you, is it?'

'I'll give her one more chance.' Feeling the silence, Temsa looked around to see Ani wearing an unsure expression. 'What's your problem? Been talking to Danib, have you? Go on, spit it out.'

Ani raised her chin, standing straighter like a soldier at attention. Her eyes focused somewhere above his head. 'Nothing at all, Boss. Huge haul. Only a few dozen men lost. And one less rich bastard in the city. No problems here.'

Temsa flourished his cane. 'That's what I like to hear, m'dear! Take note, Danib!' He clanged away, calling out over his shoulder, 'And fetch me Tor Busk. Have him meet me at the tavern. I want to see if he has another locksmith on his books.'

He could hear Ani's upper lip curl, that crackle of spit over big teeth.

'Aye, Boss.'

THE MORNING WAS THICK WITH mist. A fog had blown in from the Troublesome Sea, flooding the streets with its dank, cold vapours. It was as if some colossal, Nyx-bound sea monster had washed ashore and claimed the city for its grave.

Tor Simeon Busk hurried on, grunting and grimacing with every step. The cold played havoc with his old hips. He did not like the mist. If he had wanted cold, he would have stayed in Skol.

A shade bumbled out of the haze, arms full of crimson vegetables. Busk dragged out his knife and waved the shade to go around him. That was another reason he hated the mist. It was hard to hide in the desert sun, but mist made every shadow a waylayer, every muffled clank an approaching soulstealer.

'Away with you!' he snapped.

'Yes, Tor,' muttered the shade, noting the fine silks wrapping Busk's generously proportioned body. He did as he was told, bowing as much as his armload would allow.

'Disgusting sneaker,' said Busk as he walked on. The fact that no high-roads came close to Temsa's tavern was a cause for disappointment. He kept the dagger out for good measure. If it were up to him, he would have stayed in his tower and kept out of this dangerous fog. With the recent disappearance of several nobles, the city was growing more soul-thirsty by the week. But a man didn't say no when Boss Boran Temsa called. Unless he was suicidal, of course, or didn't know the name. In either case he would eventually be delivered, yelling and screaming. Busk knew better.

He struggled on, navigating by the blurry edges of buildings, gauging his whereabouts by the names of taverns or bazaars. Nothing appeared solid. No direction seemed certain. He heard the rumble of carts go by him, but no detail other than a passing shadow. A few drunkards staggered into his confined, hazy world. With a shake of the dagger, they dispersed like blown seeds in search of a new home.

At last, the slanted edges and sharp point of The Rusty Slab reared out of the mist, like a mountain too perfect. The pyramid's lights were either still glowing from the evening before, or had been lit uncomfortably early. In the haze, they were like arachnid's eyes, observing Busk's approach. He aimed for the tall thrust of stone that gave the building a front. Its flat face bore carvings of merry scenes and a long sign brayed the tavern's name and ownership.

As Busk made it to the ramp of the door, a man came flying past him. Literally. He didn't touch the sand for several yards. Somewhat startled, Busk looked up to discover Miss Ani Jexebel standing over him. The sleeves of her tunic had been bunched up, showing off the scars and black swirls of ink that decorated her bulging forearms.

'And stay out!' she barked at the man she had forcibly ejected, then nodded absently to the tor. 'Busk.'

'*Tor* Busk, madam. I have a title for a reason.'

'And I've got two fists for a fuckin' reason. Want me to use them?'

Busk looked at the aforementioned fists, clad in leather and bone gloves. 'No.'

'Then in with you. Temsa's been waiting, and that's something I wouldn't make him do, if I were you.'

He took her suggestion, stepping into the tavern and onto a sticky sandstone floor. The mist had crept in, drawing a haze around the whale-oil lamps. The staff who ambled about between the patrons were all alive; not a shade amongst them. It was as if Temsa didn't trust a shade to serve a drink.

The huge shade, the one who insisted on all the battle armour, was waiting by the stairwell. One humongous hand held the curtain open while another beckoned to him. Busk went ahead, treading the dark stairs in the blue glow of Danube, or whatever his name was. Busk's footsteps were lost amidst the heavy, rhythmic clanking following close behind. His breath hung in the frigid air that wafted from the giant.

The chamber was also dark. Temsa was sitting behind his desk, enwreathed in a thick cloud of smoke. A pipe bowl hovered near his lips, lighting just his crooked nose and sharp eyes. There were dark bags of tiredness beneath them. One single hair escaped from the coiffed slickness on his balding scalp, and dangled over his lined forehead.

A smoke ring came bursting out of the cloud and floated towards Busk. He broke it with a flick, wrinkling his nose. He knew better than to engage in such foul habits. Busk tried a polite smile, but his crotchety mood interfered. 'You called?'

'Tor Busk. A pleasure, as always.' Temsa's voice was deep with smoke and tiredness.

'It would be, if not for the early hour.'

'Would you have preferred night?'

'I would have preferred an armed escort, rather than a sole and rather surly messenger.'

'You have guards, no?'

'Guards, indeed. With eyes, ears and wagging tongues. People in this city spend secrets like silver. You know that.'

Temsa chuckled. 'Next time I'll have Ani accompany you. Ashamed to be seen with me, Tor? Not like you.'

'*Wise* to not be seen with you. Rumours are rife at the moment. Talk of rampant soulstealing and nobles disappearing without claims. I don't need any suspicion in my direction. As such, I'd like to keep our business as quiet as can be.'

Temsa leaned forwards, blowing his pipe to make his face blossom. 'Wise, indeed. Please take a seat. I know how badly your hips ache on the colder days.'

The brute of a shade placed a chair next to him, and Busk chose to sit. 'What can I do for you?'

That darned metal foot stamped on the stone and a few grubby men came forth with bundles wrapped in palm fronds.

'Our latest pickings. I saved the best for you,' said Temsa.

The trip was starting to appear worthwhile. The soulstealer had been busy. Four – no, *five* – bundles were brought in. One at a time, they were opened and spread before him, showing off trinkets of red and yellow gold, brass, copper, argent silver, and platinum from Belish. There were jade necklaces, elaborate sundials, bracelets, armbands, curved ceremonial daggers, silk knots and weaves, a turquoise necklace, and even a lone Skol signet ring. Normally they came in pairs.

Busk's eyes tore themselves from the bundles and back to Temsa's waiting gaze. 'A good haul!' He dug into his pocket and withdrew his lens: a miniature spyglass made of bronze and crystal. He wedged it into his eye socket and began to examine more closely. He spoke as he worked. 'Necklace is fake. Phylan earrings, worth a few silver. Nice turquoise here.'

'There was another matter I was hoping you could assist with,' said Temsa.

'Mhm?'

'The matter of a locksmith. You know that trade better than I do.' It was true, though it sounded like it irked Temsa to say it.

'Thought you were using that woman?'

'Tooth.'

'Quite.'

Temsa blew a great fountain of smoke as he leaned back into the shadow of his enveloping chair. 'I believe she is reaching the limit of her usefulness. She's good for most jobs. Knows her way around a door. But when it comes to the vaults you tors and tals can afford…' He sucked his lip. 'Lacking.'

Busk looked up from a small silver toy made of cogs and springs. 'And why would you be interested in what we tors can afford?' He felt a prickle along his shoulders; perhaps it was the chill of the shade standing far too close for comfort.

Temsa chuckled again. It was a horrid, scratching noise that did nothing to put a mind at ease. 'I wouldn't worry yourself with the details, Busk. These days I find my souls farther afield, outside the main districts. Outsprawls on occasion. I just need a locksmith that won't disappoint me when it's crucial. Understand?'

'For vault-work you'll need somebody good. And I mean *good.* Maybe one of the best. There are only a few locksmiths in the Reaches that could lay bare most Arctian locks. A Skolwoman is the best, or so my associates say. Everass, I believe her name is, but she's in high demand and somewhat picky. Besides her, there are a few Krassmen, Scatterfolk or a duo from Belish.'

'Have you used any of them in the past?'

'No.' It was the truth. Busk's past as a fence had introduced him to a range of both shady and colourful characters, but no locksmiths of the calibre he had recommended. That was the point. Nobody in this business made a recommendation they couldn't be held accountable for. 'I don't know any of them.'

Temsa waved his pipe. 'Of course not. You're "legitimate" now, after all. An art-merchant. Wasn't that what you were posing as, last time we spoke?'

'A broker. And there's no posing.'

'Still sounds like a fence to me.'

Busk ignored him. He picked up a stone box inlaid with gold and weighed it in his palm. 'Almost a deben, by my guess. Dozen silvers for that one.' If he listened carefully, he could hear a scribe hovering behind a drape, scratching away with a reed.

A cloud of smoke blew over him. 'What about your associates? Is there somebody who could introduce me?'

Busk shook his head as solemnly as he could. 'Not for what you want, Temsa. There are, however, a few people I haven't spoken to in many years. They might have better knowledge than I.'

'Then I'll wait to hear from you. You'll be discreet, I assume?'

Busk levelled his eyes at the man. 'Would you expect anything else from me?'

There was a contemplative puff of the pipe. 'You haven't disappointed me yet.'

The tor nodded as he moved on to the next bundle. He found something curious there. 'What are these?' he said, half to himself.

'I was hoping you could tell me.'

Busk turned the tiny shapes of metal and coiled springs over in his hands, peering closely with his lenses. He hummed absently, needing time to think. He recognised the pieces instantly. Not just through their shape or design, craftsmanship or material, but by the minuscule scratch on one strip that looked like half a handle; a scratch with a file-like edge that ground at Busk's thumb. It was writing, but not Arctian glyphs or Common. These were Krass letters. A small *C*, followed by a *B*, if Busk was not mistaken.

'Writing implements? No. Handles for something. Perhaps clockwork of some kind. Look like old Skol runes...' His voice trailed off. 'Where did you find these?'

Temsa clucked his tongue. 'Now, now. Where's that discretion, Tor?'

Busk held up his hands. 'Curiosity got the better of me.' He placed them back on the desk. 'Only, it might help me narrow them down.'

The soulstealer worded it well. 'A leftover from a poor soul that wandered into the wrong part of the docks. Smith of some kind. No longer with us, unfortunately.'

'Smith? Hmm. Tools, then, I'd guess. Maybe for a jeweller, or sculptor, or some peasant usage. My apologies.'

'Shame,' Temsa sighed.

'If you allow me to take them and give me some time, I'll find out the answer. At the very least, the metal will be worth something.'

Temsa leaned out of his smoke and scraped all but half a dozen of the metal slivers towards Busk. 'I'll keep the rest here, for a time. You go ask your questions,' he said.

'I shall, rest assured.'

Busk got to the task of examining the other items, and within ten minutes he was done. The scribe produced the total and soon the tor was counting silver pieces across the desk.

When his business was concluded, Busk stood and slid the metal pieces into an inside pocket. Temsa stayed in his chair. His pipe had died, and now his face was almost invisible in the smoke and gloom.

'Well, then. A good day to you, Boss Temsa. I will have my shades pick up the wares. Let me know when you have more to buy.' He bowed before heading for the door.

'Locksmith.'

The word stopped him, foot hovering over the threshold. 'Beg pardon?' Busk looked over his shoulder. Temsa hadn't moved. He wondered if he were even making eye contact.

'A locksmith. You'll find me one, yes?'

Busk tried a smile. 'I'll do my best.'

'That's all I ever expect.'

Busk said no more and took the opportunity to leave. The big shade lit the way down the stairs and escorted him to the doorway. Ani still lurked there, on the lookout for more men to catapult into the road.

They bade him no farewell, only silence and stares. Busk kept a stately pace until he rounded a corner. It was then that he hurried homeward as quickly as his old hips would allow him.

Though the mist had still yet to burn away under the morning sun, it wasn't his dagger he clutched close to him now, but his pocket, and the metal strip that lay within it.

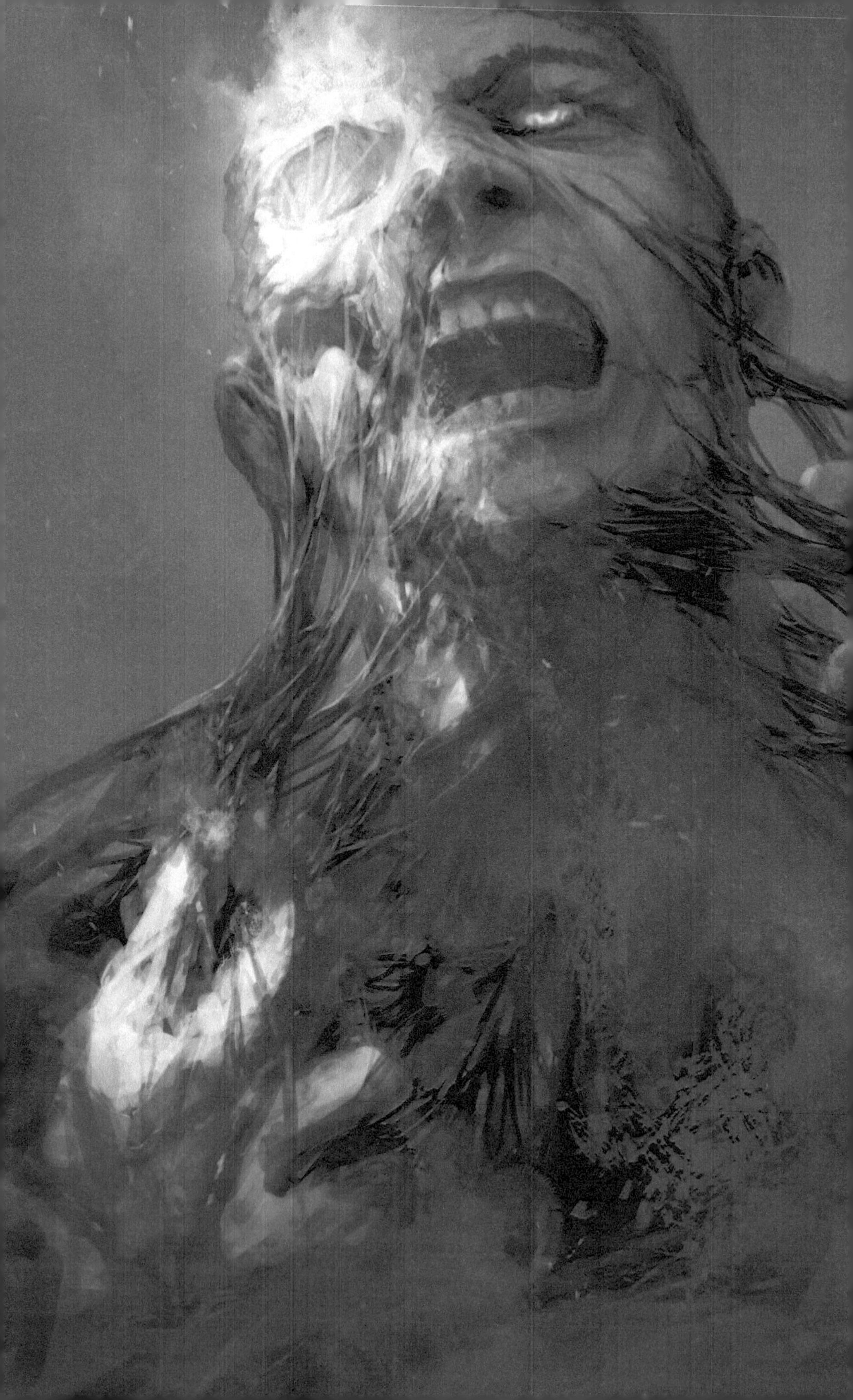

CHAPTER 12
MOTIVATION

There are many ways to deal with a recalcitrant house-shade without damaging them permanently. Many shades can continue to work just as well without certain appendages. Hanging by copper-thread rope for several hours is also highly recommended. Or a good old-fashioned beating with a thin rod can work wonders!

FROM 'YOU AND YOUR SHADE', AN ARCTIAN SCROLL ON THE TRAINING OF HOUSE-SHADES

IGNORANCE IS BLISS, SO THEY say. In my opinion, whoever said that must have been deaf, mute, blind and most certainly a fucking moron. They might have been happy knowing nothing, but unanswered questions plagued me, along with a boredom that stretched with the hours. Bliss was a foreign creature in the house of Horix.

I'd been confined to my alcove since the accident beneath the widow's tower. Not a word, not a whisper, not even a fleck of spit in my direction. The fact I had not suffered alone was small comfort. Almost all the house-ghosts had been stuffed into their hollows and told not to move. A scant handful of others shuffled about their duties, passing us occasionally with scowls, as if we had been given a holiday. It felt more like punishment to me.

For the duration of our penance, all manner of hammering and crashing carried on below us in the roots of the tower. It was something to do with the accident, and the nine dead guards who had been dragged out into the sun, bloody and crushed and bent at odd angles.

Curiosity had always run hot in my veins. Questions such as *how does this work?* and *what's behind there?* had largely run my life before now. It was the foundation of my occupation, why I had fled my home at a young age in search of greater things, and never looked back. Kech's knife might have taken away my body, but my soul and all its foibles had survived. I stewed in a state of agitation, burning with desire to know what was happening below and yet unable to find out.

Prisons work on a similar principle. It isn't the company that punishes the incarcerated, or the squalor or ill treatment. It's the fact the world still churns on beyond the walls, and the prisoner is no longer a part of it. I hadn't felt more like a prisoner since being locked away in Temsa's cages, and I have seen my fair share of cells in my time.

In truth, wanting to know what Horix was up to was all a distraction. The voice of the dead guard had disturbed me deeply. Not simply because it had come from beyond the grave, but because it imbued on me a responsibility I did not want. I currently had enough weight on my shoulders. I did not need some jabbering nonsense about floods and chaos weighing me down. And yet, when I closed my eyes, all I could see was a dead man with half a skull, staring at me with bloodshot eyes. I could hear that voice between every flurry of hammering. It underlined all my twitching, all my fidgeting, and gave my angst a dark shadow. Responsibility had been chasing me my entire life, and so far I'd managed to outrun it. I refused to let it catch me in death.

Bela had become fed up of my agitation. Every noise brought my head snapping around. Every muffled shout caused me to nibble at my cold, vaporous lips.

'Will you give it a bloody rest, Jerub?' Her eyes glowed like a gas flame.

'Aren't you curious to know what happened to those men? What's going on down there? What all that noise is?' I asked her.

'No.' She looked away, hiding her lies. 'Not curious about any of it.'

Any kinship in being both caught and sold by Temsa had vanished in the first days of entering Horix's tower. She was no more helpful than the others.

'I am,' ventured the waif of a ghost several alcoves down. He was a new and wide-eyed arrival; a victim of an accident involving a salt barrel being hoisted into an attic and a rat-nibbled rope. An honest ghost, the Krass called that: one who hadn't been escorted into the afterlife by cold steel, but by simple accident alone. It still counted as turmoil under the Tenets. Honest ghosts had their downsides, however. Accidents can be messy. The young Arctian man was a zig-zag in shape and half his previous height. His spine was bent savagely in several places, and his head skewed to one side. He wore a heavily-patched smock – which was more like a blanket with holes in – to hide whatever bones had burst through his body before the barrel was done with him. He must have been sold cheap.

I jabbed a thumb at him. His name refused to stay in my mind. 'See? Whatshisface is.'

Bela snorted. 'It's pointless to wonder. We're house-shades. It's none of our business.'

'It's every bit our business. There's something dangerous in this tower, and Vex and Yamak and Kalid are hiding it. Didn't you see the bodies that came out of the widow's cellars?'

The eastern blood erupted in her. 'Scared of dying twice, Krassman? Are you that weak, *fitja*?'

I tried to match her eyes. I was normally the sarcastic or quietly brooding kind of debater, but death had changed my flavour, turned me bitter.

Before I could school the Skol bitch on the particulars of her pigsty of a homeland, or inform her of the crossbred slurry that ran in her veins, something held me still. Silence can be just as loud as cacophony.

The hammering had stopped cold, no sputtering out. Nothing but motes stirred in the tower. I held my breath even though I had none to hold. 'They've stopped.'

Bela turned her back on me in a huff. I flicked my fingers at her as I stepped forth. The crushed ghost followed suit, poking into the corridor.

'What do you suppose they've been doing?' he said in his gargled voice. He was Arctian, judging by his accent.

'Fixing whatever broke, I'd wager. Something important.' *Something secret.* This was my mystery, not this newcomer's, but as I looked over my shoulder at the young chap, all bent and limp, I remembered the words of my long-dead master, Doben, the man who had taught me ways to break a lock *Never do a job alone. If you get caught, the other man makes an excellent decoy.*

'What's your name?'

'Konteph. Well, that was my life-name. Can't remember what they call me now.'

'I'll call you Kon.'

The man shrugged at an angle. 'Fine.'

'Do you fancy a walk, Kon?'

The man seemed fond of shrugging. Taking it to mean 'fine', I took the lead and let him shuffle behind me. Bela tutted at us, once for every step we ignored her. She resorted to hissing threats.

'You'll be sorry!'

Kon wavered, but I beckoned him along and together we crept to the mouth of the corridor. We hovered there behind silk drapes and listened for sounds. There were none, and it emboldened me. My last foray had been useful, after all. It had got me in front of Widow Horix.

My feet fell as softly as shadow on the stone steps. Even my glow diminished, as if my tense posture took up too much energy for light. I took it as a bonus, and sucked in my belly a little tighter.

'What were you, Kon? Before all this?' I asked of him in a whisper. Something to distract myself from the aching silence.

'Worked for the Chamber of the Grand Builder. I was a minor acolyte. Was working my way up though, slowly but surely.'

'Doing what?'

He scratched his head, as if memories of his life were fuzzy. His vapours around his shaven skull stirred. I saw the faint mark of a glyph tattooed in dark blue on the back of his head. 'Carrying plans about, mostly. Fetching the teas. Drew a spire once.'

'I see. What happened?'

'Was wanderin' back to the architect's office when I heard a shout from above. Something real heavy hit me from above and behind. I felt something in my back pop and then my face hit the flagstones. Next thing I knew, I woke up in some dark room as a shade, dripping with Nyxwater. So I'm told, this barrel of salt was being hoisted in a tal's tower. The old rope snapped and down it came on yours truly. Before I could say a word, I was on a wagon and off to the soulmarket. All very sudden.' He blew a sigh. 'And you?'

I paused, wondering which lie to tell today, the force of old habits, but something in Kon's eyes made me choose the truth. They had a simple faithfulness in them, like the eyes of a puppy. I found it easy to confide in him, and it felt good to

'A thief. And a damn good one at that. I came to Araxes for work but got my throat slit instead by a soulstealer gang. All very sudden indeed. And I'd had high hopes for this journey.'

'You're Krass?'

'I am. From Taymar, a place between the mountains and the sea.'

'Then why'd you come here, to the Arc? Wasn't there any work for you at home?'

I paused, my hand idly passing over a vase sat upon a pedestal. I watched my cold fog its surface. 'Not for me.'

'Wh—'

Several floors below us, there came a clank of a heavy door handle and the stairwell shone bright green, ghost and lamplight intermingled. Kon's eyes grew so wide I thought his vapours might tear.

I was already making for an adjacent corridor. 'Here!'

Kon hobbled into the dark behind me. There were shelves of dinnerware and pottery, but no alcoves nor cupboards besides a small niche for discarded smocks. We ducked amongst the hooks, making them jingle, and tried to cover our glow with cotton. For a second time that night I held a pretend breath as I listened to the scuff of boots and faint trudging of the many dead.

There were more tonight, or so my ears told me. Guards as well as ghosts. It only served to stoke my curiosity. If more ghosts were needed, why had I not been picked? It served them right for me to resort to sneaking, or at least that's what I told myself in an effort to curb my jealousy.

A house-guard traipsed into the hallway, brass oil lamp aglow and waving about. Fortunately, he wasn't a thorough employee, and after five paces he decided he'd looked hard enough and went back to the stairwell.

Kon and I waited for an age, face to face, with me matching his buckled posture to fit into the narrow space.

'I think it's time,' I said when I'd had enough of his blank staring. Even for a ghost, the young man seemed pretty soulless.

Another shrug. 'Fine.'

I wondered what he was getting out of this besides company. He looked more afraid than excited. No doubt my wraithlike face wore the same narrow-eyed impassive look I'd favoured in life. I had no reflection to check, after all, but I was well-versed in creeping about towers in the darkness. It felt pleasurable to be doing it again.

Going back to the stairs, we kept to shafts of moonlight and lamp-glow as the floors came and went. Although the lower levels glowed with lamps, I spotted only a handful of guards keeping watch below us. They patrolled around the spiralling atrium in pairs, and near the ground floor, we hovered on the stairs to watch their movements. All we had to do was wait and pick our moment to dash across the marble. I fixed my eyes on the tall, triangular doors to the cellars, on the far side of the atrium.

When our opening came, we scuttled down the remaining stairs with haste. Kon was slower than I was, and kept trying to stick to the shadows. He was still fresh, dead gods bless him. Ghosts are fainter in bright light, especially in the orange glow of whale-oil. Step by step, he fell further behind me.

By the time I'd pressed my hands to the cellar doors and inched one half open, he was only halfway across. A shout came ricocheting across the soaring hall. He froze, as any guilty man would, and I chose my moment to act, swiftly ducking through the door. Kon's eyes were wide and begging in the brief moment I met them before shutting the door with a soft click. Without hesitation, I scurried down a curving flight of steps, dark and lampless.

When you're in the business of breaking into things and profiting from their contents, guilt is like mould. It is either a fungus that slowly withers away through starvation, or a rot which grows into a beast that consumes you. It all depends how much you feed it. By the time I'd reached the bottom of the stairs, where the air had grown cool and heavy with dust, I'd forgotten Kon almost completely.

A bang from above had me running faster, down a sloping corridor that opened out like a funnel. I found myself in a room clogged with dust and little light besides my own. All the lights had been snuffed bar one: an oil lamp on the far side of a sea of wooden barrels. I walked amongst them, trailing fingers over pickaxes and hammers and the bent heads of nails. Everything was clogged with rock-dust and damp sand. I felt like choking, despite my lack of lungs and the particles wafting through me.

I knew better than to dally. Beyond the containers and tools and the lonely lamp, a rock-hewn arch led me deeper into a dark tunnel reinforced with stout props and beams. The going had a distinct downward slope to it. Already I felt as if I were a hundred feet underground. There were no lamps lit here. My skin lit the walls an eerie glow, and the unknown beyond my light made me wary.

The tunnel had an exit like a black maw, yawning wide. I stood at its edge to find a wooden ramp reaching down into the darkness. The walls were sheer and disappeared beyond the reach of my light. I felt a thickness to the air, as if it had been stripped of its quality. It was warm and muggy against my cold. Things dripped in the darkness and the echoes betrayed the size of the place. It felt like I stood in a cavern.

I shuddered as I imagined the infinity of the walls and the press of dead bodies and shouting voices that would appear at any moment.

With a wordless grumbling, I set foot to the ramp. I made it a dozen paces before footsteps and lamplight tumbled down the tunnel. I collapsed into a crouch so rapidly that it would have torn the crotch of any trews asunder. Fortunately, I was not wearing any. Unfortunately, however, I had no hiding place; I could only tuck myself under the railing of the ramp, clench my soft teeth and—

'What the fuck do you think you're doing?'

The copper gloves grabbed me tightly, making me yelp. Colonel Kalid stood over me and promptly delivered several smart blows to my nose. I splayed on the floor, eyes crossed. The sting of the metal rang through my head, as if I was the clapper of a great bell.

'You again, Jerub!' I recognised Vex's braying voice.

'A troublemaker, to be sure.' Master Yamak was there, too.

'I'll have words with the widow.' The looming shadow above me was poised to strike again. My glow carved out the colonel's stern features and made pinpricks of his irate eyes.

More boots sounded on the stone. The rough hands hauled me up to my feet and I received another blow to the gut for my troubles. I was taken back to the room of barrels and Kalid left me against one. The three stepped away to discuss me like a piece of meat.

'Reckon he saw anything?'

'Too dark.'

'Did you see anything, Jerub?' Kalid shoved me. The knuckles of his gloves sizzled against my vapours.

'Nothing!' *Just the outline of a crane-like contraption, reaching into the dark.* Unimportant.

'What's to be done?' Vex sounded eager.

'The sarcophagus.'

'I concur.'

'Only thing for it.'

'Whassat?' I croaked.

I received no answer, and instead was thrown towards the stairs, where guards waited with copper-thread rope to bind me. They dragged me face down, shins dragging, while Kalid and the others marched behind. I could have sworn Vex was rubbing his hands with glee.

At the south side of the tower, a cellar had been dug into the foundations. After two sets of winding stairs, there were storerooms where the walls were lined with all sorts of crates and bric-a-brac. I was shown to one with little ceremony. I waited in the darkness until the lamps were lit. All I could make out was a great lump sitting in the centre of the room under a tarpaulin.

In Krass and Skol, where indenturement had yet to consume society, those who had died in turmoil were tossed into the Nyx unbound. Those who died naturally got a coin in the mouth and had Nyxwater poured over their graves, or were buried by its banks, just as my parents were. We did it just like the ancient tribes did, before the Nyx became capable of binding, before the Tenets were written and ghosts were forced to arise from their slain bodies. In the east, we used shallow pits or boxes known as coffins.

Kalid dragged the tarpaulin away, and as it turned out, the sarcophagus was one of these coffins. It was a relic rather than a replica, if the merchant in me was right. It was made of plain yellow sandstone, once polished but now chipped and rough. Atop it, the image of a deity I didn't recognise had been scratched into the stone: some posing skeleton with an elongated jackal or anteater's head. Half the detail had been lost to time.

The size of the sarcophagus instantly concerned me. It was clearly from an age when men and women were of shorter stature. I had thought the punishment silly, at first. A stupid game, like locking a scampish little brother in a chest. But the more I stared at its dimensions, the more I began to fidget, and curse this jackal god. I recognised none of the Arctian glyphs that might have told me his name.

As the stone lid was raised by straps and pulleys bolted into the ceiling, those around me delighted in watching my expression fall. The lid was thicker than I'd thought, chiselled with a lip that dovetailed with the body and made the inside shallow. *Exorbitantly shallow.*

Despite my struggles, I was pushed into the sarcophagus and made to lie face up, arms bound across my chest. I could feel the cold of the stone against my own chilly vapours, and that unsettled me more. I thrashed, but the colonel's copper gloves held me down.

Kalid waved his hand to the men on the ropes. 'Down it goes!'

'How long?' I asked. The lid descended in tiny increments, pulleys squeaking.

Vex leaned over me to smile. I stared into his dark sockets. 'Few days ought to straighten out a fuckwit like you. Maybe a week.'

Even though the lid had barely touched the coffin, I could already feel its weight on me. I began to thrash.

'I was lost! I didn't mean—'

Doooooom. The coffin shook as the lid fell shut, sealing me in the dark.

I must have wriggled for an hour, perhaps more, as I tried to push the lid with my knees and forehead. My shoulders were already pressed to the stone, my head and heels too. I could have licked the stone in front of my face without stretching. My belly brushed it constantly. I felt suffocated, squashed, blind and paralysed all at once. It was torture of a variety I had never endured: feeling as though I was dying all over again and yet remaining impervious. This was a new circle of hell.

When at long last my panic began to subside, when I began to give in to the helplessness, I became aware of the silence. My scratching and thrashing had distracted me from the fact the stone permitted no sound nor light.

Any silence longs to be filled, and a lonely mind is wont to fill it with thoughts and made-up whispers, as if the nothingness is too unbearable. It's how dreams are made before sleep claims you, but I had no sleep to save me. Instead I lay there for untold hours, unable to stop my own internal rambling. It was far from meditation. Perhaps it was the closeness of the stone, or some spell of that accursed sarcophagus, but my thoughts were of the dark and damning kind. I realised then that this was not a torture of the body, but of the soul.

Instead of knives, I cut myself with old memories. They were dredged up and shown to me like a fisherman displaying bursting nets. Instead of poisons, I made myself sick with all my bad choices. Over and over again, around and around. I was trapped in a prison again, one of my own making. One of pure thought and imagination chalked onto the blackboard darkness, as half-formed and as vaporous as myself.

I am a boy again, picking at mushrooms under an oak as a storm crackles above. Behind, leaves are running down mountainsides, chased by the dry wind. A voice calls me.

I am a young man, fingers racing against an hourglass and the tininess of cogs, the fickleness of springs.

I am at the bank of the Nyx, standing over a pair of rune-scratched slabs dusted with sand. My fists are clenched, as numb as the two headstones that bewitch my eyes.

I am struggling to breathe through a straw pillow as a hand throttles me from behind. Another pins my arms. I am sobbing but he doesn't stop.

I am running, lockpicks grasped in my hand, chasing the flailing straps of a wagon while dogs bay behind me. A hand reaches forth to clasp me by the wrist, and I am free.

A woman is walking away from me, satchel slung over her shoulder, a horse trotting by her side, shod hooves crunching on the day-old snow and ice.

Bars trap me, and despite my insistence of innocence, many voices are laughing. They laugh and they laugh, fingers pointing and spittle flying from rotten teeth.

A bearded old master knuckles his brow as the picks in my hand break time and time again in the lock.

I am a young man again, kicking at a hay bale with the kind of angst only teenage years can bring.

Somewhere nearby, I hear a braying cackle. My fists are as numb as headstones.

And around I went.

CHAPTER 13
FAVOURS OWED

The origins of the Cloud Court are founded in loneliness and fear. In 473, Prince Jural, Empress Basilis' murderous son, came to the throne too early and too violently. The first succession by murder in thirty years turned the noses of the nobility, mostly through jealousy. To favour them, Jural built his own court of sycophants. In the end, he allowed them to get too powerful, to run districts, to get too close, and it led him to the same fate as his mother: an asp in the bedsheets. The new Talin royal line began with his death, as did the Cloud Court.

FROM 'A REACH HISTORY'
BY GAERVIN JUBB

MAY YOUR REIGN BE LONG and prosperous, my emperor, powerful of strength and mind, lord of all the sun touches. May both the living and the dead remember your name throughout all ages to come.'

Sisine waited for the two knocks to come, but nothing stirred besides the flames of the lamps above. She bent a knee to the marble again, her silks rustling.

'May your reign be long and prosperous, my emperor, powerful of strength and mind, lord of all the sun touches. May both the living and the dead remember your name throughout all ages to come.'

The wait was torturous.

'May your reign—'

The hatch slid open with a clang, and the scroll was pushed through.

Sisine reached out to take it, but held herself back. She leaned closer. 'Father?'

The scroll shook as if the hand that held it was unnerved.

'Will you not even speak to me? Your own daughter?'

Only a muffled cough answered her.

'You're a coward!' she hissed, but before she could go further, the hatch shut with a clang.

Sisine snatched the scroll up and strangled it, wishing it was the emperor's neck. Hands shaking with anger, she got to her feet and ripped open the scroll to see his decrees. The ink was so fresh she smudged half a sentence with her thumb. Her lips moved silently as she read.

Sisine looked back to the Sanctuary door in all its glinting complexity, and the great diamond that glowed at its centre. How many times had she stared at it? Wondered at its thickness, its keyholes and mechanisms? What manner of man was left behind it, possibly staring back at her? Almost five years had passed and not once had he left it, preferring to stay alone and untrusting. The Sanctuary had been his insurance, and yet it appeared it would now be his downfall. That was the only explanation for the nonsense scrawled on the papyrus.

The emperor has finally lost his mind.

There, in the golden glow of the door's metal, the empress-in-waiting smiled.

'Guards! The door!'

THERE WAS NO IDLE NATTERING in the Cloud Court that day, no heckling. Just the intense stares of the impatient. Their eyes rested not on her, but on the scroll, like stray dogs watching a butcher's bloody hands at work, waiting for a juicy morsel to drop. She knew it wasn't the Nyxwater that gripped their attention today. Today it was something more sinister.

Sisine took her place between the pillars, bowed to the empty throne and cleared her throat, a habit she had grown accustomed to. Normally it brought a begrudging, bickering quiet, but this morning it was unnecessary. She could have heard hair grow in the silence.

The empress-in-waiting looked again at the words. Her tongue traced the edges of her teeth as she drew out the silence, making them wait.

'The emperor's decrees are as follows!' she said at last. 'His first order: the expansion of the Outsprawls must continue to the east another three miles.'

The collective moan was deafening. Clenched fists filled the air. Shouts rained down.

'What of the murders?'

'Has no word of them reached the emperor?'

'Secondly!' she yelled over them, wanting her father's drivel to be heard. She'd soon grown tired of shielding him, playing his lackey as her mother had. 'Secondly, the royal falcons are to be restocked, ready for the late hunting season!'

This time, not a serek was left sitting. Some even began to leave, filtering away to the doors that led them out and down to the Piercer's mighty lifts.

The scroll met the floor with a loud crack. It skittered over the marble, bringing the entire court to a standstill.

'The emperor could not care less about this city!' she yelled. A curious murmuring washed over her, just as she'd hoped. 'The emperor has lost his mind!'

A few backsides began to touch seats again.

'That is what you are all thinking, correct? Whispering between yourselves? Well, Sereks, when I read these words, I wonder the same as you. I wonder why he will not listen to his daughter's pleas. To the pleas of his sereks or his city. And then I remember why!'

Boon, as predicted, was the first to speak. He was still standing, arms folded across his golden chains. 'Please do elaborate, Highness.'

Sisine sighed for effect. This speech had been long rehearsed in the polished silver of her mirrors.

'It is simple! The emperor's mind is clearly occupied with matters further afield. I believe it is not disinterest, or madness, but trust. He leaves it to us, his family and advisors, to handle the preservation of this great city while His Imperial Majesty deals with the expansion of this empire's borders. Why else would the empress feel comfortable leaving so suddenly if we were not capable of speaking for the emperor when he cannot speak himself? After all, we would not want our emperor to be embarrassed, would we, sereks of the court?'

A resounding, 'NO!' echoed through the great hall. They understood her just fine. They could sense the power was shifting, and they were fools enough to think it flowed in their direction. Sisine fought the urge to grin. She was set on playing the reluctant yet dutiful champion.

'Then let the Cloud Court speak its mind as it was meant to! Tell me your districts' wishes and I will see that the emperor's will is executed forthwith. Serek Boon, no doubt you have something to suggest?' She chose to give him first pick. It earned a smile from the intolerable shade.

'These recent disappearances concern us most, Highness. There have been four altogether, two in the past week. The tors and tals are becoming skittish, and I may say the same for the court if the disappearances continue. Order must be maintained in this city.'

Sisine could have laughed. There was no order in Araxes and they all knew it. What Boon meant was *control.* Four nobles dead, their half-coins gone, but still no official claims. Only whispers and rumours. It seemed a newcomer had entered the game, and they were intent on ignoring the rules, what few and laughable rules there were between the nobles.

'What say the rest of you?' She opened the floor and was immediately pelted by hearsay.

'Tal Urma's guards said she went in her sleep and has been bound by some distant cousin. He'll now be managing the estate.'

'How convenient, I say!'

'They are saying that Merlec simply "tripped", if you believe that. His house-shades have already disappeared! His tower is empty!'

'It stinks of criminal activity.'

'Uppity soulstealers, I would say.'

'But is it several, or one?'

Sisine raised her hands. 'I shall have the Chamber of the Code and Chamberlain Rebene's scrutinisers look into these deaths immediately. Under order of the emperor.'

A young serek spoke up, another of the few free shades that sat on the court. Her long flowing hair moved as if she were underwater. 'And what of the Nyx?'

The empress-in-waiting shook her head. 'The Nyxite prices were raised as promised. You need not worry about this so-called drought, Serek Hamael.'

Apparently, they did. The Cloud Court bent her ear for another hour, each of them eager to have their voices and needs heard. It was worth the verbal torture. Sisine placated them with promises here and assurances there. When they finally grew bored of bleating and whingeing, she bade them a good day and watched them file from the chamber with their cocky smiles and satisfied rumblings. All except Serek Boon, who strode down the lofty marble steps and made his way towards Sisine, hands clasped behind his back and a serious expression on his mottled face. No guards stood with him. None but the royal family or the Royal Guard were allowed to set foot on the floor of the court.

A phalanx of them moved to make a fence of spears between her and Boon. They were shades, all of them, bound to her father. Sisine felt their cold draught wafting over her feet.

Boon bowed low. 'Your Highness.'

'The court has adjourned, Serek, and you greatly overstep your boundaries.' She could have had him skewered right there and nobody could have disputed it.

'If I may.' Boon held up a finger and Sisine noticed several sereks lingered on the balcony, looking on with blank stares. When his eyes came back to her, they were full of blue sparkle. 'You play a very good game, I must say.'

Sisine raised her chin. 'You accuse me of playing games with this court, Serek?'

Boon chuckled, keeping his voice low. 'This is a room made for games. Why else are we here? We do nothing but argue over decrees we have little say over, and yet we play out tradition because it means – let's be honest, Empress-in-Waiting – we get to look important. You and I. The sereks. That is the luxury of the rich, is it not? It is all a great farcical game, but it continues because it works. The emperor's Sanctuary has kept a truce between us. You know that as well I do, and yet today you shook that truce. A bold move, if you ask me.'

Sisine stared at him over the guards' gleaming helmets. 'I believe it is about time this city saw some boldness in its leadership. And no, I did not ask you.'

'Change is only good in the eyes of those it benefits, Highness. Some of us have sat in this court for decades—'

'Five of them, in your case.'

Boon smiled. 'Quite. And in that time, we've seen little change. Your grandfather, your father and your mother have always kept the Cloud Court at arm's length, and wisely so. Why? Because it maintains the balance of the game. It keeps you royals royal and the rest of us anything but. Balance makes us content, makes us forget that the throne…' He paused to gesture to the nearby empty seat of marble. '…is always there to claim. Yet today, you chose to start speaking for the emperor. To start making promises. I find promises are like wild jackals, Empress-in-Waiting. Have you ever kept jackals? I have. They are savage yet intelligent beasts. Keep them fed and you have loyalty. But take that hand away and… well. Savage, as I said.'

Sisine grinned right back. 'This room might be for games, Serek, but this house – *my house* – is one of daggers. I was born and raised here. You should not forget that if you are intent on making open threats.'

Boon held her gaze, then relented with a bow. 'Only a kind warning to tread carefully, Highness. I would never dare threaten the empress-in-waiting or His Imperial Majesty. But there are other souls in the Cloud Court who might. Some who grow ambitious.' He had no cocksure look on his face now. Just a pout. 'On the matter of family, has there been any more word from your mother the empress? When can we expect her return?'

'She is still in the eastern lands,' Sisine replied coldly. Bezel had yet to report anything about her mother's whereabouts. In the meantime, she saw no reason to destroy a perfectly good explanation. 'It seems she will be some time, Serek Boon. Plenty of time to get fat on scraps from the royal table.'

He caught her meaning and withdrew. Her guards escorted him out, all bar one. The gold-clad shade hovered by her side, motionless. She clicked her fingers in his face. 'Fetch me Etane.'

After a snap of metal heels, the guard sprinted away and she was left alone to tour the marble ring of the Cloud Court and ponder alone while Etane took his sweet and merry time. Though she wove an erratic path across the vast floor, she found herself coming to a halt in front of the emperor's throne. Its design was simple: two rectangular armrests, a soaring back that had the look of a mighty scroll hanging open, and a flat area for the royal arses that graced it. It was in the material and the details that the grand chair impressed. The entire throne was carved from one block of exotic turquoise quartz, made to reflect the souls that the Arctian Empire had been built on. The stone was glasslike, pellucid, and as colourful and changeable as the Troublesome Sea. Where the sunlight caught its upper edge, the marble faded to the green of sandy shallows. At its base, where its dais unfurled in steps, it was a fathomless cobalt.

Into the throne's polished surface had been written the names of every emperor or empress that had claimed it, and their dates of ruling, no matter how briefly. A thousand years of binding and back-stabbing had produced a lot of names, and some had ruled for days only, if not hours. Glyphs and old hieratic script crowded the tall scroll and most of the arms in no discernible order.

Sisine firmly placed her foot on the second step. She leaned down, reaching out a finger to a wide space across the base of the throne. A copper-painted fingernail traced her name in large, proud glyphs. The more she wrote, the harder she pressed. Her teeth creaked as she clenched her jaw.

Before she could finish, doors thudded behind her and Etane came shuffling into the Cloud Court. He was shining bright as if he were irritated. He'd chosen an eye-wateringly colourful waistcoat and pantaloons today. From a distance, it looked as if a Belish peacock was running wild about the Piercer.

'You called, Your Wondrousness?'

Sisine withdrew from the throne, like a child caught with half a stolen biscuit. She pressed her fingernail against her palm instead and felt it snap under the pressure. 'There you are! Serek Boon thinks he can lecture me as if he were a tutor and I a mere child. But that's not even half of his gall! No, he plays the friend while he is most likely plotting behind my back!' she vented.

Etane looked up to the vacant benches and hummed. 'Productive session, was it?'

'Boon wouldn't risk speaking to me alone unless he was trying to steer me. Or goad me in some way.'

'Looks like it's working.'

Sisine was pacing now, repeatedly picking at the jagged end of her nail. 'I want you to find out who's behind these murders. I need to know whether it's Boon. Or another serek. I will be the one inciting havoc, nobody else!'

'I've told you, princess, all your spies came up empty. Whoever's behind it all, they've either got a lot of coin or a lot of fear keeping lips sealed.'

'Then I want you to look into it personally. I don't care if you have to talk to every last contact you know, if you have to put that giant sword of yours to use and threaten people, if you have to walk to the Outsprawls and back. I just want this murderer found.'

'And what about Basalt? Unlocking the Sanctuary? And—'

'Forget him! The Sanctuary is impossible to crack! We should have realised that sooner. Circumstances are changing.'

'I think we're heading in the wrong direction. You'll overreach. We should be busy finding another locksmith instead of—'

Sisine jabbed her now bleeding finger at him. 'I am no *girl*! And I am tired of you advising me on matters you think I need advising on! There is no "we", only I. You are but a house-shade! I am the Empress-in-Waiting, and I have everything under control.'

Etane rolled his eyes. 'Fine.'

She brought her face close to the shade, feeling his cold mist against her nose. Her voice was restrained but no less angered. 'You should know better than to refuse me. You think yourself above the other shades. Family, even. But you forget your half-coin lingers in the royal vaults, just like all the rest.'

Etane looked sheepish. 'Yes, Princess.'

'Have Chamberlain Rebene and the Chamber of the Code also start investigating the murders. Immediately. That will keep the sereks quiet.'

'Yes, Princess.'

'Now go. Get out there and find this murderer by any means necessary.'

'And if—'

'*When*.'

'When I find them, then what?'

Sisine was already making her way to the doors. She flashed him a derisive look over her shoulder, as if it was the most obvious answer in the world. 'Then I want you to invite them here, of course. To the Piercer.'

Behind her, Etane bowed, hands wide and head low. 'As you wish, Your Gloriousness. As you wish.'

'*MEAT*, SHADE. I SELL MEAT, not fuckin' hearsay. Go on, half-life, away with you!'

Of all the things Etane missed about his flesh, the ability to spit on market scum like this was high on his list.

'A pox on your mother.'

'What did you say to me? I ought to—'

'I serve the royal family. You'll do nothing but watch me walk away,' Etane snorted, tapping the gold feather on his breast, and then the ornate hilt of the sword poking over his shoulder. The blade was huge, reaching almost to the back of his knees and wider than a barbarian's palm. A faint mist emanated from its crossguard, as if its metal was frozen. It was an heirloom of the Renala family line, gifted to him from the Piercer's armouries as long as he played bodyguard. Over the decades, Etane had come to know it like a limb. He had even given it a name: Pereceph.

The other vendors had listened in, and half had already turned their back on him. He tutted at them and chose another direction.

After relaying Sisine's orders to Chamberlain Rebene, Etane had wandered the Core Districts, the High and Low Docks, the Spoke Avenues, the Fish District, and the factory yards. It had taken almost the entire day, and now he stood on the boundary between the Spice Groves and King Neper's Bazaar, hoping to pick up gossip by chance.

Instead, he stared at passersby, feeling useless and bored. He had spoken to a dozen of his trusted eyes in the city, several scrutinisers, and even one Core Guard captain known for gathering rumours, but all Etane had rounded up were the same stories, over and over. All of them contradictory.

It was a gang from the Outsprawls.

Desert witches, I'eard.

Or maybe a rich tal, making a move.

It's that Scatter Prince Phylar, insinuatising himself into the city.

Etane couldn't decide which tale was the most ridiculous. And so there he stood, where the meat stalls rubbed shoulders with spice merchants, leaning under the shade of palm branches. He watched the bustle around him with half-closed eyes, listening to the roar of commerce. The bright colours became a blur. He imagined he could smell the earthy stench of spices and cloves wafting from the Groves. It had been far too many decades since he had.

A gaggle of men distracted his gaze. They rested under an archway, dabbing their faces with colourful silk cloths and pulling faces at the powerful scents. Their suits were dark cotton and cut in a business-like style: sharp folds of cloth that reached to the knees. Their hems were of gold, red or blue depending on their station or bank, but all wore the rising sun of the half-coin on their breast. Grey felt hats, conical in shape, perched on their heads and wobbled as they chatted. Etane caught snatches of gossip, interspersed with numbers and statistics.

Bankers.

As he was thinking they had ventured far from Oshirim District, the explanation for their wandering came running up. It was another banker, clutching a papyrus package stained dark with bloody juices. The man seemed pleased, but the others wrinkled their lips and shook their heads.

Unimpressed and eager to leave the stinking stalls, they bustled in a westward direction, back to their desks and vaults, no doubt. Etane followed, more out of boredom than anything as substantial as suspicion.

He trailed them at a good distance, keeping an eye on their grey felt hats over the busy crowds. He would lose them on one street, gain on them in the next. The going was slower for him than it was for them. Workers carrying bundles and hand carts barged him aside without a word, paying no heed to his rich trappings, the giant sword slung across his back, or his golden feather.

Etane glared at the gold plume on his chest, lodged between the bright swirls of his waistcoat. He had despised it his entire indenturement. The gold might have been shit-brown for all the difference it made. It marked him only as royal property, not as free, and that meant precious little on Araxes' streets. *Fuck all*, as the Scatterfolk would say. A bound shade was a bound shade no matter what house owned him or what he wore, always second class to the living. Only free shades could command some respect with their white feathers.

He looked to a gaggle of nearby indentured, prising apart broken flagstones outside of a shop. Their vapours were caked in dust, their faces grim, and their master standing over them with a copper-tipped whip. In the Cloudpiercer, Etane at least had some status. Out here, he was no better than these half-lives.

The bankers took the Avenue of Oshirim and Etane negotiated the mobs to follow. He felt the cool of a shadow fall on him as he passed beneath the great statue of Oshirim, god of the afterlife. Worn down by the wind-blown grit, disfigured by time and vandals, the dead god watched over the streets with gouged-out eyes. His mighty flail, once held towards the sun, lay at his feet. Before the empire, Oshirim had defended Araxes against the desert sands. Now he peered sightlessly into the distance, trying to spot the city's end.

Host to Araxes' financial powers, Oshirim District spread like the spokes of a cartwheel behind the god's back. Towers of grand proportions made deep canyons of even the widest streets. Squeezed between them were stouter, shorter buildings. They bore signs for insurers, sigils, lesser banks, mercenary agents, and vaultsmiths. Huge palm trees lined the streets, splashes of green against the gold and ruby awnings that offered shade for the crowds, though it was scarcely needed in the buildings' shadows.

The cut of cloth changed within a dozen paces of Oshirim's statue. Silk and velvet abounded. Sparkles of silver, gold and platinum dragged Etane's eyes left and right. Shining armour, too, for the sellswords and house-guards trailing every noble and dignitary. Some glowed blue under the plate and scale, others had sweat dripping down their red faces. Both kinds marched in rings around their masters, holding spears out to discourage pickpockets or bandits. Broad daylight didn't dissuade a criminal of Araxes. Daylight only meant they could see better.

On one corner, Etane saw a noble in an outrageous green cape arguing with another noble with a feather hat. Their words were lost on his ears, thanks to the din of feet and voices, but Etane didn't care about them. He was looking at the small figure between them, kicking at a stray palm frond. It was a little girl, shining bright and blue outside of her yellow frock. She wore a velvet choker about her neck that did little to hide the dark bruises of poisoning. Her face was dusted with chalk and iridescent powder. A white feather hung from her chest and a wooden doll dangled in her hands.

Young shades never failed to turn Etane's stomach. 'Kill them young, keep them young' was the saying amongst some of the nobles, and what a vile logic he found it.

Their eyes met through the shifting of bodies. Etane ventured a polite smile. The girl watched him for a moment before curling her lip and turning back to her business of kicking foliage. Etane cursed her freedom behind his lips, and hurried on.

The bankers had gone. Or, more accurately, they had blended in. Etane saw another score of them ahead, all in the same dark cloth and felt hats. Before long, half the crowds wore the same outfit. The shade came to a halt and wondered whether it was time to give in. Only the prospect of Sisine's inevitable tirade held him from turning back.

He had come to the right district for finding crooks. Just as the Nyxites had claimed the right to the Nyx, so had the banks positioned themselves as the protectors of half-coins. Nobody could quite remember the point when honest vault-houses had become powerful institutions, but it had come and gone, and now the oldest banks rose as high as the towers of tals, tors or sereks. Some even challenged the Chamber of the Code and the Piercer with their grandeur.

Etane disliked the banks intensely. Even in the skewed moral landscape of the City of Countless Souls, there was still a scale to be measured against, and he placed the banks near the bottom. Any rich tal or tor with a penchant for vaults, a building big enough, and a reputation clean enough could be a banker. And why not? There was a handsome fee to be charged for protecting another's half-coins. The banks had grown fat off these spoils, making barrels of silver that their masters invested into increasing the number of shades they owned. Should a question or – dead gods forbid – a complaint ever be raised, the banks were quick to disguise the simplicity of their services in percentages and figures and sections of Code so complex they would put a Chamber magistrate to shame. As far as Etane was concerned, there was no honest labour in the siphoning of others' hard efforts. That made the banks no better than soulstealers.

The shade looked up at the gigantic spires that shaded the streets: pyramidal, punctured with windows and balconies. Their architecture, like much of Araxes, was morbid but lavish. Great gold seals decorated their flanks. Gleaming metal capped their peaks. Entrances took the form of pillars carved like leg bones or archways made of vertebrae. Multitudes of flags hung limp from rows of traditional painted skulls. Silk banners and immense carved panels bore names that had been in business for centuries.

Akhenaten's Vaults.

Setmose.

Fenec Coinery.

Harkuf's.

Flimzi Consolidated.

The Bank of Araxes.

Etane wondered how many half-coins could be counted between these buildings. How many millions of souls could be accounted for? Half the wealth of the city – nay, the Arc – lay here in this district, barely two miles square. It made him glad his own coin resided in the Piercer's ancient vaults, away from the manicured fingers of these soul-grabbers.

He clicked his fingers, but no sound came forth. *Perhaps the murderer was a bank. Or a banker.* Why else target nobles who were known for keeping their own vaults? The more Etane considered it, the more it made sense. It was how this city worked: those with power were forever hungry for more. It was power's curse. Like the ocean, once a man tastes its depths, he is drawn to discover how deep it goes, no matter if it drowns him to get there.

Etane stood in the centre of a triangular junction between three avenues. From there, he could stare at each of the enormous bank buildings and ponder which of them he should invite to see Sisine. There was no itch to scratch, but even so his finger raked the scar on his soft skull in thought.

He caught the faint scuff of feet behind him. Too close, too gentle. Etane swivelled, hand flying to the hilt of his sword. He found a shock of scarlet standing behind him. A woman's face glowed beneath a hood, almost purple under the fabric. The shade's hands were clasped within her long sleeves, and once again he found himself eyeing a white feather of freedom.

'Etane Talin, as I die and glow,' she breathed.

'Enlightened Sister Liria. It has been a long time.'

'A long time indeed. Almost twenty years by our count.' She pointed to his golden feather. 'The royal family haven't tired of your sharp tongue yet?'

He folded his arms across his chest. 'Astute as always, Liria.'

'We are surprised you are not absent along with our missing empress. Belonging to her, that is.'

Etane made a show of clearing his throat. 'I am the empress-in-waiting's now. On loan, as it were. She saw fit to leave me behind.'

Liria nodded slowly, calculating. 'You're far from your tower.'

'And you from your burrow. You are taking a risk, skirting around the edge of the Core Districts. If a scrutiniser or a Core Guard sees you…' He made a show of smacking his wrist. 'Tut, tut.'

'What brings you to the banking district?'

'I could ask you the same. As it happens, I am busy looking for a dinner guest.'

She chuckled softly. It was a cold sound, full of the sickly pride the Cult of Sesh bred. 'Is the empress-in-waiting so short on friends these days that you need to procure them from the streets?'

Etane snorted. 'This one's special.'

'Tell me, what does one have to do to earn the princess' invitation? What does it take to attract the eyes of her chamber-shade?' Liria stepped sideways, chasing his wandering gaze. 'What, do you not trust us? After all the decades we have known each other? You were a brother in our ranks for many years, Etane Talin.'

'Don't make me laugh. Trust – or rather the distinct lack of it – was the reason you fell out of favour with the royals in the first place. It was also the reason I left the Cult of Sesh.'

'We prefer to be called the *Church* of Sesh now. Cult is far too... sinister. We have never meant any harm.'

'Stop lighting black candles and chanting in dark cellars, and people might change their minds. "Cult" suits you.'

'Didn't suit you, though, did it?'

Etane looked away. 'Like I said, lack of trust.'

'Very well, but you know what we deal in. Information. Perhaps we could be of help.'

He caught her sidelong glance, and every bit of meaning it carried. 'And what would you want in return?'

Liria's eyes flared beneath her hood, as if insulted. 'Why, nothing at all. It is a gift. Once a brother, always a brother.'

'Fuck you, Liria. There is no "free" where religion is concerned. Tell me what you want in return.'

'Information, should we ever need it.'

'About what?'

'Your empress-in-waiting.'

Etane grumbled, thinking of a red-faced, golden-eyed Sisine; the spittle flying through his vapours, the scratch of her copper nails. It was mildly tempting. 'You can forget it. She is my master.'

'Like you have forgotten your freedom, Brother?' she said, nodding to her own words. 'We can remember a time when you craved it. A time when it was within your grasp.'

The shade stuck out his chin, making her wait for some time. He remembered those times well. Lost opportunities had a way of sticking in the mind. 'Times change.'

'Would you not take your half-coin now, if we could offer it to you?' Liria brought her hands from her wide sleeves and held them out, flat and empty. Etane instinctively found himself reaching out, even for nothing. Liria smirked, hiding her hands again. 'Take our information as a gift for an old brother. No favours owed. Though if ever you grow tired of your master, we shall meet again.'

Etane's impatience was growing, as was his unease. The Cult had a knack for manipulation. Their gifts had a tendency of turning into favours. In the end, it was the thought of an enraged Sisine that made up his mind. 'Enough. Just tell me.'

'You are not the only shade who turned his back on the Church of Sesh,' she said, leaning closer.

Etane scowled. 'You can't be serious. That's what you call information? I ought to—'

She stepped aside, revealing a channel in the crowds. At its end, across the other side of the plaza, he saw four figures emerge from the grinning mouth of a bank. Fenec's Coinery.

They were impossible to miss. The shade in their midst alone drew the eye: a giant, armour-clad lump of a soul, matched only in height by the brute of a woman standing on the other side of the two men.

Danib. Bloody Danib. He hadn't seen that shade in almost twenty years, when he too had been part of the Cult.

Liria whispered in his ear, 'I would be watchful of that one, if I were you. He's rather ambitious.'

As she faded into the churn of people, Etane stared at the men. One was clearly a banker, clad in dark felt and a cotton suit. The other was something else, but certainly not poor. He was wrapped in green fabric and a yellow silk sash like a lightning strike across a field. Rings glistened on his fingers. Sunlight made his leg glint with gold or copper.

The channel had closed, and Etane had to hop up and down to follow them along the edge of the plaza.

North and east they headed, closer to the docks and the sprawl of sapphire ocean beyond. Etane didn't recognise the man, but Liria's words of warning lured him on. It was a better pastime than gawping up at banks for the rest of the afternoon.

For an hour he followed the group toward Bes District. He grew used to the clanking hobble of the apparent master; the man who walked slightly ahead of the others, and swaggered more than all of them combined. Etane could have closed his eyes and followed the canter of his foot and cane alone.

But he kept his eyes heavenward. There were a few spires in this district, perhaps of trade barons, but the rest of the buildings were jumbled and piled like old boxes in a storeroom, with lines of clothes strung between them. Parrots argued on the rooftops. There seemed to be more warehouses than homes here, and the streets were flooded with indentured workers rather than guards and rich folk. The living pushed their way through as if the dead were bothersome foliage.

At a junction, the four came to a halt in front of a pyramid-shaped tavern. An entrance yawned at its base. A wide strip of stone dubbed the place 'The Rusty Slab'. Noise spilled out into the road. Guards in mismatched black armour stood about, kicking at stones.

Etane hovered on a corner, watching them climb the steps and disappear into the doorway. He kept an eye on the tavern for some time, observing the guards and counting the flow of patrons coming in and out.

Taverns were like mischief factories. The sober were fed in through the doors and with the liberal application of specialised lubricants, were ejected some time later, as pissed and rowdy as baby goats. Better yet, the products literally paid for themselves. Across the span of his century and more of death, Etane had often dreamt of another life, of one spent plying beers to the thirsty somewhere far away from the baking sun. *A simpler life.*

When the sun began to stretch out the shadows like a baker kneading dough, he left his corner and pointed his feet towards the Cloudpiercer. Before he made it to the next street, he made sure to grab a passing shade by the elbow. It was a woman with a bloated, poisoned face. She wriggled, but Etane held her fast. He nodded back towards the Slab.

'Tell me, who owns that tavern there?'

The shade, now over her initial shock of being seized mid-stride, spoke her words as if she were spitting fruit seeds. 'That place? That's Boss Temsa's. Boss Boran Temsa.'

'You don't seem to like him very much.'

'A fuckin' soulstealer like him? Rightly so! He's crooked at every angle.'

'A stealer, you say?'

'Don't you know? He calls himself a soultrader. Half the shades in the next four districts have been sold by him. Myself included. Now leave me be! Got chores.'

The shade shook free and hurried away.

'Boran Temsa.'

The name found its way to Etane's lips many times before he reached the mighty archway of the Piercer.

CHAPTER 14
STRAYS

I don't care what was taken, Crafter Yonsson, I wish to know how it was taken. You and your brother both assured me that the vault was practically unbreakable. That it would take a thief a hundred years to crack it. Well, it took half a night, sirs. Half a night for this thief to crack your vault. He did not even damage it in the slightest. I eagerly await your reply and return of the sum I paid you. You should also be aware that Reever Bornn will be asking questions of you and your acquaintances forthwith.

Letter from Bjarl Gregorn to the Brothers Yonsson, Master Vaultsmiths of Saraka, Krass

THERE'S NOTHING QUITE SO ISOLATING as not being able to count the hours or feel the passage of time. I died a second death of stillness and boredom in the sarcophagus, and made my own hell out of thoughts and memories. When finally there came a muffled yell and a sonorous grate of stone, I had almost forgotten where and what I was. So wrapped up in my internal monologue was I that it took rough and painful hands to drag me back to consciousness. Like bursting from the Nyxwater, I was thrust back into the violence of the world, and it spun my head.

They dumped me on the floor. I spread my hands out across the stone, staring at the boot prints drawn in the grit and how the torchlight made them sparkle. I had almost forgotten colours beyond blue and grey.

'How long?' My question was a whisper.

'Four days.'

'Four?' I had guessed triple that.

'On your feet!' Kalid bellowed in my ear.

I did so with much wobbling, and once there I decided some grovelling was in order. Grovelling can be infinitely useful if you can get over the shame of it. I'd learned that the hard way. 'I'm terribly sorry. I've thoroughly learned my lesson. I'll never step out of line again.'

Kalid pushed me under an archway and up a flight of stone steps. 'You're damn right you won't, half-life. But you're not done yet. Vex has asked for you be put outside.'

'Outside?'

'Like a stray dog. Fitting, seeing as you have a habit of wandering where you're not wanted.'

I had no words. I was merely glad to be free of that abominable stone prison. I stayed silent as they stripped me of my smock and scarf.

Outside was as scorching and bright as the sarcophagus had been cold and dark. The sun was at its zenith, beating down on the city with casual ruthlessness. I looked up at the sheer walls of the tower and followed them to the crystal blue skies, cloudless as ever.

My brief moment of appreciation was shattered by a heavy rope being slung about my neck like a python, and two big hands forcing me down next to a stake driven into the cracked earth.

'Stay, dog,' said Kalid. He allowed himself a chuckle before he left me alone.

I looked around the long, flat garden, if a walled-off patch of scorched dirt and a few furrows of waxy-leafed plants can be called a garden. The shade of the palms didn't reach me; at least not yet. I'd have to wait for sunset for that. A few ghosts in grey smocks and hats tended the vegetation. Aside from sideways looks, they paid me no heed.

It was strange: I felt the heat, but not as a temperature; I still felt deathly cold as always. Instead of burning me, the sunlight made me feel thinner, as if I were evaporating. It wasn't painful, but it was deeply unsettling.

'Still better than the fucking coffin. Still better than the fucking coffin.' I repeated that to myself like a mantra. If the other ghosts heard me, they stuck to their pruning. I was jealous of their hats, wide-brimmed and flat like plates, and I hated them for working under dappled palm-shade while I boiled like a puddle in the desert. Though I knew I was made of nothing but soul, and only misty in form not substance, I swore my throat felt parched. I longed for a sip of water.

I couldn't decide which was worse: having no sense of time at all, or being able to watch the minutes limping by, marked only by the creeping of the sun. Treacle replaced the sand of the hourglass. At least now, back in the bright shining world, free at last, I felt the spell of the sarcophagus fading. With the fog in my mind clearing, my thoughts turned to the excavation beneath the widow's tower, and the picks and shovels I'd seen piled there.

"Suspicious" didn't even begin to do the grimy scene justice. A tal had no business digging clandestine holes under her mansion.

Over the course of an hour, I boiled it down to two guesses: Horix had either struck gold, or she was tunnelling somewhere. I thought of the city layout, trying to apply my bearings to her underground workings, but it was pointless. The subterranean stairs had twisted too many times. In any case, I knew the bitch was up to something shady.

I knew then that I had lied to Colonel Kalid. I had little, if any, intention of staying in my damnable alcove. I pulled at my stake again and wasted time by thinking up foul names for the sun.

It was early afternoon when the cat came snaking through the garden, black as night, yellow eyes searching. Some of the ghosts tried to shoo it away, but all they got for their troubles was vicious hissing. I had often believed there was language in a cat's mewing and yowling. I wondered what curses it spewed now. Cats are spiteful creatures; I had no doubt they would make milk curdle if they could speak Common.

A dog. Now there was an animal that could be relied on. A hound knows the value of a human besides opening doors and providing mice. I'd had a dog for a time. I hadn't wanted him, but life sometimes chooses a path for you, despite your best efforts. His name had been Troge. "Faithful" in Krass tongue. I should have called him Brute, since the puppy who had crawled his way to my doorstep with two broken legs had turned into a hound of fearsome size and muscle. Mountain mutts are like couches with hairy legs. In the end, he caught the spittle-rage and I'd had to have him speared. It was one of those memories that never failed to cut me, no matter how many years I spent trying to blunt it.

The black cat wound its way towards me, eyes fixed on mine. I stared it down. It looked mangy, with one tooth poking above its gum and a scant number of crooked whiskers. It walked towards me with disjointed steps. I waved my hands at it, but the creature came to a stop just out of arm's reach and set its arse to the sand, becoming a little tower of black fur.

Closer up, I could practically see the fleas frolicking through its dusty coat of wiry, midnight-coloured hairs. Part of its left ear was missing, and there was a child's sketch of scars across its muzzle. Though its eyes were piercing and bright, the rest of it seemed half dead, broken in some way.

It yowled at me, low and sorrowful. Then it retched, head down and bony shoulders arched. Bones crunched. I recoiled, thinking it diseased.

'Go away!' I flapped my arms. The other ghosts were looking at me.

Another yowl, guttural this time. It retched again, and again, until it was gagging with deep throbs. There was a splat as a ball of hair and blood met the ground. The cat shivered, its entire body blurring for a moment, and then it sat again.

'That's better,' it said, purring.

Sand scattered in clouds as I scrabbled away, testing the length of my leash. It was miserly, to say the least. My legs flew from under me and my tongue stuck out as the copper fibres strangled me.

The cat spoke again. 'Horush said you would be skittish.' Its voice was hoarse, like papyrus being torn. To confuse me further, it sounded female.

It was official. Either the sarcophagus had addled my brain, or the desert sun had cooked me to madness.

'Have they taken your voice, Caltro?'

My mouth flapped at the use of my name. 'I…'

The cat came closer, winding about the stake like a needle through wool. 'You're not mad, you know. At least not completely. Everybody needs a dash of madness.'

'I—'

'It's normal to be afraid, too. Human.'

The cat's skin and fur seemed too baggy, too lacking in lustre for my liking. I swear I could hear gristle clicking with every sinuous movement.

'I'm not afraid. It's not every day a cat decides to speak to me, is all,' I lied.

She locked eyes with me again. 'Then perhaps this is not every day.'

'Are you trapped in that body?' I knew of strangebinding: the old fashion of ensnaring human souls in other forms, like owls or dogs or horses. Pets, instead of slaves. The Reaches had outlawed the practice several centuries ago, and yet I heard some lived on throughout the world.

'No. I can come and go as I please.'

'Then what are you? No more riddles.'

'I am older than the desert. I walked the earth before the moon was built of dust and shatter. Before the seas learned to roar.'

'I said no more riddles!'

'We are the old gods, Caltro. I am who you called Basht.'

I scoffed. 'The gods are dead. Even if they weren't, you are not one of my gods. How do you know my name, beast? What witchcraft is this?'

'You call us dead. We are more… silenced. We still watch on. We know all that live and die.' The cat looked up at the empty sky, as if the answer lay somewhere in its sapphire wash. I followed her gaze, clueless.

'Enough! Enough of this cryptic shite. Speak plainly, or don't speak at all. What are you truly?'

The cat lowered her head. 'Making sense is difficult. We speak an older tongue than you. Over great distances. Horush said you were confused. Though he used… different words. "Useless" was one.'

I wanted to strangle the answers out of the creature. 'Who the bloody fuck is Horush?' My volume brought a few more stares from the gardeners, but all they saw was a ghost and a cat.

'He came to you some days ago, in your measuring. Through the eyes of a dead man. It is the only way he could speak to you across the… how do you say it? The divide.'

'Speak to me? Confuse me, more like. Just like you, another figment of my imagination come to taunt me. Stress. That's what you are. A manifestation of all the shit stepping off that ship has brought me. Nothing more. Leave me the fuck alone.'

Basht growled at me, impossibly deep for a creature of her size. She stretched out, tail high. In the angle of the sun, I saw her shadow spread, and in that moment I saw no silhouette of a cat, but of a lion, bristling with fur. The look in those yellow eyes was a killer's gaze.

I tugged at my leash again.

The cat's face was starting to sag, and yet she still managed to raise a lip and show a rotten tooth. 'Do not test me, boy. We come at far too great a risk and effort to waste time. I am calmer than my brother. That is why I have been sent. Horush had too much… emotion.'

'What do you want from me?'

'Your help, Caltro Basalt. Salvation. You are our spear in this fight. Our shield against the coming flood.'

'You talk of fighting and floods and chaos, but I have no idea what or who you want me to fight.'

The cat growled again. 'One of our brothers seeks to destroy us. It is he, his followers, you must stop.'

'And who are they, exactly?'

Basht spat the words at me, shaking her head all the while as if none of them were right. 'Fanatics. Zealots. Devotees. They seek to finish off what our brother started. To ruin this world. To flood it with the dead. We sent you back to fight them.'

I shook my head, partly because it sounded utter rubbish and partly because I abhorred the idea of fighting. Not through any righteous sentiments of pacifism; it's more that my tubby frame has never lent itself well to being nimble and quick with a blade. I make a wonderful target.

'But I'm a locksmith, not a soldier.'

'That is why we chose you. Even a mighty fortress can be conquered with the opening of a single door, Caltro, and there are many doors you have yet to open.'

I patted at my vapours. 'Like this? And I don't know if you've noticed this leash, and the fact I'm a half-life—'

'A boon, though you see it not.' She prowled again, stiffer this time. I realised the cat was dead, merely animated by whatever unearthly creature resided within. *Like the corpse in the courtyard.*

Basht was speaking again, interrupting my horror with more riddles. 'And you know, like I, that there are doors that do not look like doors, yet can be opened with a key just the same. We have given you the key, Caltro. A gift. All you have to do is use it.'

'I have been given nothing.'

'Have you not?' she purred, eyes widening. I saw the deadness behind them, but on the surface they glittered. I saw not a cat, but a raging beast, mane flowing and muscles shuddering. I heard a roar stretch across an empty plain, heard it echo over and over in my ears until my chest reverberated with it.

I saw myself, gawping at me as I snarled. I felt the heaviness of fangs in my mouth, the press of fur around me, the hot breath panting over a lolling tongue. I felt a savage hunger in my belly. I longed to test my jaws on the blue form before me.

A jolt shook me free of that strange fantasy. I was back in my own form, staring down at the black cat. The creature was now slumping to the ground.

'Find Sesh's followers,' said Basht. 'Stop them. Save us.'

Her will left the creature. The cat's eyes rolled up and the body fell to the sand, dead once more. A lone black fly began to buzz around it. I hoped that my punishment wouldn't last more than a day, or that somebody would come take the cat away. I hadn't the stomach for maggots, even in death. As the flies began to gather around it, my gaze wandered anywhere but the little corpse while I mulled the cat's words over.

Nothing about my situation was normal, but there was still a line to be crossed between it and the absurd. This was nothing but absurd. No, it was tosh. Utter horse shite. It was some tavern song I had heard once, dug up by stress and made a reality. It certainly sounded like one of the old ballads: dead gods inhabiting dead things, spinning me yarns of fanatics and doom and devouring floods. In those songs there was always some great ruin, and one special moron who just so happened to have the power to fight it. I refused to be that moron. If I had any great power it was self-preservation, and that required ignoring heat and stress-induced illusions.

And yet somehow I could not shake the vibration of the roar from my chest, nor forget the stupid look on my own face as I stared back at myself, clearer than any reflection. I had been as foreign as a stranger in the street. As separate as the sky and the dust.

I shook myself, feeling weak under the sun. I hummed to quieten the cat's words. It was a habit I had never been fond of, and it brought me a few looks from the garden ghosts, but it did have wonderfully distractive properties.

VEX LOOKED THROUGH THE GRILLE, his blind eyes staring past the gold filigree at the pale, moustached, and haughty face beyond.

'Yes?'

'Fetch your mistress, shade. Tell her Tor Busk has come to pay a visit.'

'I'm afraid Widow Horix is not accustomed to hosting unannounced callers.'

'Then announce me, and I shall be welcomed.'

'I—'

'Did you not hear me, shade? Fetch your tal.'

'Of course, Tor Busk. Wait here, please.'

Vex tried to swing the grille shut, but the tor's hand found its way into the gap. Finding his fingers pinched, he seemed to be regretting his decision, but he did not move. The guards either side of the door bristled, but the shade waved them back.

'You expect me to wait here, out in the sun?'

Vex held back his scowl. 'I'm afraid so, Tor. I am under explicit instructions.'

The indignant grunt was muffled by the thud of the door closing. Vex hurried for the stairwell, winding up and up until he was knocking at his superior's door.

'What?' came a grunt.

'It's Vex, Master Yamak.'

'In!'

The room was wreathed in trails of incense. Yamak had the appearance of a sweaty boulder, perched at a desk. He was dabbing a reed at a large scroll. He seemed engrossed in his task, eyes low and narrowed at the sprawl of numbers before him.

'We have a visitor,' said Vex.

The man's head snapped up. 'What?'

'Tor Busk. Here for the widow.'

'Well, he can't see her.'

'He's insistent.'

'Blasted tors, thinking they own this city.'

'Don't they—'

'Yes, all right!' Yamak slammed down his reed, spattering ink across the scroll. He cursed under his breath before hoisting himself to standing. He wiped a hand across his brow, his hand coming away dripping. 'Make him wait in the atrium under guard. I'll go see the widow.'

Vex drifted back down the stairs. He took a stand between the guards and, after checking the straightness of his robes, had the doors opened wide.

Before Vex could bid him enter, Tor Busk strode into the atrium as if it were his own, sweeping his cape from his shoulders and draping it over the nearest spear. He wore a golden waistcoat that strained at the buttons and a baggy suit of bleached white cotton. A pointy hat perched atop a thin mop of greasy hair. His pale skin was that of the far north, and it had taken on a pinkish hue rather than a tanned brown.

'My guards and I will take some water,' he announced, gesturing to the small entourage that followed him in: a half-dozen rented soldiers in bright scale plate and toting short spears. They stood like river reeds on a calm day, waiting for a breeze. The sweat ran from beneath their bronze helms. Half of them were Scatterfolk, and apparently still getting used to the sun.

Vex had a deep bowl and several goblets fetched from the pantries. The tor let his guards test the water first, and then wet his own chapped lips.

When Busk had wiped his moustache, he made for the stairs. Vex and the house-guards had to stand in his way. 'My mistress has been informed of your arrival. She has asked that you wait here.'

Busk puckered his mouth into a shape resembling an arsehole, but he stayed where he was. He occupied himself by gazing up at the spiral interior of the tower.

'Fine tapestries. Phylan, I would guess?' He pointed to a pair of scarlet banners hanging far above them.

'You have a keen eye, Tor.' Vex was unimpressed. The tapestries were covered with the swirling language of the Scatter Isles. A child could have identified it.

Busk crossed his arms. 'How long will she be?'

'As long as she takes.'

'Are all of Horix's shades as impertinent as you? I'll have your name.' His face was reddening, his silly pointy hat wobbling.

'It is Vex, Tor. And neither the Widow Horix nor her household are accustomed to receiving unannounced callers. I'm sure you are aware of the dangers associated with unexpected guests. These are greedy times.'

Busk's northern skin was flushing pink. 'Now you imply I have nefarious intentions here? How dare you!'

'He dares, Tor Busk,' said a thin voice from above, 'because I have taught him to dare.'

The tor immediately threw himself into a low bow, almost losing his hat. Vex stood aside to let the widow descend.

'Tal Horix, my lady. Forgive me. I am unused to such candour from a half-life. I prefer the indentured in my home to be more silent.' Busk shot a look at Vex.

The widow's black frills swirled around her like ink drops in water. Her cowl was high and tied about her wrinkled chin. Her hands, as always, were hidden in sleeves large enough to accommodate a strongman's thigh.

She paused a few steps from the marble floor, looking down on Busk and his entourage with an expression that betrayed nothing. 'The nature of your sudden visit, Tor Busk?'

Busk bowed low. 'I beg forgiveness for the suddenness. I am here under a matter of urgency regarding one of your recent purchases.'

Vex frowned. *Now the man is all graces and smiles.*

'Which would be what?'

'It is a matter best discussed in private.'

'Privacy can be a costly thing.' Horix held his gaze for a moment, testing. Vex wasn't sure what she saw, but it seemed to reassure her. 'We shall speak in the lower dining hall.'

'My gratitude, Tal Horix.'

With much rustling of frills and skirts, the four of them trod the stairs to the middle of the tower, where a large room looked out over the muddle of adobe and sandstone. Yamak had arranged for guards to stand around the edges of the hall, between velvet couches and ivory tables.

Once seats had been taken on opposite ends of the dining table, Vex took a stand by the widow's elbow. Tor Busk gestured at him without using his eyes.

'The matter is a private one.'

'Vex has served this house for almost twenty years. He can be trusted,' replied Horix with a tut.

'I see.' Busk spread his hands out across the mahogany. 'It's come to my attention that we often visit the same soulmarkets. While I know you are a discerning buyer, I'm afraid many of the traders don't share your scruples.'

'Speak plainly, Busk. I haven't the time for empty chat. You clearly have a reason for being here. Get on with explaining it.'

His rings drummed on the wood. 'Very well. I believe you've recently bought a shade who was illegally bound.'

'I did not know you worked for the Chamber of the Code, Tor Busk. Or should that be Scrutiniser Busk?'

He flattened his hands on his more than ample belly. 'Call me a concerned party. I would hate to see your proud name sullied by rumours.'

'Rumours are fleeting fancies, Tor Busk. I care for more permanent things.'

'Be that as it may, it disturbs me to know the markets are selling stolen souls. It disturbs me more to know that you might have an illegal shade within your house. You and I both know plenty of tals and tors have fallen foul of poor purchases and succumbed to the plots of soulstealers, or spooks. I'm worried for you, Tal Horix.'

She cackled at that. Vex allowed himself a tight smile.

'I appreciate your concern, Tor Busk, but it's unfounded and frankly naive to think the soultraders are completely honest.' She wiped imaginary tears from her face. 'Tell me, who is this shade you're so concerned about? And how did you come to know about him?'

Busk sighed. 'I have made the same error, I'm afraid. I bought a house-shade from the same batch of Boss Temsa's stock. Kech was his name. He has been recalcitrant, constantly arguing for his innocence. Have you experienced the same?'

Horix shrugged. 'I can't say I have.'

'Well, I intend to take mine back to the soulmarket and demand a refund from Boss Temsa. I would be happy to do the same for you, Tal Horix. To save you the trouble and embarrassment.'

'How charitable.'

Busk shook his head. 'I am not one for charity, madam. I would happily purchase him for the same price as you bought him and reclaim the cost at the market.

'A him, you say?'

'A Krassman, or so my research has told me.'

'I do not buy Krassmen.'

Tor Busk paused for a long time. Their gazes duelled over the table top, one set of eyes dark and shadowed, the other narrow and blue.

'My research—'

'Has clearly counted for nothing. You are mistaken, Tor.'

Busk was not done. 'Tal Horix, I believe him to be dangerous. Kech has told me his story. He is *very* dangerous, in fact. A reputed killer in his country. He was fleeing to the Arc. You have no doubt heard the same stories as I. Stories involving shades of a similar ilk rebelling against their masters. With bloody results, no less.'

Though Vex straightened, the widow was motionless. 'I see. And why is it that you are suddenly so worried for my safety?'

'You are a well-respected member of the noble class, Tal Horix. I wish only for you to see your… sixtieth birthyear?' He went as far as to wink at the mistress. 'You can consider me an ally. Friend, even.'

She offered him a thin smile.

'Are we in accord? I have taken the liberty of drawing up the agreement. All legal and binding. Sigils from Galiph & Sons provided the service.' The tor was already digging in his pockets when Horix stood.

'I think not, Busk. You presume too much and seem to know very little. I think you are mistaken about my purchases. If I were you, I would look to your own stock before worrying about mine. And as for friends and allies, they are a weakness in this city. I'd expect a tor like you to know that. As such, I thank you for your visit and bid you a fine day.'

By the look on Busk's face, he looked as if he'd just been dipped into a pot of boiling oil. Even his guard, standing behind his shoulder, had to stifle a snigger. Vex smirked.

Busk was forced to stand and trail in the widow's wake. She led him to a skinny bridge spanning the tower's hollow core and overlooking the atrium.

'I—' he began, but Horix cut him off.

'You're most welcome for the water.'

From the bridge, Horix watched him stamp all the way back down the stairs, embarrassed and no doubt privately fuming. When the door finally slammed, far below, Vex swore he heard her old face creaking into a smile. It was desperately brief.

'Bring him to me,' she snapped.

'Who, Mistress?'

'The Krassman. The one you've been punishing.'

'May I ask why, Widow Horix?'

She shot him a look that would have skewered a rat at a dozen paces. 'No, you may not, shade. Find him.'

'He's in the garden, Mistress. Tied to a post.'

Without a word, Horix bustled past him, a storm cloud of frills and wayward ribbons. He made to follow once again, but she waved him away, swiping at him with her long, copper-painted nails. He bowed profusely and ducked into a nearby corridor. He listened to her sharp footsteps descending, and groaned.

'She don't like you much, does she?' asked a voice. Vex heard the sniggers coming from the alcoves around him.

Vex turned to find a crumpled, half-folded shade staring at him, wearing a goofy smile. Others were chuckling away to themselves.

'Fuck you! Fuck you all!' Vex adjusted his cloak. 'Double duties, the lot of you!'

I FELT THE SHADOW FALL over me before I heard the footsteps: a welcome smidgeon of shade in the late afternoon sun. I waited for my visitor to speak, not wanting them to move. Although I felt nothing but cold, I swore the sun was boiling me alive, stealing my vapours.

'Who are you, half-life?' The voice was a crow's caw, and I knew who it belonged to without turning.

'Jerub.'

'No, your other name. When you were alive.'

I took a while to answer. If I were alive I would have been busy finding the saliva. Instead I was simply trying to remember. Dazed, I watched the other ghosts scuttling past, bowing and scraping, their arms full with baskets. My head lolled in their direction.

'How many of us are there?'

'What?'

I looked at her then, gazed deep into her dark hood to meet those flint eyes. 'How many of us do you own?'

It was her turn to pause. 'Sixteen thousand.'

I felt like curling up. I felt groggy, as if I'd spent a day propping up a tavern bar. 'Sixteen…'

'Thousand.'

'All here?'

'Do you see sixteen thousand shades in this tower?' she snapped. 'I have businesses. Makers and sellers. Now give me your name, *ghost*, or I'll leave you out here for another week. You won't be worth a sack of last season's grain when I'm done with you.'

'Caltro. Caltro Basalt. You might have heard of me…'

'Where are you from?'

I swayed. 'What are you… what are you building?'

'Answer me!'

'Taymar, in Fault province. Near the Kold Rift.'

'You said you were a smith? Vaultsmith?'

'Locksmith. Best in all the Reaches.'

She spat something green on the sand between my feet. I stared at it dully, confused why there was still a dead cat slumped by my feet.

'Lies!' she cried.

'Truth...'

'Why did you come here? What were you running from?'

'Not running. Not this time. Appointment. In—'

Whump. My vapours collided with the sand as my concentration failed me. I became limp, seeping slightly across the grains.

'Fuck!' I heard the widow curse before she screeched for assistance at the top of her lungs. I blinked and found myself surrounded by shades. Vex was there, and I felt something dripping on my face. A shiver ran through me, rippling across my body, as if the sun had fallen behind a cloud or a rooftop. I fell with it into a dark space. Five faint stars shone down. A single bright point at their centre sparkled at me.

CHAPTER 15
GHOULS

On inspection of your forces, Your Majesty, we have numbered the living at two hundred and fifty-four thousand, Thirty-six hundred men and horse or insect. We have numbered the half-lives at one million, three hundred thousand and six hundred.

LATEST COUNT FROM THE CHAMBER OF MILITARY MIGHT, ARCTIAN YEAR 1001

THE SUN'S BRUTAL RHYTHM HAD grown easier with time. It was useless to oppose the monotony of sunrise and sunset. The stark mountainside became a place of opposites: day to night, hot to cold, blinding bright to deepest dark. But it was predictable, and anything predictable can be managed. Time, and lack of options, helped.

What was not predictable was the stench of Farazar's body.

Nilith had never known a body could stink so in the desert heat. It was not uncommon to see a beast felled by the sun on the streets of Araxes, and for the corpse to linger there for days, filling the air with its reek. However, she had never had to share a horse's back with one for days on end and get to suffer the entire spectrum of putrefaction. Just as she was getting used to one kind of smell, another came along to make her gag. Farazar's wine- and fat-pickled body had also begun to squelch with the jolting of Anoish's trot. As much as she tried to listen to the sand scattering in the hot breeze, or the hoof beats, even the grumbling of Farazar's ghost, she still heard it.

The nights on the soaring slopes of the Firespar had become hallowed periods, where the body could be put away somewhere at the edge of the firelight, and a squelch-free silence could reign. It was also a chance to rest her leg, which, although healed by the beldam's charms, still ached from being dangled against the horse's side all day.

The slopes had not yet proven challenging. They were simply winding, with the path chasing back and forth through grey-brown shale to lessen the angle. Without feeling like they'd climbed at all, they could now stare down at the vast expanse of desert below them, where foothills were mere pimples and the dunes just cracks in a yellow palm.

That night, the moon and stars illuminated the vista, showing them a handful of other campfires far in the distance, shining against the inestimable wasteland. The soft glow of a town or quarry shone in the east, at the limit of the horizon. A thin, charcoal line of a river-rift meandered between the dunes, heading north and east.

In the west, a few soultrains or nomad caravans weaved back and forth. Nilith could even see the specks of gazelles or giraffes galloping across the salt flats. Perhaps sabre-cats pursued them, or jackals. If she peered closely enough, she swore she could see faint violet lights hovering between the dunes. They were the lures of dunewyrms. Like fishermen and baited hooks, they dangled their lights from a stalk to attract prey, waiting patiently until something became curious enough.

Nilith's fire was hidden behind a rock, out of view of any watchful eyes immediately above and below. The hot breezes of the day had turned cold, and they whipped at the flames in jealousy.

Much to Nilith's contentment, Farazar had stayed quiet for several days now. Perhaps he too had heard the squelching of his body and it had unsettled him. He spent the nights brooding with his back to her and knees drawn against his chest. Once he had tried to sit out on display, glowing like a beacon, but his weak attempt at betrayal had been swiftly quashed and criticised.

The night passed in shattered pieces between brief periods of sleep. Her unease kept her up. Once, she awoke to find Farazar pacing around the fire. She watched him with droopy eyes until he noticed her gaze, huffed, and went back to his brooding.

When morning broke over the side of the old mountain, the light pouring into the barren gullies dragged her from her shallow dreams. After taking a moment to relieve herself behind a nearby boulder – a curious black thing that looked half-molten – she roused Anoish and strapped the stinking body across his rump. She retched on her empty stomach. For some time, she had to stand quite still with the waterskin clasped in both hands.

Once the nausea passed, and with two strips of shirt stuffed up each of her nostrils, they continued the climb. Farazar took the lead today, eager to be far away from his corpse. Nilith wished she could do the same, but she needed her strength. The water was running low and her supplies were beginning to dwindle. Unless the old mountain had a spring at its peak, she would need every ounce of vigour to press on, and that meant riding.

Dawn became early morning, and the rousing sunrise grew into a sharp, angry heat. It was as if the sun lived a whole life each day: the harmless dawn cheery as a newborn, the morning and midday sun a hot, youthful angst, and the evening a regal slide into the horizon. Nilith waited all day for its passing.

The turns began to grow tighter and the angle of the path sharper. The Firespar had finally started to test them, and by early afternoon, the sweat poured from her and Anoish. The endless winding became disorientating, and when combined with the stink, Nilith found herself curling up on the horse's back, filling her nose with his musty scent.

An hour later, the path forked, splitting into three like a trident spearing the mountain. One led west, another east, and the centre aimed straight up towards the ragged summit and the pass that led through its crater. It was the shortest path, but it was also the most dangerous.

Now that she stared up it, following its zig-zag tendencies and noting how far away the sharp crown of black rock still seemed, Nilith felt dizzy. She swayed against Anoish's neck. She turned to look over her shoulder, but found the slope fell away at an alarming angle. The country far below was wrapped in a haze of heat and dust. Nilith put a hand to her forehead.

'Trouble, wife?'

Farazar's croaking voice brought her round. 'None, thank you.'

'Which way, then?'

'Straight up. The hard path. The dangerous path.' She could feel Anoish grumble through her backside, and the grind of his molars, too. The horse was far too smart for his own good.

'Good. Maybe you'll fall and break your neck.'

'I keep telling you, if you want to spend the rest of eternity as the whipslave of some mountain bandit, be my guest. Remember that, before you try to attract attention again.'

Farazar fell back into his silence and began a slow trudge up the middle path. Nilith took a moment to water Anoish and herself before nocking an arrow to the string of her borrowed bow. It was a small thing, fashioned from dark wood and springbok horn, recurved and bent with gut-string. And should she run out of arrows, her knife sat at her side, the scimitar tucked into the corpse-wrappings behind her.

There was nothing to do but continue. She held tight to the horse with her legs, laying the bow flat on her lap, and endured. A mountain was simply a test of moving one limb in front of the other in the right direction, its height measured only by the number of repetitions needed to reach its peak.

Nilith gave up on counting by the time she reached six thousand, and those were hoofsteps. The landscape below had become smaller and less detailed, yet the jagged ridge still towered over them, as though it had barely moved. It was infuriating. She found herself clutching the copper coin looped around her neck, remembering the meaning of resolve.

The mountainside became more hostile the higher they climbed. The iron colours of sand and rock faded into black and sun-baked grey. Boulders perched on knuckles of folded rock. It bubbled here, seeped there: so full of movement yet all frozen in time. Great whorls and pockmarks interrupted the path, and the earth was scorched black wherever the stone had spread. Nilith could smell a faint sulphur on the breezes.

'I thought this mountain had died a long time ago,' she said to Farazar, still a dozen paces ahead.

He sighed. 'They say the earth never truly dies here. They say the Firespar will roar again, one day.'

'So you do know something of your country after all.'

He muttered something about wives and beheading.

Anoish was tired long before the sun had sunk behind the slope. His hooves were used to plains, not crags as steep as stairs. No steppe-hoof, this one. Half their path faded to darkness while the other half blazed a dark orange. Nilith cast around for something resembling a hollow, somewhere she wouldn't roll to her demise down the craggy slope in the middle of the night.

The light had almost disappeared by the time she decided it was useless. The slope looked like it had taken some ancient and magnificent hammer blow. There was no camp to be found amongst the jagged boulders, pumice and broken rock.

'We press on,' she said as she slipped from Anoish's back. The horse whinnied his gratitude and she patted his pronounced ribs.

'In the dark?' Farazar had a point; no moon had risen yet.

'We still have stars, and you'll light the way for us, won't you? Warn us of any craters or holes that could lame our good horse?'

'Or bandits.'

'Fear not, Farazar. You know I can defend myself. And you.' She patted the corpse without thinking and quickly withdrew her hand.

'Hmph.'

And on they went, with Farazar walking ahead of Nilith while she guided the horse. As night claimed the sky, his glow grew brighter, and with the added shine of the stars they kept up a good pace.

Conversation was non-existent; there was just the occasional mumble of a pothole or rift in the path. Anoish was clearly eager to avoid injury as well, and did a fine job of staying calm. He had grown used to the shade's presence in the last week. He must have sensed Farazar's uselessness, or the constant derision in Nilith's voice. He ignored him as much as she did.

The pace slowed as the slope arched its back. There were a few places where they had to scrabble up the detritus of old landslides. Anoish whinnied in panic as the stones crumbled under his hooves, all pumice and shale. Nilith had to shove her shoulder into his flanks to help him onto firmer ground.

They reached the lip of the crater in the night's darkest hours. In the starlight, they found it a hollow, vacant place. It stretched in a teardrop shape, a mile or two across at its shortest point. Jagged spires of rock stood around its edges like the surviving pillars of a hall with its roof blown off. Several of the structures must have rivalled Araxes' mansions for height. They all leaned at an angle, away from the centre of the crater.

Beneath them, the rock fell away, grooved and scorched like the inside of an old cauldron. Occupying a hollow in its centre was a small lake, still and as silver as mercury in the starlight. Between it and them, a forest of fang-like rocks protruded from the crater's floor, pointing at the stars.

It may have been a trick of the dawn, or compensation for the dark of the crater, but Nilith could have sworn she saw a faint glow to the north, where the city lay.

She shrugged off her cloak and handed it to Farazar. 'Put this on. Wrap it around you.'

'I refuse.'

'Do it.' She shuddered in the chilly breeze.

Farazar obeyed, slipping on the cloak and hugging it about him. It was almost as if he'd missed the touch of clothes on his body. After much complaining, he'd apparently grown used to his nakedness.

The descent into the crater was precarious, with Anoish almost tripping on a wobbling boulder. Thankfully, the ground was quick to level. Black sand hissed underfoot. Pebbles crumbled into ash, and the fine dust swirled about them like a sea mist.

They weaved their way through the black fangs. Their stone had escaped the harsh bite of the wind, and the glass-like facets had not dulled. The faint glow escaping Farazar's cloak made their surfaces dance as if they dripped with oil. Their tall points blotted out the stars, so dark they were edgeless, looking like voids in the sky.

There was a heat to the ground that kept Nilith's shivering at bay. She could feel it in her feet, or through her hands when she pressed them to the ash. She was grateful for it.

She kept her eyes on the silver lake, visible in portions between the standing stones. Her hand kept reaching out to the diminished waterskin dangling from Anoish's side. She could feel the horse's pace quicken every time he caught sight of the lake's glint.

'Steady now, boy,' she whispered, plucking the skin from its rope and holding it tightly.

A stench of sulphur hit them hard as they emerged from the stones to cross the open earth to the lakeshore. It put a halt to the horse, but Nilith was too thirsty to stop. She bent to the water's edge and found herself coughing at its reek of acrid salts. It made the dead body smell like perfume. She reeled backwards, holding her breath until she was several yards from the water.

'Well, fuck that,' she said between coughs.

'It's not advisable to drink the water,' said a voice behind her. 'Poisonous, eh? Eats your skin.'

Nilith's knife was free of its sheath in a blur. Her other hand reached for the bow.

In the half-light, Nilith saw the form of a woman, large of build and wrapped in dusty leather armour. Smudges of ash decorated her piggish face in some poor attempt at a tribal pattern. Her black hair had been cut short and was waxed into spikes. She wore a wide grin, and though her open hands were empty, a sword hung at her belt.

'You're wise to be cautious up here, eh? Road's always full of strangers, never friends.'

'Keep your distance.'

She took a step forwards to prove her boldness. 'Looking for water, eh? The kind for you or the kind for your *ba'at*?' She used the old Arctian name for a ghost, as many desert-folk did. They were an older people, but that didn't mean kinder.

Nilith shook her head. 'I think we'll go look somewhere else.'

The woman hissed through her teeth and half a dozen figures emerged from behind the stones. They were scraggy fellows all, with either knives drawn or arrows nocked. Nilith's hand had found her bow, but she realised she would be turned into a pincushion before she could do any good with it.

The woman approached. She admired Anoish, running her hand across his rump, staying clear of his hooves. The horse shied away from her and Nilith bared a scowl.

'Fine beast. And a fine stink. Not bound yet, I see, *ba'at*?'

Farazar raised his chin as he met her painted eyes.

'What do you want?' asked Nilith. 'Gems?'

'You have them?'

'Some. Enough to pay for safe passage through your crater.'

The woman smiled, moving closer still despite the blade in Nilith's hand. 'We own nothing here. It would not be right to charge you for something we don't own, eh?'

Nilith narrowed her eyes. 'What if I pay for protection?'

'From what?'

'From you. From wild beasts. Or perhaps I pay for some clean water.'

'Mm…' She hummed, biting her bottom lip. 'I'm not really in the business of protecting or selling things. Unfamiliar trades, eh?'

Nilith tensed her arm, ready. 'Then what business are you in?'

The woman took her time, looking around at her men, who had formed a wall around them.

'Taking what we want.'

The fist came for her gut like a triggerbow bolt. Before Nilith's blade could do more than rake the woman's arm, she was already winded and falling backwards. Two arrows thudded into the ground beside her head, and she fell still, curled around her stomach.

The woman stamped her feet either side of her face. With one fist, she seized Nilith by the collar, and with the other proceeded to beat her into unconsciousness. All she heard, before the knuckles brought the darkness, was the frantic neighing of Anoish and the stone-cold silence of Farazar. Between the starbursts of pain and spraying blood, she glimpsed him standing helpless nearby, three copper spears at his throat. His smirking face was the last thing she saw before succumbing.

'EASY, BEAST. EASY.'

The equine shrieks brought her round sharply. She flinched, finding her hands bound and her face raw. Her nose felt broken. One eyelid was a narrow slit. The other was closed shut. Her jaw refused to move.

'Calm it, eh?'

With great difficulty, Nilith inclined her head, looking over to the noise of the horse.

They had Anoish lashed to a stake with little room to move. The woman and a few of her bandits were surrounding him, hands waving in a vain effort to stop him bucking.

One man had a switch and kept lashing him across the flank, hissing for him to calm down. Nilith struggled again, forming no words but plenty of bloody spittle.

'She's up, Boss!' yelled a voice not far from her.

'A fighter, eh? Good news.'

Ungentle hands hauled her upright, resting her against her own stake in the ground. Nilith rolled her head about her shoulders as the woman approached. She felt the cold air where her clothes had been torn and ripped. One leg of her trews was missing. Her white hood and jacket were gone, as was the copper coin around her neck.

They were still on the shore of the lake. A great fire was now burning, mixing brushwood smoke with sulphur-stink. Farazar had been left beside his body. They hadn't liked the smell either, and so he was down by the water. A guard hovered a good ten feet away.

'Wha—' Words were difficult. Her lips were split; fiery every time she moved them.

'Don't speak, woman. Won't do you any good from here, eh?'

'I have coins, gems. I could make you rich.'

The woman reached inside her leather jacket – *Nilith's* jacket – and produced a fat ruby. 'You already have, and no doubt you'll make me richer still, eh? Folks in the south are growin' fond of live slaves, not shades. You seem well bred, eh? Perhaps you'll make one of the Belish dukes a good pet. You know what they say: can't fuck a ghost. Real thing's better.'

Her soot-stained hands reached out to run through Nilith's tangled hair. She was rough, tugging here and there, then she patted her on the swollen cheek.

'Pretty, too. Once. I bet, eh?' Her tongue, stained black with ash and tobacco, licked from Nilith's chin to her forehead. The cuts stung at the wet touch and Nilith recoiled. 'If you're lucky, I might take you into my tent tonight, instead of letting one of these fuckers have their way with you.'

She rose from her knees and pushed away her gathered cronies. They hooted and moaned, and Nilith heard mention of 'later' from the woman's lips.

'What's your name?' Nilith called after her, words slurred.

Her captor paused. 'I'll give you that. You're speaking to Krona of the Crater Ghouls.'

One scrawny man lingered to show some teeth and a pair of wild eyes. He was soon called away, and Nilith was left to stare at the blurry image of a campfire and listen to Anoish's whinnying. A few jagged lumps of riding beetles were dotted around, their shells glassy in the starlight. There were more figures around the fire, some not as solid as others. She saw small glowing figures wandering between the seated, ducking swipes and scattering when somebody yelled.

Children. Shades bound young, ripped from their innocence and murdered neatly. Another fashion of the Arc. It always made Nilith shudder.

The darkness called to her again, though this time it was full of voices. Conversations of coins and gems, over how much this one and that one would get at soulmarket, the braying of lewd nights, of horse meat and who had stuck a sword in whomever else.

When Nilith drifted back into the world of the living, the shouting had quietened to a low murmur of garbled conversation. The figures around the fire had reduced in number, though she could still spy the big frame of Krona against the flames. A few had passed out, bellies rising and falling with faint rumbles. The smell of pipe smoke and goat fat had replaced the stink of sulphur.

Drops of liquid splashed her face, cold at first, then stinging as it found her cuts. She hissed, curling into a deeper ball.

A man hovered over her, holding a wineskin at an angle. In the other, a white stone, presented like a trophy. 'Krona says I got to be careful with you,' he rasped. 'Gentle.'

Another dribble, another fierce surge of pain. The wine stank. She dabbed her wounds with her sleeve.

'No fun in being gentle, I say.'

A boot prodded her in the side and she lashed at it. A hand grabbed her by the hair and wrenched her head back. She saw a familiar face through the blood-matted strands. It was the grinning man with the yellow teeth, built like a rat and just as verminous.

'Get off me!' Nilith pulled at his grip. He was strong for a little man.

He showed her a knife, thrust through a leather belt at his side. 'I'll do what I please!'

Down she went, back to the dust, face first with her hands pinned behind. Her wounds ignited, white stars exploding behind her eyes. It took her a moment to feel the man's searching hands on her. She felt cloth rip at her waist and hot breath on the nape of her neck. She thrashed against his hold, but his bony legs knelt on hers, holding her down. Another rip, and she felt the night breeze on the skin of her thighs. Hot, rasping hands began to paw. A stubbled cheek pressed in close as he whispered.

'She said you'd be a wriggler!'

It is said that in moments of danger, panic hands control over to instinct. Unfortunately for the rat, Nilith's instincts were those of a fighter. And a fierce one, at that.

She ground her face against the sand, turning her head to feel the skin of his ear against her lips. She bit down as hard as her sore teeth would allow. It was enough. His screech deafened her on one side, but the more he struggled, the tighter she clamped. Nilith felt the crackle of cartilage between her teeth. Hot blood filled her mouth. She fought not to retch as she swallowed it.

He punched and he shoved but all it did was quicken the process. With a repugnant sound akin to silk tearing, half his ear came free. He reeled backwards, haemorrhaging crimson.

Nilith spat the flesh to the ground and struggled to her feet. Now she was tall enough, she slid her hands up and over the stake. Behind her, the guard had heard the screeching and was marching up the lakeshore to investigate. There were shouts coming from the fire, too.

To her surprise, it was Farazar who acted. With a hop and a leap, he reached the guard, hooked his hands around his elbow, and swung the man towards the water. It took some tugging, and all the ghost's momentum, but he went stumbling face-first into the water. It was deeper than it looked, and for a moment Farazar's guard was completely submerged.

He reared from the waters with a choking scream. Steam emanated from his body as if the water was hot, and Nilith heard the faint hiss of burning. His clothes peeled away from reddened skin in smoking shreds. He went down again as he thrashed his way shorewards. Mistimed gasps filled his lungs with the acrid waters. When he reared up, she could see his eyes had melted down his cheek. He died as his hand touched the shoreline, raking four furrows in the grey sand with bone rather than flesh.

Nilith raced for the corpse, still bundled in its wrappings. She skidded short of the water, spraying sand, and grabbed the scimitar from the folds. She grasped it with two hands and ran towards the horse.

The first man was stopped short with a vicious slash across his stomach. His drunken eyes rolled up as his body fell to the floor, chasing his spilled guts. Farazar was now following at her heel, and he scrabbled away from the body like a pigeon from a cat.

'You should have picked a different path!' he screeched.

The others were approaching now. An arrow zipped by, followed by an angry shout from Krona.

As soon as Anoish's tether was slashed, the horse turned so Nilith could jump onto his back. She galloped him the short distance back to the body. Farazar even helped to sling it over the horse's back.

There was no time to tie it, and so with one hand gripping it tight and the other entangled in Anoish's mane, Nilith kicked them into a gallop. The horse brayed as somebody grabbed his tail, but a vicious kick freed him. Within moments, they were flying along the shoreline.

The breeze slapped Nilith in the face, pointing out every cut and bruise in cold detail. Howls chased them, and the slaps of feet on sand. Arrows began to fly again; not the sharp kind, but blunt ones with hardened bags of—

One clapped her in the base of the skull.

—sand.

Her vision swam. She slumped across Anoish's neck, and as much as he tried to hold steady, she tumbled from his side. Sand might be soft to feet, but was hard as rock at high speed, and she rolled several times before coming to a flailing stop.

The last thing she saw was Krona's blurry face, grinning once more, a stubby bow clutched in her hand.

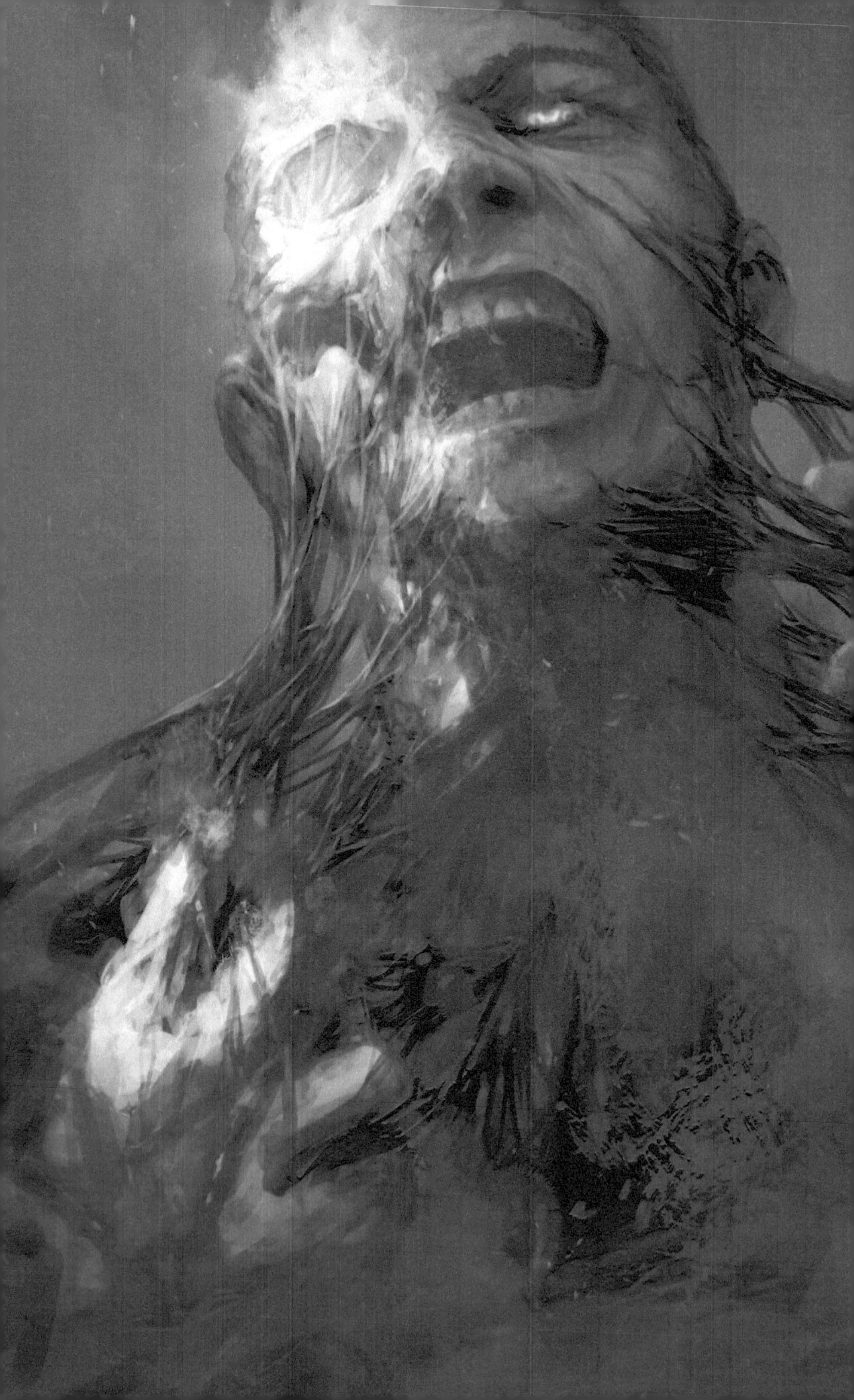

CHAPTER 16
A TEST

When life gives you lemons, seek sugar from death instead.

POPULAR SAYING AMONGST
Free Shades

THIS PIECE OF FESTERING CAMEL cunt?'

Charming.

'Yes, Vex. For the dozenth time. She's chosen him.' Yamak crossed his flabby arms, like an open gate closing in Vex's face. His bone and gold bangles clinked.

I couldn't have been more entertained by this. Since being hauled into the dark and cool of the sandstone several days ago, I had been hounded by the ghost. Had he breath in him, it would have been falling on my neck. Instead, he had a spiteful heart, and it was my pleasure to watch it be stamped upon.

'Why?'

'Widow has her ways, you know that!'

'Tor Busk said he was dangerous!'

Yamak wiped sweat from his furrowed brow. The drips stained the scrolls spread over his desk. He had made a cursory effort to hide their contents, but I could still see the scattered lines of diagrams and plans. 'And Horix says otherwise,' he said.

'But I am the one who tends her! This cretin doesn't know shit about—'

'Enough, shade! You forget yourself.' Yamak cleared his throat. 'It's already done. You're reassigned to oversee the kitchens.'

That's beneficial. The kitchens were six levels below, and as I didn't eat, Vex poisoning me was out of the question. Though there was plenty of copper down there…

Vex bowed his head, finding a spot on the floor in which to bury his empty gaze.

Yamak beckoned to me and I did my best to avoid shouldering the ghost on my way past. But alas, I'm often a victim of my worse nature. In my defence, I only brushed him. Barging anything is tough without skin or bones. It made my point well enough, and Vex muttered something foul at me in Arctian.

I followed Master Yamak to the very peak of the tower. Every door was opened for me and every step I took was echoed by half a dozen of Kalid's soldiers, none of them shades. Their plate armour clanged musically.

Horix was waiting for me in her library, curled like a cat in a chair. Her frills were cast wide about her, black as an oil slick. Her chin rested on her fist and a pair of crystal spectacles pinched her nose.

For a library, the place was pretty sparse when it came to scrolls or books. The shelves appeared to be largely reserved for tallow candles. The sunlight had been shut out behind two triangular skylights, but it was far from needed; the candles burned almost as brightly. I felt the thickness of their smoke in the air.

'Have the gates been sealed as ordered?' she asked.

Yamak bobbed his sweaty head. 'Yes, Widow.'

'Then you may leave us.'

'As you wish.'

With a short bow, the man was gone, leaving the doors closed and the guards behind. They fanned out behind me, short spears tucked into their sides, held low but ready.

I was guided towards a velvet-clad chair. I sat, hands folded on my lap, back still bent from a strange tiredness that I hadn't shifted since my punishments. I felt as though the sun and sarcophagus had stolen some of my soul, and left a weakness in me instead.

Waiting for her to speak, I let my eyes wander over the golden glyphs on scrolls and book spines, the white marble and bleached bone shelves spread around the walls like honeycomb, and the candle flames looking like hot jewels.

Horix spoke quietly, as if I was sat closer to her. 'You don't have to look so worried.'

'I'm curious, rather than worried. Not unless you want to put me back in that coffin again.'

'The sarcophagus. Yes. One of Master Yamak's suggestions. Cursed stone, or so he tells me. Not many of them left any more despite being all the rage in the western districts several years ago, I hear. Now they have a new fashion. They string a shade up by the legs and dangle them in a bucket of water. You can't drown, of course, but most shades don't remember that while you're trying to choke. Especially the fresh ones.'

I stared at her and wondered if this was a threat.

'Have you ever been to the Outsprawls, Mr Basalt?'

My name caught me, as if reminding me of a dream erased by the light of day. It seemed Jerub had died in the garden. 'No.'

'Frightful places, they say. Rife with crime and poverty. But I disagree. I think they are rich with ideas, with life. People living in hard places and hard times tend to take extraordinary measures for an easier life. For instance, in the south-eastern Sprawls, where the creeping sand can swallow a building in a night, the beetle-farmers have realised that planting palms and ferns keeps the earth in place, and provides something to fight the sandstorms. Hardship breeds ingenuity, don't you find?'

'I guess.'

'Take your situation, for example, Mr Basalt. You've had a run of bad luck lately, would it be fair to say?'

'If we are talking fair, I'd wager dying would rank as some of the worst luck there is, Mistress.'

'And yet here you are, in a hard place and a hard time, doing anything you can to make your life easier. Even if it does mean poking your nose into places that don't concern you.' The cackle that followed her words was odd, and not purely through its brevity or high pitch. It was mismatched with the veiled reminder that she was in charge. 'That's why you are sitting here now. To see if I can offer you something to help you. Is it not?'

'I am here because you summoned me to do a job.'

'And I bet you didn't complain once, hmm?'

The old bat had me there. The sparkle in her raisin-like eyes told me she knew it.

'What are you building in the cellars?'

She snapped two bonelike fingers at the guards. 'Leave us.'

They hesitated, worrying too much to be obedient. I wondered what it was about this crone that inspired so much loyalty and care. It couldn't have all been down to silver coin.

When the last boot had disappeared behind the door, Widow Horix inched to the edge of her seat and pushed herself up to take a predatory tour of the shelves. Her movements were stiff, as if she hadn't got up in some time. She had the look of an old panther patrolling her territory.

Her fingers hopped between the edges of scrolls. 'I like stories, Mr Basalt. Do you?' she asked, ignoring my question.

'I did, once.' As the years claimed more and more of me, I found that almost all stories have an unhappy ending for at least one character. My problem was that it was always the character I identified with most. In fiction, people like me always seem to be rather expendable. And lo, I sat there as glowing proof.

'People say a story is a window into another mind, another world. I believe they are more mirrors than windows. In them, we glimpse ourselves dressed up as the characters. And like any reflection, the truth we see can be hard to swallow. Perhaps that is why you don't like stories any more, Mr Basalt? You don't like what it reminds you of?'

I never had, not in the silver of a mirror nor in the pages of a book. But in my business, it doesn't pay to be pretty, and it certainly doesn't pay to be kind and just. Quite the opposite, in fact. 'Did you bring me here to tell me a story, Mistress?'

'No, I did not.' She levelled a finger at me. '*You*, however, were in the middle of your story before you fainted. I would like to hear the rest of it and see what it shows me.'

'I'll warn you, it doesn't have a happy ending.'

'I have seen many a year pass by me. I am sure I can manage.'

'With all respect, why would you care about my story?'

Horix gave me a haughty look. 'Because I believe it might just interest me.'

Things are only interesting to rich people when they either cost them or make them money. 'There's not much to tell, to be honest,' I lied.

She spoke to me as a teacher would a petulant child. 'Let me start you off, Mr Basalt. Surely even a Krassman knows the Tenets of the Bound Dead? The laws written a thousand years ago, to govern the binding and ownership of shades?'

I crossed my arms. 'Of course I do. Everybody does, thanks to the Arctian Empire's influence.'

Her words chased mine, monotone and automatic. 'They must die in turmoil. They shall be bound with copper and water of the Nyx. They must be bound within forty days. They shall be bound to whomever holds their coin. They are slaved to their master's bidding. They must bring their masters no harm. They shall not express opinions nor own property. They shall never know freedom unless it is gifted to them… Am I making myself clear?'

I was starting to think she was, but before I could speak she answered for me. The widow took long strides with each word until she was practically under my nose, staring up at me from beneath her cowl.

'In summary, you are nothing to me besides a *yes, Mistress* or a *right away, Tal.* When I ask a question, I expect it answered. Do not mistake my chatter and your apparent promotion for anything more than what it is: theatre, Mr Basalt. Misdirection. I have tried nice, so allow me to be direct, if you Krassmen prefer that. You will tell me your story, or I will have Kalid put you back in the sarcophagus for a week. Then I will ensure you never speak again by cutting out your tongue. Do I make myself clear now?'

The words couldn't leave my mouth fast enough. 'What do you want to know?'

'Chiefly, who you are and how you came to be in Araxes.' The widow swept back to her chair, ready to be spun a yarn.

It was time for honesty. It was not my strong point nor my preference, to be honest, but for all the black cat's nonsense, Basht had spoken the truth about one thing: every lock had a key. Cracking Horix's theatricals required truth.

'As I told you, I'm from Taymar, but I grew up near the mountains of the Kold Rift. I was born to a pair of healers who lived on the wild steppes. They had me late in life to cure their boredom and had the dream of me continuing the family trade. I preferred stealing things instead. It started with their clothes and trinkets, then food from the village markets. Enjoyed the thrill of it so much I joined a few Taymar gangs to hone my skills and my nerve. Can't count the times my father came to retrieve me from the local prisons, spending hard-earned coin on bribes or favours. I was too young to realise I was dragging my parents' reputations through the mud, towards penury. When I turned twelve, I learned of a master locksmith in Saraka and I didn't think twice about running away. I did it for me, but in a way, it was to give my parents the peace they deserved.

'Master Deben was the locksmith's name, and he taught me as his master had taught him. I spent years at his side, pushing myself onto bigger and better jobs. My parents both died the winter after. Swelterflux, the letter said, but it was their time. Quick and painless, and their ghosts didn't rise. They were buried by the Nyx under a lemon tree with a copper coin in each of their mouths, and through guilt I stayed in Taymar for almost a decade. I fell in with the gangs again, thinking I'd learned everything I needed from Deben, but I was wrong. I overreached. Overstepped the mark, and paid hard for it.' I wanted to clear my throat, as if it could help me swallow unwanted memories. 'I escaped the prisons of Taymar and went back to Saraka and Deben. Since then I've spent my whole life breaking into places that aren't meant to be broken into. I've cracked locks all across the Reaches. Mostly in Krass, the Scatter Isles, and outlying parts of the Arc.'

'And you claim you are one of the best in all the Reaches. How come I have never heard your name, as you so incorrectly assumed?'

'A good locksmith doesn't want his name to be known except by those in the business. I'll have you know my initials can be found scratched into cracked vaults across all the cities of the east. And I am the best.' Her unmoving glare broke me. 'Or I *was*.'

'Who is the best, then? To those in the business?'

I wrinkled my nose through habit. 'Maybe Evalon Everass, a Scatter wench who has a talent for pretty combination locks and never taking a job she can't crack. Style, no substance. Also straight as an arrow. Works as a "consultant", whatever the fuck that means.'

'Quite.' Horix puckered her wrinkled, slate-grey lips. 'And you have never worked in Araxes before?'

'Never, despite you Arctians having the most impressive locks in all the Reaches. But sadly you deal more in half-coins than silver. I only deal in the latter. Closest I've come is some far-flung nobles on the borders who wanted to take a shortcut in their business affairs.' If you're looking to bankrupt a rival, it's far easier to empty their vaults than to outwit them in business.

'Tor Busk. A Skolman. Ever worked for him? Is he a man who dallies in your line of business?'

We were honing in on her point, I could feel it. The name rang a faint bell, but I never forgot an employer. 'Never heard of him.'

Horix was circling me now, frills sighing against the stone.

'And you came here for an "appointment", or so you called it?'

'I was offered a job. I decided to take it.'

'Was there no work for you in Krass? Picked every lock, had you?'

'Almost.'

'Who offered you this job?'

'A…' I hadn't prepared a lie, and it showed. I also liked to keep my employers private. 'A serek, I imagine.'

'You don't *know*?'

'I don't have to tell you, Widow, that most of the jobs I get offered are highly secretive. Many clients like to remain anonymous.'

Horix tapped the tip of her nose. 'Why don't I believe you?'

'Because you're naturally suspicious?'

'Because it strikes me as odd that a man of such a methodical profession, the so-called best in the Reaches, would take a job before knowing his customer, his requirements or his price.'

I winced, feeling pinned. It was a subject I had hoped to avoid. In all my thirty-four years I had never been as impulsive as the day I strode out of the door, hungover as sin, bound for Araxes. I had chided myself for many hours in Temsa's cell for it. You could call it the City of Countless Souls calling to me, if you'd like. I call it being almost penniless and still half-drunk.

I squirmed. 'You usually find out the details in person…'

Horix clapped her hands, as if dusting me off. 'If you'd like, I can reinstate Vex and you can go down to the—'

'I... I was eager to leave Taymar,' I blurted. 'I'd disappointed some people. One person, to be exact. An earl. Unfortunately he held the ear of many influentials in the underworld. I was named. Shamed. Ruined me from Krass to Skol and everywhere in between. All because I failed to complete the job he tasked me with.'

'Why?'

Why, indeed? It was a simple question with an easy answer. I stuck by my decision, no matter how much it had cursed me.

'Because it would have meant me dying. Have you ever heard of a deadlock, Mistress? No? It is a type of lock that uses the spell of binding. It takes the soul of whoever fails to crack it. Rarer than rare. So much so that the earl had not known. I am a fantastic locksmith but I am not an idiot. When I realised, the job was over. There was an argument with some of the earl's men who had been the muscle, and that brought the house-guards down on us. In the escape, several of them were caught and hacked down. One of the men just so happened to be the earl's son, there to make sure father's money was being well spent. Instead, he spent thousands of silver ensuring I never worked again.' I paused, gathering my thoughts. Usually, I never talked this much unless I had a beer in my hand.

'Within a few months, soon enough I was out of funds and living in either a tavern or a hovel. I never did it for the money, just the challenge and thrill. I was down to my last coin when I found a papyrus scroll on my doorstep. All it said was that my presence was requested in the Cloudpiercer for a matter of employment. There was a black seal of roses and daggers that I was to present at the Cloudpiercer, and a name. Etane. As for how he found me or how he knew of me, I had been intending to ask that in person. In any case, his note came at the right time and in my eagerness to restore my reputation, I left without another thought. Besides, you don't just ignore a summons from that sort of address…' I trailed off, noticing I was reeling off excuses.

I looked up to find Horix was wearing a surprisingly toothy smile, albeit yellow and full of dark gaps. I was surprised her cheeks weren't cracking. Her grey jowls suggested they hadn't had much practice.

'Did you say Etane?' she asked.

'I did.'

'Ha!' The cackle reverberated about the room. 'Etane!'

'Know him, do you?'

Horix kept her smile. 'As you have been kind enough to answer me, I will answer you. Etane Talin is a chamber-shade. Servant and guard to the royal line of Talin Renala. That seal is an old Talin seal. He's most likely serving the empress-in-waiting now the empress has apparently disappeared. What would Sisine be wanting with a locksmith, I wonder?'

I left her to her thoughts, busy with mine. *The empress-in-waiting wanted my services.* I had expected nobility, but not royalty. I quelled my brewing frustration with the idea that the job would have most likely ended with a dagger in my back. *An Arctian would rather pay with steel than silver*, as the saying went, and the royals are the deadliest of them all.

Horix clicked her fingers at me, dragging my attention back. 'Old Etane. He died over a hundred years ago in a feud between the Talin and Renala families. Two decades ago, he fell in with a bunch of fanatics – the Cult of Sesh – along with the rest of the idiotic royal family. In Emperor Milizan's time, you would have seen their members wandering freely about the Piercer. Red robes, always shades. They were the fashion of the day, but no more. They were proven treacherous. Milizan was murdered by his son, the emperor-in-waiting, and his empress was banished to die in the wilds of Skol. The Cult was prohibited from setting foot in the Core Districts ever again. Like the rest, Etane hung up his robe and went back to being a house-shade. Now he belongs to Sisine, it appears.'

Her mood had shifted like a sea breeze. The widow had seemed pleased. Now she frowned deeply, though I hadn't the foggiest idea why. I was too preoccupied with her mention of fanatics to care. The word shrieked through my head like a guard whistle. Once again, the widow had echoed the dead cat's message.

Over the past few days, I'd tried to stick to the notion that the encounter with Basht was merely a stress-induced hallucination. However, hallucinations don't usually crumple to a heap and stick around to leak shit. I couldn't explain the voice of the corpse, either. The only other explanation was that I had been bound wrong, and apparently become some lodestone for dead things with dire, cryptic warnings. *Not gods.* I couldn't bring myself to even think the word. That was madness, even in this world of ghosts. But it didn't mean I wasn't curious to find out whether the warnings were true. To save my own skin, of course.

When Horix was done scowling, she pointed me towards the door. 'I find you interesting, Mr Basalt,' she said.

'Thank you. But about this Cult—'

'And I see no reason why I shouldn't keep you as my personal shade for the time being. Let's see what other stories come to your mind, hmm? And remember what I said: you belong wholeheartedly to me. You will not breathe a word of our conversations. Otherwise…' She let a finger dangle like a sword, its tip pointing down through the floors to a certain stone box.

Despite my questions, I held my tongue. As I reached for the door handle, she fed me another tidbit.

'Perhaps, in time, if you prove yourself, I will consider informing the Chamber of the Code of your situation.'

I smiled, hating her as a fish hates the fisherman that catches him.

That hatred comes not just from a hook in the mouth, but the submission of all hope into the hands that threaded the hook. I was either Horix's supper, or she would show kindness and release me. However, looking down into that old face, wrinkled and puckered like a pig's neck, I saw very little kindness there, only plenty of sour years. It didn't look good, but it was the only helping hand I'd so far been extended.

'Thank you, Mistress.'

'Good shade. Now, fetch me tea.'

I bowed as low as I could manage, mostly to hide my irked expression, and let her shut the door on me. The guards watched as I shuffled between them, heading for the kitchens.

'Still better than the fucking coffin,' I muttered to myself when my feet met the cold stairs.

VEX WAS FULL OF ANGRY glares and mouthed insults. He stood on the other side of the vast kitchen, arms crossed and face all ascowl at me.

At first I mouthed back gibberish, making him bob his head, questioning me silently. Then I moved so that a kitchen ghost was between us, and kept doing so until he danced just to look at me. Lastly, I simply stared, long and hard, while he got angrier and angrier. Toying with others' emotions is always good fun, especially when they can't lash out.

I was disturbed from my amusement by a faint tap on the arm. The kitchen boy had finished constructing the elaborate lunch, and with a timid voice he explained it to me. Thin slices of cured quail and heart of palm with sugared rose petals. Fruit and honey, with sour cumin yoghurt. Papyrus stems with vinegar and grains. Honeyed dates. Pomegranate tea. Beer, warm as the mistress liked it, with a silver straw.

I balanced the elaborate tray across my forearms as he loaded it, plate by delicious-looking plate. I was glad I couldn't smell the food. It would have taunted me even more.

Before I made my way out into the dark corridors beyond the heat and hiss of the kitchens, I gave Vex one last look and a smile for good measure. If he'd had skin, it would have been flushing red. As it was, he'd taken on a purple hue.

To the quiet rattle of silver cutlery, I padded across the stone. My eyes were fixed on the food, making sure none of the tea or beer spilled, or none of the dates rolled off their little plate. It was hard keeping the tray in the air, never mind level.

I paused to readjust my grip and a date decided to make a bid for freedom. It wheeled to the edge of the tray, colliding with my thumb.

With the tray safely perched on a cabinet, I had the spare fingers for the date. It was a slippery bastard, drenched in honey that my vapours could not grasp at first.

Once I had it pinched, I held it up to the light of the nearby hallway. I remembered these from life, and how their dried skin put up a brief fight before succumbing to a bite, all juicy and sticky beneath.

I opened my mouth and let the fruit hover above my lips. All I longed for was the feel of it. Not the taste, just the space it would fill in my useless stomach. I wanted to know the very act of eating one last time.

The date passed right through me: slower than falling, held back by my vapours, but surely. It dropped on the floor with a tap, and I regarded it like a turd on the marble. With a humph, I set it back on the plate, dust and all, and wiped the tray with the end of my scarf.

The part of loss that slices the deepest is that you never know which moments are the last until they've already been and gone. The last meal, the last kiss and such. What hurts is how it pales to the glorious finale you might have imagined.

My last meal had been no mighty banquet; no roast pig and buttered apples, spiced carrots, or sausage stew. My last meal had been a watered-down soup with a salty fish head in it. I remember staring at it, pondering the ugliness of things forced to live below the waves.

My last kiss had been closely followed by a slap, not a sleepless night.

My last night's sleep had been in a stinking hammock, not a feather bed.

My last words had been, 'Fuck it', not the poignant goodbye I'd never planned.

And my last rutting? Far too expensive and far too long ago to bear thinking about. Shame always grinds a sharper edge onto a memory.

Widow Horix would be taking lunch in her library, it seemed. The guards admitted me after much patting and poking of my smock and tray.

She was back in her chair, a look of impatience on her wrinkles. 'Set it down,' she ordered.

I did.

'Not there.'

I moved it.

'Now fetch the table. I don't eat from my lap like a commoner.'

The small table was brought over and placed in front of her chair.

'Closer.'

The tray came next, and after a few cursory sniffs, she tucked in.

I had expected a pinch more refinery from a tal like Horix. The Arctians are famed for their elaborate, though extremely private, balls and dinners. Manners were like keys or silver in Araxes; they got you places. And yet here was Widow Horix, slurping down the strips of meat and pickled papyrus stems as if she hadn't eaten in a week. Judging by the fact she was mostly comprised of wrinkle, that seemed entirely possible.

'On the shelf, over on the far wall. A test for you,' she said around a brown mouthful of smashed dates.

I looked but couldn't see, so I wandered closer to roam the bone shelves.

'The box.'

A small lockbox sat alone, wood engrained with silver and jade. There was a complex lock on it with three keyholes. A fine design from the last century. Scatter Isle, if I wasn't mistaken.

'You see it?'

'I do.'

'Can you open it?'

I blew a long sigh. 'That is a rim lock with rotating cylinders, and those are a triple-tumbler bolt system with sticking pins. This box is resistant to bumping, shimming, and from the look of the wood, by-passing. Yes, of course I can open it.' I patted my empty smock. 'But I don't have my tools. A good locksmith still needs his tools.'

She slurped at her thick beer through her straw. It chimed against her teeth. 'Then you fail the test.'

'I—'

'I don't believe you to be a locksmith of any worth, or even a locksmith at all.'

That set my jaw. I'd always been partial to a challenge, especially if it was to prove my worth. That was part of what had dragged me to Araxes. Some wise old barmaid had once told me it was something to do with my childhood, but beer she'd poured me had removed most of the detail from that night.

I cast around, looking for slim and slender things. The library was short on curios besides scrolls and candles, and I hardly thought the widow would be happy with me breaking things. In the end I turned to her tray, and swiped several pieces of slender cutlery. She continued to chew, her eyes following me back to the box.

The knife was thin enough, but the fork's tines were too closely spaced. Over the course of minutes, I managed to bend two until they snapped. Then I found a long pin in an old tapestry hanging in a niche and angled it into a curve. Horix watched me throughout.

With a grumble, I held the makeshift tools in finger and thumb and bent to stare into the lock. I swore my senses had diminished since dying. Which was to be expected, I supposed. It wasn't just touch or smell; closer objects were more blurred to me, sound seemed more muffled, and echoes died on the first bounce.

So it was that it took me some time to grasp the improvised tools correctly, and to hear the clicks of the pins as I gradually took their innocence, one at a time. Twice I had to start again, knocking the whole lock out of alignment. I bumbled like a freshpick, and even though I doubted Horix knew a scrap about lockpicking, she almost certainly heard my muffled cursing.

With a sharp turn of the fork tines, the first lock finally gave up. The second was trickier, and I had to bend the pin into several shapes before I heard the grate of the cylinders lining up. Another twist, and it too fell before me. The third lock took under a minute to prime the lock, and with the knife blade, I turned it open with a satisfying click. That is the sweetest sound to a man in my trade; sweeter than the cry of a firstborn child. I hadn't heard it since the ship.

But the box was empty, and it made the thief in me feel just as hollow. It was like being punched in the groin straight after a romp beneath the sheets.

I found something smug in the widow's smile when I turned to face her. She had finished with her food, and now sat with steepled fingers. Her leavings could have fed a beggar for a week.

I slammed the lid of the box. 'There. Told you.'

'It took you some time.'

'Test me on something bigger, if you like. You'll soon see.' Tasting my old life had me thirsting for more. I wondered what use Horix had for a locksmith besides the usual Arctian ambition, and whether it had anything to do with her cellars.

'Perhaps I shall, but not today. We have talked enough and I have grown bored of you. Clean up these scraps, then clean my rooms. You'd best be as good with a polishing cloth as you are with fork tines and pins, Mr Basalt.'

'Yes, Mistress,' I said with another low bow. I could play the chamber-shade while she tested me. That, in a small way, was progress.

The widow departed into an adjoining room with a snigger. 'You Krass always look like you're trying to sniff your backsides when you bow.'

CHAPTER 17

LOT IN LIFE

Another bloody layer to the Cloudpiercer, says the emperor. Just clicks his fingers like that, and off we go. He thinks that an endless dead workforce means you can build endlessly, but he don't know the work it means for us that still breathe and beat. Senseless royal twats.

FROM THE DIARY OF MASTER OPHET,
GRAND BUILDER TO EMPEROR THEPH
DURING 552-569

NILITH WAS AFIRE.

She thanked the dead gods her face was covered. Her wounds would have been seared by the sun's rays and baking sand. Instead, a cloth covered her as if she were a corpse. It had been damp in the morning, but now it was dry as papyrus.

The day was hot but dark for her. Even movement and sound caused her to flinch. She winced behind her wrappings at every shout. Whenever footfalls came near, she had to wrestle her heart back down her throat.

At least the fear kept her mind off the pain. Her head throbbed chronically. Her knuckles were raw and hot where she had tumbled. Her face was still a mass of cuts and bruises, and now it was pasted in grit. Her throat felt like a desert cave.

'Get 'er up!' There it was: the shout she had been dreading.

Sunlight blinded her as a silhouette dragged the cloth from her face. She was seized by the bonds around her wrists and waist. She scraped along the scorching black sand, finding new pains with every tug.

Blinking hard, she tried to get her bearings. The day was cloudless. The tall stones around them looked like glass chambers filled with a dark smoke. In her dizziness, she swore she saw their surfaces moving.

Krona was sitting astride a black horse, a sword across her lap and fresh ash on her face. She was still wearing Nilith's leather jacket. The rest of the Ghouls were spread out behind her on their own horses: big burly mountain creatures. A few sat atop green scarab beetles, each as tall as the stallions. Their pockmarked carapaces shone in the light, and where the sun caught an edge, the green took on a rainbow hue like oil on a puddle. The insects burbled away to themselves behind their gnarled mouths and pincers.

Anoish still had Farazar's body on his back, and was tethered beside a man with a thick bandage around one side of his head. At the back of the group, a train of little ghosts glowed faintly in the sunlight. Half of them wore rough smocks; the rest were naked. One tall ghost stood at their end, looking as doleful as his charges. *Farazar.*

Krona poked Nilith with her riding whip. 'Recognise this?' She dangled a copper coin on a chain from her dirty fingers. 'I should thank you, eh? It'll save me some silver at the Nyxwell!'

Nilith snarled and struggled as best she could. It amounted to a great deal of wheezing and more pain.

'Tie her up, eh?'

Rough rope was thrust between her wrists and tied to a horse and rider. She looked up to find a grim man with one white eye nodding at her.

'I want to be at Abatwe by sunset, understand?' Krona shouted to her gang. In the light, Nilith could see there were almost thirty of them.

A dull moan rose and fell, like a bored wind.

'Away!'

The Ghouls moved off and Nilith was yanked into a stumbling walk. She felt like a jellyfish stranded on the Whitewash Beaches, all wobbly and transparent. She found a rhythm and an angle that hurt the least, and by the time they started to climb to the crater's lip, she felt almost alive again.

Nilith didn't know whether it was the beldam's good luck or the dead gods smiling, but she thanked both repeatedly for the blessing that Krona hadn't taken her life. For a moment, she thought about trading it to be rid of the pain, but the notion was fleeting, followed swiftly by a shudder. The Krass in her cursed such an idea. Hers were a stubborn people. It was one of the reasons the Arc had yet to swallow her lands. It was a place where old traditions and customs lived on. Where religion was not a madness. Where nobles were born of silver and family, not the number of dead they owned. It was a place where if something was started, it was finished. She would not give up. Not yet.

As the Ghouls made it over the edge of the crater, Nilith looked down at their zig-zag path and the country far below it. The Duneplains looked foreign compared to the Long Sands they had left behind.

Orange, green and silver-blue; the spread of sand held no single colour from the Firespar to the horizon. Where the dunes didn't reign, scrubland and white salt flats stretched for miles. Dark flecks of nomad caravans, soultrains and flocks of ostriches kicked up plumes of dust. At the bottom of the Firespar's slopes, where the foothills gradually turned to sand, a small town had made camp over a thin black scratch in the desert. Faint roads led away from the town in various directions. They were quick to fade into the ever-changing terrains of the Duneplains.

Where the sky met the earth, there was a smudge. It could have been cloud or heat-haze, but Nilith saw it as Araxes. It must have been the city, or the Outsprawls at the very least, but the more she squinted and strained, the more her head pounded.

The rope tugged at her and she jolted forwards, almost falling.

'Keep fucking moving,' grunted the rider, spitting something black at her feet.

The morning passed much the same way, with her falling behind and being sharply tugged along. As the hours passed and the path stretched, the tugging became more frequent, until she was almost being dragged rather than walked.

She could have cheered when Krona called for a stop and for water to be passed around. Nilith was given just a sip, but to her it felt like plunging her face into an ocean. She swilled the water around her dusty mouth, soaking the grit out of the cuts and cracks.

The rest was short-lived, but it sustained her for the next few hours of descent. The mountain's shoulder kept most of the heat at bay until late morning, when the fiery orb conquered the spires of the volcano.

The northern slopes were more cratered, as if the rock beneath had either sunk or had blown forth towards the distant sea. By the look of the huge pockmarked and smoke-black boulders that decorated the slopes, the latter was more likely. The Firespar had an old reputation for violence.

Her minder was silent throughout the journey. Every now and again Krona would leer over her shoulder at Nilith and say something to the milky-eyed man in a foreign tongue. He would only reply in grunts. No words.

Nilith held her silence. She didn't imagine she would be able to speak. Her face was still swollen from her beating and her tumble from the horse. She wondered how long she had before the mess became infected.

By noon, the path was following a curving route down the hollow of the northern slope. The going was kinder here, and Nilith could lean back to let her heels slide in the charcoal gravel. It was a chance to half-close her eyes, fade into the monotony of walking, and regain her strength.

Step by step, the landscape rose up to meet them, and the ground regained a more horizontal angle. The mountain's slopes flared for miles, similar to the brim of a witch's hat in an old Krass fairy tale. Gradually, the ground turned to folds, looking like black dough mashed up by some enormous child. Nilith had to scramble over the great creases of rock with her hands tied. Here and there, where bubbles hid, the horses' hooves punctured the stone with a puff of black dust. They barely twitched; they seemed built for this landscape. Anoish was more careful.

'Lost your fight, eh?' asked Krona, interrupting Nilith's thoughts.

It took a while to make her mouth work. Her words were malformed, rusty. 'No. Just biding my time, thank you.' Escape was a word that had been stuck in her mind all morning.

'What fuckin' time? We're not far from Abatwe now, eh? I'll see you sold by sunset.'

Nilith ignored her. No threats or witticisms came to mind, which was unusual for her. She blamed the heat.

'They'll have to fix up your face. But I'll tell them I found you like that, eh?'

Nilith eyed the sword on the woman's lap. It had a knack of catching the sunlight, and had been flashing at her all day. She wondered where her scimitar had got to, and which of these degenerates had it hanging from their belt.

On and on, Krona brayed. 'I reckon fifty gems for you. Forty-five if I'm feelin' generous. I bet forty for your ghost, seeing how fresh and undamaged he is, eh?'

'Not much to share around your crew.'

'You forget the other *ba'at*. Little ghosts, eh? They'll fetch a high price in Belish.'

'Despicable.'

'Is it so? I call it fair.'

'Murdering children? How is that fair?'

'We only murdered some. The rest we found in a burnt orphanage, near-dead from sun and swelterflux. Seemed a shame to let the creatures suffer. This is giving them a chance to live on.'

'As slaves, and it is no life. It is a half-life.'

'You citykind might call them shades, but it means the same as *ba'at*. As slave. That's what the dead gods left for us, eh? It is our lot in life.'

'Only because the city and the emperor say it is.'

Krona turned and nodded to Nilith's minder. He gave her a sharp smack around the ear, making her stumble. Her halter rubbed a strip of skin from her wrists.

'Enough, eh? No politics in the desert. Sand shifts too quickly.'

Nilith said no more and got on with the business of trudging.

The Arctians say the desert teaches each person a different lesson. If she had learned anything so far, it was that she was no longer as young as she thought she was. This gruelling quest had proved that in the first week. At least today she had an excuse; she had been beaten half to death by a desert psychopath, after all. Desperate times make desperate minds, and a desperate mind will always dig up more problems in its search for hopelessness. Hopelessness is the only way to be completely free from responsibility. Age was not the issue here. This was about the ill wills of unscrupulous folk. *Wherever there are no laws, or no strength to uphold them, lawlessness will flourish. Evil will abound*, she thought. It was a simple and universal truth, and in its inexorability, chilling.

Abatwe started as a pale smear in the distance. Within a few hours of toil, it became a sprawl of dome-shaped houses and a great wooden structure built over the crack that ran through the countryside. The Ghouls followed it, but kept at a respectful distance. Nilith could only see a dark rift and heard no trickle of water over the scuff of hooves and jolting of her bones, but she knew the Nyx when she saw it.

The adobe houses rose out of the ground like barnacles stranded at high tide. She could tell they had once been a dazzling white, but the sand and wind had eaten at their facades, tanning them grey and orange. A few of the larger buildings sported limp banners on bent poles, marking taverns and shops. A few motley guards and sellswords watched on from archways, wise enough not to make a challenge to Krona and her crew.

Despite its size and dilapidation, Abatwe seemed to be a hub of business. The spectrum of cloths and colours in the streets could have told her that alone. Though the sun was starting to sink, trade was still proceeding at stalls and in small squares between the buildings. People in dusty smocks and cotton rags browsed merchants' tables full of sparkles, colours or billowing smoke. Nilith tasted spices and meat in the air, and her stomach twisted in jealousy.

Krona halted her Ghouls by a fence of bone-white wood and chose four to accompany her. Anoish, Farazar and the train of little ghosts were brought up and Nilith was tied at their end. The horse nuzzled at her as he moved past, and she ran a hand over his nose. The rat man cracked his switch, cutting a red line across the beast's flank.

'Nuff of that!'

Nilith cupped a hand to her ear, nodding at his grimy bandages. 'Pardon?'

He blew spit through puffed cheeks and puckered lips. 'Lucky you're bein' sold, you cunt. I'd have carved bits off—'

Krona clapped her hands. 'Enough, Habad! You had your chance to wet your cock and she bit your ear off. Stay quiet if you want to come along, eh?'

She led them deep into the town, to the fervent bustle of a central bazaar. The Ghouls were immediately mobbed by buyers and sellers. Nilith was pawed and poked at. Pipe smoke was blown in her face. People tapped at her arms and chattered prices in languages she had never heard. Anoish whinnied behind her as unsolicited inspections were made. She bared her teeth and hissed.

Krona raised her sword and rested it on her shoulder. A space around her small convoy immediately opened up, and they moved on unbothered.

It turned out they were headed for the wooden structure poised over the river-cut rift. It was a simple thing, little more than a tall frame hung with thick curtains. They didn't form a solid ring, but were spaced around so that corridors opened up at specific angles. At their centre, there looked to be a well dug into the rift, and a stone font decorated with a mosaic of smashed pottery. Figures in robes stood around it. A Nyxwell.

A soulmarket sat before it, like a wedge between the town and the structure. The tents of caravans and soultrains were camped around the edges of the space. At the edge of the Nyxwell, there was a large hut roofed with palm fronds. Hooded figures waited around the smoke of a small brazier. Chains dangled from their belts. A bald man in a leather jerkin sat on a stool, heating up a variety of brands. Around the hut, a score of tables had been placed in a semicircle. Some looked official, while others were being used as footstools for slumbering soultraders. A handful of unsold ghosts and town guards slumped about, looking the paragons of boredom.

Krona chose one of the shabbier traders. With a mighty roar, she upended the table and the man that sat behind it. He landed in the dust, blinking hard and wiping drool from his chin. He froze when a sword buried itself in the table a few inches from his face.

'I think you're done for the day, eh? Move the fuck on.'

The trader scurried away, his felt hat clamped to his head.

Krona kicked the table upright, and after an impressive jump, stood atop it.

'Listen up!' she yelled over the chatter of idle business. 'I got a dozen fresh *ba'at* here. None of them older than twelve. Got me a perfect shade with a body ready to bind. Got a young desert steed. And I got a live one, too. Middle-aged, needs a bit of care but that's how we found her. Do I have any takers?'

Her men toured the crowds, knocking shoulders with the other traders and their hired muscle. To reinforce her point, Krona wrenched her sword free, and let it hang by her meaty thigh. 'Like I said, any takers?'

A few men and a woman shuffled forwards, tentatively eyeing the stock. Krona smiled. She hit the floor with a crunch and began to charm her customers by poking each ghost and making up some imaginary merits.

'She's good at sewing. This one can play the arghul. He lights a fine fire, eh?'

The buyers regarded Nilith with wrinkled faces. She stared back at them with hate in her eyes.

'This one was found beaten on the slopes of the Spar. Got into a bit of trouble, didn't you, eh?' Krona patted Nilith cheerily on the arm. 'She's a good cook or would make a good guard. Failing that, a mistress, eh, men?' She chuckled. 'All she'd need is a bit of water and salve. Maybe a dip in the Well if you have the gems. That shade there is a friend of hers, too. The unbound one. Some sort of lover's disagreement, I suspect, but they'd work well as a pair.'

The buyers hummed and smacked their lips. The woman came forwards to stare at Farazar's wounds, and when he shied away, a copper switch lashed him. As Farazar seethed, Krona took them aside to barter, leaving her goods and Ghouls to camp up beside the table.

Now that Habad's wily eyes were distracted by the crowds, Nilith immediately put her mind to escaping. She sidled up to Anoish. His bonds were double-tied, but if she couldn't free herself, she could at least free him, and maybe drag her and the body with him. It took some fumbling and breathless cursing, but in the end she untethered him from Habad's ride.

'Shh.' She ran her hands down his flanks. 'Easy. Not yet.'

In an effort to get closer to Farazar, Nilith made a show of finding a place to sit. One of the Ghouls spied her, and with a click of his fingers, she sat.

'Farazar!' she hissed, a little louder than she'd have liked. He shot her a sly look and she cocked her head. He drifted towards her, coming to rest within reach.

'My ropes. They're not copper thread.'

'Don't talk to me,' he said, unmoving. Several white lines scored the vapours of his naked back.

'You helped me before. You can do it again. Now untie my ropes!'

'Because I…' Farazar flapped his mouth. 'Because…'

Nilith rolled her eyes. Even that made her head pound. 'It's either stay here and get bound and sold to someone like that, or come with me.'

Farazar scowled. She saw his eyes slip to the woman who had come to stare at him: a dark-eyed and severe-faced nomad woman wrapped in dusty yellow cloth. 'You will just bind me later.'

'At least with me there'll be a later.'

Blue teeth gnawing at blue lips. 'No.'

'It's now or not at all. I refuse to let them bind you. And I will not be branded.' Nilith bared her teeth, letting him see her frustration. 'Ropes, damn it!'

He fumbled worse than she, still unpractised with his hands, but he got the job done all the same, and just in time. Krona was returning with her arms around two buyers. One, the nomad woman, was shown to the train of waist-high ghosts, while an obese man was pointed towards Nilith and Farazar. The man's eyes roved over every inch of them. His mouldy tongue flicked out, a lizard tasting the air. Nilith clutched the stray ends of rope in her fists, making it look as if she was still tied.

'Want him as your new master, Farazar?' she muttered.

'You drive a hard bargain, Master Gleeb,' Krona was saying. 'But I'll relent. Let's fix her up and then you can decide. Be cheaper than a binding, given the rise in Nyxwater prices, eh?'

Krona hauled Nilith up by the scruff of the neck and marched her towards the structure. A man in a grey robe, a Nyxite by her guess, met them at the steps to the font. Nilith struggled fiercely, expecting a quick knife to the back of the skull and a dunk in the water. Perhaps this man preferred his slaves alive after all.

'What will it be?' asked the Nyxite.

Krona surprised her. 'Healing.'

Struggling no less at the word, Nilith was pushed up the steps and shown to the font, lined with an array of assorted pottery shards. They looked like panes of coloured sugar, arranged to show only a thin white line of grout. Below her feet, between the gaps in the wood, the rift of rock widened to reveal a dark and oily pool of Nyxwater. It was shallower than she would have expected, almost dry. There was even a rickety ladder leading down to it. Beyond the pool, the water dribbled away into another pool.

'Sit her down,' said another Nyxite, a young girl barely out of her teens. Her hands shivered as she raised an earthenware bowl. Something sloshed within it.

'Bring the conveyor.'

'The what—'

Krona's hands clamped over Nilith's mouth, and a raised finger told her to be silent.

A withered and shaking ghost was brought forth. He looked too young to act so decrepit. A design of a circle and cross had been branded into the vapours of his cheek. With great reluctance, he placed his cold hands on Nilith's face and held them there despite her wriggling. A ghost had never touched her before. She did not want to breathe, lest she somehow inhale him.

After the solid clink of gems landing in a pan, the water was forced into her mouth, foul and bitter. It almost drowned her but she did not dare swallow. It was a cruel torture to be so thirsty and to be doused with Nyxwater.

'Enough!' ordered a male voice. The water and the cold touch were removed. The ghost was barely visible now, just a blue outline being led from the platform. Nilith spluttered and spat until she had emptied her mouth.

'What the fuck w—'

Krona bent down to her ear. 'You citykind have grown too precious, too disgusted by a *ba'at*'s touch to remember what they can do, eh? What they really are. Life after death.'

Nilith had heard rumours. *Wive's cures*. Like eating an apple in a storm to cure gout. Or bathing in ox-piss to take away warts. *Nyxwater and a ghost's touch*. Nobody in Araxes would have ever stood for such a thing.

She placed a hand gingerly to her face to check she wasn't somehow bound and ghostly. She wasn't, thank the gods. All she found were the lumps of bruises and the ridges of cuts. The wounds hadn't disappeared, but they had closed up. There was no pain, just a cold numbness.

'It hasn't worked.'

Krona snorted. 'No? Just you wait. Master Greeb here will be most pleased in a day or so, won't you?'

The man spoke in a thick desert dialect. His eyes were narrow, carrying concern. 'I trust so, Miss Krona. I trust so.'

'Trust away. My word's good. And final, eh?' She patted the pommel of her sword and the man was rapidly convinced.

Nilith was forced back to the dust, where the child ghosts stood in a small group. The woman was busy inspecting them. Nilith was pushed past them and on towards the hut, where the brazier waited with its glowing tools. The sight of them stirred fear in her. Her window of escape was a hairsbreadth, her plan still non-existent. Instinct began to kick in.

'No! No! You can't!' Nilith struggled once more, but Krona held her by the neck with iron fingers and threw her to the sand before the men.

'One more for you.'

The bald man looked up, turning between Krona and the trader Greeb. He held out a reed and a dirty piece of papyrus. 'Your brand. Sketch it out.'

Greeb drew a cross with an eye behind it, and the brander sighed. 'All rather elaborate. Set her down and hold her still. Chest? Back? Arm? Face?'

'Neck.' Greeb patted his throat. Nilith knew of an artery there, and how one small cut could bleed a man like Greeb in three minutes flat. She bared her teeth as Krona sat her on a stool and clamped one hand on her bonds. With the other, she wrenched Nilith's head to the side, exposing the sweaty flesh of her neck.

It took all Nilith's nerve to sit still and wait for her moment while the man chose his brands. He brought them from the fire, glowing at their tips, and scraped a shower of sparks on the sand.

The brander looked to Krona. 'Got her? Live ones tend to squirm.'

'Just fucking hurry up, eh?'

Nilith couldn't have agreed more.

The man held up a rod with a glowing cross at one end, and advanced with it balanced on a finger. As soon as she felt the heat of it near her skin, Nilith seized her chance. She wrenched her hands from their bonds and seized the brand by its rod. Without pause, she pulled it towards her, aiming to ram it up into Krona's face, just below the eye.

It met the woman's skin with a hiss. Her scream brought the entire soulmarket to a standstill. Krona tried to lean away, but Nilith pushed and pushed, the skin sizzling and popping beneath the glowing iron. As Krona broke her hold to flail at her face, Nilith burst away and pelted towards her horse. Krona screeched like a gutted cat behind her, but it gave her no guilt to grin as she ran. A brand would be a fine addition to all the woman's tribal smears.

'Farazar!' she yelled as she spied Ghouls sprinting at her.

She knew not whether he had slapped the horse or Anoish had guessed the plan, but the beast came bursting through the crowds, sending two tables and half a dozen men flying. Nilith used all her remaining strength to bound onto his back as he passed. She clung to his halter, knuckles white, legs splayed, and rotten corpse bumping her.

'Go!' she cried, though she needn't have bothered; Anoish was just as keen on freedom, and was currently using his hooves and barrel-like chest to drive the quickest path for the open desert. Behind them, Farazar was dragged along like an anchor, bashing people aside and promising retribution at the top of his lungs.

Before she was whisked into the streets, Nilith spared a glance for Krona, still writhing and screaming in the sand, Ghouls hovering around her. Her hands were clamped to her face and the brand lay smoking beside her, turning the earth black. Nilith found the time and saliva to spit in her direction.

Anoish did her proud, and with the help of shock and local stupidity, they managed to break free of Abatwe's crowds with nobody in pursuit. Nilith kept him following the rift, with his nose pointed towards the shadow in the north, where brushstrokes of clouds lingered. In the evening light they had taken on an orange tinge, like great beacons of war.

Nilith stared at them and them only, imagining the city behind them. It was the sum of all she could bear to think about. Not the pain, not the fear of Krona giving chase, not even the elation of escape. Just a simple direction.

All else could come later.

CHAPTER 18

INVITATIONS

The orphanage, as I suspected, was no more than a front for a soulstealing operation for the murdering, binding and sale of child shades to Scatter Isle princes. They have a strange taste for young half-lives, and judging by the number we found alive, dead or bound, quite a thirst, too. You will be pleased to know I delivered the emperor's justice to the ringleader on the orphanage steps. The others have been clapped in irons and await judgement at your leisure, Chamberlain.

Report from Scrutiniser Heles to Chamberlain Rebene in year 1000

COMEDY HAD ALWAYS DEPRESSED SISINE. Romance never failed to bore her. Even epics left her cold. But tragedy? Now that was a form of theatre to be respected. Tragedy was one of the world's only constants.

Unseen drums hammered out a low thunder as the bald woman onstage reached up for an apple dangling from a silver tree. The light caught the sweat on her dark skin, betraying how much she quivered with effort. An arrow was taped to her thigh. Smears of red paint decorated her to the knee.

The *Song of Saphet* was one of loss, murder, betrayal and greed; a tale whose chief concept was that nobody learns from their mistakes, and here was Saphet herself, doing very well at not learning as she reached for a poisoned fruit.

A gasp spread around the amphitheatre as there came a snap of a branch. Saphet clutched the apple close to her chest, raising her eyes to the sun to stare at Oshirim. At that moment, cymbals crashed, and water rained down onto the stage. The stone bruised wherever it fell.

Saphet stretched high, defying the gods by showing them the apple. A dark smoke began to curl around the pillars of the stage. Lamps flashed as lightning struck. With a roar, she tore a bite from the apple and chewed it proudly, juice and morsels spraying with the rain.

The drums stopped dead. The stage went dark but for a narrow beam of light in which Saphet stood, holding her heart and throat. She fell like an axe-bitten tree, landing limp as a doll in utter execution of her art.

The applause roared as the audience got to its feet. The empress-in-waiting stood with them, clapping the back of her hands gently. There was entertainment in watching others fail, but also in the knowledge that one could simply look on from afar, untouched, and imagine oneself succeeding where the Saphets of the world failed.

Sisine smiled broadly. She was definitely no Saphet. There was a woman who was too controlled by her emotion and greed. Sisine had those in abundance, but she also had buckets of restraint. And cunning. And Etane to mop up her mistakes, if somehow she ever made one.

Speaking of the dolt, he appeared as she waved away the shades that had been wafting ostrich-feather fans to cool her. She sniffed at him. 'There you are.'

He bowed shallowly. 'I've been hard at work, Princess.'

'You'd better have. Come.'

Sisine beckoned to the shades gathered at the edges of her balcony, and they rushed forward to lift her velvet couch into the air. Etane trailing behind, she led him to the hall where drinking and wandering from table to table being adored and flattered were the post-theatre entertainment. Araxes bred such sycophants, but it did wonders for the ego.

Theatregoers, tors, tals, sereks and celebrities: they all crowded her litter before they'd taken three steps. Her Royal Guard kept them at a safe distance as she smiled down at them all. Sisine did not move from her couch, for she was above them, literally and socially, and she liked it kept that way. It took the presence of the emperor or empress to bend her knee, and both were absent.

'My Empress-in-Waiting!' cried a voice. A man she half-recognised struggled through the crowd to match her litter's pace. It looked as if he were drowning in a river of rainbow silks and gold hats, crying out whenever he came up for breath. He had the dark swirls of official tattoos on his neck and hands, and wore formal black silks.

Her guards fended him off, but he held up two hands, and clasped them. 'Please! A word with you if I may, Highness! I am from the

Chamber of the Code. High Chamberlain Rebene!'

Sisine looked around, noting the sereks in the crowd, watching on. The mention of the Chamber had pricked their ears.

'Guards, allow him to pass.'

The man squeezed through the polished barrier of plate and mail and took a moment to adjust his dark clothes before approaching to bow. Sisine waved her hand, making her many bracelets chime. 'Your need for disturbing me?'

He came closer, making the guards twitch, and lowered his voice to a confiding whisper. 'Highness, is there somewhere we might speak?'

'Of which matter?'

He bowed again. 'The emperor's decrees, Highness.'

'This way.' Sisine pointed past the trays of slender glasses of beer and wine to a secluded section, raised above the floor and ringed by more Royal Guards. Her carriers gently deposited her litter beside a golden table. Etane stood close whilst the man took a plush seat at her side. He seemed unused to a perch so soft and yielding. He had trouble remaining upright.

'Speak, sir.'

'Your Highness. I am here on account of your, or rather your house-shade's, recent message to look into this spate of soulstealing.'

'If I remember correctly, my *command* was to do a better job of upholding the Code and the Tenets in this city, and to protect the tors, tals and sereks who employ you. But you may proceed.'

The man removed his square hat and laid it on his lap. His tattooed hands had a flutter to them. Perhaps it was the warm night, but sweat crept in beads from his receding fringe of tar-black hair. A topaz hoop dangled from his left ear. 'Well, Highness, I am afraid we are unable to do what you *command* without more funds.'

Sisine had practised her mother's look of displeasure for many hours.

Head back, eyes to the point of the nose, purse the lips. 'Is that so?'

'I wish it were not, Highness, but you know how inundated the Chamber is. With a hundred districts north, south, east and west, our proctors and scrutinisers are thinly spread. Most are in the Core Districts working alongside the Core Guard, but even with their help our coffers are constantly drained, month after month. As for recruitment... It is easier to cheat, steal and murder in Araxes than it is to live a lawful life and work for the emperor or the Code. We cannot fight such a mindset without more funds to spend on bodies and equipment.'

The empress-in-waiting balanced her slender chin on a clenched fist. 'You're telling me there is a direct connection between the level of crime and the amount of silver spent fighting it?' she asked in a dry tone.

The sarcasm slipped past Rebene like a raindrop off a duck's wing. 'Precisely, Highness. I've come humbly to ask you for your, or rather your father's, assistance.'

'Nothing can be done in the meantime?'

'I have my best scrutinisers hunting down leads on these disappearances, and listening for any sudden acquisitions, but we have found close to nothing. If somebody knows something, then they refuse to talk out of fear. It's a dangerous job, asking questions. One of my scrutinisers, a man named Damses, was found dead only yesterday, his notebook taken, a knife through his face. Pardon my brazenness, Highness.'

'It's quite all right.' Sisine held up a hand for a moment of thought. She could feel the eyes of the sereks on her again, peeking over the edges of their grand shelf. They huddled in their conspiratorial little packs, eager to know what business was being done and how much was being chipped from their promises. *Like wild jackals*. Boon's advice echoed in her mind, and begrudgingly she took it, careful not to disappoint them.

'How much, Chamberlain Rebene? How much do you need?'

The reply was a whisper. 'One hundred thousand.'

'One hundred thousand silver?'

'A month, Highness. Naturally.'

'Naturally.' That was more than most chambers of Araxes required in half a year, even the Chamber of Trade. And they were at least kind enough to generate their own revenue for the royal coffers. She took a moment to process the number. The Talin Renala family was extraordinarily wealthy, but in shades rather than silver. Sisine was second only to the emperor in wealth. She had her own hordes of half-coins, businesses, a range of investments some wizened old shades managed, and even a share of the royal army. *Could she spend for the emperor as well as speak for him*? She didn't hesitate.

Sisine waved for Etane to escort the man out. 'As these are my father's commands, I am sure he has budgeted for their carrying out.' She caught sight of a bobbing, glowing head in the crowd, and an idea formed. Sisine rose. The night's performance was not over. Rebene was now a prop to her.

'Too long have the Chamber of the Code's pleas gone unheard, and all the while you fight on the frontlines of law and order. Our great empire is built upon the Code. Surely we cannot ignore those responsible for upholding it. Defending it! I will see you get extra funds, Chamberlain. In fact, I will lend several hundred shades to your cause. A dozen phalanxes from the royal army. My own soldiers, in fact.'

She said it loud enough to garner an impressed murmur from the surrounding crowd. A hush fell in their corner of the hall.

High Chamberlain Rebene came to a stuttering halt. 'Your Highness, it is strictly against the Code for the Chamber to employ half-lives. In all good conscience I—'

'And it is against my code, Chamberlain, to leave my people starved of sleep, fearing for their lives every time the sun sets.' Here she was, like Saphet upon the stage. 'I hear rumours that times are changing in this proud city. I, through the might of my father, will make sure they change for the better. Take my assistance.'

Amidst the applause and gentle cheering from the audience, Rebene shuffled backwards, eyes glued to the floor and full of sweat. 'I will discuss your kind offer with my magistrates,' he said.

'You do that.' Sisine waved her hands and a serving shade appeared with a drink. She took the flute of crystal back to her seat and beckoned Etane to join her. Not to sit, but to stand near her. Near enough to be heard, at least. From there she could watch the milling of the theatre-goers, and listen to the rustling of their voices and jangling of heavy jewellery.

'Soldiers on the streets? Those shades are numb in the brain. Skittish. War does that to a soul, whether it's wrapped in flesh or not,' whispered Etane.

'Half the Core Guard are veterans from the wars in the Scatter, dead and alive, and you don't see them going on murderous rampages. Besides, they are for show. What better to convince the populace of an emergency than soldiers on the streets, indeed? Better still, it will keep the Cloud Court quiet for a time.' She shook her head. 'Though I don't know why I should be explaining myself to you. Stop questioning me and tell me what you have found out.'

'I've found our man.'

'Who?'

'Boss Boran Temsa. Tavern owner. Soultrader, possible stealer.'

'I told you to keep looking. I still refuse to believe a lowlife, minor soulstealer is behind the disappearance of these nobles. The audacity of such a thing—'

'He's not as minor as you would think. People say Temsa owns Bes District and has dealings with the next four districts over, that he's shrewd and connected. I followed him most of yesterday. He has wagons coming in and out the arse-end of his tavern, day and night. It's likely he has both the resources and the mettle, Your Magnificenceness.'

'I still gave you a command.'

Etane sighed. 'It would have been a waste of time, if you don't mind me saying so.'

'You mind your tongue, half-life,' she hissed.

'Temsa also has a shade in his employ. A man I used to know named Danib. A shade far older than me. Died back in the year five hundred and something down in Belish, waging a one-man war against the local populace. Used to call him Ironjaw back then.'

'Sounds like a barbarian.'

'He was, at least before he met the Cult. They freed him for a time, until a few decades ago he sold his coin back into indenturement to work for the likes of Temsa. Almost unheard of, but I guess there's not much killing to be done in the Cult. He's been wetting his sword ever since.'

Sisine would have spat were she not being watched by the elite of Araxes. 'Ha! Lies. The foul fanatics know more about back-stabbing than an Arctian royal. They seduced my grandfather, poisoned my family. I will not have them spoken of.'

'You don't need to tell me, Princess. I was there, don't forget—'

She scoffed at him. 'Trust me, this house never will. It's why you still wear a gold feather and not a white.'

Etane took a moment to swallow. 'But perhaps it means our man could have a connection with them.'

Sisine's head snapped around. 'With the Cult?'

'Changes a few things in that grand plan of yours, doesn't it?'

'You don't think they were behind the disappearance of our locksmith, do you?'

'Thanks to you having the man who gave us Basalt's name killed, and the men that told him, I'd say we've been pretty discreet. Though it's likely. They have sharp ears. And I still haven't found a trace of Basalt.'

'Devious fiends.' Sisine quashed her anger with a sip of frosty spirit, sweet with fruit juices. She let the sting of it linger in her mouth.

'So?'

She tutted. 'Invite him. I will gauge the man, see what he knows. What his intentions are.'

Etane shook his head. 'You expect truth and allegiance from a lowlife soulstealer?'

'You should know better than anyone, Etane, that I spent my formative years ignoring the scrolls my tutors said I should read. Instead I spent my time reading people. This man is ambitious for a reason. I will find out what that reason is. Then I will bring him under my wing and manoeuvre him in certain directions. Against the Cult, if needed. In any case, he may be able to bring about the chaos and fear I need to drag my father from his vault.'

'And here I was thinking I did the dirty work.'

Sisine snorted. 'Now you can do the messenger's work. Go speak to this Boran Temsa. First thing tomorrow.'

'Would it not be wiser to send—'

'First thing tomorrow.'

'Aye.'

'In the meanwhile, I shall have another glass.' The empty flute dangled between her finger and thumb.

'As you wish… Princess.'

'WERE YOU BORN THICK AS donkey shite or did you pick it up along the way?'

'Boss, I—'

Boran Temsa slapped the man hard across the face, making him whimper. 'Fucking moron can't even speak properly.'

Temsa hobbled away, wiping his hands with a silk kerchief. He stopped beneath a grate in the ceiling and stared up into the shaft of white sunlight. 'Explain it to me again.'

There was much panting as he composed himself. 'Boss, I've already told you everything.'

'Danib.'

A mighty blue hand encircled the man's neck, lifted him, and pinned him to the wall. His heels drummed at the stone.

'All right!' he wheezed.

Temsa nodded, and Danib threw him across the cellar. He came to a snivelling halt at Ani's feet. She spat on him before kicking him away.

'Speak, Omat.'

He drew himself up with hands splayed, as though Temsa had an arrow nocked and trained on him.

'All right. I was in *The Jackal's Hall* with Pamec and a couple of the other lads, few days ago now. We were talking about nothing. Just rumours of the Nyxwell dryin' up and Abbas Shem's girls, down the road. You'd just paid us, see?' He paused to swallow. 'I noticed this man sitting near us, smiling every time I caught his eye. Said he worked on the docks, for the soulships that take the shade armies out to the Scatter. Said more and more were going out each day. Then he told us about a legion of the emperor's soldiers that had just returned from Harras. If they were flesh they would have been in ribbons, he said. Covered in white wounds where copper had gouged them, he said.'

Temsa waved his hand in a rotary fashion.

'So we keep talking. He buys us drinks, asks us what we do.' He smacked his lips. 'I swear we never said no names, just told him how we worked as guards for an up and coming tor. That's what we and the lads called you, Boss. No names. Said you'd just made a good takeover. Not me. Pam said it like that, so we all laughed. He did, too, and so it went. By the end of the night, he kept asking whether you had a job for 'im. Maybe as a house-guard. We thought he was joking. I hung back to give him the name of the Slab, and what to say. Then he says thanks, whispers something real smug, and walks off. I get the suspicions and grab him by the arm, and the fucker pulls a knife. I hit him, he hits me. I get out my steel and put it through his teeth. Choked him on it. I check him for stuff, as you do, and see all these smart tattoos. Then I find this scroll of notes and names. Mine was on it. Like I said, he had a ring on a chain, too, some glyph of a woman with scales and a star.'

'The dead goddess of justice, Mashat.'

'Yeah, her.'

Temsa stalked across the floor, taking his time, his steps a musical clatter of boot, cane and copper claws. Omat was quivering by the time his shadow fell over him.

'Thank you for that tale. I just needed to hear it once more to know somebody was capable of being that stupid.' Temsa brought his face close. Ani placed a hand on the man's shoulder.

'Do you know what a ring with the goddess of justice on it means?'

Omat shook his head.

'It means you knifed a Chamber of the Code scrutiniser, you cretinous cunt!'

'I didn't know he had it on him!'

Temsa stamped his left leg onto the man's sandalled foot. He screamed noiselessly, face frozen in pain. Blood pooled around his foot.

'Have you ever seen the inside of the Chamber of the Code, Omat? I didn't think so. There are stacks of scrolls and papyrus sheets so high they had to knock out two floors above the hall. Stacks so high that if the Chamber ever opened its doors, mountaineers would flood from across the Reaches to climb them. Complaints, claims, letters, cases, all piled up for eventual review. It takes years for them to migrate across the hall. They say people die in there when a stack collapses, which sometimes they do, only to be found days later.' Temsa withdrew his claw. 'And do you know the only thing that can move a case up the stacks faster than anything, Omat?'

'No?' said a quivering voice below him. Temsa was looking at Ani.

'The death of one of the chamber's own. It's like if somebody murdered one of your lads. You'd want a piece, correct? Sharpish, right?'

'Yes.'

Temsa raised his hands. 'There you have it. Now, thanks to you, good old High Chamberlain Rebene might come looking for a piece of me, put me in irons and take me to the Chamber of Punishment. Right now, he doesn't have a shred of proof, but just imagine what would happen if he found out I was blackmailing a banker's son and sigil, hmm? Just imagine.'

'Shit would go down, Boss,' said Ani.

'It would, Miss Jexebel. With great intensity.'

He strode away, leaving Omat to paw at his bloody foot and wonder whether it was the last wound he'd receive that night. Temsa had already decided for him, but he wanted to wait. A bit of grovelling never failed to brighten his day. He picked at his manicured nails.

'Please, Boss. I didn't know. I was tryin' to protect you.'

'Really? Because it looks to me like you were endangering everything I've worked for so far.'

Omat began to shuffle across the stone, wiping snot from his nose. 'Please! I'll do anything. I'll work harder. I'll keep my mouth shut. I'll keep my ears sharp and my blades sharper. I promise.'

'Ani, if you please.'

The woman took a moment to smile before grabbing Omat by the collar and throwing him against the cellar wall. A humongous axe chased him, striking him in the neck. As the echoes of the almighty clang died away, the body fell but the head stayed put atop the embedded axe blade. Omat's eyes still whirled about their sockets, his mouth gasping like a fish plucked from the water. His last moments, though drawn out, ebbed away with the blood pouring down the wall.

Ani wrenched her axe free of the sandstone and the head tumbled to join its body. She thumbed the red blade.

'Fucking Omat. Will 'ave to sharpen that now,' she said with a tut.

Temsa sighed as he fetched another kerchief for his foot. 'Well, if you will choose to be dramatic, you have to suffer the consequences.'

Ani nodded sagely. 'I suppose.'

'Bind the body and have him sold cheap. He can still be a labourer in the southern mines. Kal Duat'll take any—'

A shout echoed down the corridor. 'Boss!'

'What?'

Tooth appeared in the archway. Her heavy breathing stopped the moment she saw the body lying in two bits. 'I can come back when you're not buthy?'

'What is it?'

'There'th a thade here to thee you.'

Temsa shot a look at Danib. 'What shade? In red robes?'

'No. He'th got a gold feather, though. Lookth important for a thade. Well drethed.'

'And what does he want?'

Tooth wiggled a finger in her ear. 'I don't know. I jutht came to find you thtraight away.'

Temsa bit his lip, trying to bleed out some patience. 'I see. And why you, dare I ask?'

'Everyone elthe looked buthy.'

'Right. Lead the way,' he said, giving in. 'Danib. Follow.'

With the big shade in tow, Temsa wound his way through his honeycomb cellars and up to his office. Morning light spilled through the shutters and drapes, casting spears of smoky air.

Temsa dragged out his chair with a squeak and automatically reached for his pipe. 'Have him fetched.'

Danib poked his scarred head into the stairwell and slapped the blade of a hatchet against the wall three times. Tooth got the message and soon enough, Temsa heard feet on stairs.

Tooth came in first, followed by a smart-looking shade. Temsa wasn't sure if he'd seen the like before. The suit was ill-fitted, but of fine cloth. The gold feather on his breast glinted with metal; no cheap dyed thread there. There was a poise to the shade that betrayed some breeding, some noble blood that had once run through his body. Had he not had the mark of being bound, Temsa would have thought him a free shade. Maybe a tor.

He was currently staring at Danib. The big shade was staring right back, almost as if they recognised each other. Temsa broke the silence.

'To what do I owe this unexpected pleasure?'

'Master Temsa, my name is Etane Talin. I represent a very important figure in the city who is keen to meet you, to discuss common interests.' The accent was Arctian, but clipped, almost royal. So was his last name: *Talin*. One half of the current ruling Talin Renala family. *Etane* sounded rather familiar too, but he couldn't think why. Temsa was immediately intrigued, but he kept it from his face.

'Are they keen on beer?'

'Pardon?'

'Your employer. Do they like taverns?'

'Not particularly.'

'Smoking pipes?'

'No.'

'The bartering of souls for profitable gain?'

'She has an extensive retinue, if that is what you mean.'

'A she, is it? What I mean is, it doesn't sound like we've got any common interests at all. So the question is, why would I be interested in meeting with her?'

This Etane was a confident bastard. 'Common goals, then. And if that doesn't interest you, then how about mutual gain?'

Temsa held a taper to a lamp to light his pipe. He let smoke billow before he answered.

'Now that I like. And just who is this mistress of yours? This "very important figure"?'

The shade raised his chin. 'I trust you can keep this invitation confidential. To our two parties alone.' He looked at Danib for some reason. The big shade didn't even blink.

'Of course.'

'Her radiant Highness Sisine Talin Renala the Thirty-Seventh.'

Inwardly, Temsa felt a rare stirring in his stomach. Some might have called it surprise, joy even. Outwardly, it looked as though he hadn't heard. 'What a mouthful.'

'Excuse me?'

'Quite the mouthful! And a handful too, no doubt. I hear she's taking charge, now that the empress has disappeared and the emperor still refuses to come out of his shiny closet.'

'You put too much stock in street rumours, sir. The empress has not disappeared, she is attending to business in her homeland.'

Temsa grinned, tapping the pipe-stem on his teeth. 'Of course she has. Knowing you royals, she's likely already dead and bound.'

'Will you accept the invitation or not?'

'I will. You have me curious, and it's not every day a man of my years and my position gets invited to the Cloudpiercer to see an empress-in-waiting, now, is it? Will the emperor be joining us?'

'I'm afraid the emperor will remain in his Sanctuary.'

Temsa nodded. 'Wise man. If I owned two million shades, I'd be a hermit too.'

Etane bowed sharply and headed for the stairwell. 'Oh, and if you could ensure you are dressed appropriately for royal company, that would be most appreciated. Perhaps a smarter suit.'

With a scowl, Temsa dragged out his leg and let it thump on the desk. 'That good enough for royal company?'

The shade twisted his lips. 'Maybe a polish wouldn't go amiss. That should clean the blood off.'

'Danib, get him out of here.'

But Etane was already gone. He had been royally trained; he knew when it was time to exit somebody's presence.

Temsa chuckled to himself, bringing his foot back down with a metallic thud. 'A princess, indeed. Well, as shittily as this day began, it's certainly taken on a brighter shine.'

Danib was staring at the doorway.

'You know him, don't you, brother?'

Danib nodded.

'Let me guess. You shared some years in the Cult together?'

Another nod.

'Then you're going to write down everything you know about Etane, and Sisine Talin Renala the Hundred and Forty-Ninth, or whatever, and then you're going to have the shades pick out the finest suit they can find. Perhaps something from Tor Merlec's collection. Or we shall see what Tor Kanus has to offer when we visit him tonight.'

Danib growled like a bear catching the scent of blood.

CHAPTER 19

JEALOUSY

If you want to eat, then you'd better slit a throat.

OLD ARCTIAN SAYING

THE SUNLIGHT POURED THROUGH THE skylights like an old bully, waving through a cottage window to taunt and remind me of a past beating. It made my vapours prickle.

I withdrew the lockbox out of the rays and breathed a sigh of relief in the shadows. I glared at the empty sockets of the gold skull emblazoned on the box's top. Whatever grand name and seal had once decorated its forehead had been filed away. It was a tough little thing with a dozen different tumblers to pick, rotating on rings within the cylinder. Something from Belish, where they use tiny children's fingers for fashioning such locks.

It was the tenth challenge Horix had set me that week, each one trickier than the last. I was growing bored of her tests. All that work and I still had no idea what I was being tested for. If I'd still had skin, my thumbs would be worn and blistered by my makeshift tools. At my request, the knife had been filed and my tines replaced with a thin hook; metal from the hinge of another box I'd broken, literally speaking.

'Concentrate, Cal,' I told myself, something to interrupt the constant clicking. My mood was fouling my hands. 'Fuck!' The tumblers sprang back into place. I'd slipped and touched the spring instead. *Novice error.*

I repositioned myself over the box, faced the lock to the ceiling, and tried again.

Knife in, turn left three notches. Press. *Click.* Forwards. Right halfway. Find it. *Click.* Third tumbler. And so on, until the last two. These were deep in the lock and therefore unpractised. I used my knees to steady my arms as I slid the knife further in. I found the penultimate tumbler's notch easily. *Click.* The last had no ring; it was just a delicate matter of finding the right tumbler. There seemed to be a range. *Decoys.*

I racked my brains, imagining where all the other tumblers lay, and how they moved should the key turn. I mentally clambered over cogs and wheels; measuring and testing, drawing rough blueprints as I manoeuvred them around to examine every angle. It was a knack I'd learned largely through boredom. A young child with two vacant parents, no friends and a hundred miles of steppe to himself tends to live more in his imagination than in real life. It had given me a fiercely visual mind, and that was my strength. The key to lockpicking, pun intentional, is one part engineering, one part skill, and two parts imagination. At its heart, it's a duel of wits between the locksmith and the ingenuity of the fucker that dreamt up the design in the first place.

Only when I was certain did I turn the cylinder, using the flat of the knife as a key. There came a satisfying round of clicks as each of the three bolts fell open.

I'd gotten used to finding the boxes empty and fruitless, with no prize for me besides the satisfaction of breaking the lock. To me that was only half a prize. This box, however, held a small scrap of papyrus, flour-yellow against the pink velvet interior. A glyph had been painted upon it in red ink.

'Room?' My Arctian was no good, but it was improving with the time spent in Horix's tower. It was a tough language. First you had to crack the glyphs – all forty-three of them – and then the actual language itself. The glyphs were odd squiggles, descended from the hieratic language the Arc used to use thousands of years ago, when a Long Winter had apparently covered the land in ice. Personally, I couldn't imagine such a thing.

This was a tower of rooms. I wondered which one the leathery old bat was referring to. I decided it would be her room. It was a simple place to start.

I took the box with me, struggling to balance it on my stomach. It irked me that I had to spend eternity with my large belly. It was my fault for spending the last year patronising a swathe of Taymar's taverns. Alive, there's always a chance of change. A spot of exercise. More vegetables. Fewer pints of beer. These could all have helped me. I had never let them, and that was my own fault. Now dead, I was stuck a pudgy fellow, and there was nothing I could do save for wearing a bigger smock. Or an enormous scarf. At least at times like these, with a bit of tensing, my faithful belly formed a useful shelf for heavy things like bothersome lockboxes.

I waddled my way up the stairs, having to readjust the box twice before the summit. It was warm high in the tower, and a hot breeze wafted across my feet. Windows must have been open.

The widow was in her chambers as I guessed, gazing down at the city from her balcony. The drapes had been tugged aside yet they still danced in the rushing air, reaching towards me as I stood in the grand archway.

I was getting the feeling that Horix fancied herself quite the actress. Every interaction seemed staged, every moment with her scripted, or at the very least defined by a beginning and end that she had preordained. Even now, she was poised at the window, no doubt ready to use the vista to manufacture a point or opinion.

I waited for her to notice me. Part of me wanted to see her break form, to turn around and check her audience had arrived. To my irritation, she did not. After several long minutes, I set the box on the table with a clunk and stood before the balcony, hands clasped in front of me.

'Did it beat you?' she asked without turning. The hot wind brought me her words.

'Not in the slightest, Widow.'

'Ten boxes in a row.'

'Did I mention I was a locksmith, not a boxsmith?'

'A lock is a lock, you told me.'

'Yes, but—'

'Have you ever seen such a grand city, Caltro?'

Here we go.

'Come.'

I moved to stand by her shoulder and blinked in the bright light of the morning. The sun was behind us, but despite the shadow of the tower, the city's white roofs and mustard sandstone caught its glare.

Covering my eyes with a hand, I followed the tower's long black silhouette out into the city. Araxes roared as ever, filling the air with the sounds of commerce and life; the screeching of parrots and mewing of gulls; the dull clunk of marching feet and hooves; a thousand traders working their lungs; and the machines cranking away within factories. Every now and again I could hear a lone clang of a distant bell, or a boom from the docks. Here and there, a scream.

The Troublesome Sea ran along the horizon, reaching out west until it became a blur, indistinguishable from the yellow of the land and endless city. I looked south and tried to see the reaches of Araxes, the Outsprawls. They were as distant as the sea's horizon. Between them and me, great pyramids and knife-blade towers poked out of the dust like unreachable islands. If I squinted, I could see the orange smudges of a sandstorm against the azure sky.

Horix was playing the guide now, pointing eastwards. 'The Oshirim District, there, home of banking. The District of Bones, it was once called, when the banks began the tradition of decorating their buildings with painted skulls, many hundreds of years past. See the triangle of towers and that long avenue? That's the Avenue of Oshirim. His statue is behind that ugly lump of a building. Beyond that, the Fish District. And then the High Docks, home to some of the oldest parts of Araxes, like the Spoke Avenues that spread out from the Grand Nyxwell. Do you see?'

'I do.'

'Beyond them to the west are the Low Docks, where you came in, I believe. What was the name of your ship again?'

I'd already told her twice, and I knew her memory was as sharp as a purse-cutter's blade. '*The Pickled Kipper.*'

'Indeed. There, you see? That's Tal Fenili's compound. Cannot bear heights, that one, which is likely why she built an empire of warehouses. And there, King Neper's Bazaar. Five thousand stalls sit under those canopies, Mr Basalt. Almost a district in its own right. And beside it, the Spice Groves.'

I saw the vast sprawl of colour between the buildings, like a patchwork quilt. If I angled my head to the wind, it seemed most of the city's roar came from its direction. I should have headed there for Vex's challenge.

Her finger moved to the core of the city. 'Beyond that, you can almost see the horns of the Grand Nyxwell. Behind the Chamber of Military Might, that other great cube of a building is the Chamber of the Code Older than the Piercer, it is. The queues of petitioners and claimants and officials go around and around it like water down a whirlpool. Weeks, they can wait in those lines. No high-roads for the nobles either. Everybody queues before the Code.'

As I was debating how much I hated queues, she turned to me. Her cowl had been shoved back in the wind, and her thin grey hair was trying to escape its tight bindings. She had painted her face today. Thick black lines of paint underscored her eyes.

'They say Araxes is so vast that not even a free shade could see it all. Now there is a growing community. That oddly-shaped lump of pink over there is Serek Boon's tower, a free shade who sits on the Cloud

Council. He's not the only one. They live like any other serek, or tal, or business owner, or trader. Free of the Tenets. Is that what you want, Mr Basalt? A white feather on your chest?'

It was, but I made a show of thinking. She saw it as an opportunity to speak some more.

'After all, why wouldn't it be? Why else would you try to claim your innocence? Implore me to help you? It makes perfect sense. What else is there for you now except to be free?'

I did not want to stay in this sprawling hell. I turned my head to the wide expanse of grey between the buildings to the east. My home lay far beyond that rippling horizon.

The widow had read my thoughts. 'A home, I see. Of course, throwing your coin into the Nyx is another type of freedom, but I would guess you would rather be free to make your own choices.'

I nodded. I wanted to shudder at the thought of spending another moment in that dark, endless cavern that I knew waited beyond death. Horix had cut to the heart of the matter. 'That's what any person wants, and the only thing left of worth to a ghost,' I said.

'Naturally.' Horix turned back to the city, and half-closed her eyes. It was coming. I could feel the pause lengthen as she built to the point of all her nattering. I wondered if she'd once known a place in politics, or whether eighty or so years in Araxes had just beaten this personality into her. 'What if I were to make you free? Gift you your half-coin? It would be quicker than spending half a decade in the Chamber's queues.'

I had to keep myself from blurting out the answer. 'I would accept, Mistress. But you don't seem the sort of woman to be so charitable. At least not for free.'

Horix clicked a finger in my face before sweeping indoors. 'Very astute, Mr Basalt.' She occupied a spot on a long couch and gathered her frills about her. 'I want you to break into a vault for me.'

'Why?' I always ask. You learn to, after a while.

'The why is not part of the bargain.'

'What kind of vault?'

'A big one. Possibly one of the most complicated locks in the Arc, I hear.'

My fingertips brushed against each other, as they tended to do when I itched for a new challenge. 'Is it to do with this Cult you mentioned?' I had been eager to press her on that subject since she had first scowled at their name. She scowled again now.

'No.'

'What you're building in your cellars?'

Her fist pounded a cushion, unleashing a puff of grey dust. 'Enough! You do not have the luxury of questions, half-life. Give me an answer.'

'I'm wondering whether I have a choice.'

'I could command you, of course, threaten you, but then I would not feel obliged to reward you. I find half-lives, just like people, work better when there is something in it for them.'

I remembered the last job I had so hastily accepted. I needed more. 'I want more information. And assurances. Written assurances.'

Horix's pleasant face took on a moody slant. Her painted eyes narrowed into dark slits. 'Do you not take me at my word?'

In truth, I absolutely did not. I tend not to take the word of most people, especially those richer than me. Of which there are many. Nor do I find it easy to trust those who buy my soul at auction and lock it in stone coffins. I said as much.

'I would have thought the last few days would have changed your mind. I have even overlooked your many, many failings as a chamber-shade. You are a far cry from Vex, but you can still be useful to me. Vital, even. In return, I can be vital to you. Do not wear this opportunity out with stupidity or pride.'

I felt like smiling. In her eagerness, Horix had betrayed my position, and for once it turned out to be a rather good position. *She needs me.* Whether design or luck had delivered me to her – I was inclined to believe the latter – the old crone was up to something that required me to pull it off. I was the key to her lock.

'Will you do it?' Horix pressed me.

'Where and when?'

'The where is none of your concern, either. As for the when, it will be when I say so. Weeks, perhaps. No time at all to a creature of immortality like yourself. Now, do you agree?'

Weeks. Biting my lip as hard as I could, I decided to follow this thread and see where it led. Being needed can keep you alive a lot longer than you think, even when you're dead. At the very least, I got to find out what she was hiding in her cellars. At most, I would earn my freedom, and then my justice. All I had to do was bide my time and play chamber-shade.

'If you can write it down, we have a bargain.' Habit made me stick out my hand. Horix regarded it like the proffered hand of a leper and I took it back.

'If I must.'

'And I will need my tools.'

The widow tutted sharply. 'You can have new tools.'

'Only if my others can't be found. They are special to me.'

'You expect me to barter with Boran Temsa for them back? He's no doubt hawked them by now.'

I lowered my head. Crafting something with your own hands imbues a special kind of worth. It's why my initials had been so proudly scratched into my tools. I made a mental note to peruse King Neper's Bazaar or the markets around the docks when I was free and flush, even if there was only the slimmest of chances I might find them there.

'Will there be anything else, Mr Basalt?' asked Horix snidely. Her restraint was visible. A blue vein in her forehead throbbed.

I thought about it, but shook my head. 'Not presently, Mistress.'

'I'm glad. You may return to your alcove.'

After bowing, I went to turn, but she caught me with a tut.

'Not that way. Downstairs. Back where you belong.'

'Down…?' As her personal chamber-shade, I had been given something resembling a broom cupboard outside the door to the widow's chambers. Roomier than my last lodgings but no less degrading.

Horix chuckled like a snake coughing. 'You thought you would continue to be my chamber-shade? I wanted to watch you. I wanted an excuse to test and question you without arousing suspicion. I have done that and now our bargain is struck. You're quite atrocious as a chamber-shade, and I shan't live with that. Not one moment more. Vex has been in my possession for twenty years. You have barely been here twenty days. Until there is a vault to unlock, you will continue your duties. In fact, you may go and inform Vex for me. I believe he has just returned from the bazaars.'

With that, she left the library in a flurry of black frills. I stood alone, jaw working away, wondering whether I had heard her correctly. I could not have been "atrocious".

Just as I was about to leave, Horix returned bearing a short scroll, no thicker or longer than a thumb. She ripped a strip of papyrus from it and showed me a scrawl of Arctian glyphs and a seal of three skeletons stamped into the fibres. I tried to make sense of the handwriting.

'There. Proof of our bargain and my promise of freedom. Justice you may seek on your own.'

I graciously accepted it, and as I always do when in awkward situations, took a clumsy stab at humour. 'I will show this to my legal adviser.'

Horix snorted, crooking a finger towards the door. 'You do that.'

As I reach the corridor beyond, she yelled one final condition after me. I could not see her, but the echoes of her rasping voice chased me.

'And you are forbidden to go anywhere but the confines of this house! You are my property, understand?'

My response was flatter than the papyrus I clutched in my palm. 'Yes, Mistress.'

VEX LAUGHED SO HARD HE almost pitched into his pan of boiling water. I had half a mind to finish the job, but the thought of another spell in the sarcophagus stayed my hand.

'Oho, what a shame, Jerub! What. A. Fucking. Shame!' He punctuated his words with pokes at me. 'You had your chance and you ruined it, hmm? I should have placed a few gems on you failing, maybe even a silver. Remind me the next time the widow has a bright idea that involves you.'

What kept me calm was the fact Vex only knew half the story. 'Well, if you'll excuse me, I've been told to go rest in my alcove. Busy day tomorrow, I imagine. You never know, the widow might remember how ugly you are and change her mind again.'

Vex muttered to himself as I picked my way between preparation stations and stoves, heading for my alcove.

Bela and the others looked surprised at first, then somewhat pleased to see me. They traded smug looks across the hallway. Kon was as oblivious as ever to the petty politics of his fellow indentured. He poked out of his alcove and waved.

'Hi, Jerub. Back, then?'

'Back,' I grunted in reply. 'And call me Caltro.'

Bela opened her mouth. 'What's the matter, *Caltro*? Could the mistress not stand the sight of you no more?'

I smiled as sweetly as I knew how. 'No. In fact, I requested to come back. I was worried poor Vex might die for a second time with jealousy. And besides, I missed Kon. As for the rest of you? You can all go fuck yourselves with copper spoons.'

An uncomfortable silence fell, and I leaned back in my alcove with my cheeks bent grinning. Like Vex, they were unaware of the papyrus hidden in the pocket of my smock. I was not in the mood to be challenged any longer. I knew I was above them.

I wanted to take it out and examine the glyphs closer, to check the old bat wasn't cheating me. I would have to know my Arctian better if I were to endure several more weeks of indenturement. Bela looked up at me as I snorted. I wouldn't be staying in the putrid, conceited hole they called Araxes a moment longer than I had to. I would return home, a deader man but a freer man. Krass was not without its free ghosts. They were uncommon, but then again I'd always been an outsider. A loner. It might even suit me.

There I waited, watching the sunlight in the stairwell slip from yellow to orange. Several more ghosts joined us. They wore curious looks for me, but held their tongues after seeing the others shake their heads.

When they were bored enough to close their eyes and feign rest, I crouched down to find a suitable hiding place for my slip of papyrus. A small gap between the stone tiles was makeshift, but it would do for the moment until I found something more permanent.

I'd mastered a sort of sleep since my stint in the sarcophagus. It was the only blessing out of a mound of curses. I say sleep; it was more a trance where total immersion in my thoughts blotted out all sound, surroundings and, blessedly, the drudging passage of time. Over the past few nights, I'd trained my mind not to slip into dark places as it had in the stone coffin. Now I found I could concentrate on lighter things.

Into my trance I fell, mulling over the widow's words. My imagination accentuated her features, making her a globular mass of wrinkles, like the folded black stone of Scatter Isle volcanoes. I thought once more of her mention of fanatics, and how I'd missed my chance to ask more of them. Basht's warnings were nonsensical without something to fill them with meaning. I still needed context.

I told myself that would come with time, and instead I turned my thoughts to the widow's promise of freedom, imagining Temsa being hauled away in chains to be hung, or stoned, or whatever these Arctians did to soulstealers…

CHAPTER 20

ANY PORT IN A SANDSTORM

The Duneplains are not just dangerous due to the fauna occupying the barren stretches and salt flats – dunewyrms, skullfoxes, verminous beetles, bandits and the like – but due to its natural forces. The dunes are ever-shifting, so no reliable maps can be drawn of them. The ground is full of rifts and vents. In some places, rain has not been seen for a century. No other stretch of the Far Reaches holds such opposition and bitterness towards human occupation. It is a land meant for the dead, and the dead may keep it.

Excerpt from 'Reach Around - A Traveller's Guide to The Far Reaches'

THE WORLD HAD FALLEN ON its side. The dunes and scrub and salt plains slid by as though they fell through an hourglass. Time was not steady, but would pass in clumps and jolts. One moment she would be staring at moonlit scrub and salt, and wonder where the sun had snuck to. A blink later, and she'd open her eyes on bare desert, red and blotchy. Or a distant hill, clinging to a cliff-face of a world.

She skipped through the hours. Even the constant throb of pain was similar. It was a kind of healing sleep, and as broken as it was by the jolting of the horse, it was slowly doing its work.

Nilith had grown accustomed to slumbering against Anoish's back. She'd had to. It was the only way she could catch shuteye without stopping. The constant shifting of his muscles and shoulder blades had taken time to tolerate, but exhaustion had helped.

Even Farazar seemed tired, for a shade. Maybe he was emotionally scarred, but in either case, he drifted behind them, pulled by his unseen leash. He had been silent since escaping Abatwe, and she was glad. She had no words to offer back.

All Nilith could think of was the sound of sizzling flesh, and for once in the blasted desert, not her own. If she closed her eyes, she could still see the skin of Krona's face cooking. Bubbling. A worthy punishment for a person like her, she'd judged, but at the same time, it was another scratch in the sand. She'd hoped for stealth and speed on this journey, but all she had found were murder and delay. Desperation was twisting her into something she did not like.

Throughout the morning, whenever she had craned her neck to the heavens, she noticed a black spot wheeling overhead. A vulture, most likely, though at times Nilith swore it hovered like a kestrel or hawk. Twice she waved a feeble arm at it, and mumbled something about coming back when she was dead.

She gritted her teeth as Anoish skipped over a stone and her head came up and down with a painful thump. Nilith patted his side. She could hear his breathing becoming increasingly laboured.

It was time to be upright once more. It took some time but she got there, pushing herself up with her fists while her back clicked in far too many places. Her chest was numb, her arms limp, and yet before she massaged them back to life, the first thing she did was look behind her.

The late morning sky was stark, bereft of clouds or haze. The unhindered scorching of the sun bleached the colour out of the sapphire, leaving it turquoise. Apart from Farazar's slumped form, the horizon was empty. No dark spots in sight. Nilith felt some of the tension seep from her bones. The sun was leaning towards the west. The worst of the day's heat had already passed.

She scanned the dunes for a sign of a settlement or a hiding place. The salt flats shimmered cruelly as though they carried water, but amongst their blur she saw nothing; not so much as a rocky outcrop.

Nilith tapped her teeth together in thought, feeling the grit between them, and began to gently probe her face. Her teeth had settled back into their sockets at least. Her puffy eye was slowly deflating. Her split lip had scabbed over. Even the bruised and cracked ribs weren't screaming as much when she pressed them.

She spread her hands over the horse's sides, noting the new wrinkles in his coat where the Ghouls' switches had kissed him. There were fresh scabs there, too, and despite his whinnying when she prodded them, he would be fine. Nilith was still thanking the dead gods he hadn't twisted a hoof in the mad dash out of Abatwe.

It took an hour for a smudge of red to appear in the haze. Nilith set a course for it, hoping it was not a trick of the heat. What little luck she had left held. The smudge was no trick, but a ruined cottage of stolen quarry stone and bone-white wood. Just a broken ring of it remained. The rest had been chewed away by the winds or appropriated by nomads. It peaked in the centre like a dented crown, providing a few feet of wall and a patch of shade. A rusted cooking pot with a hole in it lay half-buried in the sand.

'Who on earth would live out here?' Nilith muttered, sliding from Anoish. Her legs were far too numb, and she crumpled into a heap. She lay there, face against the hot sand, until her blood stirred enough for walking.

She only needed to make it the dozen steps to the shade, and then she could crumple again. Fire and food, if any… they could come later. Watering herself and Anoish was more important.

Once she'd mastered being vertical, she remembered water. Her remaining skin was still tied to Farazar's corpse. It was practically empty, but she shared the remnants equally between her and the horse. He seemed as tired as she was, if not more. In fact, he beat her to the shade, taking up most of it besides a patch where she could lay her head on his double knees.

Nilith was asleep before her cheek met his bony leg. Her dreams were full of moaning breezes and the slow sizzle of the sand shifting around them. All through it, she felt as though something was brushing her cheek, like a lover's hand. Faceless people stood around her and watched her fit and shiver.

When she awoke, she found darkness above her. A cold wind had sprung up, blowing sand up and over the wall and onto her face. Had she lain there for a night it would have buried her, but for now it was just an inconvenience.

The soft glow of Farazar sat nearby, looking back the way they had come. The wind had covered their tracks. In the moonlight it kicked up skinny dust-devils and set them dancing across the cracked salt.

'Storm coming?' Nilith spoke up, her voice scratchy with the amount of sand she must have inhaled over the last few days.

Farazar shook his head, still as vacant as a blue balloon. She tapped her teeth, shuffled upright, and edged around Anoish so she could face him. The horse snuffled softly before going back to sleep.

'Feels like it. Air's hot, not cold,' she said.

'Sandstorms fade at night.'

'Maybe tomorrow, then?'

He grunted, staring off at the sliver of moon that had poked above a dune. 'Unlikely.'

Nilith tutted loudly. 'Got something you need to say?'

He spoke with an ice-cold bitterness. 'I hate you.'

'We've hated one another for years.'

'It wasn't enough for you to come and kill me. To have the audacity to bind me. No, you see fit to drag me across sand and mountain like a dead camel, right into the claws of the first bandits and backstabbers you find. I hate you for that, and more every day that you insist on this disgraceful quest of yours. You're a fucking imbecile, punishing me with your idiotic choices. And what's worse is you believe that *ma'at* nonsense will protect you, like some snaggletoothed witch in orange rags.'

Nilith ground her teeth. 'I did what time demanded of me.'

'Well, look at what your doggedness has earned you. You came all that way south to fetch me, and for what? You look deader than I do. This journey is cursed by your impetuousness. Carry on like this and you'll be hounded all the way to Araxes, never mind reaching the Grand Nyxwell in one piece. I'll be shocked if you make it to the Sprawls.'

His judgements stung her but she waited for her anger to quell. She hadn't the energy for shouting.

'So much hatred,' she said with a forced smile. 'And yet it was *you*, Farazar, who saved me from that Ghoul in the crater. Who undid my bonds.'

He snarled, clearly ashamed of himself. 'I... I swore nobody would bind me. I would rather be murdered all over again before I'm indentured to filthy bandits. Or serve some beetle-riding quarry-owner, passed on to his moron son like an antique table—'

'You've come around to my way of thinking, I see. Finally accepted your death.' Perhaps there was a chance of a peaceful journey after all. 'Why not work together? You could stop being a prick and I'll carry on getting us home.'

He shot her a murderous look, and Nilith decided humour might not be the best approach. 'Help you? How fucking dare...' He was so disgusted as to be speechless. 'I only help myself, as I have always done. This isn't over, wife. I have accepted nothing. I didn't want to be sold by the Ghouls, but it doesn't mean I will stand to be claimed by you or any other. Better to wait you out and watch you fail. Take my chance when it comes. I told you: freedom, the afterlife, or the void. I am determined to keep that vow.'

Nilith pushed herself up, and holding her nose, she moved to Farazar's corpse. 'I may have lost my copper dagger, but fortunately for me you stink like a butchered hog left out for the flies. The Ghouls didn't go near your corpse. Which means...' After some rummaging between the cloth, she dragged out the scimitar. Its copper and gold looked liquid in the afternoon sun. 'I have this. I don't need your help.'

Farazar looked smug. 'The sun really has baked your brain, hasn't it? You've already failed and you don't even realise it.' His voice was sharp, like cut flint.

Nilith didn't answer him at first. Instead she tried some experimental swings of the blade. She winced as her arm sockets protested. 'I've made it this far.'

'And still with many miles to travel. How many days do you have to bind me?'

Eighteen days. She could have probably counted the hours if she had the time and inclination. She imagined herself short of the finish line, with only a puff of blue smoke and a stinking corpse to show for all this toil and terror. It was far from the result she had dreamt of.

'A few weeks.'

'Plenty of time for you to make a mistake. Why don't you just drag me to the nearest pool of Nyxwater you can find? Be done with it instead of insisting on the Grand Nyxwell?'

'It has to be done right. You know that.'

Farazar had no more to say on the subject. He shuffled around to rid her from his peripheries and busied himself with moon-gazing. Nilith returned to her spot beside Anoish.

With her sword balanced on her lap, she watched the ghost through narrow eyes. Sleep didn't pester her. She'd had enough of that. All she entertained was suspicion and wariness of the ghost. She looked into the swirling of his skull, behind the strands of cobalt hair, and imagined him concocting ways to stop her.

Nilith spat the grit from her mouth and hunkered down out of the hot wind. At the noise, Farazar looked over his shoulder. His lone eye glared at her, then returned to the glowing heavens. Nilith squeezed the sword's hilt tighter. She had planned for this. She knew he would be a liability the moment her knife had sawn through his windpipe. There was always cutting his tongue out with copper, but conflictingly, his hate-filled protests kept her sharp, shoring up her determination and reminding her why she had planned this whole journey in the first place. Not to mention the enjoyment of poking and prodding, of telling a captive audience how wrong he was.

Perhaps Farazar had been right. Perhaps there was a lesson in all of this; one that she wanted to teach him before it was too late, final words he would have never listened to whilst alive. It would be a sweeter end, but she didn't need him to understand in order to finish what she'd started.

Her thumb whispered against the honed edge of the scimitar.

FARAZAR HAD EITHER LIED OR erred, but in any case, the sandstorm rose with the dawn. A band of orange on the eastern horizon, it rushed across the landscape like a mountain range loosed from its roots. Towers of dust curled above it like grasping claws. Here and there, yellow lightning forked between the billowing clouds, showing their insides and sending thunder rolling across the Duneplains.

Nilith withdrew her head from the lip of stone and wiped her face. She'd wrapped some spare cloth around her mouth and nose, but her eyes were still bare. 'You said there wasn't going to be a storm.'

'I said there was *unlikely* to be one.'

'We can't stay here. We'll be buried!'

'You want to go out *there*, onto the plains?'

'I saw lights there last night. Uncovered for just a moment, but I saw them through the haze.' She knew of several small settlements sprawled between Araxes and the Steps. There was a slim chance this was one of them.

'Trick of your eyes. Or a quarry. One whose masters would slap you and me in iron and copper before we blinked. Or greedy nomads looking to make some quick gems. I refuse to move.'

'What do you care?' She stared at his shoulders, hunched and glowing brightly wherever the sand punctured his vapours. Which, in fairness, was everywhere. He refused to move further behind the wall. It meant being nearer to her.

'Because there's copper dust in the air. Feels like needles, trying to scrape me away. I would rather not traipse through a sandstorm for hours on end, enduring this.'

Nilith was sure she had seen something in the early hours, to the north and west, but there was a chance that she was mistaken. It could have been a wandering ghost, or nomads, even a soultrain, and yet her doubt was trampled under the desire to prove him wrong. 'Tough. We're moving.'

Anoish, being a desert horse with the eyelashes of a camel and wide hooves, wasn't particularly fussed when Nilith poked him into action. Nevertheless, she ripped some more fabric from the bundled corpse, and wrapped some around his snout. Once she had made a crude visor for her eyes, she handed the rest to Farazar.

'Here, wrap yourself up.'

He accepted it grudgingly and slipped it over his head and shoulders like a rough cloak. He still wasn't standing, but after Nilith led the horse far enough, he decided he'd rather walk than be dragged along the sand.

The going was tough even before the sandstorm hit. Its vanguard winds whipped the dust up into their faces. Balls of scrub-grass and vegetation flew by like catapulted masonry. One struck Anoish in the side, thorns raking bloody scratches, but he ploughed on.

With every mile they battled, the sandstorm claimed ten. Soon enough, the distant band of orange had become a towering mass, higher even than the Cloudpiercer of Araxes. It billowed and surged like ochre dye blooming underwater, never staying still for a moment. Nilith could hear the deeper roar of rock and dust over the animalistic howl of the gales.

'Where are these fucking lights of yours, wife?' Farazar yelled.

'Ahead!'

They made it another mile before the sandstorm struck them. A wall of sand-laden air and wind drove them to their knees, tearing at every loose scrap of clothing, every strand of hair. Nilith had to walk at an angle to fight the gusts. Both hands were clamped over her face, and yet still the grit poured into her mouth and nostrils. She managed thin sucks of air through her lips, always one breath away from choking. If she held a foot in one place too long, the sand began to swallow it. Whenever she dared to open an eye through the slits of her fingers, she saw an angry, roiling world of orange and brown, dark as twilight. Palm fronds and scrub and pebbles from old riverbeds tore through the murk, cartwheeling at vicious speeds. One clipped her knee, sending her staggering right into the path of a ball of dry weeds. It knocked her flat and left her with blood smeared across her arm.

Direction became moot. She couldn't see ten paces in front of her. Nilith, to her shame, found shelter behind Anoish's flanks. The horse plodded on, staggering here and there but otherwise staying strong and sturdy. It did little for the violent gales, but it kept some of the dust out of her face.

She vowed to buy him the largest bale of hay possible when they reached the city. In that moment, the doubt hit her. *If* they reached the city. Barely half an hour into the storm, and she was all ready to mimic the ghost and curl up in the sand, and wait to be swallowed. Behind her, Farazar had hunkered down into a ball, succumbing to the pull of his corpse and letting himself be dragged.

Nilith cursed her impetuousness. Farazar – though she wanted to spit even thinking of it – might have been right: she didn't pay heed. She did rush in, but it had always worked. Luck had been her friend until now; a smattering of a plan had always managed to bring her through. Though the impetus behind it had been years in the making, even leaving to hunt down Farazar had been a whim riding on the back of a rumour. She had memorised her maps on the back of a wagon across the Long Sands.

Nilith clung to that dogged luck now, pushing forward in what she trusted was still north. There was nothing to be said of direction besides guesses and luck. The sandstorm obscured all.

Her first clue that she was right came in the form of a small stone wall, disguised as a bank of sand. Nilith went tumbling down onto all fours, staring at a ragged thread of garment under her fists. Anoish nuzzled her, but she patted him away. It was a scarf of some kind, half-buried. She tugged it free and it whipped her in the face.

'What have you got?' yelled Farazar.

It was a scarf. Clutching it in her hand, she pushed forwards through the raging clouds of grit. She felt as though she were being sanded away, layer by layer.

Something made of stone loomed out of the orange haze. She pressed her hand against an adobe wall, like a mother finding a lost child. Nilith lead Anoish behind a wall where the winds were lessened. Through her fingers, she spied another stone lump, and another. Six altogether, huddled around a covered well. Something was drumming loudly in the roar of sand and wind.

Nilith shielded her face and poked out to see. She got a mouthful of grit for her troubles, but she spotted a lamp hidden behind glass, affixed to the wall of the largest building. She held the scimitar at her belt and pressed on, faced into the wind now rather than traversing it.

'This way!' she called to Farazar, who had fallen behind, glad for the wall's shelter. Once again, the spell tugged him, and he came walking moodily beside her.

As it turned out, the drumming was the wind rushing through a banner. It puffed like a sail against the gales, and the thin smiling holes cut in its cloth produced low, undulating tones. It seemed to proclaim some sort of tavern, and she wondered if the noise was intentional for times exactly like this. They seemed used to sandstorms: the lamp was hidden behind a dirty pane of glass, and next to it was a door of palm-wood and rusty iron, sails against the winds. Nilith groped for the handle, found it immovable, and resorted to pounding on the door.

'Please! Help!' she yelled. Then, remembering her Arctian, '*Quia*! *Ayun khas*!'

The door shifted outwards, and a thin metal tube was poked through the narrow crack. Its eye found her and she instinctively held up her hands, wincing in the thrash of sand. Holding the tube was a thin old man, very dark of skin, matted locks of hair waving like tentacles. He was wild of eye, but a hand on his shoulder held him steady. A woman was there, half hidden by the frame. She was willowy with a proud jawline. She had the milky skin of Ede's cave-city folk.

'We need help! Myself, my shade and my horse.' Nilith let the scarf flap in the doorway and the woman took it.

The tube waggled towards the blade at her belt. With finger and thumb, she pinched it by the pommel stone and drew it out for one of them to take.

'My horse?'

The old man spoke, in a voice so deep she struggled to hear him over the din of the storm. '*Uela. Shasim.*'

Nilith got the general meaning. His words were clipped and his dialect twisted but she still understood. *Horse out back.*

She found Anoish some shelter under a stable of tarpaulin and timber at the rear of the tavern. After tying him up next to a covered barrel of fresh peelings and scrub roots, and stashing the body in the corner, she made her way inside with her ears full of Anoish's contented munching. It almost rivalled the roar of the storm and violent flapping of fabric.

Farazar was hovering in the doorway, holding it ajar. Nilith closed it behind her and shook herself. A shower of sand cascaded on the packed floor.

'My apologies,' she said, before she looked up. As she stared about at the small congregation of benches and tables, the bar, and caught the whiff of roast meat, a great weight descended from her. It might have just been the sand she emptied from her leather coat, but to her, it was the first time she'd felt remotely safe in days.

The old man had gone to his spot by a clay hearth and a table strewn with earthenware pots. A large set of scales sat before him. It was the woman who answered, standing behind the bar, hands spread wide.

'None necessary,' she said.

'You speak Common?'

'I do. It's necessary. Get all sorts in here. Traders of all sorts. Souls mostly. Welcome to the *Parched Parrot*.'

'Do you have food? Water?'

'What we can spare. The summer has been hotter than usual. More caravans dyin' in the Duneplains.'

Nilith didn't need to be told that. She found a seat at the bar while Farazar meandered through the benches. He still clutched his ragged cloth around him.

'What about a bed?' Nilith asked.

'Ah! Up!' the woman snapped at Farazar the moment his glowing arse touched the bench.

'Is there a problem?'

'His kind aren't usually welcome in town, let alone inside my tavern. But, seein' as you aren't from around here, I'll leave him be. He says a word, causes a fuss, and he's outside in the storm.'

Nilith bowed her head, glad for the rules. 'Kind and fair terms.'

'No it's not. I expect you to be payin'.' The woman put her hands on her hips, eying Nilith's dishevelled and wounded appearance. 'Do I recognise him?'

'Who? The shade?'

'He looks familiar in some way.'

Nilith watched Farazar raising his chin. 'No, he's just got one of those faces. My idiot husband. Fell down a cliff.' After a moment of condolent humming, Nilith patted her ripped smock. 'Would you accept trade?'

'Depends.'

'Well, you could have my…' Her hand froze at her neck, finding it bereft of chain and copper coin. She remembered last seeing it around Krona's neck and inwardly swore.

The woman raised a finger to the scimitar sat on the bar-top. 'How about this sword?'

'It's, er… my great grandfather's sword,' Nilith explained. 'I need it.'

Farazar cleared his throat behind her. Both she and the woman turned on him, shushing him glares.

Nilith had an idea, and pasted a look of resignation on her face. 'It would be a shame to part with it, but throw in a bath and you've got a deal.'

The woman looked as though she had just witnessed a murder. 'A bath? Are you fucking sun-cracked? What a waste of water.'

'No, madam. I'm completely serious, and I also saw a well outside. There's nothing that can make a person feel human again like steaming themselves in a bath.'

The woman shook her head. 'Bath's worth ten silvers easy. At least fifty gems.'

'So's the sword. More, even.'

The old man snorted over his pots of dust and silt.

'Give us the horse.'

'I can't part with him.'

'The shade, then.'

'I thought you didn't like shades around here?'

The woman wrinkled her nose. 'We could sell him.'

'I'm telling you: sword's worth more than both. Sell this instead. Don't trade in indentured.'

The woman picked up the blade, her brow joining her nose as she caught some foul whiff on it. Even so, she noted the black beads of obsidian around its rim, and the snakeskin handle. The blade was notch-free, and the edge still sharp… in fact, the more Nilith's gaze followed hers, the more she convinced herself the sword probably could have actually got forty silvers. At the right bazaar, of course. She just doubted it was anywhere around here.

'You really want a bath, girl?' rumbled the old man in Commontongue. 'Sure you're not sun-cracked, eh?'

'No. I simply feel more grit and sweat than person at the moment, sir. Besides I have wounds to clean.' Nilith gestured broadly to her forehead.

'Seen trouble?'

'Bandits. Stole almost everything.'

'Mmm.' That apparently satisfied the old gentleman, and he went back to tinkering with his metal tube.

The pale woman led her to a corridor with honeycomb-like rooms. 'Third one along. Simple latch. I'll bring water, food after the… bath. I don't know how much water we can spare for it, mind.'

Nilith already had one foot in her room. 'Anything will be fine.'

With the door closed, she found her sand-stuffed mattress and collapsed into it. The room was barely a large cupboard, but to her it was a palace; somewhere away from the vengeful fists of the storm. She could hear it moaning through the shutters on the far, or rather not so far, wall. It yanked at their hinges with every gust.

The woman returned swiftly with a pitcher of water and a cup, both made out of toughened camel hide. Nilith thanked her before proceeding to drink the entire pitcher in one go. She felt the silt washing around her mouth, but she didn't care. She had swallowed enough sand already; a little more was worth slaking her powerful thirst.

While she was waiting for her bath to be drawn, she returned to the main room. Farazar now lurked in a corner, arms folded. He still wore his makeshift cloak, looking like a stubborn child with the last candied fruit being asked to share. His eyes were slitted and jealous, and she decided to leave him be. He knew better than to interfere.

The woman poured her a glug of dark liquid, and slid the cup along the bar. 'On the house.'

Nilith sniffed it, and it burned between her eyes. 'What is that?'

'Shame-juice, Old Fen calls it. It's *ammita.* Distilled from beer, and other things.'

Despite the dubious explanation, Nilith wasn't one to be a bad guest, and so she knocked the viscous stuff back in one go. It felt like swallowing a sword. The taste was aniseed and bitter salt. It clawed its way into her head and dizzied her within moments.

'Dead gods' piss, that's strong.'

Old Fen chuckled to himself over on the table, and she grew curious of his tinkering.

'What is that thing, old man?'

'This?' He held up the tube, then knocked a bowl with a bone ring. 'Or this?'

'Any of it.'

He looked like the sort of man who enjoyed an audience. Nilith had found that people who owned inns, or those that frequented them more than their own homes, were only ever there to tell their own stories, not to listen to others'.

'Ahem, well. It's all rather complicated,' he began.

'Don't let 'im fool you. It's not witchcraft or wizardry. What did you call it? "Science", is it?'

'Don't ruin it, Eber, let me talk.' Fen bobbed his head. 'That's what the Chamber of Thinking used to call it. *Sahr*,' he said in Arctian.

'Science? Sounds like the word for magic.'

'Same thing to those that don't know better. What looks like magic is just science we don't understand yet.'

Eber rolled her eyes and poured herself her own shot of ammita. Nilith took a seat across from the old man and began to sniff the small earthenware dishes. They were a spectrum of colours, from pitch to lavender, mustard to crimson. Some smelled like salt. Others sulphur.

'You can make all sorts of magic with these. For instance, pinch of this and that over a flame, stretch out a wineskin into a balloon over it, and the skin'll fly on its own.'

'No.'

'Surely. It's all from thousands of years ago. The ancestors, you know them?'

'We all have ancestors. Mine were likely different.'

'Well, here's another example. They didn't fight with swords, see. Not *just* with swords. They had something else.' Fen went to work, taking an empty dish and sprinkling small amounts into it. Yellow, black, grey. With his leathery fingers he mixed up the powders, doing so with utmost care. Nilith saw Eber watching, bored as though she'd seen this a score of times.

A quick flick, and Fen dashed the powders into the hearth. The small flame that had been burning there flashed into life, burning bright white and reaching up to put fresh scorches on the adobe wall.

Nilith had been expecting some salt-trick of a beldam, not an explosion. She was shocked. 'What in the Reaches?'

Fen rubbed his blackened fingertips together. It was only then she noticed half the fingers on his right hand were missing; just puckered nubs. 'Makes you think, don't it? Possibilities. The oldest nomad songs say they had great machines called caloms. Could shoot chunks of rock, tear a man in half.'

Nilith pointed to the thin tube, made of battered lead and twine. 'Is that what that is?'

'A small one.' The old man held it up. It had a latch on one end, and a hole nearby with a lamp wick curled over it. 'Put the powder in, then a little pebble.'

'Or a gem. That was a waste, wasn't it, Fen?'

He ignored Eber, continuing with his lesson. 'Then you can stuff a bit of cotton down it, stop it coming out. The hole means you can light it. Push the wick down and boom.'

'What happens to the pebble?'

Eber cleared her throat, tapping the edge of the bar. Below her long fingers, there was a splintered hole the size of a coin.

'Dangerous.'

'Ain't it just?' Fen wiggled his stumps. 'That was the first try. Wood don't work for caloms. If I can just show it to somebody in the city – somebody rich, with an eye for science – I could make my coins, be a tor in a tower before I die.'

Nilith ignored the dry cough coming from the corner of the room. She could see the hope running through Old Fen's eyes, like sand through the waist of an hourglass.

'If I had the gems…' But the Ghouls had taken them all.

'Ha!' Fen snorted. 'All the travellers say that.'

Nilith leaned forwards, fixing him with a stare. 'I know a few people. When I'm done with my business, I'll try to come back here. I'd say come with me, but it's dangerous. Too many have died already.'

'Connected, I suppose? Know all the right people? Heh, you traders spin some yarns.'

'I'm no trader.' Nilith paused, wondering what was worth sacrificing to gain the man's trust. Both the fighter and the opportunist in her saw the potential of this fire powder, and it had ignited her intrigue. It could change the world. 'I know Araxes inside and out. I know great minds that would boggle at this. Traders with hundreds of ships. People who would lick their lips at such a demonstration.'

'And criminals? Terrorists? Soulstealers? Warlords? Who's to say which hands should hold this powder?' He grabbed a handful and let it sift through his remaining fingers.

Nilith had to smile. She leaned back. 'You make a fine point, sir. Perhaps such things aren't worth the silver or gems.'

Fen's reply didn't make it out of his mouth. Eber rapped her knuckles on the bar. 'Bath's done.'

Nilith could have kissed the woman. Perhaps the ammita had gone to her head after all.

After stowing Farazar in her room, she followed Eber to a small hollowed-out chamber with a door to the outside, where a large trough lay steaming. A fire heated the room, and over it pots and pans of dirty water. Eber poured a few in before she vacated. Nilith caught her murmuring before she shut the door.

'Sword better be worth it.'

The first dip into a bath was always the most special, followed closely by complete immersion. Nilith didn't waste any time achieving both, disrobing and then quickly plunging herself in.

She found baths to be odd things; so luxurious and innocent, and yet all it took was a mere duck of the chin, a few long moments, and they could drown a woman. Pleasure seemed always so intertwined with danger.

The hot water put all of that out of Nilith's mind. It made her sweat, but the warm embrace dissolved the tension in her limbs, calmed her heart, and made her head loll against her chest.

Whether it was the release, how sweet peace could feel, or the stress finally catching up with her, but she began to shake. Her eyes stung. The water splashed as she scratched the sand from her arms and neck, tearing at her hair to rid her scalp of grit. Half-formed words streamed from her mouth.

When finally her breath ran out, she fell still, heaving to the rapid beat of her heart. Under the shadow of her tangled, raven hair, she stared down at her face in the rippled water. The stiller she was, the clearer it became. The Nyxwater had sealed her face wounds. The bruises and great bags under her emerald eyes remained. A tooth was missing in the corner of her mouth. One eye was still intent on staying bloodshot.

Nilith lay back with a shaking sigh. She knew any moment the waters would start their inevitable turn to cold, and so she lapped up every scrap of heat. She did not care about the scratch of silt and wood under her spine, nor the flinches of pain coming from every blister on her sun-roasted shoulders, nor the fact she was in a trough, nor the fervent rattling of the outside door… all that occupied her was the stillness of the water wrapping her. No trot of a horse. No ache from looking over her shoulder constantly. No sharp wind pushing her onwards. Just stillness.

Nilith must have stayed in those waters until they were cold.

CHAPTER 21
HYPOTHETICALLY SPEAKING

The scrutinisers were a Chamber initiative that started several hundred years ago. They were torturers and interrogators originally, and only the Chamber knows truly if they still are. A force of law and order, they call themselves. I'd call them a waste of air. A show of authority for the sake of fulfilling authority's need to show authority. Cyclical lies, friends! Pomp and trivialities!

FROM A SPEECH BY CONDEMNED SOULSTEALER AND ANARCHIST WINSON DANK IN 870

SISINE PACED. SHE WAS FOND of pacing. It quelled what lesser folk might have described as nerves. Hers was a higher plane of fidgeting; a necessary sprightliness. She had the weight of an empire on her back, after all.

'Where is he, Etane?'

The shade sprawling on a velvet bench wore a weary look. Sisine was glad that for once he was dressed in the manner his position dictated: a long robe, charcoal grey and adorned with the royal colours of turquoise and sandy yellow.

'He should be here soon. He said he'd come.'

'Soon is not a time. And as of now, soon is late. I cannot abide—'

Etane cut across her. 'Lateness. I will remind him when he gets here.'

Sisine swung past him to prod him with a finger, and the sharp copper thimble on its tip. 'You've grown sullen of late. More recalcitrant than usual. What is wrong with you? Should I be concerned? Must I have you sold?'

Etane scrunched up his face. His blue vapours etched faint wrinkles. He had been around fifty when he died, but to Sisine he looked much older. Perhaps shades did age on some level, through toil and time. The years will always leave their marks on souls.

She halted and crossed her arms with a crackle of silk. 'Spit it out.'

'It's this business with Temsa and his shade. They can't be trusted, and yet you seem to be barrelling towards friendship.'

'I do not "barrel", shade. I manoeuvre. I sidestep. I parry. And it is not friendship I seek, but a temporary ally. One I can control as long as I need him. One who can graciously take a fall if the need arises.'

'And this Danib—'

'The mute you say has sold his coin back into indenturement.'

'Him. I never trusted him. He was with the Cult of Sesh for hundreds of years. You don't just leave the Cult after that long.'

'Is that so?' Sisine raised an eyebrow.

Etane shook his head, chewing over his words. Before he could give them voice, a timid knock sounded at the great door in the next room. He practically flew from the bench to answer it.

'What is it?' he hollered through a peephole.

The voice was muffled behind the wood, steel and ivory. 'There's a visitor for Her Highness! Won't give us his name. Middle-aged, short. Beard. Cane and... eagle foot. Got a big shade and a guard with him. Looks suspi—'

'Admit them!'

'You serious?'

'Admit them, man. On the empress-in-waiting's orders!'

'Right away!'

When Etane came ambling back, she prodded him again, in the centre of the forehead. He winced, and she saw the pale flash of anger in his eyes.

'You're a fool if you think I can't see it, old shade. I've spent years watching the tics and shrugs of sereks who think silence is a shield from their lies. You doubt me, your own master, and I find that intensely disturbing. You do not get to doubt me; you simply follow orders,' Sisine told him. 'I will not have your foul mood interfering with this evening. Understand?'

Etane tried a bland smile. 'As you wish.'

'Good. Now fetch me this man.'

The shade went into the next chamber and laid hands on the door's locks. After a glance through the peephole, he cranked them. Six sharp metallic twangs sounded before the door swung open with a hiss. The clank of armour spilled through the gap, and moments later, a score of guards filed into the opulent parlour and took their places around the walls. They were dressed from scalp to sole in silver and blue steel, with their shortswords already half-drawn, in true royal tradition.

Sisine took her place on a long couch, slightly reclined, but still straight as a spear. One elbow up, hand against her face, and the other idly waving a thin silver flute of spiced wine. The Arc lived off beer, and that was what made it common. She was better than that.

Etane had remained outside in the hallway, waiting for Temsa to ascend to the highest reaches of the Piercer. Even with colossal clockwork lifts and a thousand shades winding levers above and below, it took an age.

When finally Etane appeared at the door, Sisine put on a pleasant smile; one she had tailored over the years. The trick was to reveal just the right amount of teeth. She wanted to appear warm yet aloof. Confident yet disarming. But as Boss Boran Temsa entered her chambers, she found it a struggle to maintain any kind of smile at all.

The man must have been two thirds her height, bent of back and leaning on an ornate onyx cane. Her eyes roved from his greased hair to the sharp beard framing thin lips and a gold-speckled smile; from the wrinkles of his years to his clothes of fine black and grey silk; and finally, to the source of the strange clanging noise.

His leg.

It was an eagle's foot, cast in gold and copper and attached just below the knee. Four talons spread out from the ankle, curled and sharp, and scratching at the marble with every step. What had happened to the customary ebony or mahogany leg, she had no clue.

Her mother had once told her that short people should always choose short guards in order to appear taller. It was a matter of fashion in Araxes, yet Temsa had thrown that to the wind.

He was dwarfed by his companions, looking like the river at the gutter of a canyon. They loomed at each of his shoulders. One was a paler woman with tight braids and broad, tattooed shoulders to match her height. The other was a shade in full battle armour, standing almost seven feet tall.

This must be Danib. Now he stood before her, she did find something familiar about him. She pondered if she had seen him during her grandfather's flight of fancy with the Cult, when she had been just a tiny girl.

'Your Highness,' Temsa said in a voice aged with smoke and drink and harsh words. He bowed deeply, and stayed in that position so long Sisine wondered if he was having trouble coming back up. But he did, and she nodded her thanks.

Unlike most visitors to her chambers, Temsa's eyes didn't once creep to the grand balcony, or the silken drapes, or the gilded arches hanging above them. They were fixed on hers, unblinking and curiously confident. Almost excited. Usually her guests were more prostrate and quivering.

'Allow me to first say what an honour it is to be invited to your royal chambers, and to be in your presence,' he said.

She waved a hand at a matching couch. 'Boss Boran Temsa, it is a pleasure also. Please, sit. I'll have my chamber-shade, Etane, fetch you some wine.'

'Don't mind if I do.' Temsa removed his long coat and handed it to Ani with a flourish. Etane moved past Danib, keeping his eyes low even though the big shade watched his every movement. He poured Temsa a glass and returned to the adjoining room.

Temsa sipped the wine daintily, but his breeding showed through him smacking his lips. 'A fine drop. Skol?'

'You know your grapes. Irenna. Ten years old.'

'I believe one needs to if they intend to spend coin on their juices.'

Sisine was struggling to keep her gaze from straying to the leg.

Instead she gestured to the two giants. 'Won't you introduce me to your companions?'

'Of course. Might I present Miss Ani Jexebel, one of the finest warriors the Scatter Isles ever birthed. And Danib, a very old and close associate of mine. With no disrespect to Miss Jexebel, he is quite possibly *the* finest warrior in all of the Arc.'

Sisine watched their reactions. Jexebel seemed to have trouble understanding, but the gist was enough to make her frown. Danib was featureless; a glowing blank canvas.

'Bold claims, Boss Temsa,' she said. 'Might I ask why they are not out fighting for their emperor against the Scatter Princes with the rest of our fine warriors?'

Temsa grinned, showing off several gold-capped teeth. 'Ani, because I pay her better, and Danib because I am his master. Through silver and copper they are devoted to me and I feel safer for it. Dangerous days in this city, wouldn't you say?'

'Indeed.'

A silence fell, pregnant with polite shuffling and sipping of wine. Sisine decided to lead.

'You may be wondering why I invited you here.'

'For mutual gain, or so your shade informed me.'

'That is true, in broad terms. Advancement, evolution; these terms would be more accurate. I can tell you are a man who is a forward thinker. Not one for normality.' She motioned towards the leg. *She had to know*. Even if it was merely morbid curiosity.

Temsa played dumb for a moment, looking at his glass before his lap. 'Oh! The leg. Of course. Quite the conversation piece, wouldn't you agree?'

He was more confident and – dare she think it without shuddering – *charming* than she had expected. Temsa had swaggered into her rooms as if he dined with royalty every other week. He was no serek, no tor, and yet here he was, sipping wine with the empress-in-waiting and no sign of a tremor in him. Sisine wondered whether the royal reputation had slipped, or if this man thought far too much of himself.

'It is not a glamorous story, I'm afraid, Highness. Simply an accident of my own causing. As a lad I worked as a whale-fisher on a proud and honest boat. We made a killing two ways, we used to say. First at sea, then at land when the silver was divided up. Problem was, such work gave me a thirst for gambling, and I spent most of my pay in card-dens and fight-pits. You must be aware of what it's like in the outer districts, where the Chamber of the Code's power is fainter than here in the Core. I fell into debt with a man named Roph Khanet. A dangerous man. Sold weapons to anyone with a purse big enough, regardless of loyalty. As I couldn't pay what I owed in silver, I had to pay with my flesh. He sent a man named the Butcher to me one night, and he left with one more leg than he arrived with.'

Sisine leaned forward, wine hovering at her lips. She knew that learning a man's past could tell a lot about his present, and more importantly, his future. 'Surely that is not the end of the story? Etane tells me you are a wealthy businessman, and growing wealthier every day. How does one grow such an empire from such poor beginnings?'

Temsa shook his head. 'How else does one succeed? I dusted myself off and improved. I learned the cards. I learned the cups. It took me a year to start running my own rackets, taking cuts on games. I used the winnings to buy property. Buy and sell, buy and sell. That was my trick. Three years later I took my vengeance on Roph Khanet and his Butcher by buying and burning his prized card-den to the dust in the space of an hour. They just happened to be inside it at the time. A decade later, I have turned from trickery to honesty. I am proud to run a tavern and a profitable – and very legal – soultrading business in Bes District. The leg is now a reminder that from loss comes strength.'

'To strength, then.' Sisine held out her glass, and he touched his to it with a clink. 'Leave us!'

Temsa flinched ever so slightly as she barked her order. The shining guards hesitated. Etane appeared around the corner.

'Your Highness?' he asked.

'Guards! Leave us!'

They left at a creeping pace, wary of the company they were leaving their empress-in-waiting in. Sure enough, they filed out. The door lingered open behind them.

Etane pursed his lips. 'And me?'

She beckoned the shade to her side. 'Stay. As can your companions, Master Temsa, if you trust them?'

'With my life.'

The door was locked, and Sisine turned to face Temsa. Danib and Jexebel moved forwards to stand behind his half of the couch.

Something heavy and metallic grated in the next room, and Etane appeared with his huge greatsword. Not a curved Arctian sword, but a straight, double-bladed weapon of the Scatter. One side was sharp steel, the other dipped in copper. Its weight did not seem to bother him. Sisine knew it to be called Pereceph; something to do with a dead mother or wife. She couldn't remember, let alone understand why anybody saw the need to name a weapon.

Etane took up a position by her side and rested the sword's point between his feet. He stared at Danib, then Jexebel, and waited for his mistress to speak.

'A hundred years dead amounts to a lot of spare time. Before he was killed in a coup between my ancestors, the Talin and Renala houses, Etane here was a prince by all rights, and a champion of the sword. He still is in death. Practices every day, don't you, Etane?'

There was a whoosh as the shade swung his sword in an arc. She could have sworn she heard its metal whisper.

Temsa's smile had hardened. 'Why the warning, Highness? I thought it was business we were talking?'

'No warning. Business it is. However, I thought it might be useful to point out Etane's history, seeing as it intertwines with your Danib's. It seems they were both members of the insidious Cult of Sesh at one time, which I believe you are aware of. I cannot help but question whether there is still a connection there. Before I speak further, I must know if you have had any dealings with the Cult. If so, then Etane here will be happy to escort you from the Piercer.'

Temsa held her gaze. 'And here I was thinking nobles and royals never talked straight.' He finished his drink and returned the glass to the table. He crossed his leg, letting it shine in the bright lamplight. 'Rest assured, Empress-in-Waiting, that my dealings with the Cult amount to selling them a few shades and trinkets here and there. Sometimes they pay me in tips for good sources of shades.'

'Legal sources.'

'Of course. Poor-houses, building collapses. Hospitals and the like.'

Sisine smoothed out her skirts, humming. 'As you likely know, the Cult are far from favoured by the Talin Renalas and the Cloud Court. Not after they weaselled into my family and turned my grandfather Emperor Milizan to religious madness. It took his death and my grandmother's banishment to see the royal line put right again. I will not stand for a repeat of history.'

'I'm aware, Highness. I remember applauding the rumours of the Cult's culling, and when I heard how swiftly your father introduced their backsides to the flagstones. I know your proud line, descended from the bones of the dead gods, would never stoop so low as to consort with fanatics and madmen again. Or criminals, for that matter.'

Sisine raised her glass. 'Speaking of criminals, I hear other rumours of tals and tors going missing. Of them dying suddenly. Of guards posted at empty mansions and towers, with no explanation besides scant letters. Most strange is that no claims have been made on their fortunes as yet, not by family nor associates. What half-coins they kept in their own vaults have gone. Those they kept with banks linger in their vaults, yet to be legally transferred. It smacks of criminality to say the least, but unlike any Araxes has experienced before. What have you heard of such things, Boss Temsa?'

He sucked air through his teeth. 'Well, to tell the truth, Your Highness, not much. We soultraders and businessmen keep our ears to the washing lines. I have heard of the disappearances, but nothing as to who's responsible. I would have heard of it sharpish. So far, the washing lines have been quiet.'

Sisine bowed her head in disappointment. 'A pity.'

'I imagine it has the Court ruffled.'

'That is not the pity of it.'

'No? What is?'

She sighed. 'Araxes is diseased at its core, and yet the ones with the power to change it pretend nothing is wrong. The sereks prefer to spend their time bickering, my father still refuses to leave his Sanctuary, and my mother has seen fit to flee. As shameful as it may sound, the murders have turned heads when nothing else could. This level of chaos might actually be good for the city, if it were to continue. Even escalate. I am keen to congratulate the man or woman behind it.'

Temsa clearly tried to hide his smirk, but the glint in his tiny eyes betrayed him. He thought on her words for a moment. 'It's a sad time for a grand city such as ours when its redemption requires murder to achieve.'

'Indeed. But these are flights of fancy in any case. Surely such a task would be impossible. Bold though this man or woman might be, I would wager it has been luck so far. I doubt they have the reach, the information, or even the resources to keep up such work.'

'You might be surprised, Majesty.'

'How so?'

Temsa cleared his throat, leaning to the edge of his seat. 'Even after binding a few tors and tals, ransacking several towers, I would wager this enterprising person – likely a person of the lower hierarchies – won't be rich enough for their liking. They'll want more. But more means greater danger and more attention from the scrutinisers and the Chamber of the Code. If they're wise, they will play it safe and slow, or call it a day altogether. Unless…'

Despite her love of theatre, Sisine had never been one for blatant fishing. Such a practise was below her. However, she knew the meaning of a wriggle on the line, and gave in. 'Yes?'

'Unless such a person had a benefactor. An equal-minded person in the upper reaches of the city. Somebody of importance and clout.'

Sisine nodded slowly. 'How interesting.'

'I find it so.' Temsa waggled his glass. 'More wine, Etane?'

Sword kept firm in hand, Etane poured out another measure for both him and Sisine.

'How would a benefactor help such a person?'

The man held out a stubby finger, counting. 'They would provide names. Addresses. Information on the stepping stones to causing the necessary… chaos. Names that are known for relying on their own vaults and locks, rather than the banks'.'

'Easy for somebody in a high enough position. There is a saying in the Piercer: it is everybody's business to know everybody's business.'

'A wise motto, Your Highness.' Temsa thumbed his goatee. 'And of course, assurances would be needed.'

'Absolutely. These sorts of things need to be protected, kept quiet.'

'Indeed. And trust. And free rein.'

'Not to mention compensation.'

That stopped Temsa with his mouth half-open. 'Compensation.'

'On both sides, I would imagine. Shades for the one party, perhaps, in return for information. And for the other, for dirtying their hands, well, they can keep whatever else they claim.'

'A Weighing.'

Sisine had to swill her wine back into her flute. 'Excuse me?' She saw a slight dip in Ani Jexebel's forehead.

'What better disguise is there? Surely a person taking such dark and dangerous strides would stay in the dark, not assume his – or her – place in the order of things. No tor or tal would be so bold and daring. You nobles love to play your games far too much.'

Sisine waited, thinking hard about which strings could be pulled, which mouths might be silenced. For days she had planned this out in her mind, but Temsa's proposal was an uneven flagstone, and it had tripped her.

'I believe it would be far more dangerous. A higher profile brings higher scrutiny. Such a sudden rise would be subject to investigation.'

Temsa snorted. 'Psh. Forgive me, Majesty, but the Chamber is paralysed by processes and backlog. The Chamber is a toothless wolf. It looks the part but it lacks the bite. Most tors and tals have yet to realise this, and so they still believe that bold, hostile takeovers will result in punishment. At least public shaming. With the right sigil and the right bank, depositing stolen half-coins that weren't already banked isn't a problem. Small deposits attract no attention; neither do certain transfers with the right documents. Weighing them and making them official isn't the problem either. Neither would a few transactions here and there. It's keeping the rumours from spreading. That's what'll bring the

Chamber crashing through a door. That's where the benefactor comes in, and it's less suspicious to protect a fellow noble than somebody lowly.'

That was how he was doing it. Forgery and blackmail. Banking in increments to avoid attention. It also explained why he hadn't already claimed the dead nobles' half-coins from their bank vaults. He had been waiting for protection. Sisine wasn't sure whether he had slipped or was simply being honest, but she gladly took it in her stride. She couldn't help but imagine the stacks of half-coins no doubt stashed beneath his tavern, waiting to be banked.

'It sounds needless to me.' She tapped the spine of her flute with her copper nail.

'What is the point in building an empire without enjoying it?'

In that moment, Sisine understood the man. He was no different from the sereks of the Cloud Court. He wanted what all in Araxes longed for: more. He wanted to have a name. A title. A tower of his own.

'Should this be the case, complete separation would be a wise idea,' she said.

'I would agree.'

'No public contact nor conversation.'

'Oh, I don't know,' Temsa chuckled between sips. 'If the person in question makes serek, a public argument could be useful to prove the opposite.'

Sisine almost choked on her wine, but she covered it well. She decided to reel in her catch. 'Well?'

Temsa looked between her and Etane. 'Well, what?'

'Do you know of such a person who would be willing to take such a chance? Hypothetically speaking, of course.'

He shrugged, a gesture she had always hated. It was neither yes nor no, and as such not an answer. 'I would have to ask around.'

She narrowed her eyes. 'Ask around? I imagined you to be discreet.'

Temsa got to his feet abruptly. 'I might know a man. Owns a tavern. Successful soultrader. He might be of use to you. Hypothetically speaking.'

With that, he drained his glass and reached for the coat hanging from Jexebel's hands.

'I thank you for the wine and glorious company, Highness, and bid you a good evening,' he said loudly, with another deep bow. 'I will be in touch soon.'

Sisine watched him go with a mouth that didn't know whether to hang or clamp shut. Danib looked back over his shoulder with a blank look. It was for Etane, not her.

When the door had shut, and she heard the clank of armour escort Temsa away, she turned to Etane. He was already looking at her, lip starting to curl, a dry mirth in his eyes.

'I do believe we have our man. The agent of chaos that we need.'

'And you think you can control him?' he asked.

Sisine lobbed the wineglass at him. It smashed against his robes, staining the turquoise a deep purple.

'OUT!'

'PRETTY YOUNG THING, WAS SHE not, m'dear?' Temsa asked of Ani, who had taken on a slouch.

'What?'

'Pretty young, I said. Those royals and their bright eyes.'

'Pretty young is all. If I took an axe to her skull I reckon feathers would spill out instead of brains.'

Danib grunted, the closest he ever came to a chuckle.

Temsa wagged his cane. 'You underestimate her. She is quite the player of games. You'd almost think it ran in the family.'

Temsa shaded his eyes to stare at the sky, and the beautiful evening it was turning out to be. Not that Araxes knew much else besides the occasional sandstorm and sea-squall, but the factory smoke was blowing out to sea for a change. The only thing that marred the dusty purple were the high-roads, spearing the base of the Piercer.

'The air's fresh. I think I'll fetch a litter back to the Slab.'

Temsa clanged down the wide steps of the Cloudpiercer, making passersby look on with confusion, and in some cases, horror. He lifted his chin. It had been a good day, and he liked the attention.

A line of armoured carriages and litters waited at the edge of the street. Their carriers were shades, bent of back and a faint purple in the fire-glow of the sky. They lazed about, muttering, though as soon as Temsa came near, they began to perform.

Heels were clicked, hands waved, and glowing smiles beamed. Prices came rolling in; special offers, or promises of a sturdier ride than the next fellow. No doubt they were all comrades in servitude, but right now they were fierce competitors. Beggars squabbling over an apple.

Temsa chose two sturdy fellows with quiet voices and not much to say. Temsa sat in their chainmail- and velvet-lined litter, and they pulled the canopy over its frame to give him some privacy. Danib and Ani took up positions to walk either side. He stared out at them through his linen windows.

'Danib always looks depressed, but your face is unusually down-turned, Ani. Even for you.'

She worked her mouth, finding her words.

'Think you made a mistake, Boss.'

Temsa waited for the explanation. She complained about nearly everything, but never his decisions. Not once. He realised he needed to listen.

'You gave away too much. Moved too quickly. Spoke too plainly.'

'I haven't agreed to anything, m'dear. And as for our conversation, purely hypothetical. You heard the young empress-in-waiting.'

Ani kicked at a stone, catching a pedestrian on the ankle. There was a yelp of indignation, but the moment the man saw the size and meanness of the offender, he apologised and hobbled on.

'Still,' she mumbled. 'You don't know her. The richer they are, the more devious they've had to be to get there. She's the richest of the lot apart from the emperor.'

'We don't know the Cult's intentions either and yet we partnered with them.'

'And now you're working against them with her. Too many people in one bed.'

Temsa laughed. 'The older I get, m'dear, the more I find you can never have too many people in your bed. You can always kick them out. What you've got to watch out for is being kicked out of beds that aren't yours. I can handle the Cult.'

'And the princess? You think you can manage her alongside the sisters? You're stepping between the hammer and the anvil, Boss.'

'And yet I am uniquely positioned to keep the two at arm's length. They'll have no clue until I want them to. All I need to know is their end games. It can't just be power. Power isn't enough for people like them.'

'People who want titles? Like you suddenly seem to want?'

Temsa rubbed his beard. 'Shit. Have I made another mistake, Ani?'

She growled. 'We always worked from the shadows. Better that way.'

'Well, you'd best polish your axeheads, because we're moving into the light. Sanctioned. Supported. Official. I told you before: no more alleyways, no more small banks or stuffing half-coins into cellars. We'll take what we want and get to smile at the ball after we do it.'

Ani just shook her head, clearly finding it all a bit too much. Temsa waved a hand at her. She'd come around eventually, when she was buried in coin, swimming in axes. That would grease her wheels. She was too short-sighted to see it now, but she would.

'And you Danib? You think I've made a mistake as well?'

The mighty shade just shrugged. Temsa couldn't make anything of it, but he knew it wasn't excitement or pride. None of what he was feeling.

'Let's not all cheer at once, shall we? I think I'll bask in the glow of tonight's success alone.'

With a flick of his wrist, two linen strips descended to block them out. Danib's glow still permeated the thin cloth, as did Ani's smell of sweat and steel-oil, but at least he didn't have to see their grumpy faces.

'Carriers, onward!' He poked his head out of the window as the litter lurched. 'You two can take your time, see the city. Maybe get it into your thick skulls that things will be changing for the better. That way, you'll be in better fucking moods when you return!'

Ani and Danib's sullen looks followed him all the way to the next corner.

CHAPTER 22

OLD FRIENDS

By decree of the empress, Arctians are discouraged from the practices of deadbinding or strangebinding. The Tenets of the Bound Dead do not account for these practices, and as such they are an affront to indenturement itself. Souls are to be kept in the shade form rendered by the Nyx, and not placed within another object, alive or inanimate.

Royal Decree dated the month of Tawab, Arctian year 850

NILITH AWOKE WITH A START, unfamiliar with the trappings of sackcloth and blanket. She pressed her hands to the walls, feeling how cold they were, and flat. Nothing like the dark cave mouth she had been dreaming about.

Farazar was still holed up in the far corner, by the door, squinting at her in a beam of sunlight breaking through the shutters.

'Time?'

'An hour or two past dawn.'

'Shit,' Nilith cursed, throwing herself from the cot and towards her smock, freshly washed and repaired, and a spare cloak and trews from Old Fen. They had more new cloth in them than old, but she was grateful for it.

'So ladylike,' sighed Farazar.

Nilith strode into the bar, finding a few others scattered about the place, hunched over cups. Eber nodded to her, paler still in the daylight streaming through the open door. The old tinkerer had disappeared with the sunrise like a vampyre.

'Will you be wanting breakfast?' Eber asked.

Nilith shook her head. 'Just supplies, is all. Something that'll travel.'

'I can spare a few bits of tack-bread, maybe an orange. There's water in the well, and a fresh skin too, which I'll throw in for not causing any trouble, and for keeping Old Fen occupied. One of these days he'll blow himself straight to the afterlife. And this tavern along with it. Speaking of…'

Eber reached beneath the bar and produced a small leather pouch with a long loop of string choking its neck. It thumped on the wood.

'He left this for you. Some of his powder. Said to show it around the city. That you seemed the sort to know what was right and wrong.'

Nilith found a smile tugging at her mouth. She hung the pouch around her neck and tucked it under her mended smock 'I hope he's right.'

'Dead gods be with you, then.'

'And with you, Eber.' Nilith moved towards the door, but caught herself. 'There might be one thing else.'

Eber narrowed her eyes, suspicious.

'Could you spare a knife or other blade, hopefully copper?'

'Mhm.' The woman seemed to understand perfectly. 'All I got is a fork.'

'That'll have to do.'

With the makeshift weapon tucked into her pocket, Nilith strode into the day. Wincing at the sunlight, she fetched Anoish from the stables, half of which had been torn away in the night. The horse didn't seem bothered one bit, still chewing at some remnant of the bucket, staring at her, a look of calm boredom in those dark eyes. Dust clung to his eyelashes.

He dragged his hoof along the ground as she approached, making a mark. 'That's right,' she replied. 'We're moving on.'

Strapping the body back onto the horse was a task neither of them enjoyed. It was almost enough to ruin her morning and last night's bath in one fell swoop. Though the sandstorm had blasted a lot of the smell away, dark stains were seeping through the rags in patches, and the softness of the body turned her stomach.

Farazar had appeared around the corner, staring dolefully out into the desert between the buildings. Now in the daylight, Nilith saw they had found a small town, complete with a central meeting circle and well. The buildings were like adobe tortoise shells, half-swallowed by orange sand. She could smell the char of smiths' fires on the morning breeze; the tails of the storm.

'Onwards, then?' she asked of him.

He grunted some manner of reply before taking up a cross-armed position. He wanted to be dragged today, it seemed. Another useless protest.

Casting a leg over Anoish, she settled down into what was by now a very familiar position. She swore she had made an arse-shaped mould in the horse's back.

At first the sores complained, reminding her of the flight from Abatwe. As she left the town, Nilith threw a look south, where the desert rose up in one enormous yet incredibly gradual slope towards the Steps. They still dominated the horizon behind them. The Firespar looked ashen grey in the haze. There was an orange tinge to the air, of dust still yet to settle.

Once more, she and the horse fell into the rhythm of the journey, nodding heads together as hooves rose and fell. Dried salt and scrub plants, long dead and dried out, crackled beneath him. Nilith let herself fall into a daze as the heat rose. The hood sewn into her cloak did its job of keeping the sun at bay, but not its heat. She still cooked, same as ever, only now she had the white crust of the salt flats to reflect it. She closed her eyes and let Anoish do the navigating. The clever beast had realised it was north they were heading, and stayed true, wavering only at noon when the sun was at its hottest.

Farazar decided to talk just as the sun began to slip west. 'You do realise you've given up your only defence by trading that sword?'

Nilith had, and said as much.

'What will you do if we meet more bandits?'

'We'll have to run faster, won't we?' she replied, patting the horse. He whinnied in agreement. The stripes across his flanks were still healing.

'Foolish bitch.'

'Would you rather I planned and plotted like a true Arctian?'

'If it means not being bound to some greasy-fingered bastard of a merchant, then yes.'

'Always thinking of yourself.'

Farazar hissed again. He clearly had an axe to grind today, and was keen to see it razor sharp.

Some of his fire had returned, it seemed. 'You're one to speak. You seek to further your own gains by binding me,' he snapped.

'Do I?'

'Don't make me laugh. I know you do this for yourself. What else could be worth all this effort?'

'There are many ways to be rich, husband. Something you never learned.'

He fell silent, but no less sullen. He stared at her, arms crossed, his feet carving slight furrows as he let the magic pull him. His glow was bright against the sun.

'You will see, Farazar. You will see with your own eyes,' Nilith told him.

She turned back around, and a spot of something caught her eye in the sky above. A wheeling dot, wings flared on thermals. She shaded her hand and decided it was too small and fast for a vulture. It was the same creature that had followed them for the last few days. There were still no shadows on the southern horizon, but it still put her hackles up.

'Let's keep going. In silence. It's much better with your mouth closed, dear.'

Farazar obliged her for the time being, and she fell back into the monotony of trotting. Only this time, she kept one eye on the sky and its dubious inhabitants.

They had journeyed two miles when the rock struck her in the back of the head. The hood absorbed some of the blow, but the missile was sharp and she sprawled against Anoish's neck with a cry. The second caught the horse on the back end, making him jolt into a gallop. Nilith was tossed from his back, coming down hard on her side. Her bruised ribs lit up anew.

'You…' she wheezed.

Farazar was standing over her. Her thrashing legs barely held him back, glancing off him or passing through his frozen outlines. She scrabbled backwards as he held up another rock with both hands. His eyes were practically aflame, they glowed so brightly. In that moment, Nilith saw why the ancestors had feared ghosts so much, before they had learned to tame them. The horror of his snarling image, even in daylight, was chilling.

It would have stalled her, powerless against the blow, if Anoish hadn't barged Farazar aside. The ghost flew one way and Anoish trotted another, standing in front of Nilith like a guard dog. She pulled herself to her feet and patted him on the chest as he stamped and trumpeted.

Drawing the copper fork from her sleeves, she rushed to Farazar, who was gathering himself together in frantic movements. His rock had rolled away.

She dug the fork into his flailing foot, making him yelp. Again, into his thigh, as she worked her way up him. His frigid hands gripped her, angry enough to hold her but lacking the corporeal strength to do anything about stopping her.

Once more the fork found his vapours, and once more he cried out. He finally fell still at the sight of the fork protruding from his chest, with Nilith's hand wrapped around it. Her sweating and grim face was just beyond.

She felt the blood trickling down her neck as she held the piece of cutlery there, making his vapours glow white. Bright cracks had appeared around the fork's tines. He trembled with the pain.

Before she could drag it from him, something feathered and full of screeching appeared between them. Talons clutched her hand, making her release her hold. Both she and the ghost scrambled away from the furious thing, their fight forgotten in the confusion. It was a falcon of some sort, but it refused to stay still long enough to know more.

'What the f—'

'Run!' it yelled at her, in a small voice but not without depth. It must have been strangebound, but it had been years since she had seen something of the like.

'Run?'

'As fast as you bloody well can! You have bandits closing in!'

She stared south, rigid with fear, but there was nothing on the horizon but a smudge of black smoke.

The tavern. It had to be. It made no sense for bandits to burn a town unless they were angry about something, like giving shelter to an enemy. Nilith thought of Eber's kindness, and Old Fen. She bit her lip until her eyes began to water. She wondered if they had managed to run.

'The Ghouls. They're chasing us,' she breathed.

The falcon was still screeching. 'Sixteen outriders, with twenty-three more behind. Half a day and closing. Your choice.'

Nilith needed no further explanation. Snatching up the fork, she was atop Anoish in moments. She kicked her heels into his sides to spur him into a gallop.

The little falcon flew alongside, still flapping furiously.

'Who in the Reaches are you?' she yelled over the rush of air and hooves. Sand flew at her face.

'Not that way! There!' The bird swung across her, heading slightly east.

'But the city is that way.'

'The city is fucking all of it, woman! There is a river this way. And a barge.'

Nilith shook her head. 'I don't do barges!' She knew of the river, and yet she had chosen horseback for the shorter and more direct route. The river ran a wriggling path northwest until halfway through the Duneplains, then curved east and far too out of the way. Not to mention full of rapids and meandering curves. Besides, water was not a strong point for her. 'I can outrun them.'

The falcon perched uncomfortably on the horse's head, mottled wings wide. 'Then you're a fucking idiot.'

'Who are you to speak to me like—'

'Because I want to help and you're not letting me.'

'Who are you?'

'Not important right now. You just ride. Follow me!'

With that, the falcon soared into the wide blue and became a distant speck above. Nilith guided Anoish in his direction. Both their hearts pumped hard, both trying to outdo one another. Farazar was half-running now, half being pulled along. His hands were clutched to his fresh wounds, head bowed, but he was still running. Their goals had aligned once more, it seemed.

Putting aside the madness of following a talking falcon she had just met, she pressed on. This time she kept both eyes on the bird.

The distant haze coalesced into a dark band with each thunderous stride. Another ravine perhaps, or a band of grass along a riverbank. Behind them, the column of smoke slanted at an angle, reaching further into the powdered blue, like a mighty finger pointing accusatorially at her.

It didn't take long for their pursuers to appear. They were mere smudges in the wobble of heat, but they grew stronger quickly. The higher ground must have given them sight of her, and it had spurred them on.

It spurred her too, and she kicked Anoish into a frenzied gallop. It felt as though they raced between the teeth of a vice closing.

With time, the dark band became clearer: it was a narrow canyon with rocky edges. It looked like a colossal and jagged smile curving into the distance. The edge of it swung out towards them, like a rope trailing from a fleeing carriage.

As they flew past a makeshift signpost – just a collection of pointy rocks and driftwood – she recognised the glyphs for 'water' and 'boat'. The falcon had steered them true. Nilith pushed Anoish harder.

Even though they were still a mile away, a small hut came into view, guarding a long sweeping ramp down to the river. The waters must have spent millennia digging down into the rock to make that canyon, but away from the sun, the river had survived the desert. She could see the blue sparkle between the dun rocks.

'Yaah!'

Nilith caught the cry on the wind and turned to find the bandits were gaining. Their horses were taller, longer-legged stallions. Their scarab beetles were just as fast. She could hear the drumming of their hooves and feet. She blessed Anoish, but he was no stallion, though he seemed to have the heart of one.

The falcon plummeted from the sky like a falling spear. It flared its wings barely a yard from the ground and looped up to fly by her side again. 'There is a flat barge tied to a jetty. Big enough for twenty and cargo. An old man lives in the hut, but he'll be too slow to stop you.'

'Won't they kill him?'

The falcon clacked his beak angrily. 'Or they'll kill you. Your choice!'

The deaths of Eber and Fen, never mind the townsfolk, were already resting on her shoulders. She would be damned if another soul had to die that day because of her mistakes. Nilith felt a fresh sweat eke out of her brow. It felt cold against the hot, rushing air.

Once more she kicked at the horse. Anoish sensed her desperation. He pushed his head out and leaned into his gallop a little more. She felt his flanks shiver with exertion as she flattened herself to his back. She listened to the wind howl alongside the frantic drumming of hooves.

Farazar was far behind, but she heard his yelling all the same. A quick glance saw him kicking up as much dust as possible, all the while hollering to her how close the bandits were. The old bastard had his moments; the yellow cloud of dust he'd created blotted out the Ghouls, hopefully choking or blinding them in the process. Nilith twirled her finger in a circle, telling him to keep at it.

She almost flew from Anoish's back as the beast skidded to the doorstep of the hut. She had to hug his neck to keep from falling.

'Old man!' she yelled between gasps. A figure was already standing in the dark of the open doorway. An old trident preceded him, glinting in the sun where it wasn't rusted. 'You have to run! There are bandits coming!'

The old man poked a raisin-like head out into the day, staring past her elbow at the diminishing cloud of dust, and the black shapes spread across the sand. Their cries were a rising roar.

'We need your barge!'

'I don't want no trouble!'

Before he could slam the door, Nilith had leapt to the ground and closed the distance to the doorstep. He half-heartedly thrust his trident at her, but with a sidestep and swift yank, she'd disarmed him. He stood, hands clasped, defiance etched deep into the wrinkles of his face.

'They're bringing trouble, whether you want it or not. Come on!'

'This is my home! I ain't no coward. I've run this barge for eighte—'

'Nothing to do with cowardice, old man. They'll kill you just to better their moods. Come with us! There's no time!'

Nilith had to drag him from the hut. She thanked the dead gods he had shrunk with age. It took almost no effort to place him on the horse.

'Hold on.' She slapped Anoish on the arse, and with a desperate whinny he raced for the river.

Nilith raced after them, feet pounding the gravel, her chin now permanently affixed to her shoulder. The Ghouls were eating up distance. There must have been a hundred yards left between them, and that was crumbling despite each dogged lunge. Farazar whipped past her, a smirk twisting his lip. She hefted the trident in her hand as a warning, but he was already out of reach. This was no time for his trickery.

She heard Krona's voice rise above the rumble, a crack of lightning amidst thunder. It sounded twisted, muffled, but it still found Nilith's ears.

'Run 'em down, eh!'

The bitch was still alive.

Sweat began to pour. Nilith pushed her legs as hard as she could manage. The slope was gentle, but unkempt with rocks and discarded timbers. She almost tumbled twice staring back at the pursuers. She managed to find her balance through fear and panic alone, her body acting without her.

'Run 'er down!' The shout was closer now. 'Get that bitch!'

Krona was sat up in her saddle, squinting against the wind. An enormous bandage wrapped her face, but at its edges, Nilith could see how black and warped the skin was. Ugly black veins traced her neck where the char had spread. A thick mace was held in her hand, spiked like a beach urchin. The look in her good eye told Nilith she thirsted to use it.

Anoish and the bargeman were already at the water's edge. The barge was a simple flat thing, rectangular and raised at the edges in some places like a shield. She saw the old man's hand flashing over the mooring lines. Farazar was tackling another knot. Anoish had already found his spot at the far edge of the barge.

The falcon screeched above her as it dove out of the blue. Once again he flared his wings, this time in the face of an oncoming horse. His beak raked its head, talons grasping at its eyes. The equine scream that followed told Nilith the falcon had claimed a prize. She looked back to see a horse writhing atop its rider and the hawk turning skywards, a bloody eye clutched in his foot.

'Keep running, you moron!' he keened.

The tumble had bought her a handful of yards, no more. As other Ghouls collided with the horse, Krona and the others careened around it and bore down on her.

'Push off, push off!'

The bargeman's shouts stopped the breath in her throat. She would have to jump. That cold sweat streamed down her cheeks.

As Nilith's feet pounded the wood of the small jetty, she heard hooves clatter close behind her. She readied herself for the jump, eyes fixed on the bargeman's extended hand, a few yards out into the river. Her legs had become numb pistons. Her right arm was the wing of a windmill in a storm. The other gripped the trident so tightly she swore she would snap its wooden pole.

'Yah!'

Nilith heard the whoosh of the mace as she leapt; felt the coldness of its spikes kiss the back of her neck. There was nothing she could do but will herself to be the first mortal to fly.

The bargeman leapt back as the trident's points slammed into the wood. River water cascaded as Nilith collided with the side of the barge. She immediately scrambled aboard, fingers pulling splinters from the deck. The frigid water had stolen her breath, and she gasped for air.

Behind her, three horses and riders tumbled into the water. The beasts churned the river to a frenzy. The men's shouts were garbled as their armour and weapons dragged them down. Krona was clawing at the jetty pilings, heaving with anger, spitting river water and curses. She spared one hand to point at Nilith, bent double on the barge. Nilith thought it was a toothless threat until she heard the twang of a bowstring, and the first arrow thudded into the wood beside her foot.

'Down!' she yelled, throwing herself flat. More arrows clattered to the deck as she crawled under the lip of the barge's sides. The craft was gaining speed, but not quickly enough to stop the arrows raining.

Farazar was glued to the deck beside some enormous paddle. Anoish pressed himself as low as possible, but he made too easy a target. An arrow sank into his back leg, and he started to convulse, kicking out and splintering some of the deck. Nilith gritted her teeth as she waited for the arrows to stop, her heart clenching with every bray of pain.

The old man yelled in her ear. 'Still him, woman! Before he tips the barge!'

As soon as there came a halt in the barrage, she rushed to him and lay hands on his back. It was no use: he would not stay still. He almost bucked her into the water when she tried to touch the arrow.

Whispers spilling from her mouth while the shouts and threats of the Ghouls filled her ears, she held the horse by the neck and shut her eyes. It took several tense moments while the last few arrows zipped and splashed around them, but eventually he calmed enough to lie flat and catch his breath. White saliva covered his lips.

'Easy, boy,' she muttered into his ear. Staring over his mane, she looked at the now distant jetty, where shapes were still being pulled out of the water. Their voices echoed down the narrow canyon. Only then did she let out the breath she'd been holding, and allowed herself to sag to the deck next to Anoish. She let the pounding of her heart fill her head and flushed cheeks. Her vision blurred with every beat. She wondered if there was anybody else out there, undergoing the same hardship at that same exact moment. Then she remembered she was in the Arc, and that the answer was obvious.

Farazar was pitching a fit. 'They'll just follow us, you fucking idiots,' he was saying, now up and marching around the barge. 'They'll stand on the edge of the rock and shoot down at us.' He kicked at a discarded arrow. 'Copper tip! Why didn't you build a boat with a roof, you camel-brained twat?!'

The bargeman said nothing. Instead, he concentrated on the tiller and paddle, working more speed into his vessel.

'Does he not speak Common? Arctian, then! *Faran esa m—*'

Nilith pushed herself upright. 'Farazar! Shut it! I will have words with you, but not now. You sit down and stay quiet.'

The ghost ignored her, continuing his marching instead. Silently, however.

Nilith went to stand by the bargeman, eying the rushing waters behind him warily. She lowered her voice to a whisper. 'Despite his foulness, he raises a good point, sir. I would wager they have plenty more arrows. Those men will shoot down into the canyon.'

'Will they now?' he replied, a deep frown doubling the cracks of his sun-baked forehead. His voice was shaky with age, but his calloused hands were as steady as the river's flow.

'Fifty years Ghyrab's been sailing the Ashti, and every passenger I've taken on has thought they knew more 'bout her than me.'

'The Ashti? Your barge?'

'No, the river! Means "defiant" in my tongue. She defies the sands. She hides down here in her canyon, where nobody can touch her. See?' The man pointed ahead, where the Ashti took on a wavering curve. Where the river showed its back to the striped sandstone, it had cut a notch in the rock tall enough for a horse to stand, and deep enough to hide the barge in its shadow.

Nilith smiled at the old man. 'You know your river.'

'They'd have to cross to have a shot at us. Ain't no bridges for a while. This bend goes on for miles before she curves back toward the city and reaches Kal Duat. No bandits welcome there.' The man shook himself as though he'd remembered something important. 'In the meantime, you got some explaining to do! Why are you bringing all this trouble on me?'

'They robbed us in the mountains,' Nilith began to explain, but he only had eyes for the river.

There came a flutter and a thud from beside them, and they both looked down to find the falcon sat on the wood.

'That was me, old man. I told them to take your barge.'

The old man shuffled away, holding his hands in a circle.

'Oh, for fuck's sake, man.' The bird hung his head. 'I'm a strange-bound shade, not one of your old dead gods. What is it with desert-folk?'

The bargeman wasn't convinced and edged closer to the tiller.

The falcon hopped away, beckoning with a wing. 'That's a regular occurrence. Something to do with a legend about one of the dead gods taking the form of a falcon. Hush, or whatever his name was.'

'Horush,' suggested Nilith.

'That's the fellow.'

The falcon led her closer to the barge's edge, but Nilith stayed a few yards back, watching the waters run past with a curled lip.

'Don't like the water?'

'Not fond of it.' *Petrified* would be more accurate. If she wasn't exhausted, she would have been shivering. As a girl, she had almost drowned in a mountain river just like this one, chasing her father's hunting party.

'Guess that's why you weren't planning on this route?'

'That and it being less direct than a horse.' Nilith narrowed her eyes. 'Who are you? Why are you helping me?'

The falcon cackled, a strange, whispering sound. 'My name is Bezel, and I only help myself. I'm not helping you.'

'Then I'll rephrase, you impertinent creature. Why are you here?'

Bezel's black eyes were unreadable, nothing human in them besides the intentness of their stare.

'Because your own daughter – my master – has ordered me to find you.'

Nilith tensed. 'And now that you have?' she asked tentatively.

'Now that I've found you, and seeing as you are clearly in need of my help, I think you can make me a better offer.' He clacked his beak as Nilith took a seat on the deck, her brow deeply furrowed. 'After all,' he said, with all the confidence of a predator, 'why deal with a princess when I can negotiate with an empress?'

At the tiller, Ghyrab choked.

CHAPTER 23
NEW FRIENDS

In cases of impasse at a hearing or claim against illegal binding of shades, the favour of the magistrate will always reside with the living.

ARTICLE 21, S4 OF THE CODE OF INDENTUREMENT

WITH A SIGH, I SETTLED down into my alcove, feeling thin and as if I desperately needed to sweat, but couldn't. The other ghosts milled about, spending the time we had been given muttering about me, no doubt. I couldn't give a toss for their words, and instead shuffled backwards until my shoulders met the stone.

Two days had passed in which there had been no word from Horix. The widow had stayed ensconced within her uppermost chambers. The ghosts continued to tread the stairs at night, and I had continued to be on my best behaviour. Knowing an end is in sight will lighten any prison sentence. Weeks, she had said. I could handle weeks, if it meant freedom. Months, maybe. Years, I baulked at. Time is heavy in great quantities. What mattered was that I had my writ, and I had taken a step towards justice. Even if it took another step, and another, I was making progress.

Kon passed by to grin lopsidedly at me. No words, just a wave and a smile. The dullard was perfectly suited for indenturement. He seemed totally unaware of his plight, as if he'd been born a ghost and slave. I wouldn't be surprised if he was the sort with the audacity to sing or whistle while he worked. I did not know; Vex had separated the two of us since our late-night excursion. His alcove was now on the far side of the tower.

I waited for the others to retreat into their hollows before I began to claw at the wall. A light sprinkling of dust alighted on my fingers and mixed with my vapours. With a pinch and a bit of jiggling, the slip of papyrus came free. I paused, listening for signs of movement, watching the pattern of sapphire light on the floor. My secret was safe.

I settled back to read it again. I had made out several more of the glyphs, and indeed it did speak of freedom. I thumbed the three skeletons, watching the glow of my fingers beneath the fine papyrus. I lit each of the glyphs before I folded it away, and held it to my head, wondering how such a tiny piece of paper and some scribbled ink could hold so much power over me and my future. The old stories talk of a magic in words, written or spoken aloud. They say that magic died long ago, but at that moment I was not convinced.

'Weeks,' I whispered to myself. I could endure such a stretch until the widow was ready for me. Though my curiosity constantly tugged at me, I could play the nice house-ghost and fulfil my duties. At the very least, I knew I couldn't be worked to death.

I didn't dare to speak it aloud, so I mouthed it to the papyrus as I stashed it back into the crevice. It seemed I was finally turning this whole eternal enslavement malarkey around. Not completely, as my fate still rested on the widow and her obscure chore, but my luck, for the first time since being dead, seemed to be improving.

There came an abrupt clang from the far end of the corridor. Voices with commanding tones. A few ghosts came past. Kon came wandering back, seemingly lost. He was scratching his head even though he clearly had no itch.

'What is it now?'

'Supposed to go downstairs,' he said. 'Some work to do in the stables. Beetles and horses need cleaning.'

Bela came past, a sour face for me. I got to my feet, slyly checking the papyrus was out of sight. One by one, two house-guards worked their way down the corridor, plucking ghosts from their alcoves and pointing them to the stairwell.

'Go on, off with you.'

'Move, shade!'

When it came to me, being one of the farthest alcoves, I stepped out to join the train but received a wallop to my chest instead. The heavy copper staggered me. The guards said nothing, one following, one staying to hold me back.

'Not you,' he muttered. 'You stay.'

None of the ghosts saw me remain, and when the guard was sure I wasn't going to move, he pushed me once more for good measure and sauntered after the others. I listened to the clunking of armour and muted thud of feet recede downstairs.

'Fine, then,' I muttered to myself. I crossed my arms and leaned like a village lout against the stone. For an hour I waited to be fetched, but nobody came. When I got bored, I settled down into a crouch, and told myself that the widow had some more tests for me.

By the time the last light of day faded to black, I was deep in a haze of thoughts. It was why I nearly jumped out of my smock when cold hands shoved me awake.

The hollow eyes of Master Vex stared back at me, our blue noses almost touching.

'This is all very sudden,' I said. 'I normally expect dinner before romance.'

'I've been thinking,' he hissed. If he'd had spittle it would been decorating my chin.

'Dangerous pastime that, Vex. Could you step back a little?'

He came closer, pressing me against the wall, fingers at my scarf. His vapours were stronger than mine. 'That's *Master* Vex to you, Jerub. I've been thinking that you've been having it too easy.'

'Have I?' I wouldn't have called the last few days easy whatsoever. Vex had put me and the rest of the ghosts through rigorous cleaning routines, scouring half the tower into a sheen. I didn't think it possible for a ghost to get blisters, but I swore I was coming close.

'Clearly the work I give you is not enough, otherwise you wouldn't be swaggering around, acting far too full of yourself. I think it's time to teach you a lesson in humility. Come on. This way.' He pulled me from my alcove and pushed me down the corridor. Faint starlight and city glow spilled down from the distant windows above, but all I could think of was a stone coffin or a stake in the sun.

As I turned left up the stairs, hopeful for chores upstairs, Vex moved to block my way.

'You'd be so lucky. The widow has no need of you tonight. I have another job for you instead.'

Play the nice house-ghost. 'Fine. Whatever you say.'

I trudged down the steps, wondering what in the Reaches he could need from the base of the tower. To pass the time, I thought I'd see if I could bring the man round. Having a nemesis is far too tiring for me. It's why I became a locksmith, not a warlord. Doors and vaults hold no grudges once they've been broken, and don't put a knife through you while you sleep.

'You don't have to hate me, you know. I didn't ask to be given your job, and now I'm back in the alcoves I'm no threat to you.'

'On the contrary. You're a threat to this entire household. I know all about you and your criminal ways.'

I wondered if Horix had shared her knowledge, or if he had concocted his own half-accurate rumours. In any case, I really was no threat. I was no murderer, just a thief, and the only thing worth burgling in this tower was my half-coin. I had already considered that countless times, but not knowing where it was and not having any tools were slightly prohibitive. Horix had kept my makeshift ones.

'What do you mean?' I challenged him.

'Keep walking.'

'I don't know what nonsense you're on about, Vex, but I'm just here to get on with indenturement. No more shenanigans. No more nonsense. Tal Horix has put her faith in me. I would be stupid to spoil that, wouldn't I?'

The shove sent me skittering down two steps. 'If she had faith in you, she would have kept you as her chamber-shade. There you go again, thinking far too highly of yourself.'

I held my tongue about my promised freedom.

We descended until we ran out of stairs and entered the grand atrium. Vex pushed me towards the main doors, which were oddly unguarded.

'Where are we going?'

'I told you,' he hissed in my ear. 'I have a job for you. Another errand, like last time. We need supplies from the bazaar in the next district. And not "we". Just you.'

'Alone? It's past sunset.'

'No rest for the dead, shade. The City of Countless Souls never sleeps.'

I shrugged him off. 'No. Tal Horix has forbidden me to leave the tower.'

Vex snorted. 'Has she, indeed? Get it into your thick head, Jerub. You have no importance here. She doesn't care a fucking button for you.'

'Maybe we should go ask her, then,' I snapped at him. 'See what she says.'

Vex reached to throttle me. 'I've spent the last two days telling her what a liar and a charlatan you are. You're no thief. No locksmith. You're a washed-up failure with a cut throat. She's seen you for who you are and changed her mind. She will find a replacement for you like *that*.' He snapped his fingers in my face.

I bared my teeth, silently cursing him for interfering. He was ruining my progress, changing my fortunes without me. 'There is none better than me.'

'See? Yet more lies.'

I clenched my fists as he pushed me outside.

The courtyard blazed with fires in iron cradles. Several house-guards stood swapping tales and guffaws at the entrance, but they had not seen us. Vex thrust an empty basket into my hands and led me to a side door sandwiched between two pillars. It was a heavy thing of barred iron but it had a simple key. Vex jiggled it in the sand-rusted lock and showed me the street beyond.

'Go.'

I shook my head, holding my basket like a shield. 'No. I'm not going anywhere except back to my alcove.'

'You'll do what I tell you! What Tal Horix tells you!'

'No. I want to hear it from the widow herself. I refuse to believe you.'

A copper spike appeared in his hand and waved at me menacingly. It looked suspiciously like a kitchen implement.

'Go.'

It took me a moment to say it, with that spike inches from my face. 'No.'

Vex slashed at me, and I stepped into the doorway.

'You want to spend another night in the sarcophagus? Horix has given me full permission to—'

'Fine!' The very mention of the stone coffin put a shiver in my vapours, which for a ghost is an extremely unpleasant feeling. *Could the widow really be so fickle*? I didn't believe it, or I didn't want to believe it. 'What do you want?'

'Salt. Twenty debens,' he replied.

I waited, but nothing more came. 'Anything else?'

'Rough papyrus. Wire brush. And palm oil.'

'What a farce,' I grunted as I stepped into the street. The chill had not left me yet, and I tensed as I walked out into the long shadows of early evening and stared at the bruised sky.

'Better hurry, Jerub,' Vex advised, before shutting the gate with a barely stifled snicker.

I yelled into the wood grain, 'It's Caltro!'

Vex was clearly trying to fuck with me; get me in trouble, get me lost, or worse. I debated whether to just sit there and wait, or walk around to the guards and say I had been locked out. I still wore the widow's macabre seal on my breast, beside the black feather. There was also the alluring opportunity of showing Vex up once more.

'Vindictive bastard,' I cursed him as I chose to start walking. You can take all the vintage wines and golden drapes and thoroughbred stallions and put them in a flaming boat out to sea. Proving people wrong is the finest luxury in life. It's the very essence of lockpicking.

Like my last excursion, I would fetch the salt, all twenty bloody debens of it. I would get the sponges and the wire brush. Even the fucking palm oil. I would place the basket at his miserable feet with a smile so triumphant he would turn purple with rage, and then I would tell Horix exactly how much of a snake her prized Vex was.

With a straight back and almost a swagger in my walk, I struck out along a bright and wide avenue that faced the sunset. It was with the same amount of swagger that I walked straight into the black sack swooping over my head.

The stars vanished in a blink.

Something hot and heavy clamped around my neck and waist, then my legs.

I felt the world topple as I was lifted up like a tied boar.

Somewhere beneath me I heard a reed basket splinter beneath booted feet.

In that moment, I had the brief opportunity to wonder why my time in the Arc had so far been nothing but a progression of poor decisions.

One after the other, stacked like the cards of a deck.

Just as I was about to start vocally voicing my complaints, a fist or a club struck me in the head. It must have been wrapped in copper, whatever it was. I gasped as sharp fire spread down my back. There came another to make sure, and then I was left to lie limp in my kidnappers' grasp as they began to run.

'Fuck it,' I sighed to myself beneath the sackcloth.

The story continues in

Book Two of the

CHASING GRAVES TRILOGY

For all of my books, fantasy worlds, social media, Patreon and Discord, wander over to:

www.linktr.ee/bengalley

ACKNOWLEDGEMENTS

They say nothing worth doing ever comes easy. Sitting here, gawping at the final version of *Chasing Graves*, wearing a manic yet relieved grin, I'm inclined to agree. In many ways, this book was a big challenge for me as a writer. *Chasing Graves* is a mix of POVs, it's my first first-person protagonist, and I managed to build a larger cast of characters than I've ever worked with before. It's also the first time I've written a whole series in one go without publishing any of the volumes.

When I first set out to write *Chasing Graves* in 2017, I was somewhat daunted by my own ambition, but determined to tell the story that had been loitering in my mind since The Emaneska Series, begging to be written. I realised that if I had a lot of plates to spin, I would need a hefty amount of feedback to keep my imagination on track.

Many friendly faces stepped in during the early stages to help me shape this book, such as my ever-patient girlfriend Rachel and my good buddies Ben, Lucy, and James, who endured numerous hours of me yammering on about ghosts and death and Egyptian mythology. A special thank you also goes out to fellow fantasy author Phil Tucker, who provided feedback on the all-important opening chapters.

I would also like to thank my fantastic beta readers. As always, they were instrumental in road-testing *Chasing Graves*. Out of the kindness of their hearts, they helped me trim the fat from the plot, and their detailed feedback formed the foundation for the final version of the book. My thanks go out to Shane S, Kartik N, Richard H, Leann H, Rusty and Teri M, and Jordan T.

I can't possibly go any further without thanking my irreplaceable editors, who essentially keep the world from knowing how terrible at grammar and spelling I truly am. Huge thanks to Andrew Lowe, who was a big help on the first draft, and to Laura M. Hughes, who put the very final touches to the book, and did a grand job of it, too. I'll be forever grateful to Laura for opening my eyes to my apparent obsession with the word 'gurn'.

A gigantic fist-bump goes to artist Chris Cold, who produced the artwork for the *Chasing Graves* cover, and what an astounding job he did. I still find it difficult to take my eyes off it.

It was also a pleasure to work with typographer Shawn King once again. I still owe him a big flagon of ale for the work he did on *The Heart of Stone* and *Shards*. Considering what he's done with the *Chasing Graves* cover design, I think I now owe him a whole barrel.

I also want to thank my fellow fantasy authors who, throughout the writing and editing of this book, have provided me with constant motivation. They have always been there to push me on and lend me enthusiasm whenever I find myself running on empty, and they continue to inspire me daily with their achievements and passion. They are too many to mention, but the Terrible 'Ten' know who they are.

The same goes for the wonderful individuals who make the fantasy genre such a vibrant community. The following people and blogs were more than enthusiastic about getting their hands on the first copies of *Chasing Graves*, helped me to reveal the cover, and provided the first ever reviews. I want to thank Tam of the Fantasy Inn, Jennie Ivins from Fantasy Faction, Mihir Wanchoo from Fantasy Book Critic, Adam Weller, Emma Davis, and James Tivendale of Fantasy Book Review, Petros from BookNest, Adrian of Grimdark Magazine, Esme of The Weatherwax Report, Bob from Beauty in Ruins, Lynn of Lynn's Books, Wol from The Tome and Tankard, Timy of RockStarlit BookAsylum, Petrik and Haïfa of the Novel Notions team, and last, but far from least, Lynn from the Grimmedian. Your support will forever be deeply appreciated.

And that brings me to you, the reader. I've been writing and publishing for almost 10 years and I don't think I will ever get over receiving emails, reviews and comments from fans and readers. Your support and enthusiasm consistently spur me on, and this author thanks you from the bottom of his black and twisted heart.

– Ben Galley

ABOUT THE AUTHOR

Ben Galley is a British author of dark and epic fantasy books who currently loiters in Vancouver, Canada. Since publishing his debut Emaneska Series, Ben has released the award-winning weird western Scarlet Star Trilogy, *The Heart of Stone*, the critically-acclaimed Chasing Graves Trilogy, and the Scalussen Chronicles.

When he isn't conjuring up strange new stories or arguing the finer points of magic systems and dragon anatomy, Ben explores the Canadian wilds, sips Scotch single malts, and snowboards very, very badly. One day he hopes to haunt an epic treehouse in the mountains.

SUGGESTED LISTENING

Below you'll find a Spotify playlist that is a tribute to the various songs that inspired, fuelled, and otherwise invigorated me during the writing of the *Chasing Graves Trilogy*. I hope you enjoy it.

Matter
ARCANE ROOTS

In Cold Blood
ALT-J

Everlong
FOO FIGHTERS

Cold Cold Cold
CAGE THE ELEPHANT

Pardon Me
INCUBUS

Lost On You - Elk Road Remix
LP, ELK ROAD

Saturnz Barz (feat. Popcaan)
GORILLAS, POPCAAN

Broken People
LOGIC, RAG'N'BONE MAN

King of Wishful Thinking
GO WEST

Ocean View
ONE DAY AS A LION

Drift
HANDS LIKE HOUSES

Silence
OUR LAST NIGHT

Monstrous Things
PICTURESQUE

Back To Me
OF MICE & MEN

A Light In A Darkened World
KILLSWITCH ENGAGE

That's Just Life
MEMPHIS MAY FIRE

Cycling Trivialities
JOSÉ GONZÁLEZ

Set Free
KATIE GRAY

Hurt
JOHNNY CASH

Chalkboard
JÓHANN JÓHANNSSON